Elizabeth H. Winthrop

Elizabeth H. Winthrop was born and raised in New York City. She studied English and American Literature and Language at Harvard University and graduated with distinction in 2001. In 2004 she gained her MFA in fiction from the University of California at Irvine, and in 2005 she received the Schaeffer Writing Fellowship. Her first novel, *Fireworks,* was published in 2006. She currently lives in Savannah, Georgia.

Also by Elizabeth H. Winthrop

Fireworks

Elizabeth H. Winthrop

December

SCEPTRE

First published in the USA in 2008 by Alfred A. Knopf
A division of Random House, Inc.

First published in Great Britain in 2008 by Sceptre
An imprint of Hodder & Stoughton
An Hachette Livre UK company

First published in paperback in 2009

5

A CIP catalogue record for this title is available from the British Library

ISBN 978 0 340 96143 8

Typeset by Hewer Text UK Ltd, Edinburgh
Printed and bound by Clays Ltd, St Ives plc

Hodder & Stoughton policy is to use papers that are natural, renewable
and recyclable products and made from wood grown in sustainable forests.
The logging and manufacturing processes are expected to conform
to the environmental regulations of the country of origin.

Hodder & Stoughton Ltd
338 Euston Road
London NW1 3BH

www.hodder.co.uk

For my parents

I

ONE

Saturday

I

Wilson's got his arm deep in the twisted mess of wires, pipes, and tubing that festers there beneath his truck's dented hood like the intestines of some living thing. He gropes at the undersides of things, trying to find whatever leaking crack it is that's caused him now to fail inspection twice. That and the broken hinge of the driver's seat, which he keeps upright by stacking milk crates behind it.

"Damn truck," he mutters. "Goddamn." He says it though he loves this truck, he wouldn't ever trade it in. It keeps him busy on the weekends; it's a project, a chore.

Today is Wilson's birthday. He looks younger than his forty-two years, and in many ways he feels it. He feels the same as he always has, all his life, same as he did as a kid stalking through the woods with a BB gun or a young man drunk at a keg party, and so sometimes he doesn't recognize the city businessman he's become, with a weekend house in the country, a wife, a child who breaks his heart. He'd always thought by the time he got to somewhere around forty-two he'd be ready to accept stiffening joints and graying hair, wrinkles and cholesterol pills, but when these things apply to him he feels as if there's been some mistake; he's not quite ready for them yet.

He pulls his arm out from under the truck's hood and starts to wipe the grease from his hand onto the rag he's taken from the bag of them in the hall closet: old clothing ripped into neat squares. He stares absently at the truck's engine as he rubs the rag over his fingers one by one, then he shuts the hood. He'll have to take the thing in to the shop, he thinks; he's no mechanic. A breeze chills him, and he looks at the sky. The clouds are low and rolling. Fall leaves ride the air, and he imagines gulls at the nearby shore coasting the wind. Late autumn always fills him with something like fear, or dread, or sadness; he's never sure how to label the feeling. It's an awareness of the inevitable impending dark, barren cold of winter, which when it comes is fine, he knows, and eventually ends. Still, he shudders.

Firewood, he thinks. He should chop some firewood. He's bought a new rack to store it on outside this winter, with a tarp attached to keep it dry; he assembled it last weekend, and now it needs filling. He should bring some wood inside, too; it's getting cold enough for a fire, and Isabelle loves a fire. She'll sit in front of one for hours, reading, or drawing, or staring at the flames, rotating her body when one side gets too hot. Like a chicken on a spit, he once said, which made her laugh.

He walks to the garage for an ax. He tosses the dirty rag he's holding into the trash can, which is nearly overflowing with cardboard, Styrofoam, wood scraps, newspapers, empty paint cans and oil bottles, and other rags like this one. He stares at the newest rag and tilts his head in recognition. The rag is flannel, printed with purple alligators. It's from a nightgown he brought back years ago for Isabelle, from a business trip to where? Spain, or maybe Portugal that time; he can't remember. But he does remember buying it, calling Ruth back in the States to make sure that he bought the right size, and the right size slippers to match.

He takes the rag from the trash can and holds it in his hand. He considers folding it up, tucking it away somewhere, but then he sees no point in that. He hesitates a second more, then tosses it back into the can, lifts his ax, and goes outside.

Ruth stands over the kitchen sink peeling carrots. "I thought I'd make split pea," she says. "A huge vat of it that we can keep frozen and warm up, you know, on those Friday nights when we get here and it's late and cold and the furnace is out or the pipes are frozen. I feel like that happens more and more each winter, but wouldn't it be nice to have a warm bowl of soup? That and a fire, if your father ever gets around to chopping wood." She puts the last peeled carrot down onto the pile of them stacked on the cutting board and watches the skin spin down the drain as she runs the disposal.

5

"You know," she says, chopping the carrots into coins, "your uncle called this morning. He's convinced he's under surveillance. He's being buzzed by black helicopters. He's counted thirty-six since yesterday." She wipes the hair from her forehead with the back of her wrist. "And," she says, "he thinks Ronna's mind is being poisoned." Ruth looks up. "Because she uses aspartame, not sugar." She pushes the carrot coins to the side of the cutting board and reaches for an onion.

The kitchen opens onto the family room, the rooms themselves separated only by the wide counter where Ruth stands. She looks up over the counter and into the other room, where her daughter sits at the table, her head bent low over her sketchbook, a pencil clutched firmly in her hand. She looks stern with concentration, and Ruth can tell by the whiteness of her fingertips that she is pressing the pencil hard against the page. She is framed by the picture window, and her silhouette is dark against the sky behind her, its steely canvas broken only by the jagged limbs of the apple tree, Ruth's favorite. Bare long before the other trees this fall, the apple tree is dying, Ruth knows. Wilson wanted to cut it down, but she wouldn't let him.

"It's dead, Ruth," he'd said.

"It's not dead," she'd said. "It's dying. Let's just let it die."

The winter will kill it, she suspects. It's meant to be a bad one.

"Do you know what my mother said to me on her deathbed?" Ruth asks, flaking the onion's skin away. "I asked her, I said, 'Mother, what am I going to do about Jimmy?' And she looked at me, and she smiled, and she said, 'Ruthie, I don't know, but he is your problem now.' And, my God, words have never been truer." She picks the knife back up and holds it above the onion, then she pauses. "I'm just not quite sure what I'm supposed to do." She lowers the knife onto the onion. "What do I say about thirty-six black helicopters, for instance? Do I say I see them, too? That everyone does? Or do I tell him he's delusional?"

Ruth steps back from the onion to dry her eyes. Isabelle has not looked up. A large pot of water on the stove has finally come to a boil, and Ruth pours several bags of split peas in. "There," she says. "That should last us for a couple months at least. Maybe even all winter. Though I'd like to make lentil, too, at some point." She turns back to the cutting board. Her daughter hunches over her sketchbook, very still except for the slow and deliberate movements of her drawing hand.

"I'd like to see what you're drawing, Isabelle," Ruth says. "When you're finished, if you want to show me."

Her daughter says nothing, though Ruth didn't expect an answer. Isabelle hasn't spoken for nine months now. She has been to countless doctors and psychiatrists, but nothing seems to help, to penetrate the silence. Ruth is sure that she is somehow responsible.

There are images that haunt and tease: Isabelle at two, sitting alone on the edge of the sandbox in the same blue overalls every day, watching as the other children play; Isabelle at four, sitting small among her preschool classmates, glancing often at Ruth with her book in the corner to make sure she hasn't left her there alone; Isabelle in tears on her first day of kindergarten when finally Ruth arrived to pick her up, ten minutes late. Isabelle had taken literally her teacher's joking threat to turn the stragglers into chicken soup, and she had nightmares for months. Of all days, on that day, Ruth should have been on time. And maybe she shouldn't have stayed with her daughter at preschool, the only parent, until April, when Isabelle was finally ready to let her go. Maybe she should have gotten into the sandbox with her daughter and helped her to make friends instead of allowing her to sit as a spectator until she was comfortable. She's read countless books on parenting, trying to figure out just where she went wrong, and how she can make it right. Each book tells her something different: she should discipline, she should tolerate, she should encourage independence, she should allow for dependence—and each book points to a mistake. Where she should have tolerated, she disciplined instead; where she should have disciplined, she didn't.

She lifts the cutting knife and begins to chop the second onion. She hears the back door whine open and waits to hear it close; it doesn't. "Shut the door!" she yells. "You're letting out the heat!"

8

Wilson appears in the kitchen door with a bundle of firewood in his arms. "What are you making?" he asks.

"Split pea. Could you please close the door behind you when you come inside?"

"My arms are full. And I'm going right back out," he says, passing through the kitchen into the family room. "I'm going to bring another load in."

"Yes, well, in the meantime I can already feel the draft."

Ruth sets her knife down and goes to shut the door herself. When she comes back into the kitchen, she sees Wilson crouched at the hearth, building a fire. "It's fire season, Belle," he's saying. "I thought you might like a fire. Doesn't that sound good?"

Isabelle doesn't look up from her drawing. Ruth watches as Wilson balls up newspaper to set beneath the logs. "Don't forget to open the flue," she says.

Wilson says nothing. When the wood catches flame and a steady fire is going, he stands up and takes a step backward.

"It's nice to have a fire," Ruth says. "Thank you."

Wilson brushes his hands off on his thighs. "I'm going to bring a few more loads in," he says.

"Why don't you sit down?" Ruth says. "Why don't you relax, read the paper or something? It's the weekend. It's your birthday. We don't need more wood right now."

"Might as well, while I'm at it," Wilson says. "And I need to get the logs I just cut under the tarp before it starts to rain." He looks out the window. "It looks like it just might rain."

"Maybe snow," Ruth says. "Wouldn't that be exciting? Maybe if it snows you could even sled tomorrow, Isabelle."

"Or we could build a snow fort. Remember that one last year?" Wilson says, going over to stand by his daughter's side. Isabelle slides her hand over the drawing. Wilson's face goes slack. "Sorry," he says quickly. "I'm not looking." He ruffles his daughter's hair and hurries through the kitchen for the door.

"Wil," Ruth calls after him. He turns in the kitchen doorway, his face red, whether with cold from outside or heat from the fire or something else Ruth can't be sure. "I made reservations at Luigi's. For seven o'clock."

Wilson nods and smiles stiffly. "Great," he says. "Sounds good."

If it does anything, it will snow. Even with the gloves he wears for handling firewood, Wilson's fingers have gone numb. He throws the last of the wood onto the rack and covers the pile with the tarp. He straightens up, pauses to catch his breath. Across the street and down aways, he can make out a moving truck beeping its way backward down the driveway toward Mr. Sullivan's old house. He sniffs, takes the ax from where he's rested it against the side of the house, and brings it into the garage where it belongs.

The garage is a mess. There are boxes of who knows what stacked ceiling high and piles of other clutter: garden hose, sprinkler, paint cans, drop cloths, bicycles and tire pumps, croquet set, deflated basketball, old moldy hammock. There is no room for a car in here, though there could be room for two. He should make room. He should clean this garage out. If it's going to be a bad winter, truly, his truck might appreciate the shelter of a garage. His truck would probably be in a lot better shape if it had wintered in garages all its life. This is something he should do, before the snow, before it's too late, right now.

He decides to start with the clutter, since he can't get to the boxes until the clutter is cleared away. He pulls garbage bags filled with clothes for Goodwill off an old loveseat and brings them outside, then he pushes the loveseat itself out into the driveway. He brings outside old paintings leaned up against the wall; these are mildewed, and wisps of a spiderweb stretch across the corner of a frame. He drags out the hammock, the croquet set, several pairs of rusted cross-country skis, bent poles, an old sled. Behind the box the birdhouse came in, he finds a familiar box that he'd forgotten. It contains a zip cord to be stretched between two trees and a swing to ride between them. He'd bought it for Isabelle last year for Christmas, but somehow it hadn't made it under the tree.

He opens the box and unpacks the wire and the swing. The set comes with hooks to drill into the trees and, according to the directions, setup looks easy enough. Wilson steps outside the garage and surveys the edge of the woods behind their house for suitable trees to stretch the cord between. There are two that look solid enough, the space between them clear of other trees and long enough for a decent ride. He takes the power drill from where it sits on the shelf, a tape measure, and the box with the zip cord out to the trees. He measures exactly seven feet up from the ground and makes a mark on each tree with one of the hooks; seven feet is high enough that Isabelle will be able to dangle without needing to lift up her legs and low enough that if she were to fall she'd be okay. He goes to drill the hook holes, but the power drill is dead. He takes it back to the garage to charge it, but this zip cord is something he wants to set up now, not later, so he goes back to the trees with a large screw and screwdriver and starts to drill the holes by hand. The wood is hard, and his fingers are numb, but slowly, stubbornly, he twists the screw around, around, around.

"Wilson!" he hears Ruth's voice calling from the driveway. He looks toward her and blinks, unsure of how long he's even been standing at this tree. Isabelle is standing at her mother's side. "What are you doing?" Ruth says, gesturing at all the junk he's left out in the driveway.

Wilson sets his tools down and walks toward his wife and daughter. "I was cleaning out the garage," he says.

Ruth looks past him toward the tree he's been working on. "Looks to me like you've made a mess of the driveway and are busy communing with a tree."

"I found a zip cord. You know, one of those things you ride between the trees? I thought I'd set it up for Isabelle."

"I see."

"And the power drill is dead."

"Right. Well, we're going to the grocery store. We shouldn't be more than an hour, but I've left the split pea simmering, so could you go in and give it a stir once or twice?"

She opens the door to their station wagon and gets in. Isabelle gets in on the other side, and they drive away. Exhaust lingers in the cold air even after Wilson can no longer hear the car's engine. He breathes on his hands to warm them, and turns back to the tree.

"I spoke with Dr. Kleiner after your appointment yesterday," Ruth says. She glances over at her daughter in the passenger seat. Isabelle stares out the side window—or rather at it, Ruth thinks; she can't see through it for the fog gathered on the glass. "He says he's not sure he's the right doctor for you, and he thinks we should find someone else." She turns the defrost on high, keeping her eyes on the road ahead. It's a narrow, tree-lined road with blind curves. Ruth drives fast. "He says it takes two to make progress. You can't draw water from stone." Ruth sighs and lowers the defrost. They come around a bend in the road and up suddenly on the tail of another car. Ruth brakes and frowns. "Fucking asshole," she mutters.

She's quiet for a minute. "Look, Isabelle," she says. "If you don't want to speak to me, and you don't want to speak to your father, fine, but please, please try to cooperate with the doctors. Dr. Kleiner was what, the fourth? They just want to help you. I want to help you. Your father wants to help you. We all want to help you. We love you. Don't you want to get better? Don't you want to get to the bottom of all this shit?" She looks at her daughter hopefully. Isabelle sits like stone.

The two ride in silence for the rest of the drive. Ruth grips the steering wheel hard. She is angry at these doctors. All of them, it seems, have given up on Isabelle after little more than a month, each sending her on to another doctor who after a month will send her on to someone else. Ruth tries to explain to them that Isabelle is shy, that it takes her time to get comfortable, that if they only gave her a little bit longer she might warm up to them, might give them her trust. Dr. Kleiner had used the phrase "lost cause." The recollection makes Ruth fume. That was the only diagnosis he could come up with, since no one can seem to find anything "wrong": it's not Asperger's, it's not autism, it's not anything that can be tested for and named. As far as Ruth and Wilson know, there's been nothing specific to catalyze it, no trauma or abuse. *Lost cause*. She pulls the car into the grocery store parking lot and parks with a lurch. Her daughter is no lost cause. Ruth will not give up. She looks at Isabelle. "We're going to beat this thing," she says. "Now let's go shopping."

Wilson has gotten about a half inch into the wood when he finally accepts the futility of trying to bore these holes by hand. He goes into the garage to test the power drill, but it's mustered enough juice for only a feeble whining spin. He squints at the label; it takes two to three hours to fully charge. And it is not for dental use, thank you. He sets it back in the charger and surveys the garage and the things he's dragged outside. He's lost enthusiasm for this project; he knows from times past that cleaning out a space just makes room for more clutter in the end. And what does it matter about the truck? One more winter won't kill it, and if it does, well, the thing's pretty much had it anyway. What he should do, Wilson thinks, is get himself a sports car or a motorcycle. He's a middle-aged businessman, after all, and don't middle-aged businessmen do these kinds of things? Though he doesn't know quite what he'd do with a sports car or a motorcycle. He wouldn't dare tinker with either of them as he does his truck, and it's the tinkering he likes best.

A gust of wind blows dry leaves and sharp air into the garage. Wilson shivers. Already it's starting to get dark. Wilson looks at his watch: three thirty. Ruth and Isabelle should be back soon from the grocery store. Wilson remembers the soup.

* * *

Ruth hands Isabelle the grocery list. This is always how it goes: Ruth pushes the cart up one aisle then the next while Isabelle runs through the store finding all the items on the list and brings them back to the cart, where she arranges them with scientific precision; their cart is always neatly packed. Isabelle has retrieved almost every item on the list and the cart is nearly full when Ruth reminds her to get ingredients for cake. "I didn't write them on the list because I didn't want your father to see. But we need to make a cake to bring to the restaurant as soon as we get home. Or you need to. We always said when you were eleven you could do the whole thing yourself, didn't we?" She thinks, hopes, she catches the trace of a smile on her daughter's face. Isabelle's specialty, learned from Ruth, is devil's food cake with vanilla icing, raspberry jam between the two layers. Isabelle knows where to find what she'll need; she leaves Ruth in the produce aisle to get them.

Ruth pushes the cart to the side of the aisle and out of the way of the other shoppers while she waits for Isabelle to return. She looks at the neatly stacked groceries in the cart in front of her and tries to remember when her daughter developed this grocery store habit. Three years ago? Four? Ruth wonders if she should have taken such perfectionism as a sign that something wasn't right. If she had, then maybe things wouldn't have gotten to this point. And even if she hadn't taken that as a warning sign, surely she should have worried more when her daughter insisted on moving her mattress into the middle of her bedroom and taking the frame away to make things "safe." And certainly she should have thought twice when, at eight, Isabelle cultivated the ability to speak backward. Too many times these thoughts have crossed her mind, and she is getting tired of them.

She wonders what would happen if she rearranged a box or two. She wonders if Isabelle would notice. Looking around her first to make sure her daughter is nowhere in sight, Ruth puts the Triscuits where the raisin bran had been and the raisin bran in the Triscuits' spot. Just a subtle change. The two boxes are about the same size, so the overall arrangement of things hasn't been disrupted.

Isabelle returns with a box of devil's food cake mix, the icing, and the jam. They already have the eggs and oil at home. She puts the icing and the jam with the other jars—peanut butter, pickles, and pasta sauce—in the child seat, but then she pauses when she goes to put the box of cake mix in among the other boxes down below. She stares into the cart, then slowly, deliberately, puts the Triscuits and raisin bran back into their original positions. She finds a spot for the cake mix and looks Ruth hard in the eye. Ruth feels herself blushing. "Isabelle," she says. She wonders if she should make up an excuse: she was just reading the backs of all the boxes as she waited and must have put them away wrong, she thought the yellow of the Triscuits box would look better beside the red of the

Cheez-Its box than the purple of the raisin bran did. "I'm sorry," she says, but Isabelle is already headed in the direction of the check-out lane.

Wilson is staring into the flames and listening to the hiss and pop of the wood when he is startled out of thoughtlessness by the sounds of his wife and daughter returning with the groceries. He turns around. "My goodness it's getting cold!" Ruth says, bustling inside, her arms full of bags. Isabelle follows, carrying bags of her own.

"Is there more in the car?"

"There is," Ruth says. "But we can leave it in there. It's all coming back to the city with us. I've brought everything we need for now and everything perishable in, I think. I hope."

Wilson nods.

"But what you can do," Ruth says, setting her bags on the counter, "is put the stuff you left in the driveway back into the garage. Because it is supposed to snow, we just heard on the radio."

"That's right," Wilson says. He'd forgotten about his unfinished project.

"And take your time," Ruth says, holding up the cake mix while Isabelle is in the fridge.

"Right," Wilson says. "Of course." He heads through the kitchen, giving his wife a kiss on the cheek and his daughter a kiss on the top of her head as he passes.

"You're probably going to want a scarf and hat!"

Ruth calls after him. "They're in the box on the top shelf of the closet!"

Wilson goes outside without these things, though in the time he's been inside it has gotten colder, and dark, too. Wilson rubs his hands together and lugs all that he's left in the driveway back into the garage. He tries to arrange it all neatly this time—organized clutter is better than random clutter, he figures, and he's meant to take his time.

He looks at his watch when he's put everything away. It's taken him less than an hour, not long enough for Isabelle to have made and iced a cake. He surveys the garage, lit dimly by a single bulb, and his eyes fall on the power drill. He picks it up and tests it; it's charged and ready to go. He'll finish up with the zip cord, he thinks. Sure, it's dark, but he can bring a flashlight. And he likes the idea of doing something for Isabelle at the same time that she's inside doing something for him.

He takes the power drill and flashlight out to the edge of the woods. He stands still for a minute and listens: the wind in the trees, the weary creaking of branches, coyote. There is no moon.

He holds the flashlight under his chin and uses both hands to drill into the tree. What took him the better part of an hour by hand just to start takes him all of three minutes by drill to complete. He screws the hook into the hole he's made and yanks on it with all his weight to make sure it will hold. He puts a hook in the second tree about fifty meters away and returns to the box to read the instructions for the next step. This involves stretching the wire taut between the trees, from hook to hook. His fingers are numb, and he can hardly feel the wire in his hands, but finally he manages to attach each end of the wire to a hook. His neck is stiff from holding the flashlight, but he is satisfied. Last, the swing goes up. This Isabelle will ride back and forth, from tree to tree, pushing off on one tree and zipping to the other. First time she does it, he and Ruth should probably stand one of them at either tree to catch her in case she crashes. He remembers crashing his fair share on these things.

Putting the swing on the wire is the easiest part. Wilson steps back and admires his handiwork. He is pleased. Probably, he thinks, he should give it a test run, just to make sure everything is solid and ready for Isabelle to ride in the morning. He turns the flashlight off and sets it on the ground by the power drill. It is so dark he can hardly see the swing in front of him, but he feels his way onto it and with his feet pushes off hard against the tree. Next thing he is flying through blackness, the air cold in his hair, his heart pounding. He keeps his legs stretched out in front of him and ready to cushion his collision with the second tree, which he doesn't see until the moment he hits it, and then he pushes off to soar back through the darkness to the first tree.

"Wil!" He hears Ruth's voice calling him. "Wil!" He lets the swing come to a stop and looks toward the house. The windows are lit, and he can see Ruth silhouetted in the doorway.

"Yeah!" he calls. He is out of breath.

"It's time to get ready for dinner!" she calls. "We need to leave in about twenty minutes!"

He finds the ground with his feet and makes his way to where he's left the drill and flashlight. He picks them up along with the zip cord box and wrapping and heads inside to get ready for his birthday dinner.

Their table isn't ready when they get to the restaurant. The hostess offers to seat them at another table, but Ruth has requested the table in the alcove specifically for the occasion.

"Another table is fine," Wilson says.

"Another table is not fine, Wil. It's your birthday." Ruth crosses her arms. "We'll wait at the bar," she tells the hostess.

Ruth has two vodka gimlets. Wilson has a scotch. Ruth orders Isabelle a Coke with grenadine. That's how she asks for it, "a Coke with grenadine," instead of asking for a Roy Rogers, which, as Isabelle has told her many times, is the correct name for the drink. Isabelle says nothing.

Almost an hour later, they are finally seated at their alcove table. Ruth is hungry; she hasn't eaten since breakfast, and she gets crabby when she hasn't eaten. Wilson knows this and asks for a bread basket and menus right away. "And a vodka gimlet, please!" Ruth calls after the waitress. "I could eat a horse," she says.

The waitress returns with Ruth's drink, bread, and menus, and they are silent as they scan these, though they have been to this restaurant many times.

"Mmmm," Ruth says. "I'm not sure whether steak or pasta sounds better. They both sound good. What are you going to have, Wil? They have crab cakes as a special appetizer tonight."

"Do they?" Wilson asks. Crab cakes are his favorite.

"I read it on the specials board as we walked in. They must have known it was your birthday."

Wilson smiles. "Must have."

"I think I'll have the steak," Ruth decides, closing her menu. "And a Caesar salad to start."

"That sounds good," Wilson says.

Isabelle has taken a red crayon from the dish of them on the table, but instead of drawing on the kids' placemat she's been given, she draws directly on the sheet of white paper covering the tablecloth.

"I don't know if you should draw right on there, Isabelle," Ruth says.

"I'm sure it's fine," Wilson says. "It's paper. They replace it between meals." He lifts the corner of the paper as proof.

They are quiet for a minute, and then Ruth clears her throat. "I've been thinking," she says. "I've been thinking maybe we should go away this summer. Africa, maybe. I'd like to go to Africa." She stirs her drink. "You've been to Africa, haven't you, Wil?"

"Seventy-five," he says. "My father took me."

"Well, I'd like to go to Africa. I'm sure it's more beautiful than I can imagine. What do you think, Isabelle? Would you want to go to Africa?"

Isabelle switches crayons, red to black.

"Tell Isabelle what Africa's like, Wil," Ruth says. "Tell us about your trip."

Wilson shifts in his seat. He tries to catch Ruth's eye, fails. He glances at his daughter. Her head is bent over her drawing. "Well," he begins. "It was a long time ago. But I remember it was very hot. It was hot, but we had to wear pants because of the rattlesnakes. Or something. I think it was because of rattlesnakes." He pauses. "There were giraffes," he says lamely. "And lions . . ."

He is relieved when the waitress returns to take their order. Ruth orders her salad and steak, and Wilson orders crab cakes and linguini.

"And what would the young lady like?" The waitress turns to Isabelle. Isabelle stares at the table.

"Isabelle," Ruth says. "Tell the waitress what you'd like to eat." Isabelle stares at the table.

Wilson opens his mouth to order for her, and he feels Ruth's foot hard against his shin. He looks at her, and she gives him a warning look.

"Should I come back?" the waitress asks.

Wilson clears his throat. "No," he says. "She'll have the chicken fingers."

"Chips, fries, or coleslaw?"

"Fries," Wilson says. "And I'd like a glass of red wine, please. Whatever the house merlot is."

"Let's have a bottle," Ruth suggests. "It's your birthday. We should celebrate."

"A bottle, then."

They are quiet after the waitress leaves.

"You know," Wilson says. "I think we might have new neighbors. I saw a moving truck over at Mr. Sullivan's this afternoon."

"And what were you doing at Mr. Sullivan's?" Ruth asks.

"Nothing. I wasn't. I saw from the driveway when I was doing the firewood."

"Who are they? Or he, or she?"

"I don't know. I just saw the truck." Isabelle has looked up from her drawing, and the curious look on her face makes Wilson desperate to go on. "It was a big truck," he says. "Maybe it's a family. It looked like a family-size truck. Or like a truck that would have a family's worth of stuff in it."

The waitress returns with their wine, and in the time it takes to taste and pour, the subject of the moving van seems to evaporate; Ruth is buttering a piece of bread from the basket, and Isabelle has returned to her crayons. Ruth sets the buttered bread on Isabelle's bread plate.

"Presents!" she says. She bends down and pulls a gift from the shopping bag at her feet and hands it to Wilson across the table.

"Here?" Wilson says.

Ruth gives him a look. "Yes, here."

Wilson swallows and tears the wrapping away. Inside is a box with three two-way radios, high-tech walkie-talkies. Ruth smiles. "They're for skiing," she says. "We can each carry one on the mountain when we go, in case we get separated or go on different runs or something."

Wilson looks down at the box and pretends to read the side. He wonders if there will be any skiing this year. It is something Isabelle has always loved; he taught her when she was four, and he's fond of saying that she took to it like a fish to water.

"Isabelle picked them out," she says. "It was her idea."

Wilson wonders if there is any truth to that. "Well, thanks to you both," he says, and leans over the table to give each of them a kiss.

Their appetizers arrive, and they eat in silence. Before either Wilson or Ruth has finished, the waitress appears with the main course.

"My," Ruth says. "That was awfully quick."

The waitress looks worried. "Should I bring it back later?" she asks. "I don't mean to rush you."

"No, no," Wilson says through a mouthful of food. "It's fine. Just set it down."

"How were the crab cakes?" Ruth asks when Wilson pushes his empty plate aside.

"Mmm," Wilson says. "Delicious."

"Good."

They start in on their main courses. Ruth looks up from her steak and sees their reflection in the alcove window, the three of them bent over their dinners, their faces flickering in the light from the candle. They could be anyone, she thinks. They could be their old selves. She blinks at the reflection. Behind it, outside, snow is beginning to fall. "Look," she says.

Wilson turns in his seat to look; even Isabelle looks up from her chicken fingers. "I see a snow fort in our future, Belle," Wilson says.

"I think I made that split pea just in the nick of time," Ruth says, picking up her fork again. "Just in time for winter. We got cocoa at the store today, too. That was Isabelle's idea."

"Always thinking," Wilson says. He pours more wine for both himself and Ruth.

"Speaking of split pea," Ruth says after a minute, "did I tell you what my brother's up to now?"

Wilson looks puzzled. "What does Jimmy have to do with split pea?"

"What?"

The waitress interrupts to ask them if they've finished. They are quiet while she clears.

"What?" Ruth repeats once she has left.

"You were going to tell me about your brother," Wilson says.

"Oh!" Ruth says. "Well, he's currently convinced that 'they' are spying on him. Via black helicopters. Thirty-six since yesterday, though now it's probably more." She sits forward. "He wanted me to advise you against aspartame. Or saccharin. Whichever it is. It's altering Ronna's mind."

"Jesus," Wilson says.

"Not only that," she says. Her voice is loud. "But

he's had Harry, you know, that bizarre friend of his, stalking Ronna. Or *following,* as he says. Into *adult stores.*"

Wilson clears his throat. "Maybe," he says, "we should talk about this later."

Ruth stares at him and sips her wine. "Why?" she says.

Wilson stares back at her.

"Because of Isabelle?" Ruth says. "You think she shouldn't hear about these things?"

"I'm just saying that maybe we should talk about your brother later."

Just then the restaurant lights dim, and a little group of waiters and waitresses cross the room with Wilson's birthday cake. The rest of the diners join in singing. "Happy birthday to you," they finish, setting the cake in front of Wilson.

He and Ruth both stare at the cake, which Isabelle had carried on her lap in the car on a plate covered with a blue cake lid. It is lopsided, and the icing is thick. Isabelle has decorated the border of the cake with a flowering vine encircling, in the middle of the cake, the word *Sorry.*

"Make a wish!" their waitress says.

Wilson hesitates, blinking at the flames. Ruth touches his hand on the table, and he blows the candles out. "We can cut it ourselves," Ruth tells the waitress, and the flock of singers disperses. "Here's a knife," Ruth says, handing it to Wilson.

He holds it above the cake and pauses. "It's a lovely

cake," he says to Isabelle. "And I bet it tastes good, too. Thank you."

Isabelle sleeps stretched out on the backseat as they drive home. Ruth falls asleep in front, her hand on Wilson's leg. Wilson concentrates on the road and as much as is illuminated in the pocket of light the headlights afford. The yellow line curves and straightens, telephone wires belly down and then sweep back up between the poles along the road, snowflakes flash toward them like sparks. It all looks the same along this road; Wilson can't be sure where between the restaurant and home they are, won't know until suddenly out of the darkness their house appears, windows lit and warm. And it will appear, he knows, and the thought is comforting—they'll have a fire, maybe some hot cocoa, maybe Wilson will bring out the slides he has from Africa—but until then, Wilson will keep his eyes on the road.

II

She *is* sorry. Now she is.

Isabelle lies on her back in the dark. She hangs her head over the bed's edge and feels her cheek skin sink into her eyes and the veins in her forehead start to bulge. Gravity pulls her lips slightly apart, and her teeth dry in the air. On the ceiling, she has pasted glow-in-the-dark stars in the pattern of an August sky: Cassiopeia, the reclining queen; the Big Dipper, low on the horizon; Cygnus, with his swan wings wide. Orion is shouldering his way into the sky of her ceiling, but his three-starred belt is in another hemisphere, where it is daylight still. He is a winter figure; she knows that if she could see the stars outside tonight, he would be directly overhead. She rolls her eyes toward the window. Her father has left the porch light on for her as a night-light. Snowflakes coast through its glow.

She shifts her focus from the snow outside to the window sash, which her father sanded flat and painted blue after last winter, when they arrived one Friday night and found a squirrel had come down the chimney into Isabelle's room. Her door had been shut, and the terrified squirrel had chewed at the window sash for three or four days, trying to get out. Isabelle opened the door to her room that night and turned on the light; the squirrel cowered in the corner of the room. The sash was gnawed and blood-stained; the window glass, too, was smeared in blood. Her father had gathered the squirrel up in a bath towel, and Isabelle had offered it milk and nuts. It wouldn't eat. Her father promised her that in the morning they would take the squirrel to the vet, but by morning it had died.

That was the first day she remembers experimenting with silence. She had cried and cried when she'd looked into the squirrel's box beside her bed, not because the squirrel was dead—she'd expected that—but because of how it had all happened, the senselessness of it, how it was just a squirrel, looking for nuts on the roof one day, then the next day toothless and bloody and terrified, and then the next day dead in a shoe box by a girl's bed. But how could she explain that? What was there, really, to explain? Silence had been easier.

Upside down, her brain begins to tingle and her vision starts to pixelate. She blinks once, twice, and then she sits up and rubs her eyes. She pulls her covers back and steps into the slippers she's left on the floor by her mattress, opens her bedroom door, and walks softly down the hall, past her parents' room, and down the stairs.

Ruth hears her passing footsteps. She waits to hear the whir of the fan that comes on with the bathroom light, the gentle clink of the toilet lid raised; instead, she hears Isabelle descending the stairs. She opens her eyes and waits until she hears the footsteps reach the ground floor and fade down the hall until she gets out of bed herself and follows. She is cold in her silk nightgown and bare feet, but she doesn't pause to find her robe or slippers. The stairs creak; she knows from Isabelle that to walk quietly she must put her weight on the edge of the steps, where they give less. She presses her body against the wall and makes her way slowly down. Halfway she pauses. The hallway downstairs is cast in a dim glow from the closet light. She watches the blurred shadow of her daughter on the hallway floor and listens to her rummage. After a minute, she hears Isabelle's footsteps again, slower now, and heavy. Ruth watches her pass by the foot of the stairs to the porch door.

Isabelle wears Wilson's warmest down parka over her nightgown, and a pair of his boots with feet as long as her shins. She's put on the fur hat Wilson brought back from a business trip to Russia and Ruth's fleece-lined leather mittens. One of these she takes off for a minute to grip the door handle, then she steps outside into the snow and pulls the door quietly shut behind her. Ruth descends the rest of the staircase and hurries to the door, worried that Isabelle might have already vanished into the darkness. But when Ruth looks out through the door window, she sees by the porch light that Isabelle's footprints lead only to the steps that lead down to the lawn. Isabelle sits there with her chin in her palms looking out into the darkness, snow collecting already on her head and shoulders.

Ruth stands at the door for some minutes watching her daughter watch the snow, wondering whether she should go to her, usher her back to bed. She wonders what Isabelle is thinking as she sits there, or whether she has let her mind go blank. Ruth would like to go outside and ask her. She would like to go outside and sit beside her daughter and say, *Isabelle, tell me what you're thinking,* and she would like for Isabelle to answer, *I am thinking about my drawings,* or *I am thinking about Africa,* or *I am thinking about the cold,* which now, sitting there bare-legged in her nightgown and Wilson's parka, she does not even seem to notice.

But if Ruth did that, if she put on her own boots and jacket and went outside to sit beside her daughter, none of that would happen. Instead, Isabelle would go back inside, or she would stand and walk out into the night, or, maybe worst of all, she would let Ruth sit beside her in what has come to seem a deafening silence. Ruth puts her hand against a pane of the window's glass and holds it there above her daughter's body. She sighs, and after a minute she takes her hand away and walks down the hallway to the laundry room, where she pulls one of Isabelle's nightgowns from the dryer. The one her daughter is wearing now will be wet.

She pauses at the porch door before going back upstairs. The mark of her hand is still on the glass, traced in a blur of fog. Outside, Isabelle sits motionless, her chin still resting in her hands. Ruth turns and goes quietly upstairs. She walks to Isabelle's room at the end of the hallway and spreads the dry nightgown on her bed before returning to her own room.

Wilson has rolled onto his back and is snoring loudly. She slides into bed beside him; he is warm. She slides closer against him, nudges his shoulder.

"Wil," she says. "Wilson."

His breath catches in his throat, and his eyes open.

"Roll over," she says. "You're snoring."

"Sorry," he says. He rolls onto his side, facing away from Ruth, and she presses her body against his, her arm wrapped around him. Her breath is warm on his neck and still smells like wine from dinner. He looks out the window beside the bed and watches the snow fall beneath the single streetlamp mounted to a telephone pole. He has always liked this streetlamp because, he figures, it is theirs to the extent that it is there only because their house is. In the city, the streetlamps are anonymous and everywhere; they don't care for whom they shed their light.

Wilson blinks. He is wide awake now. He tries to let himself be lulled by the falling snow, by the infrequent sweep of headlights from passing cars, by Ruth's breath against his neck, even now and slow with sleep. He glances at the clock on the bedside table. It is still his birthday. The blue of the clock numbers reflects in the glass of water beside it and casts in a neon glow the folded piece of white paper Wilson has set there beside his wallet and the car keys. He has looked at this paper many times tonight already, but he reaches for it on the bedside to unfold and scrutinize again.

He looks at the paper, ragged-edged and palm-size, by the light of the clock. A lion drawn in red looks back at him, his huge mouth open in a gaping roar. His teeth are sharp, his mane wild, and his mouth tunnels into blackness. He is sitting underneath a black tree, one that is low-branched and reaching from the sweep of wind cutting across the plain.

After they had paid at the register for dinner tonight, Wilson returned to the table to leave the tip, though he had the cash to leave it to begin with. But he wanted the excuse to return to the table alone; he wanted to see what Isabelle had drawn, what she had covered with her plate while they ate. He returned to the table just after it had been cleared, and the busboy was about to strip the paper off the table when Wilson stopped him and quickly ripped his daughter's drawing from among the wine stains and cake crumbs surrounding it.

He squints at it now again and wonders how his daughter knew to draw the tree that way. He wonders what else she knows if she knows what a tree looks like in Africa, little things, like what a cactus looks like in the desert, or how to draw a Buddhist temple. He wonders what else she's learned from those books of hers. He holds the drawing closer to his face. Africa. Maybe it's not a bad idea after all. He makes a mental note to dig out his slides from the attic tomorrow, if they're there, to maybe contact his travel agent this week.

Outside, Isabelle shivers once, not so much with cold—she is warm inside her father's down—as with the idea of it, the idea of nighttime, darkness, snow. She's not sure why exactly she's come out here, and so to give herself some sense of purpose, she's told herself that she will not go in until the footprints she has left across the porch have been snowed over. She peers over her shoulder. She hasn't been out for long, but already the snow is doing its work and the footprints behind her are losing definition. Across the street and beyond the roadside trees, she can see Mr. Sullivan's old house. Normally nothing but a hulking black shape at night, tonight the downstairs windows glow, and smoke whips from the chimney. She vaguely remembers the quiet ambulance that came to take

Mr. Sullivan away, and how her father had explained to her that he had died in his sleep, which was the best way to die. It strikes her that Mr. Sullivan was the last person to light a fire in that fireplace until now, and maybe the last person who had touched the light switch, or used the bathroom, or run his hand up the banister. She would never want to live in a house where someone had died.

A gust of wind roars through the upper branches of the trees, loud as a passing train. There was a time when she might have been afraid of that sound, afraid to be out here in the dark alone. She might have jumped at the crack of branches breaking under snow, or the hoots of owls or howls of coyotes or the marble pairs of eyes she sees frozen by the porch light even now on the edge of the woods. None of these things scare her now. There is comfort in her silence, a sort of safety, an invisible wall between her and the world that makes her feel untouchable. That is partly why she chose it, she thinks. Though maybe it has really chosen her; she hadn't realized she would become trapped, unable to break out. She has lost control of her control. This is why she is sorry; she knows she is causing her parents pain.

She stands and steps out of the glow cast by the porch light and into the darkness beyond it. Placing one foot carefully in front of the next, Isabelle walks slowly in the direction of the apple tree, lifting each foot gingerly so as not to step out of her father's overlarge boots. It is less dark out here than it looked from the porch. Her breath catches what light there is and glows a gentle bluish white as it curls from her mouth. She wonders what happens to a breath when you can no longer see it, whether it adjusts itself like a chameleon to the cold until it's out of sight, or whether it spreads too thin to see, or whether it is taken in by unseen things around her in the way she takes in air.

She crosses the last few yards to the apple tree and then stops in the snow to look up at it. It looks thin without its leaves, sickly; it lost a limb to gypsy moths last spring. They'd covered the tree entirely, those parasites. She'd crushed a dozen with her hand trying to climb before she realized they were there. The thought, or maybe the cold, makes Isabelle shudder, and she continues on her missionless mission around the apple tree and back again to the porch. She steps in the footprints she's already made so as to leave as much of the snow untouched as she can. In the morning, she'll shovel paths through the yard for her parents and herself to follow if they want to get to the tree, or the swing set, or around the house. She doesn't like a field of messy snow.

She resumes her seat on the porch steps, where she'll have to wait for just a little while longer for her initial footprints to fill. She looks over her shoulder to measure the snow's progress. Her footprints are only shallow indentations now. Soon, she thinks. Soon.

Ruth wakes up to the sound of pots clanging and the smell of bacon. Wilson is incapable of quiet cooking; it sounds like a bad percussion band rehearsing when he is in the kitchen. But she is not really annoyed. She is accustomed to this Sunday-morning noise and welcomes it as part of their weekend routine, just as she welcomes the thermos of coffee Wilson has left by her bedside, and the paper on the bed beside her, and the knowledge that downstairs her daughter and husband are cooking breakfast together.

She props up the pillows behind her and pours herself a cup of coffee from the thermos. Outside, the snow has stopped and lies nearly a foot deep, it looks like. Winter is early this year, which likely means it will indeed be a bad one, as they've predicted, and snowy. Isabelle will need new boots; her feet have grown since last year, evidently enough that last night she found her father's large boots more comfortable than her own. Ruth blows on her coffee and takes a sip. She considers picking up the paper, but decides against it; she is content to sit and listen to her family downstairs: the pop of the biscuit tube being opened, the crack of eggs against the bowl rim, the whine of the oven door pulled down, a bowl being slid across the countertop, the hiss and spit of sausage in the skillet. What is missing, Ruth thinks, is the sound of voices. She never could make out what they were saying, but she used to hear the hum of voices, laughter, the occasional shriek from Isabelle as she dropped an egg or backed away from the hot splatter of sausage grease. Now the only human sound Ruth hears is the occasional murmur of Wilson's voice. She sighs and sets her coffee down. She hears the microwave beep, the smell of burned bacon now wafting up the stairs.

Downstairs, Isabelle watches her father leave the sausage frying in its pan and answer the summons of the microwave. "Shit!" he says, pulling a smoking tray of bacon out. "Pardon my French," he says. "I burned the bacon." He looks at Isabelle. "Why did the bacon burn?" he asks. "I put it in for five minutes, same as always." Already, Isabelle has taken the bacon package back out of the refrigerator and begun to peel away nine strips, three for each of them, and to lay them out on a paper towel. "Thanks, Belle," her father says, taking the bacon tray to the garbage and dumping the burned batch in. He sets the tray down in front of her, and she transfers the bacon-laden paper towel from the counter to the tray. She watches her father reload the microwave. "Three and a half minutes ought to do it, I guess," he says, punching the numbers in. "And the sausage is about ready, and," he says, peering into the oven, "the biscuits should be just a few more minutes, so any time you want to do the eggs."

Isabelle heads directly to the stove, where she's left ready a bowl of six cracked eggs beaten with a little bit of milk. It has always been her job to cook the eggs. She cuts a pad of butter from the stick, just exactly as thick as the tip of her finger, the precise amount that will coat every inch of the pan without leaving too much of a melted pool at the bottom. As soon as the butter has melted, she gives the eggs a final whisking and then pours them slowly in, stirring them carefully with a large wooden spoon.

Wilson watches his daughter at the stove. He has set the table and brought the sausage over, along with a pitcher of orange juice. Isabelle's hair is ratty in the back from messy sleeping, and she scrambles the eggs before her with a constant, even motion. The biscuits are probably ready to come out, he thinks, but for him to get them Isabelle would have to step away from in front of the stove, and this would break her rhythm. Another minute won't burn them, he thinks; he'll let Isabelle finish her eggs.

"Good morning." He hears Ruth behind him and turns around.

"Hi," he says.

"Thanks for the coffee," she says, kissing his cheek. "Did something burn?"

"The bacon," Wilson says. The microwave beeps again. "But I've done another batch." He opens the microwave and takes the bacon out. It is perfectly done. "This must be a new kind of bacon," he says. "It cooks fast."

"No," Ruth says. "It's the same bacon we always get."

"I don't think so," Wilson says. "Three and a half minutes, and it's done."

Ruth sighs and shrugs. "I don't know what to tell you. It's the same bacon."

Wilson puts the bacon on a plate just as Isabelle is scraping the eggs into a serving dish. She covers it with a towel so the eggs stay warm and brings it to the table. Wilson quickly goes to the oven to take the biscuits out; they are slightly overdone and the bottoms stick to the cookie sheet.

"They're the same biscuits, too," Ruth says. "Everything's cooking quickly today," she says. "Maybe it's the snow."

Wilson shrugs and puts the biscuits into a basket, and the three of them sit down at the table in the family room. It has always amused Wilson to watch Isabelle eat this breakfast. She carefully constructs each bite, making little sandwiches of egg and bacon between two tiny layers of biscuit. These she salts individually and dips in maple syrup. She is deliberate, methodical, her face a study in concentration.

He clears his throat. "Good eggs, Belle," he says.

"They are good," Ruth says. "It's all good. Thank you, guys."

"It snowed a lot, huh," Wilson says. "What would you say, eight, ten inches?"

"Oh no," Ruth says. "I'd say a foot, at least."

"Maybe," Wilson says. "How about a snow fort later, Isabelle?" he says, though the minute he says it he wishes he hadn't, or that he hadn't phrased it as a question, which he knows will go unanswered. Instead, he thinks, he should have made some sort of statement, like *Later, I am going to build a snow fort, if anyone is interested*. But already he's posed the question. It hovers. He shovels a bite of food into his mouth. "If it's the right kind of snow, I mean. If it's too light, it won't stick—but if it's light, it'll be good for sledding, so we could do that. I'm going to do one or the other anyway, if anyone's interested." But this, too, makes him uncomfortable once uttered. Because what if Isabelle is not interested? He imagines himself alone out on the lawn, making snow bricks for a fort, or whizzing solo on a saucer down the hill across the street.

He thinks of Africa. "Oh, also, I thought I would dig up those slides of Africa. I think it actually might be a good idea for a trip." He looks at Isabelle for some reaction, but she is busy peeling back a layer of biscuit.

"You should do that," Ruth says. It pains her to see Wilson so powerless in the face of their daughter's silence. "I'd like to see those slides," she says. "I think it would be funny to see Daddy as a teenager," she says. She wants Isabelle to smile for Wilson; he is trying hard, she knows. "Picture it, Isabelle." Both Ruth and Wilson look at their daughter. Isabelle reaches for the salt.

Ruth sips her coffee. "Wil," she says. "Didn't the vet call and say we could pick up Maggie early?" Maggie, their Newfoundland, has been at the animal hospital since Thursday, when she had a tumor removed from a lymph node on the side of her neck; they are scheduled to pick her up on Tuesday.

Wilson regards his wife, mildly alarmed. "Did he?" he says, looking her searchingly in the eye.

"Didn't he?" Ruth says, giving him a look. "He said we could get her tomorrow, right?"

Wilson hesitates. He is about to say that no, the vet said no such thing, that Ruth must be mistaken, but then he follows his wife's gaze toward Isabelle, who is looking up hopefully at him from her breakfast with what he's sure is the trace of a smile in her eyes; she loves this dog more than almost anything in the world. He swallows. "That's right," he says. "The vet said that you and Isabelle could pick her up tomorrow." He looks at his daughter, and she is smiling. He looks at Ruth, and she is smiling. Wilson smiles, too.

IV

All day, she has not been able to get the knot with which she woke out of her hair. She hasn't tried that hard, she thinks; she'd worked at it for only a few minutes before breakfast, and then she'd spent the better part of the day drawing in her sketchbook, a charcoal drawing of her mother at the kitchen counter.

She props herself up on the sink in her parents' bathroom, leaning in toward the mirror so that she can better see the knot in her hair. She has charcoal on her face, she notices, but when she goes to rub it off she only spreads more on; her fingers are still black. She hops down from the sink so that she can wash her hands, and then she leans back in toward the mirror, frowning as she pulls at her hair. The knot is a stubborn one, and it is difficult to have to work from a reflection; when she means to move her right hand, she moves her left, and when she means to move her left hand, instead she moves her right. She grits her teeth in frustration and unleans herself from the sink. Out the window beside her, she can see the back of Mr. Sullivan's old house. The kitchen door opens as she's watching, and a man steps outside, followed by a smaller person, she can't tell whether a boy or a girl for all the layers the person is wearing. Her initial feeling is one of curiosity, but this is immediately replaced by dread. One time, in the past, she might have delighted in the prospect of a playmate just across the way, but now, under the circumstances, her mother will want her too badly to be friends with this other child. She can feel her mother's hand on her neck even now, guiding her through the door, brightly making introductions while Isabelle herself withers in shame that she will not speak and yet withdraws further into her silence anyway, removing herself as best she can.

The small person lies down in the snow and makes a tidy angel, just as Isabelle would do. The man helps the angel up, and they disappear together around the side of the house.

She looks away from the window and back at her reflection—at the charcoal still staining her face and the knot, which only seems bigger now than it did before. She takes a breath and turns to the medicine cabinet behind her, but she pauses before opening it up. Their medicine cabinets are never well supplied, especially in the country. Her father keeps them stocked with stomach things—antacids, laxatives, and Pepto-Bismol—but always she has to search when she needs tweezers to pluck a splinter, or a needle to dig one out; there are rarely things like Band-Aids and ointment. And so, she thinks, the chance of her finding scissors in the cabinet is slim. If, as she suspects, there are no scissors inside, she will go downstairs and get her mother's help, but if she does find scissors, she tells herself, she will cut her hair.

She is not sure whether the feeling is one of horror or excitement when she pulls the cabinet door open and sees, on the topmost shelf, behind a years-old bottle of calamine lotion, a pair of scissors. Her heart flutters as she reaches for them; they are sewing scissors, and they are rusty, but they are scissors. She takes them from the shelf and turns back toward the mirror, blurring her eyes at her reflection. She lifts the knotted lock of hair and holds it between the scissor blades, hesitating before she cuts and blinking her reflection back into clarity. She wonders how long the hair she is about to cut has been with her. Her hair has gotten long; the very ends of it have surely been with her for years, since Maggie was a puppy, since her grandmother was alive. She swallows, wavering for a moment in her resolve. But she *has* to do this now, she thinks; she made a bargain with herself and took a gamble, and the scissors were there. Now she has no choice but to cut her hair.

She should start feeding Isabelle orchid food, Ruth thinks, tying the spike of an orchid to a stake, the spike now grown too long to support itself, heavy with buds ready to bloom. This is the second time this year that this orchid has flowered, and the one beside it has been in blossom for three months already. Maybe if she added a little fertilizer to Isabelle's cereal in the morning, Ruth thinks, she'd be growing, too. She finishes tying the spike to the stake and straightens up to look at the bench of orchids before her. She looks at the clock; it is getting late, and they need to get moving if they're going to make it to the Christmas tree lighting. She curses herself for tending the orchids only at the last minute; she still has several to water, and, she notices, the moth orchid at the far end of the bench badly needs clipping.

Wilson bursts into the kitchen from outside, where he has started to load the car. "Crates ready to go?" he asks.

"They are," Ruth says, not turning from the orchids to face him, though she can see a reflection of him in the glass of the window above the plants. "You left the door open," she says.

"Well, I knew I was coming right back out," Wilson says, "and that I'd have my hands full."

"Still lets the heat out," Ruth says, bending over to clip a dried sheath.

"Right," Wilson says. She hears him lift one of the crates she has packed with food to bring back with them to the city. She sets her clippers down and picks up the watering can, trying to remember at which orchid she left off in her watering in order to tie up that spike. She hears him leave the room and go outside; she listens for the sound of the door closing, but she doesn't hear it. She shakes her head, feeling the draft around her ankles. She puts the watering can down and goes down the hallway to shut the door herself, but just as she gets there, Wilson is coming inside.

"The door?" Ruth says.

"I was coming right back in. That was thirty seconds."

"Yes, but the heat."

"We're leaving anyway."

"Well, the orchids aren't. And I need to get them watered before we leave, and we need to leave if we're going to make it back in time for the lighting, so just do me the favor of shutting the door behind you so I can do what I need to get done."

"Fine, Ruth," he says, exaggeratedly pulling the door closed behind him. "Is your bag ready to go?"

"It's upstairs."

Wilson turns to the staircase; Ruth returns to her father's orchids. Her orchids, she corrects herself, but she will always think of them as her father's orchids. She remembers his greenhouse when she was growing up, the earthy smell of it, how she had helped him each summer to carry the plants outside and hang them on the branches of a tree—just as Isabelle helps Ruth do the same now, she thinks, and she wonders if someday Isabelle will be the one to water and feed these orchids.

The watering can is almost empty; Ruth brings it to the sink to refill. She hears over the sound of running water Wilson's footsteps on the stairs and then in the hall. She turns the water off so that she can listen for the sound of the door, and again, she hears it open but she doesn't hear it close.

"Goddammit!" she mutters. She sets the watering can down hard in the sink and turns to storm outside, the bottom of her cardigan catching on the hook of an orchid hanger as she passes and pulling the orchid to the floor. The pot breaks; the soil scatters. Ruth presses her hands hard against her eyes and sucks a breath in through her teeth. She stands for a moment, trying to calm herself, and then, slowly, she lowers her hands and opens her eyes.

She takes a dust pan and brush from beneath the sink and returns to her orchids. There is a spare pot with the fertilizer underneath the bench, at least, Ruth thinks, though she knows she won't have time to adequately repot before they have to leave. She crouches down by the mess and is starting to sweep the dirt and wood chips up when Wilson comes back into the kitchen.

"The goddamn door," Ruth says.

"Look, Ruth," Wilson is saying. "I have things on my mind, too. I'm sorry the goddamn door slipped my mind."

"Two minutes after I reminded you, Wilson!"

"What can I say? Look—" He stops midsentence.

"Look, what?" Ruth says. She looks up at him; the expression on his face is one she doesn't recognize, a combination of horror and bewilderment, and it makes Ruth's heart skip. "What, Wil?" she says, and she follows his gaze to the doorway behind her, where Isabelle is standing in her parka, her backpack on her back, her tote bag in her hand, her hair a feathered mess of what it used to be.

In their rush to get to the Christmas tree lighting, Wilson has managed to forget his gloves. He could have sworn they were in the pockets of his coat, but all he has found there is the crumbling dog biscuit he's worrying now between his fingers, his hands shoved into his pockets to keep them warm. He stands with Ruth and Isabelle at the back of the crowd of carolers where there is more room; between the songs he can hear the honking of cars detoured around the block, which has been closed off to traffic to accommodate the crowd. It is windy tonight; his ears and nose are numb, and the bare branches of the trees around them reach northward with each gust of wind.

Wilson tries to look at the crowd, or else at the steeple of the church before them, or down at the pavement, or at streetlamps casting light on them all, but his gaze returns again and again to Isabelle. She hasn't worn a hat tonight, and her hair looks even wilder in the wind than it does inside, the short, uneven chunks of hair whipping around her face. He will get used to this short hair, he tells himself, and it will be better once Ruth has taken her to get it evened out; still, it unnerves him not to recognize his daughter; she looks like a stranger.

The voice leading them in song announces over the loudspeaker that next they will sing "It Came upon a Midnight Clear." Ruth looks at Wilson; she knows it is his favorite carol. He smiles at her and opens his mouth to sing along as the music begins, but as soon as Ruth has turned her eyes forward again, he lets his mouth close; he does not feel much like singing. Ruth is singing wholeheartedly, it seems, though Wilson doubts that she's singing with genuine enthusiasm as much as she is out of stubbornness, out of a need at times to ignore what isn't right, to keep on going. He lets his gaze drop again to his daughter. She is not singing either, which is, of course, no surprise; she is not even mouthing the words. She has rolled the evening's program into the shape of a pencil, and she holds it to her chin, looking thoughtful, but her eyes vacant, her hair in all directions.

The song ends and it is announced over the loudspeaker that it is time to light the trees. Normally at this moment, Wilson lifts Isabelle onto his shoulders so that she can see the trees light up over the heads of all the people. All around him, he can see children sprouting up from the crowd as their fathers shoulder them, and he looks again at Isabelle, wondering what he should do. He should be like Ruth, he thinks, and lift her as though nothing is wrong—but, he thinks, what if she does not want to be lifted? He can imagine crouching down before her so that she can climb onto him, and Isabelle shaking her head or merely looking away, and he can imagine the pity that would be on Ruth's face then. But what would be worse than if Isabelle rejected his offer would be if she accepted it just to spare his feelings. Isabelle would do that, he thinks; he does not want pity from his daughter any more than from Ruth. And it wouldn't surprise him if she didn't want to be lifted; he's not sure what she wants, these days, except to be silent. No, he thinks, he's not going to force anything; he isn't going to take the chance. He doesn't have it in him.

The church bells begin to ring loudly; Wilson looks up at the steeple. It is white and looming, stark against the orange city sky. He squeezes Maggie's biscuit tight in his fist, and then he becomes aware of a pulling at his pants. He looks down in surprise; Isabelle is by his side, looking up at him. His heart aches then; it aches because he knows that somewhere inside this silent girl with untamed hair is his daughter, and it aches with guilt at sometimes forgetting that. She is Isabelle, he thinks. Of course she would want to see the lights go on, of course. He squats down; Isabelle swings her leg around his neck, and then he stands, quickly as he always does, to thrill her.

"See all right?" he asks, turning his neck as best he can to look at her for an answer. She nods, her eyes fixed in the direction of the trees. He cannot see, but he knows what it will look like. He knows that the trees along the entire length of the avenue will flash on at once, that everyone will cheer, and then the crowd will begin to scatter. He knows that they will pick up a pizza on their way home, as they always do on this night, that they will eat it at the kitchen table, and that after that they will go their separate ways. Ruth will read for a bit before going to sleep, maybe, and Isabelle will draw—but maybe she will sit with him to watch a Christmas movie before she goes to bed. And then Wilson will be the only one up. He will set the coffeemaker for tomorrow morning, and he will do whatever dishes have been left undone. Not everything is wrong, he thinks, and he squeezes Isabelle's ankles with his bare, numb hands.

TWO

Monday

I

Isabelle wakes up without opening her eyes. She can tell from the color of her eyelids that it is no longer fully dark outside. She hears a bus groan to a halt at the stop outside their building, and the hiss as it kneels to take on passengers. A driver leans on his horn; another driver joins in, then another, and another in an awful, dissonant chord that when it stops seems to leave the street quieter than it was before. A doorman whistles down a taxi. Somewhere in the distance, a car alarm sings a melody that Isabelle knows by heart.

Her guess is that it is 6:22. She can't remember the last time she's woken up outside of the window of time between 6:07 and 6:26; there is something in those nineteen minutes that will not let her sleep. She opens her eyes and looks over at the clock: 6:23. A good time to wake up, she thinks; 6:23 is a pleasing arrangement of numbers, cooperative, balanced, and straightforward: six is two times three. She takes this as a good sign for the day to come.

Her father won't be in to wake her for another hour, but she is glad to wake up early. This hour is stolen time in which she can live secretly while the world thinks she's asleep and so pays her no attention; she is in its blind spot. She is free to lie in bed and think, or not think, though she's not sure if not thinking is really possible—how could one be aware of the state of unthinking if one isn't thinking about it? No one would know about it if it really exists, because they wouldn't be able to consciously experience it without thinking. It's as confusing to Isabelle as the idea of nothing, because by its very name, doesn't nothing become something? The world seems full of these contradictions.

Isabelle stares at the ceiling. Her ceilings in the city are taller than her weekend ceilings, which she could easily reach to decorate with stars by standing on a chair. She's managed to get a few stars on her ceiling here by balancing them on the end of a bamboo stick and raising the stick above her head, but this technique has proven difficult—most of the stars fall off the stick before reaching the ceiling, and she can't affix the stars that do make it all the way up with as much precision as she'd like. What she needs, she thinks, is a ladder; the whiteness of her ceiling is enough to drive her crazy. If whiteness even exists—it seems another impossible thing in the world, like nothing and unthinking. White to her isn't white at all when she looks closely—it is an infinite collection of flashing speckles. She couldn't begin to name all the colors she sees in the ceiling now.

She shuts her eyes as lightly as she can, and she stares at the light filtering red through her eyelids. The redness gets deeper and darker the more tightly she closes her eyes until finally it goes purple, and then brown, and when she quickly loosens her eyelids again that brown flashes into a putrid yellow, which fades into green as she repeats the process. She tightens and loosens her eyelids in rapid succession, letting color after color burst into her brain until she is dizzy and her eyes begin to hurt. She rubs them vigorously until her vision fizzles into gold-colored squares that linger in her line of sight even after she has opened her eyes again. She waits as things slowly come back into focus. She can hear her parents' voices now, murmuring in their bedroom; she can't help but feel disappointment that the morning is no longer hers alone, though still—she looks at the clock—she has more than a half hour until her father comes in to wake her. She pulls the covers up over her head.

Wilson and Ruth still have their alarm clock set for 6:45, which is when they used to get up to get Isabelle to school on time. They could sleep later, now, at least by half an hour, but they stick to the habit of routine. They wake to classical music and the cold; Ruth likes to sleep with the window open wide, even in winter.

"Jesus," Wilson says, getting immediately out of bed. He pulls on his robe and steps into his slippers. "I can almost see my breath in here." He shivers and crosses the room to shut the window, glad that the dog is not here this morning to be walked. Ruth switches on her bedside lamp and reaches for her glasses. She props the pillows behind her and yawns.

"Winter has arrived," she says, in some form of agreement with her husband.

Wilson rubs his hands together and goes out into the hall. He retrieves the paper from where it's been delivered by the doorman at their front door and goes into the kitchen to pour the coffee that's already waiting, hot and fresh. This coffee machine is new and has an automatic timer. Wilson's ordered a milk frother, too, but that hasn't yet arrived. He loves gadgets—kitchen gadgets, camera gadgets, TV gadgets, car gadgets—and lately he's begun to simply buy them for himself. He used to present them to Ruth for Christmas or her birthday—a knife set, a paper towel dispenser, a bagel slicer, a banana hanger—but she found these gifts insulting, "gifts for himself in disguise," she called them. But they've come in handy, Wilson thinks, lumping sugar into their steaming mugs. They don't have to wait for coffee to brew in the morning anymore. He's able to take a single paper towel neatly from the roll instead of two or three to wipe up the coffee he spills on the counter, and right now, he notes, there is a bunch of bananas ripening on its hanger.

He takes the coffees and the paper back to their bedroom.

"Thanks," Ruth says, taking her coffee. He gets back into his own side of the bed and opens the paper.

"What section do you want?" he asks.

"Metro," Ruth says. "You can start with the front. I'll read it later."

Wilson hands her the metro section, and they both disappear behind their walls of paper. Wilson has balanced his coffee mug on his chest; instead of reading he watches the steam from the coffee's surface curl between him and the words on the page. The bottom of the mug is hot, but it feels good.

He hears Ruth set her paper down. "Wil."

Wilson wraps a hand around the mug to steady it and takes a breath. He clears his throat. "Yuh," he says, not lowering his own paper.

"I thought this afternoon I'd take Isabelle to get boots, and then on the way home I thought we'd pick up Maggie."

Wilson waits behind his paper.

"Would you do me a favor and call the vet to let him know?"

"Ruth," Wilson says. He lowers a corner of the paper to look at his wife. "Don't you think the vet told us Tuesday for a specific reason? That Maggie might need until then to heal enough to come home?"

"Oh, come on, Wilson. Monday afternoon, Tuesday morning. It's a matter of hours. You really think it will make that much of a difference?"

Wilson shrugs. "I don't know," he says. "But frankly, I don't want to have anything to do with it if it does."

"Isabelle is under the impression that Maggie is coming home today."

"Yes, she is, and how did that happen? Look, Ruth, this is your thing, you do what you want. I leave it entirely up to you."

"Why am I not surprised," Ruth says. She picks her paper back up, and Wilson sets his down.

It's after seven now, but outside the light is still dawnlike and dim. Winter is so sudden, Wilson thinks. Just last week there was a day warm enough that he could leave his overcoat at home; now the sky has come down on them. The branches of the trees that grow in the courtyard outside their window are covered in a layer of ice and clack in the wind. Chimney smoke is whisked from the roof of the building beyond. Outside, the snow already will be lying in gray, dirty piles along sidewalks otherwise salted bare of snow. Maybe he'll walk to work through the park, Wilson thinks. The park will be empty and quiet on a day like this one, the snow still mostly clean except for urine holes burned in the snow by dogs, cigarette butts, bits of litter.

He sets his coffee on the bedside table and throws the covers back. Ruth lowers her paper again. "You getting up?" she says.

"Yuh," Wilson says, stepping back into his slippers as he stands. He crosses the room to his dresser, where he's left the list of things he has to do today. He's got a ten o'clock meeting, twelve phone calls to return and eight to make, a lunch with prospective clients, the dentist at two thirty. He'd forgotten about the dentist, and the thought soothes him somewhat. He enjoys going to the dentist. He enjoys having no choice other than to recline, to be still, to shelve all duties for an hour. He could use a visit to the dentist about now.

He sets the list down. Beside it, Isabelle's lion lies folded into fourths. He lifts the paper and opens it to stare once more at the roaring red lion, the gaping mouth of blackness. He's not sure what it is about the drawing that compels him to keep it like this, to look at it again and again the way you do some novelty whose magic hasn't yet worn off. He refolds the drawing and sets it back on his dresser. He clicks open a pen and adds "Africa?" to his day's list.

II

Isabelle gives her mother seven minutes to remember anything she may have forgotten to take with her and return to the apartment. Though Isabelle wonders whether her mother truly forgets things or forgets them on purpose so she can return unexpected and catch Isabelle doing whatever she does when she's alone.

Her mother left this morning at 8:42. Isabelle glances at the clock on the microwave: 8:47. She erases Maggie's left eye from her drawing; four times now she's attempted it, but still she can't get it quite right. She sets her pencil down and unfastens the photograph of Maggie from the corner of her sketchbook. She holds it away from her and squints at it, trying to figure out what it is about her dog's left eye that is so much harder to capture than the right. If she can identify specific differences—if one eyelid sags lower than the other, if one has longer lashes—then maybe this will make it easier, she thinks. But as she studies Maggie's eyes, she can pinpoint no distinct differences; the eyes just *feel* different to her. She refastens the photograph and looks again at the clock: 8:49. The elevator is quiet in its shaft beyond the kitchen wall, and Isabelle judges that she is truly alone now, that it is safe to play.

She leaves her sketchbook on the kitchen table and walks to the apartment's other end, the formal, unused end with large windows, stiff sofas, long drapes, a piano. She shivers as she approaches the instrument and blows on her fingers to warm them; it always feels cold to her in this room. Her piano teacher has stopped coming to the house. But after five years of study, she knows how to read music and figures she can teach herself. In the three months since the summer, she's been learning Beethoven's *Moonlight Sonata*.

She sits down at the bench and immediately begins to play. No scales, no arpeggios, no chords of warm-up at all. Her mother will be back in less than an hour; she doesn't have time for anything but the music.

The sound of the notes is sudden and loud in the silence of the apartment, and so Isabelle starts softly, easing gently into the piece. There are still sections where she stumbles, where her fingering is wrong, but finally she can make it through from start to finish with enough fluency that the sonata seems to cohere into something she can listen to as well as play. Somehow, it is more pleasing to hear the melody coming from beneath her own fingers than it is to hear Horowitz play the same notes on the stereo. His version is flawless, elegant, perfectly tempoed; hers, while bumpy at times and unsure, is her own. She can control the tempo, the volume, the duration and strength of the crescendos, which when she hears them played by others often seem understated, begging for more sound. It makes her feel somehow swollen inside as she plays, as if she might burst. Sometimes, like now, it makes her tired.

She nears the end of the first movement and slows her fingers down. She plays the last notes slowly, gently, and then puts her hands in her lap. She listens for the groan of the elevator, for sounds of her mother, but it is quiet. Sometimes she feels guilty not to share this music with her mother; her mother used to love to hear her play. But she can't help herself. She can't help but deprive her mother of that satisfaction, and it makes Isabelle not like much who she is, at least that part of her. She could keep playing right now, she knows. She could play even after her mother has returned, but she won't. She could, but she can't.

Ruth sits in the lobby of Isabelle's school waiting for her nine o'clock Monday meeting with the headmistress. In a canvas bag at her feet are all of Isabelle's assignments from the week before, completed and ready to be handed in. When she leaves, she'll take home with her

Isabelle's graded work and another week's worth of assignments that she knows her daughter will finish in a day. She should stop at the bookstore, too, and pick up some new books; right now, Isabelle is devouring anything to do with World War II. In the past month she has read a biography of Patton, Stalin's journals, and a Japanese historian's account of Pearl Harbor. Before World War II, her interest was the Roman Empire, and before that, Emily Dickinson. Sometimes Ruth wonders where her daughter came from.

The snow has made many students late today; the subways are running slow and the traffic is thick. Ruth watches the latecomers hurry inside, stamping slush from their boots and peeling off the leg warmers they've worn beneath their uniform skirts. The receptionist tells them to sign in at the front desk; they are late and have missed roll call in their homerooms. The girls unbutton their jackets and pull off their hats; their faces are red and wet. They talk about the snow as they pass through the lobby, about sledding the day before, about how long their subway sat stalled in the tunnel, about their math test today. They compare the weights of their backpacks and discuss today's cafeteria lunch, which is pizza. They talk about some new movie that Ruth has never heard of.

Her own daughter is warm and dry and quiet, probably where Ruth left her after they'd finished breakfast, at the kitchen table at work on a drawing in her sketchbook. This one she didn't shield from her parents; when Ruth peered over her shoulder,

61

exaggeratedly so as to make clear that she wasn't trying to sneak a look, Isabelle moved her arm away and pushed the sketchbook forward. Taped to the top corner was a small photograph of Maggie, the same image being slowly realized in pencil on the page beneath. "That's great, Isabelle," Ruth had said, and she meant it. "Wil, take a look at Isabelle's drawing." Wilson turned from the sink where he'd been rinsing off their breakfast dishes. He stood and stared at their daughter's drawing. Ruth thought she saw a pained look flash across his face. "It's good, isn't it?"

Wilson paused. "It's remarkable, Isabelle," he said.

Now, in the school lobby, Ruth looks up at the sound of her name. The receptionist is looking toward her. "Mrs. Mason is ready to see you."

"Thank you," Ruth says, and she ascends the flight of stairs to Mrs. Mason's office.

"Mrs. Carter," Mrs. Mason says. "Good morning."

"Hello," Ruth says. She takes a seat across from Mrs. Mason at her desk. The desk is wooden and wide; it separates the women by four feet at least, Ruth thinks. She takes Isabelle's finished assignments from her bag and piles them neatly on the desk before her.

"Coffee? Tea?" Mrs. Mason asks.

"Thank you, no," Ruth says. She wonders why Mrs. Mason even bothers to ask anymore; she can't remember one time she's accepted the offer, except for her first time in this office, and then she had said yes to coffee only because Wilson had. That was nearly a year ago, she thinks. They had been called in by the school because Isabelle, in the middle of gym class, had burst into tears while jumping rope, because, she'd finally been able to utter, there just didn't seem to be a point. Jumping rope one minute, the next minute sobbing so hard the teacher could hardly understand what she was saying. A little nihilist, Wilson had said to Ruth later. Until then, they had never before had to go in to discuss their daughter except for the standard parent–teacher conferences, and Ruth had thought they probably wouldn't have to again. And maybe, if she'd taken the meeting more seriously, she wouldn't be here each Monday now. Maybe, maybe, maybe. At every fork in the road, she's chosen the wrong path, and here she is. She stands up to slide the stack of papers across the desk. "Isabelle's homework," she says.

"Mrs. Carter." Mrs. Mason clears her throat. "I'm not sure how long this school, in good conscience, can continue on in this arrangement."

Mrs. Mason is clearly expecting a response, but Ruth won't give her one, not yet. She crosses her arms and waits.

Mrs. Mason clasps her hands before her on the desk. "Isabelle," she says, "is not technically a student at this school."

"Oh no?" Ruth says. She feels herself grow hot inside and wills herself to stay calm.

"Quite frankly, no," Mrs. Mason says.

"Have we not paid her tuition?"

"You have."

"Hasn't she done all the work?"

"She has."

"And hasn't she scored flawlessly on every test and assignment?"

"This is not a question of Isabelle's intellectual aptitude, Mrs. Carter."

"My point," Ruth says, "is that Isabelle is receiving an education, taught largely by herself to herself. Meanwhile, you are receiving her tuition money as if she were here learning from the teachers and eating the school's food. I'm not sure I understand the source of your discomfort."

"Mrs. Carter. Isabelle has not attended school for nearly nine months now."

"I am aware of that."

"We allowed her to pass on into the sixth grade— despite the fact that she missed the last months of fifth—with the understanding that she would be physically returning to the school in September."

"And she will," Ruth says. "We're working on it. Believe me."

"Mrs. Carter, it is now December."

"It's barely December," Ruth says. "She needs time. She needs patience. It's not easy."

"I recognize that it's not easy. But we've also been patient to the max. It might be time to make certain adjustments."

"Adjustments?" Ruth says. She clenches her jaw. "Please, Mrs. Mason, listen to me. You know Isabelle. You know how she is. What if she were to get over this, whatever this is, and were ready to return to school? Imagine how poorly she'd do if she had to negotiate an entirely new and different institution. Imagine how poorly she'd do even if she returned here, but hadn't been allowed to keep up with the work, if she had to repeat a year, meet new students."

Mrs. Mason puts her hands to her lips and sighs. "Mrs. Carter," she says.

"Mrs. Mason." Ruth's voice is quiet now. The tremble in it makes her blush. She hates to beg, but they are talking about her daughter. She is frightened for her daughter, frightened at the thought of the school pulling away. "Please," she says. She looks Mrs. Mason hard in the eye.

"Can you give me an honest estimate of how long this might take? Of how long it will be before Isabelle would return? I've seen copies of the last few doctors' reports, and it doesn't seem promising."

Ruth opens her mouth to speak. She wants to tell Mrs. Mason that it should be any day now, that Isabelle will be talking again, that she is making progress, that she is on the mend. This is what she's been telling herself these past nine months, but suddenly these words, even as they sit on the tip of Ruth's tongue, ring hollow and meaningless. She drops her hands into her lap and shakes her head. "No," she says. "I cannot give you an honest answer."

"Mrs. Carter, I understand how difficult this must be for you. But at this point I am going to have to say that unless Isabelle can physically return to school— speaking—in January, she cannot enroll at all."

"But—"

Mrs. Mason lifts a finger. "School is not only about academics. It is about social growth. It is about interaction with others. Meanwhile," she swivels in her chair and takes a new stack of assignments from where it sits on the radiator behind her, "here are the assignments for this week." She slides the pile across the desk toward Ruth. Ruth glances at the spelling list on the top: *decision, incision, license, precise.* She looks at the stack of homework on Mrs. Mason's desk, the last stack she will bring home for Isabelle, and part of her wonders if there is even a point. What difference is one more batch of homework going to make? For Ruth, Isabelle's homework hasn't been as much about the work itself as much as it has been a sort of promise or hope that Isabelle's silence is temporary, like some prolonged flu, and that soon she will be back at school. And even though she has been expecting this news, this untethering, the idea was easier to swallow than the fact of it.

She looks up at Mrs. Mason, whose eyes are filled with a pity that makes Ruth blush again. She can hear through the door behind her the sounds of girls in the hall—a shriek, and then laughter—as a class lets out, and this makes things almost worse. Mrs. Mason looks with annoyance toward the door, and then she stands and starts toward it to quiet the girls; Ruth almost stops her. She does not want Mrs. Mason to chastise the girls for her sake; although her daughter might be silent, she can handle the sounds of other children. But she catches herself before she says anything; of course Mrs. Mason would ask the girls to be quiet in the hall, no matter whom she was having a meeting with, and Ruth scolds herself for being so self-absorbed.

She can hear Mrs. Mason in the hallway now, reminding the girls to use their indoor voices when indoors. "I shouldn't be able to hear your voices from behind a closed door," she is saying. Ruth pictures the girls standing sheepishly in the hallway, their unfinished laughter thick in the air and that much more urgent now that it is not allowed. At this moment, Ruth thinks, Isabelle would be the one unable to contain herself, and even if she'd been only chuckling or grinning before, she would burst into uncontrollable laughter that wouldn't stop until Mrs. Mason had left. She used to bewilder Ruth in elevators, this way; oftentimes when they got into a crowded elevator, Isabelle would succumb to a fit of laughter, much to Ruth's embarrassment and the bafflement of the other passengers. And then, as quickly as it had come upon her, the laughter would subside as soon as the elevator doors opened. It's funny, Ruth thinks, how something she used to dread so is now something she would welcome.

Mrs. Mason resumes her seat and folds her hands together on her desk. "I'm sorry for the interruption," she says. She clears her throat. "Now, Mrs. Carter, I think we've covered the bases. Are there any questions you have? Anything I can help you with? There are alternative schools you might consider, if it comes to that, schools geared toward helping children with psychological problems. Dr. Greene, our school counselor—"

"No," Ruth says. "It hasn't come to that."

"Well then," Mrs. Mason says. "If any questions arise later, questions or concerns, please don't hesitate to call."

"Thank you," Ruth says.

The hallway outside Mrs. Mason's office is empty when Ruth emerges; the girls have all gone into their classes. She looks at the lockers along the wall, and the mural across from them. She runs her fingers over the mural; it had been a class project for Isabelle's class last year, she remembers, and she steps back to look at the thing, which normally she hurries by, eager as a student herself to get out of here as quickly as possible. It is of a city, not New York, but an anonymous city with crooked brick buildings and pigeons on rooftops and taxis and hot dog vendors and businessmen and a line of schoolkids headed toward the park, and there, Ruth notices, stepping nearer to the park, underneath the largest tree is a big, black dog—Maggie, she thinks. Unmistakably Maggie.

He should have walked after all, Wilson thinks, shouldering his way through the midtown crowd from the taxi to the door of his office building. In the end it would have been faster than sitting in a damp cab in traffic so thick it took four rotations of a light sometimes to make it a single block, the chatter of foreign tongues crackling loud over the taxi radio as the cab driver slurped coffee and ate a pungent early-morning hot dog. He might be in a better mood if he'd walked; the helplessness of being stuck in traffic puts him in a foul temper. He could simply have paid the driver and gotten out at any point along the drive to walk the rest of the way, but then he would have felt somehow incomplete, able to say neither that he'd walked nor that he'd ridden to work. But why should this bother him? Why this need always to follow through? Why should he be so haunted by things left undone? He thinks about the weekend and the state of the garage, the piles of crap that he should have thrown away instead of dragging back inside. The thought of all that clutter makes him anxious. He'll deal with it next weekend, he thinks. He'll make it the weekend's project.

He unbuttons his overcoat as he waits for the elevator beside a dozen other businessmen and -women. They stand in a shallow pool of slush melted from their rubber overshoes, briefcases in one hand, umbrellas just in case in the other. Wilson sets his own briefcase down. He takes a pen and his black book from his shirt pocket. "Garage," he writes on his weekend list of things to do, and he's just tucked his pen away when the elevator bell rings and the door opens and the herd files in.

The air in the elevator is hot and thick and smells of breath; Wilson tries, as he watches the numbers blink past floors as they slowly ascend closer to his own, not to breathe. Everyone around him is silent, their heads upturned as they watch the elevator's progress. He wonders what Joe, the front desk guard, must think as he monitors the screens that show the insides of each elevator, what he must think as he watches them all standing side by side and looking longingly upward as if to some elevator god.

Wilson's office is on the fifteenth floor, which bothers Isabelle no end because, she says, his floor is not the fifteenth floor; it is the fourteenth, and the fourteenth is the thirteenth. Thirteen is Isabelle's favorite number because she feels sorry for it. She feels sorry that people are so scared of it that they do things like skip from twelve to fourteen when numbering building floors, as if calling the thirteenth floor the fourteenth makes it something other than what it is.

The elevator stops to let people off at eleven, twelve, and finally fifteen. Wilson excuses himself as he makes his way past the remaining people and walks the short distance down the hall to his office. The receptionist is not at her desk; he can hear her at the Xerox machine in the back room and is grateful to slip into his own office unnoticed. He shuts his door, hangs his coat, and sits at his desk, where a list of calls to return awaits. He scans the list and then lets his eyes wander to the stack of portfolio binders he must read before tomorrow, or at the very latest the next day.

He opens the first portfolio on the stack. The endless numbers there swim before his eyes, and he blinks. The wind outside moans its way through the alley between his building and the next, and the rope of a window-washing platform taps against his window. He looks at the rope, and then at the building beyond it, at the meeting gathered around a glass conference table on the fifteenth—or fourteenth—floor inside. He glances at his watch; he has a meeting of his own in forty-five minutes. Maybe it would be a better use of time only to make phone calls until then, he thinks. He reaches for the receiver. Isabelle stares out over his shoulder from a photograph beside the phone. He pauses to study the picture. She was maybe five when the photograph was taken. She's standing in a white sundress among boulders orange with evening, and she's got a serious, faraway look on her face. The sun glints in her eye, and her cheeks are red. Wilson isn't sure what he so loves about this photograph; his daughter isn't laughing or smiling or standing on her head or doing anything people in pictures ordinarily do. But there's something about it anyway, something about it that seems to truly show Isabelle as she is. Is—or was?

Wilson swallows and picks up the phone his hand has been reaching for all this while. He tucks the receiver under his ear and flips his black book open to his list of telephone numbers. The first call he needs to make, he thinks, is to the vet.

III

"Driver," Ruth says, leaning forward from the backseat of the taxi. "Is there a reason we're going down Park? Lexington is always much faster."

"No, ma'am, Lexington slow today. Lexington no good."

"Well, Park doesn't seem to be moving any too quickly either. Could we give Lexington a try, please?" She sits back. Even if Lexington isn't moving any more quickly than Park Avenue, they have been crawling down Park for twenty minutes now and Ruth is ready for a change of scenery. She is tired of block after block of pristine brick buildings, the ladies in fur coats huddled beneath their awnings as doormen stand out in the traffic, blowing their whistles fiercely at cabs that clearly are all occupied. On Lex at least there will be other things to look at: banks and delis and nail salons and pizza joints and bars and coffee shops and florists, the disoriented faces of subway riders coming up into the cold from the hot air underground. Plus, she thinks, the shoe store is on Lexington anyway, so they have to go over there at some point.

The driver passes the next cross street without taking the left that would bring them over to Lex. Ruth sits forward again. "Driver," she says, and she can't hide the irritation in her voice. "Lexington, please, or you can let us out right here, free of charge."

The driver mutters something that Ruth can't make out. He flicks on his blinker signal and takes the next

72

left, hard, so that Ruth has to brace herself against the seat and Isabelle is pressed against the door.

"Thank you," Ruth says. She wants to add something else, some verbal equivalent of taking the turn too hard, but she doesn't have the energy.

She glances at her daughter. Isabelle is flushed with—what?—cold or embarrassment, likely the latter, since the heat in the cab is on full blast. Isabelle has always hated it when Ruth directs the drivers of the cabs they're in. She thinks that it's rude, presumptuous, that since the cab driver is just that—a cab driver—he'd know his way around the city better than Ruth would. They've argued about this many times before. That's one plus to Isabelle's silence, Ruth thinks—no lip—and then instantly she feels guilty for the thought. There are no pluses to Isabelle's silence, not really, not at all, especially with the school now pulling away. Her heart drops all over again to think of it, and her eyes quiver in renewed panic. She's got to get Isabelle speaking again. Somehow, she will.

Ruth pulls off her gloves and unbuttons her coat; she is suddenly hot, nearly sweating. "Goodness," she says brightly. "It's warm in here to be wearing all these layers." She looks at Isabelle as if she expects her daughter to respond. Isabelle stares out the window, her mop of hair wavering with static. "But it certainly is cold outside, so I guess it's just a trade-off," she continues. She hates the sound of her own voice, the meaningless words. She turns to look out her own window, trying to will away her gathering tears. She takes a deep breath. "But won't Maggie be excited!" she continues. "I've never seen a dog happier in the snow. She's like a pig in mud. If she seems up to it, let's walk her home this afternoon. You'll have your new boots, so we'll be all set." Ruth's voice cracks with these last few words, and so she stops speaking. She watches a man in a long trench coat and overlarge white-furred earmuffs pay a shivering Korean man for a dozen pink roses from the flowers that, even in winter, they keep outside the deli windows, protected from the cold only by a clear sheet of plastic.

Wilson squints into the glare of the dentist's lamp only inches from his face. He can feel its heat, and when he listens closely he can hear its electric hum.

"That might be a little close, huh?" A pair of rubber-gloved hands grabs the lamp by the handles on either side and pushes the thing away until Wilson can relax his eyes. "That's better. Now sit forward for me for just a sec."

Wilson lifts his head as the hands slide a white paper bib around his neck and then smooth the crinkles out across his chest.

"Now"—a masked face comes between Wilson and the lamp; two blue eyes blink at him over the mask's top—"open." Wilson drops his jaw. He feels his lips crack in the stretch, the corners of his mouth splitting in a way he knows will leave him little sores. Fingers pull his lower lip down, his top lip up, his cheek away from his back teeth. The bitter taste of rubber fills his mouth. "Uh-huh." Wilson listens to the hygienist breathe, in-out, in-out, in-out, through her filtered mask. "Gums look a little worse for the wear. Any bleeding when you brush?"

Wilson nods.

"Uh-huh." The fingers leave his mouth. Wilson hears the squeal of wheels as the hygienist slides the stool over to the counter to make marks on Wilson's chart. He hears the scrawl of the pen, the click as it's closed, the squeal of wheels as the hygienist returns. Again the eyes come between Wilson and the lamp. They blink. "Open." Wilson again drops his jaw. "Wider, please." He cringes as his lips again crack. His eyes follow the shine of the mouth mirror as a hand brings it toward his mouth and again pulls his cheek away from his teeth. His eyes cross slightly as he watches the other hand bring a pick from the tray toward him and into his mouth. Wilson shuts his eyes. The hygienist prods his teeth with the pick one by one. Her breathing is loud, and every fifth breath or so seems to be a sigh. Wilson feels the pick stick in five of his back teeth, which since his last visit have become soft with rot. The hygienist grunts as she prods at each of these, rolling her stool to the counter to circle the corresponding teeth on Wilson's chart. Wilson opens his eyes.

"Five cavities."

Wilson nods slightly.

"Awful lot of plaque, too. Do you floss?"

Wilson nods again.

"And does it bleed when you floss?"

"Sometimes."

"Uh-huh. Well. Removing the plaque may be a bit painful, especially with the condition of your gums. They're receding. Tooth roots are exposed."

Wilson nods. He has heard all this before. He knows he brushes too hard. He knows he should use a soft-bristled brush, but he prefers the medium-bristled anyway; it feels, to him, more effective.

The hygienist holds up the mouth mirror and a hooked scaler to scrape the plaque. "Open."

Wilson opens. This time, his lips don't hurt him. He stares at the hygienist's eyes as she works. They are an icy blue with a small ring of brown just around the pupil. A blood vessel has burst in the corner of the left eye, bright red against the white. This happens to him, too. He watches the skin between the eyes crease as the eyes narrow and the scaler digs deep, it feels, beneath his gum. He can taste blood, metallic like the tools, but warm. The scraping of the scaler against his teeth is loud in his head. Saliva gathers in a pool beneath his tongue.

"Okay. Spit." Wilson sits forward and spits into the white plastic sink beside him. He watches blood and chunks of gum swirl with the constant stream of water down the drain. The hygienist hands him a small cup. "Rinse." He rinses, spits, and sits back. "Okay, open."

* * *

The shoe store is stuffy and crowded with after-school shoppers. One corner of the room looks more like a playground than a shoe store: there is a small plastic slide, and there are puzzles, blocks, Nerf balls, and a basketball hoop maybe three feet in height. Isabelle sits on a bench on the other side of the room beside her mother, waiting for the next available salesman to help them. She's selected two pairs of boots from the assortment of them mounted on the wall; one is the type you pull on and off, like her last pair, which Isabelle doesn't like because each step seems to tug her socks down farther around her heel and she can never seem to get the boots off without her socks coming off along with them. But unlike her last pair of boots, this pull-on pair is fur-lined, and Isabelle can't resist. The other pair she's chosen is rubber at the foot and leather up the ankles. This pair laces up; they are a small version of what her father has.

In the same corner of the room as the toys is a popcorn machine and a stack of paper cones. Isabelle eyes the popcorn, the salty yellow kernels glowing under the light that is keeping them warm. She watches as a boy scoops popcorn into a cone, salts it, and hands it to his younger brother beside him. The younger boy watches the older one scoop another coneful up for himself, absently tilting his own cone as he stares. Popcorn kernels spill onto the nubbled carpet, the same kind they have at school, Isabelle notes, where already other kernels lie stale and smashed by heels.

The older boy turns from the machine and starts to cross the room to where he'd been sitting earlier, his younger brother in tow. He lifts three kernels from the cone with his tongue. Isabelle's mouth waters. She looks from where the boys sit with their popcorn back toward the machine itself.

"Do you want some popcorn, Isabelle?" her mother asks. Isabelle quickly drops her eyes to her lap. "It's free," she says. "You can help yourself." Isabelle tugs at a hangnail, and then she sees her mother's hand cross into her field of vision and press down on her own. "Don't pick," she says gently. "Do you want me to get the popcorn for you?"

Yes, Isabelle thinks. *Yes, I do—will you please?* She looks at her mother's hand on her own. Her mother's hand is thin, and her pinky finger hooks inward in the same way that Isabelle's does, so that when she holds the fingers of one hand together, the pinky fits neatly against the contours of the ring finger. Isabelle can see in her own hands and her mother's how the fingers must have been first a solid unit in the womb, separating later, sometime before birth; they still fit neatly back together like an easy puzzle, or the continents of the world.

"So sorry to keep you ladies waiting," a voice says. Isabelle looks up. A balding, heavy-set man with glasses stands before her and her mother. "Busy afternoon in here. What can I help you all find?"

"First thing, actually, is a restroom," Ruth says.

Isabelle looks up at her mother, alarmed by this.

"Of course." The salesman points through a pair of swinging doors. "Follow that hallway to the end, bathroom is the last door on your left."

Isabelle watches her mother disappear through the swinging doors, and her heart quickens. She feels hot, and she clamps her teeth together.

"What are we looking for today, huh?"

Isabelle stares at the swinging doors flapping back and forth until finally they're still.

"Boots, is it? These boots here?"

Isabelle stares at her feet. She is wearing an old pair of Tretorns; slush has seeped back as far as the laces. They are dirty and worn.

"These are a good choice," the man says. "Two very good pairs of boots, and I believe we're fully stocked. They just came in this weekend. Perfect timing for the weather, huh?"

Isabelle looks at the man. He's standing apelike before her, looking at her hopefully. The few strands of hair he's got left he's combed across his bald crown; some of them are out of place. She looks him in the eye and he drops his gaze.

"Well," he says. "I guess a good place to start is by measuring your feet." He pulls a stool in front of her and sits. "So if you just step out of those and stand . . ." Isabelle removes her sneakers, straightens her socks, and stands. Her socks are wet, too. "Sure is time for some boots, I guess," the man says. "Got some wet feet there." He bends down over her feet, adjusting the measuring device around her left foot. His shirt is coming untucked from the back of his pants, and his lower back is damp with sweat.

Isabelle looks up at the sound of the doors swinging on their hinges as her mother emerges from the back; she is eager for her mother to return and relieve this man of his discomfort. From in front of the doors, her mother signals with a single finger lifted that she'll be another minute. She holds an invisible phone up to her ear. Isabelle narrows her eyes. Her palms begin to sweat.

"Looks like you're a two this year." She looks down at the salesman, who is looking up at her from where he's crouched on the ground. The back of his neck is wrinkled into rolls. "That sound about right?"

Isabelle says nothing. Ordinarily, she would nod; she would acknowledge him in some small way. She doesn't mean to make him so uncomfortable. But she can see her mother throwing glances in her direction as she talks on the phone behind the register—if she's talking to anyone at all. Isabelle suspects that she's pretending, and even if she's not, her mother has left her alone with this man on purpose, so that she will be forced to talk. She stands there, silent.

"Well, I'll be back with those boots," the salesman says, breathing heavily as he stands up.

Isabelle watches him go into the back. She breathes deeply, trying to control the waves of anger that cause her heart to beat so hard and fast that she is almost frightened. She blinks slowly, staring straight ahead.

The salesman returns with two shoe boxes tucked beneath one arm and a coneful of popcorn in the other hand. He holds the popcorn out toward her. He smiles almost shyly as he waits for her to take the cone from him. "I thought maybe you'd like some popcorn," he says. "It's good popcorn." Sweat beads on his brow, and his chest heaves, up and down, up and down. Isabelle feels sorry for this man. She is sorry for what she is doing to him. She is sorry for what her mother is doing to him. She wonders if he has children at home, and imagines her own father in this man's position. She would hate whatever child made her father feel this way.

"Here," the salesman is saying. "I mean, if you'd like it." He sits on the stool in front of her, peering at her over the boxes on his lap, his arms reaching over them with the popcorn still held out.

She swallows and reaches for the cone.

This sound, this vibration—it is the low rumble of an outboard motor. Yes, that's what it is. It spreads loudly through all of Wilson's body; he can feel the noise tingling even in his fingertips, and he knows that when it stops, when the engine is turned off, he will feel it for a while even still. The air is neither hot nor cold; it is the temperature of nothing, so comfortable that he's not sure where his body ends and the air begins. The sea is flat, today, glassy still and empty, though he knows that later, sometime in the afternoon, a sea breeze will kick in and the bay will then be triangled with sails they'll watch from the terrace as they drink iced tea brewed with fresh-picked mint. But right now, it is only the three of them cutting fast through the water, Wilson standing at the helm steering only slightly to avoid the lobster pots that float boldly on the water's surface, twisting gently on their tethers.

Ruth sits on the seat in front of him. Her hair is fastened up with bobby pins, and she holds a straw hat—one of her mother's—to her head. She wears a bathing suit and a loose translucent beach shirt, which flaps in the boat's wind. Her legs are propped up on the rail; they are brown with sun, and her toes are painted red. Wilson watches as she reaches down into the cooler beside her and pulls out a Beck's for each of them. She holds her own between her legs as she lifts his up to him over her head. He reaches over the console and squeezes her shoulder, takes the beer.

Isabelle is on her knees on a cushion up in the bow, her face tilted into the wind. Her hair has come unfastened and lashes salty and yellow around her head. She is wearing only a bathing suit, which is all she ever wears in summer. This one is striped in different shades of blue. Every now and then Wilson can hear snatches of Isabelle's voice carried backward on the wind past his ears; she is singing a song he cannot make out, but still, she is singing, and this, and the sun, and the boat's breeze, and the rumble of the motor spreading all throughout his body soothe him.

Then, suddenly, the motor stops. Wilson's body tingles with the memory of the sound, and the new silence rings loudly in his ears. Ruth is gone. Isabelle is gone. The boat, the sea, the sun: all of it is gone. Wilson opens his eyes. One gloved hand pulls an electric toothbrush from his mouth while the other uses a straw to vacuum up the toothpaste and saliva collected beneath his tongue. Wilson blinks.

"Okay," the hygienist says. "You can go ahead and rinse and spit, and then Dr. Falco will be in to see you and schedule a time to fill those cavities."

"We're done?" Wilson says. He can't hide the disappointment in his voice.

"We're done."

On the way home from the shoe store, and from Bloomingdale's after that, they stop at the vet to pick up Maggie, whose early release Wilson evidently arranged despite his reluctance this morning, as Ruth learned when she had called earlier to arrange for it herself. She glances at her daughter, who is clutching Maggie's leash with two hands, pausing whenever the dog finds a place to sniff, which is nearly all the time.

We're never going to get home at this rate! she wants to say, but she does not want to transform the calm, contented look on Isabelle's face back into the dark, awful scowl she wore at the shoe store, and then at Bloomingdale's, where every Christmas dress Ruth suggested Isabelle try on was surveyed with a skeptical frown. Ruth pictures with annoyance last year's Christmas dress, which she had, as she does every year, sent as a hand-me-down to Wilson's niece, assuming that by this Christmas Isabelle would have outgrown it. She ought to have outgrown it, Ruth thinks, but then again, when it comes to Isabelle "ought" means nothing.

"Shit," Ruth mutters, feeling the slushy water of the puddle she hadn't noticed seep into her shoe. "Goddammit." She looks down at her feet with irritation, and then at Isabelle and Maggie, who have paused just behind her. Maggie is intent on a shoveled mound of snow, and Isabelle has bent down to tie the laces of her new boot, which have come undone and are wet from dragging through the slush.

She takes Maggie's leash and watches Isabelle work the laces, her bare fingers raw and red as they fumble numbly with a knot. No gloves and no hat, Ruth thinks, shaking her head. She laid them out for her, but Isabelle opted not to wear them; now, Ruth can tell from the color of her fingers and her red-rimmed ears, Isabelle is paying the price. Three times Ruth watches Isabelle drop the lace with one hand to sweep the unruly hair from her face, only to have to begin again the bow she is trying to tie; finally Ruth squats down to tie it for her. "Gloves, dear," she says. "Gloves would help."

They both stand when Ruth has finished, and before heading on, Ruth pauses to look at her daughter, her red face and that mop of hair. She has offered to take Isabelle to get it evened out, or shaped into some semblance of a haircut, but Isabelle has declined, and Ruth doesn't have the energy to fight her. If that is

84

the way Isabelle wants her hair, for whatever reason, then fine. And if she doesn't want a Christmas dress this year, then that's fine, too. Ruth pictures Isabelle at any of the Christmas parties they usually go to each year, dressed among the suited guests in blue jeans and a flannel shirt, her hair wispy and electric with static. How will they explain this silent child at their side while in the other room the rest of the children have gathered to suck on their candy canes and watch Christmas movies? What on earth will they say? How much easier, she thinks, if this silence had a name, something technical and scientific that in a single word would sum up this enormous, amorphous, nameless thing!

"Come on," she says, taking Isabelle's hand, though she says it more to herself than to her daughter, a reminder to keep on going.

Isabelle follows, or, rather, she lets herself be led, taking in everything around her as if she hadn't seen it all before. Steam curls from an open manhole in the middle of the avenue; men in hard hats stand around it, feeding some kind of hose down to the worker below, the top of whose hard hat Isabelle can just see jutting up from underground. Construction barricades block the area from traffic; drivers honk at the delay as the flow of traffic slows to maneuver its way around the site. The sidewalk is congested, too, with holiday vendors; at one table, a vendor sells art books wrapped in plastic, and at another table an Asian man with no hat or scarf himself, Isabelle notices, is selling the very things he lacks. He must be cold, she thinks; she is cold without a hat or a scarf. But part of her understands why the man might suffer the cold even with all the wares before him, as if by donning a hat or a scarf when he has started the day without he is somehow surrendering—though to what or whom, Isabelle isn't sure. The cold, maybe, or the wife at home who advised him to dress more warmly, or to himself for giving in to the temptation of warmth the goods that he is selling provide.

"No, thank you," she hears her mother say, and she turns to look with alarm from the Asian man to the person her mother is addressing in a tone of voice that seems to Isabelle bordering on rude. A man has stepped into their path and opened a briefcase of knockoff Rolex watches; her mother drops Isabelle's hand and instead grips her shoulder, steering them both away from the man and then around the corner onto a side street.

"I can't stand Lex, sometimes," her mother says, slowing her pace as they make their way west on a street tranquil by comparison to the avenue they have left behind. "Too much for Maggie to smell, too." She takes Isabelle's hand again. Isabelle glances backward over her shoulder, disappointed by the turn they have taken. The smell of a vendor's honey-roasted nuts wafts after them like a tease. Isabelle breathes it in greedily, searching for the smell with every breath until she is sure that it is gone. There are no vendors on Park or Madison, she thinks, no crowds like the one they have left behind—but then as her mother takes the right turn up Park Avenue, Isabelle's resistance gives. Park offers its own spectacles. She studies the molding and stonework of each building they pass, her head tilted back so that she can look as high as the topmost story where the stonework and carvings are the most elaborate. She compares the awnings of the buildings—some are green and some are gray, some have a ridged border and others are straight across, and they are all shaped differently, too, whether arched or square. Gray and arched, she thinks; gray and arched makes for the best-looking canopy.

She lets out a contented breath and looks down at the sidewalk passing beneath her feet. This particular sidewalk is the city's standard sidewalk—a gray-white ribbon of concrete with scoring every four feet or so—and comfortingly familiar. But there are other types of sidewalk, too, Isabelle thinks. There are those hexagonal pavers on the park side of Fifth, and the redbrick sidewalk outside the Met, and her favorite, the rose-colored marble slabs around the Cooper-Hewitt, smooth enough to slide on when it rains. And on leafy side streets like their own street, the concrete is broken, ruptured by tree roots, and sometimes, just sometimes, you come upon a textured sidewalk inlaid with shells. Maybe these are actually her favorite, she thinks; she likes to imagine from what beach the shells might have come.

She feels her mother squeeze her hand. "Let's cross here," her mother says. Isabelle looks up at the street sign; already they are almost home. She steps off the curb after her mother, pulling her hand free to run it through Maggie's fur before putting it in her pocket to warm it for a while. She steps only on the white rungs of the crosswalk painted on the asphalt and then, when they are once again on the sidewalk, she allows each foot to fall only and exactly once inside each square of the concrete, and she counts the squares as they go—twelve, thirteen, fourteen—and then, with a start, she looks up. A large bus has pulled up along the curb just ahead of them, and through the cracked windows Isabelle can hear the voices of girls calling, *Maggie! Maggie!* She stops dead; her mother keeps walking for several yards before she realizes that Isabelle is not following her.

"Oh, for heaven's sake," she says, putting a hand on her hip. "What is the problem?"

Isabelle stares up the street at the girls leaping from the bus in their basketball uniforms, being delivered back to school from some away game, their mouths smeared with chocolate icing from the cupcakes someone must have brought for a postgame snack. If things were normal, she herself would be coming off that bus, eager to get to the safety of her bedroom. The past hours would have been spent being bumped and yelled at by girls bigger than she, dizzy in the fluorescent light of an unfamiliar gymnasium, undoubtedly cold in her shorts and netted jersey, the screech of sneakers against the varnished floor grating in her ears. Why on earth had she ever subjected herself to any of that?

"Maggie!" the girls are saying, a handful of them gathered around her dog, a familiar sight from the soccer games to which her mother always brought the dog along to watch. From yards down the street and in the failing light, Isabelle watches, her eyes narrowed. She can see the girl who was her closest friend, Caroline, whispering in the ear of a girl she doesn't recognize, a new girl, Isabelle thinks. Caroline had sent her letters for a while when she first stopped coming to school, but not since before the summer. She looks different to Isabelle, maybe because of her haircut, but then when she looks at others of her old schoolmates, they look different, too, all of them familiar and foreign at once, the versions of themselves that might appear in dreams, themselves, but not themselves.

"Isabelle!" her mother calls, gesturing her over and at the same time alerting the girls to Isabelle's presence. They stop their chattering and cries of *Maggie!* They fall silent and stare in Isabelle's direction, as if she were some strange specimen, or a ghost returned from the dead. Isabelle drops her gaze to the sidewalk.

"Hi, Isabelle," one girl calls, and a few others mutter the same. Isabelle does not look up. Her whole body is hot with shame. She does not want to be seen this way. She does not want these girls to think of her this way, because then it will be harder to return to the way she used to be, which she can hardly remember herself. It wasn't all horrible, she knows. It wasn't all cold gymnasiums and competition. There were times when she roughhoused on the bus with the rest of them, had cupcake-eating contests, threw cookie crumbs into the open windows of nearby taxis. That is how she wants these girls to think of her. That is the self she wants to return to, when she can. But for everyone to see her like this—it adds weight to her silence, a weight that is harder to get out from under. It makes it more permanent; it makes it more *who she is*.

The basketball coach gathers her team together and leads the girls across the street toward the school, where their parents are waiting to fetch them. In the relative quiet, Ruth walks the few steps back to where Isabelle stands frozen, and tries to take her hand. Isabelle yanks it away and hurries in the direction of home, her eyes on the ground all the while. Ruth watches the small, hatless creature of a child stalk away, and she feels her heart sink. She hadn't exactly planned on such an encounter—how could she know the basketball team would pull up just as they were passing?—but she had known that in coming this way the possibility of such an encounter did exist, and she had taken that chance. Part of her thought that coming by the school might be a good thing for Isabelle, might remind her of the world she's left behind; she hadn't meant to rub that world in Isabelle's face. Yet again, Ruth thinks, she has fucked up.

She thinks back to the earliest days of Isabelle's silence, and how she and Wilson had thought that the silence was reserved for them, and that Isabelle was herself at school. This was maybe a month after the jump-rope incident. How humiliating it had been to be called into school that second time! *Are you aware that Isabelle is not speaking?* Mrs. Mason had asked. Of course they were! But not that she wasn't speaking at school! Not that she wasn't speaking to her teachers and friends! It was that afternoon that Caroline, over at their apartment for a prearranged playdate, appeared in the doorway of Ruth's study and asked if she could please go home.

"Are you all right?" Ruth had asked. "Are you sick?"

Caroline had looked at the floor. "I'm okay," she said. "I'm just ready to go home."

It had all happened so quickly, the silence, Ruth thinks. Though had it? Had she and Wilson just been oblivious? They had. Of course they had. And now things have come to this!

Ruth watches Isabelle vanish around the corner, and she hurries after her, dragging Maggie along. When she rounds the corner herself, she is almost surprised to find that Isabelle has not disappeared entirely, following her voice into whatever void it's gone to, but there she is, hunched and quick and silent against the cold, hurrying in the direction of home.

The midtown streets are crowded. From behind, the pack of businesspeople waiting to cross the street looks vaguely cartoonish: a collection of broad shoulders all cloaked in shades of brown, whether leather, canvas, or fur, their breaths hovering as a single cloud above them like a blank speech bubble. If he were to draw this cartoon, Wilson thinks, he would have them pawing at the slushy ground with their feet, anxious to be released into motion by a green light. Maybe he'd also give them spears and shields with which to face the oncoming crowd crossing the street the other way.

The light changes and the flow begins. A moving truck halfway down the street is blocking cross-street traffic, which is backed up as far as the crosswalk, where a turbaned cabbie flinches and shrugs in apology at the mob rushing around his cab, some of them banging the hood or the trunk of the taxi with their fists as they pass, as if the cabbie has put himself intentionally in their way. Wilson takes a breath and joins the flow, no longer bothering after all these years of living in the city to excuse himself if he bumps shoulders or steps on a heel. He keeps his eyes lowered. Everyone wears galoshes.

It is only a few blocks to the bookstore. Inside, he pulls off his gloves and scarf and unbuttons his jacket. He scans the signs hanging from the high ceilings above the various sections of the store: FICTION, COOKING, PHOTOGRAPHY, SELF-HELP, TRAVEL. This last is the section Wilson is looking for. He tucks his gloves and scarf into his pocket, takes off his jacket and slings it over his arm, and takes out from his breast pocket the piece of paper on which he has written the names of several books on Africa recommended by the travel agency. He locates four of the seven of them, which is more than he would have even hoped for; it seems to him that whenever he goes to any store looking for something specific, whether a book, an album of music, or a shirt in his size, it isn't there. That four of the seven books he was looking for presented themselves, and that he didn't have to ask a salesperson, or place a special order, seems to him a good sign—or what someone who believed in signs would take to be a good one about Africa.

Wilson brings the books to the bookstore café upstairs, where he buys a coffee and settles in at a table by the wall of windows that faces the street. From above, the crowd passing by on the street below looks somehow more orderly than it did from the ground; the sets of heads and shoulders, which is what the people look like from up here, flow against one another smoothly; there are few collisions, and all seem to move at a uniform pace. For just a second, he thinks he sees a head that might be Ruth's, and his heart quickens with the desire to knock on the window, to somehow get her attention from up here or to run outside to meet her, though by the time he'd make it downstairs and outside he knows she would be gone, swallowed up by the crowd. His feeling of desire transforms into one of helplessness, and then into relief because he knows, and has known all along, that the passing head does not belong to Ruth. Ruth, he knows, is probably at the vet, or maybe home from the vet with Maggie, presenting her to Isabelle in the hopes that the dog might get her to speak again, or at least to smile. Something that Wilson himself should be able to do. Something that he *will* do, he thinks, opening the first book in his pile.

IV

Ruth sits at the kitchen table and watches Wilson at the sink, finishing the last of the dishes. The room seems to waver in the light tossed by the unsynchronized dancing of the candles Isabelle placed around the room and lit before dinner. Neither Ruth nor Wilson has blown them out and turned the lights back on, even though Isabelle has been in bed for nearly an hour now.

Wilson is methodical in his washing: silverware first, then glasses, then plates, all rinsed and then put into the dishwasher; next the pots and pans that must be washed entirely by hand and left out on the rack to dry. His shirtsleeves are rolled up, his watch set on the counter beside him. Ruth has always teased him about his thinning hair, which in truth has been more wispy and fine than thin, but from this angle, in this light, that spot at the back of his head, the spot where his cowlick stands tall in all the pictures of Wilson as a boy, really is beginning to show signs of becoming bare. Ruth watches as Wilson sets the salad bowl upside down on the rack and reaches next for the lasagna dish.

"Don't bother with that one," she says. She overcooked the lasagna just a bit, but enough so that the topmost layer of cheese burned against the side of the casserole dish. "Just let it soak."

Wilson leaves the dish soaking, though he hates not to leave the sink empty, and dries his hands. "Should I open some more wine?" he asks.

He returns to the table with a bottle of red and two new glasses. Ruth watches as he pours, unsure how to tell him what she ought to have told him the minute he walked through the door. But before she could get to him, Isabelle and Maggie had skidded down the hall and Wilson had been ushered away to see Isabelle's new boots, and Ruth herself had been left in the kitchen alone with her cocktail and the scent of lasagna, glad that at least Isabelle's father could bring a smile to her face after the afternoon's multiple fiascos—the shoe store, Bloomingdale's, the basketball team. But now she wouldn't blame him if he were incredulous that she has let so much time go by since her meeting with Mrs. Mason to say anything to him—though she had *tried*, she thinks, and would have, if he returned her goddamn calls!

She thinks of this afternoon, when she'd tried to call him for the third time today from the shoe store to tell him the news, and how she'd been filled with a senseless, startling rage at the receptionist's report that, yes, his conference and his meeting were both through but now he was at the dentist, and that, yes, she had let him know that Ruth had called but would be sure to leave another message. And then there'd been Isabelle, across that stuffy room, standing stiff and sullen as the sweating, tired salesman measured her feet, throwing her mother furious looks that made more clear to Ruth than words that leaving her daughter alone like this had been a huge mistake, though she'd hoped that maybe, maybe while she was gone, Isabelle might talk, might be forced to talk. And then there'd been the matter of the vet, about which Wilson had been so utterly uncooperative; now it was up to her to get Maggie released a day early, and of course it would be *her* fault if the vet said no, you must wait until tomorrow; *she* would be the source of Isabelle's disappointment when all she wanted to do in the first place was make her daughter happy. She had stood there fuming as she flipped through her little red book for the number of the vet. She'd planned on simply appearing there and acting as if they'd expected to pick up Maggie on Monday all along, but this idea had come to seem foolish—better to make up an excuse, that they were going away tomorrow early and so needed to get the dog tonight.

She dialed and smiled hopefully at her daughter as she waited through several rings for someone to pick up. Across the shoe store, Isabelle glared. But then, when Ruth finally got through, the receptionist told her that Mr. Carter had already called and arranged things, and Maggie was waiting even now to be picked up.

Ruth rubs her eyes, exhausted, unsure what the hell she feels—annoyance at Wilson, or gratitude, or guilt—she's all over the place.

"Wil," she says.

Wilson pushes her wineglass toward her and sits down. He looks at her, and there is something about his eyes that saddens Ruth. It isn't that they are slightly bloodshot, which they are; nor is it the small crust of sleep that Ruth scoops from the corner of his eye with her pinky. Neither is it the way his eyes have sunk these past months deeper into shadow or the way the crow's feet reaching from the corners of his eyes have become sharper, more pronounced. It's something she can't quite put her finger on, or maybe it is all of these things together that speak so clearly to his weariness.

"Thank you for doing the dog," she says. "Thank you for arranging that after all."

Wilson sips his wine. "It was nothing," he says. He sighs. "You had me worried with that look."

"What look?"

"I don't know. Whatever look it was."

Ruth hesitates. "I saw Mrs. Mason today. She can't go back to school in January."

"What?"

"Not unless she's speaking."

"They can't."

"They can. Can and are. We have *got* to get her speaking by then. I don't know what else we'll do!"

"Christ," Wilson says. And he says again all he can think to say. "They *can't*."

"Wilson."

The idea frightens Wilson inordinately; it is as if the ever-thinning carpet they've been floating on has disintegrated completely, leaving them in a terrible free fall. Even though Isabelle isn't attending school now, she is at least associated with a school, doing the homework a school assigns; she has at least a modicum of normalcy in her life. For the school to deny her that, for the school to give up on her—it angers him that they would see her as a lost cause this way. She is not a lost cause, he thinks, and *he* will *not* give up on her. His mind begins to race: through his mind flash images of women with long, sagging breasts and collared necks, of flies buzzing around the carcass of a zebra, of plains so vast you can almost see the earth begin to curve; he thinks of Isabelle's lion lying folded on his dresser.

"Maybe," he says, his mouth dry, "maybe we should go in January. I mean, if she's not speaking. But if she hasn't spoken in nine months, why would she now? What's going to change in a month? We should think about that. January. It might help."

"What?"

"Africa!" he says. "I spoke with the travel agent today, just to test the waters. I mean, since we were thinking about it. And I went and looked through some travel books. I was thinking June initially, like you said, but hell, a trip like that might just do it!" He's not sure why it is he feels this way, but Africa— the idea of it, the images this afternoon, Isabelle's drawing—Africa is full of promise. It is bright. It is open. It is huger than silence. It is all that is left.

"Since we were thinking about it? Wilson, what are you talking about?"

98

"It was your idea," he says. "The other night. You brought it up."

"Africa? Wilson, I was making conversation."

They are silent. The flame on the candle by the sink shrinks and sputters out as Wilson watches.

"Africa is not the answer, Wil."

"Then what is?"

Ruth sighs. "I wish I knew." She pauses. "And anyway, we don't even want to have to think about being in Africa in January. That is *not* where we want to be. We want to be back to ourselves. We want Isabelle to be in school." Ruth pauses. "We *need* it."

They are quiet.

"She's got an appointment with another shrink on Wednesday. Maybe he can get her talking by January."

"Another one?"

"I told you the last one gave up."

"And what if he can't? What if he's just as useless as all the others?"

"He comes highly recommended. He's dealt with this kind of thing before." She's not sure how she thinks she'll persuade Wilson when she isn't convinced of anything herself.

Kind of thing, Wilson thinks. He pushes back his chair and hurries to their bedroom, returns with Isabelle's drawing. "Look," he says, unfolding the drawing and handing it to Ruth. He turns on the light and stands above her as she looks down at the drawing. "Isabelle did it at Luigi's the other night."

Ruth stares at the lion, at its mouth open wide, its deep black throat. It is a troubling image. "And you think this means she wants to go to Africa?"

Wilson shrugs. "Maybe. I don't know. I don't know what it means."

Ruth folds the drawing back up and hands it to Wilson.

"No," he says. "Keep it. Maybe this new shrink can explain it. Or something. I don't know." He turns the light off. Ruth looks up at him. The reflection of candlelight trembles in his eyes.

"I'll show it to him," she says.

Maggie plods into the room and leans against Wilson's leg. He strokes her absently and finishes his wine. "I should probably take this beast out."

Ruth nods. Wilson pushes back his chair and walks into the hall. Maggie has moved over to Ruth now and rested her chin on Ruth's knee as Ruth scratches her behind the ears; Wilson waits for a minute in the doorway and watches them before calling Maggie after him.

Ruth puts her finger to her lips, gesturing in the direction of Isabelle's room just down the hall.

But Isabelle is awake still. Sleep tonight seems impossible. She lies on her side in bed, facing the clock, watching the colon blink between the numbers that stand for hours and those that stand for minutes. She hears her father call for the dog, and then she hears the rattle of Maggie's collar and the clumsy sound of her paws against the carpet as she scrabbles down the hall, always eager to go out in snow—only eager to go out in snow. She hears the elevator groan in its shaft as it ascends to their floor, and then she hears its doors thud shut with a sound that seems to Isabelle somehow final. She shudders and rolls onto her back, takes a breath, and then gets out of bed. She crosses through the unlit room into the bathroom and sits down on the lowered toilet lid. The bathroom tiles are cold beneath her feet, and so she pulls her knees to her chest inside her nightgown. The room is cast in a tinny glow from the streetlamps outside, and the blurry shadows of the topmost branches of the huge oaks that line the park waver on the ceiling. A garbage truck squeals to a stop outside; she listens to the hiss and steam of its iron arms as they close in around garbage bags piled on the curb, the rumble of the garbage tumbling into the truck.

She looks at the mirror above the cabinet in front of her. She is too low to see her own reflection, but she can see the wall behind her, and a drawing hanging there that her father did in pencil years ago. She squints at the drawing in the mirror; she has not looked closely at it for some time. It is of their apple tree, and it is perfect. It is fading and a little bit water stained, and she thinks that tomorrow she should take it down and put it somewhere safe, since now the apple tree is dying. She lowers her eyes from the mirror to the cabinet, behind which she keeps all her old sketchbooks. She loves to go through this cabinet, but she will not do it often; to go through the cabinet is a special treat, a special activity that if done too much will lose its magic. Right now she knows too well what is inside: old bath toys, shells that she collected from Hilton Head, a box of rocks she collected at her grandmother's house after she died, a mustard-colored basin her parents bathed her in when she was a baby, an old set of curlers, a sewing kit, a box of bobby pins and barrettes, sample perfume vials. She wants to forget about these things, so that in a few months, some day when she is at home alone, she can rediscover them all.

She loves to rediscover things: letters in the folds of old books, money in winter pockets, the playbill from the circus in the bottom of a drawer. She wills herself to forget the details of the photographs in the album of her parents' wedding, or the contents of books in the locked bookcase in the hall. She takes more pleasure in rediscovery than in discovery itself, the mixture of newness and familiarity that rediscovery affords. Someday, she thinks, she will rediscover her voice. She thinks of the winter before, where she left her voice, and how some days the prospect of waiting for even only an hour to pass seemed like a lifetime, and how she started to feel better once she'd resigned herself to silence, once she'd made a game of it. It was one thing that she could control; it was one thing that was hers. That first day had been February 29, 286 days ago. It wasn't a real day, anyway, she'd figured, a day not to get out of bed, to eat, to drink, to speak. And that silence—it had given her something to live for, became an addiction. What she should have done, she thinks now, is set a limit for it. She should have allowed herself a day of silence only, maybe two, three, or four, or allowed herself only one day of silence a week. But she hadn't, and the longer the silence has gone on, the greater an issue it has become. She can't bear to think of the attention words would bring her, the looks exchanged at words coming from the silent girl's mouth. Yes, in trying to withdraw, she has called too much attention to herself; no one is going to ignore the fact of her silence. *Hello* used to be so easy, and part of her longs for that time when it was. She should get it over with, just speak before the days between her old self and the self she has become are too many to overcome; the problem is that she's afraid it might be too late. It is too late. She can't even bring herself to speak aloud anymore when no one is there to listen.

She stands and goes to the window. It is windy, and small flakes of snow whirl in the air. She can see her father and Maggie at the edge of the park, waiting in the pool of light from a streetlamp to cross the street toward home, Maggie's head pointing into the wind, her father in a hat and flapping scarf, his shoulders tight against the cold. The light changes, and their shadows grow before them as they pass out of the streetlamp's glow, coming closer to the building until she cannot see them anymore.

THREE

Wednesday

I

The rug in the waiting room is Oriental and patterned in a satisfyingly complicated design, more complicated even than the design of the rug in their dining room at home, which Isabelle has spent hours memorizing while lying under the table with Maggie. Maggie lies always in a spot one third of the way down from the top of the rug and one third of the way over from the rug's left edge; she has worn the blue spidery shape there thin. This rug, the one in the waiting room, has similar spidery shapes, but really Isabelle can't call them spidery, because they have twelve legs, not eight. The length of the rug is twice the width, and when Isabelle breaks the rug neatly into imaginary squares, she can see how certain squares consist of the same patterns as others, but inverted, or colored differently, and suddenly the overall design of the rug seems much more simple, the making of a rug like this more manageable, something that Isabelle, if she knew how, could do. What puzzles her most about this rug in the end is the part of the rug that seems at first the easiest to understand. She blurs her eyes at the outermost border. It consists simply of interlocking triangles, the blue triangles coming down like the top teeth in a grimace, the red ones standing up like the bottom teeth. The question she can't answer as she looks at the border is which color is the border's background? The blue or the red? The background of the body of the rug is clearly a bronze color on which the spidery designs have been laid; but as for the border, do the blue triangles rest on a red background, or the red triangles on a blue background? In her mind, it must be one way or the other. To think of them both as triangles and neither as the background unsettles the rug somehow, but to decide which is which seems as impossible as deciding which came first, the chicken or the egg.

Isabelle moves her eyes from the edge of the rug to the dark panels of the hardwood floor beneath it, which themselves end at the wall just beyond the rug's edge or else disappear beneath the thick wooden door of the office into which this new doctor has led her mother. She can imagine her mother sitting there, her purse at her feet and her back straight, the doctor far off across the desk between them. She imagines the knuckles of her mother's hands white as she balls them into fists or else grabs at the arms of her chair; she imagines the sound of her mother's grinding teeth. She imagines the psychiatrist's diplomas on the walls, the photographs of his children on his desk, the ink blotter, the paperweight, the wall of books on childhood trauma and emotional disorders, the same titles she sees in every doctor's office. To think of it all makes her tired.

She is right in what she imagines; the desk between the doctor and Ruth is wide, there are the wall of books, the diplomas, and the paperweight. Ruth is sitting up straight in her chair, her purse at her feet, anxious as she waits for this new doctor finally to speak, to say something beyond the formalities. Ruth watches his eyes move quickly back and forth across each page as he thumbs through an open folder on his desk. Finally he clears his throat. "An interesting case, your daughter," he says. "I've read through her file," he says. "I've read through it quite carefully, and it's an interesting case."

"Interesting?" Ruth repeats. "Meaning?"

"Well," the doctor says, setting the folder back on the desk, "it's been nine months of silence, is that correct?"

"Yes," Ruth says.

"The symptoms and clinical observations aren't at all consistent with a diagnosis of autism. There is nothing clinically wrong."

"Correct."

"And she's seen, what, five, six other psychiatrists?"

"Four."

"And none of them have been of any help to Isabelle."

"She's very stubborn," Ruth says. "She has a will of steel."

"Ah," the doctor says. "First and foremost it is paramount not to blame the patient in situations like these. It is not because she is stubborn that none have had success with her; it is not because she does not want to speak."

Ruth looks at this man, this Dr. Steingold. "Then what? Why? If she *wanted* to speak, then why wouldn't she speak? I don't think she *wants* to speak."

"I've seen cases like this before," Dr. Steingold says, pushing back from his desk. "Not necessarily cases of silence, but withholding of other sorts—some children will not, say, make a bowel movement; others will not eat."

He looks at Ruth. She nods. "Yes," she says, urging him on.

"Habits that seem derived of stubbornness yet that are really beyond the patient's control."

"And so what do you do?"

"This is where, in a case like Isabelle's, things become most tricky. With other children, you help get at the *why* of things."

"How?"

"You talk. You listen, and you talk. You *discuss*."

Ruth feels her heart fall. This doctor, it seemed, was taking a new direction with things; now they seem back to square one—the only way for Isabelle to speak again is to speak about why she won't.

"And the difficulty with Isabelle—"

"Is that she won't speak," Ruth interrupts. "She can't talk, you can't listen, the two of you can't

107

discuss." She cannot hide the frustration in her voice.

"Exactly," the doctor says. He sniffs. "And in the weeks or months preceding this silence, did you notice anything unusual? Could Isabelle have experienced some trauma? Was there anything that could have precipitated this? I'm sure you've been asked these questions over and over again, but I have to ask, you understand. Perhaps something will occur to you now that hasn't before."

Ruth sits back in her chair. She *has* been asked these questions, again and again. Isabelle's silence had started as joylessness, in Ruth's mind. She pictures Isabelle sitting among springtime bloom at the Conservatory Garden, blaming her watery eyes on allergies when she'd never in her life had allergies before. She thinks of Isabelle's habit of retiring to her room before the sitter had arrived whenever Ruth and Wilson went out at night, leaving the puzzled teenager who'd come armed with cookie dough and games sitting in their living room as if alone. She remembers the time she scolded Isabelle for not saying *thank you* to the ice cream man at Russo's, thinking her silence simply rudeness. Isabelle had cast her eyes downward, had let the ice cream melt down the sides of the cone before finally tipping it into a garbage can. Ruth had been so frustrated! If only she had paid better attention to these moments, these quirks. "Well," she says. "There was no specific event that I can think of. That I know of."

"But there could have been."

"I suppose. But it was gradual. It wasn't sudden."

"What do you mean by gradual?"

Ruth shrugs. "She just started speaking less and less. She seemed sadder and sadder." Ruth blinks. "Which I suppose I mistakenly interpreted as adolescence. And then she wasn't speaking at all." But when that really was, she can't be sure. In her mind, the beginning of Isabelle's official silence was the day that she and Wilson were called again into school and informed that Isabelle wouldn't speak there, either. In a way, it was Mrs. Mason who had made it official: *Are you aware that Isabelle is not speaking?* It was in Mrs. Mason's office that everything solidified, where their lives switched tracks: no speaking meant no more school, which meant no more work for Ruth, though the work of poring through psychology books and dragging Isabelle from one shrink to the next has become work enough. Ruth swallows. "You know, I can't even remember the last word she said. I don't remember the exact day."

Dr. Steingold clears his throat and flattens his lips sympathetically. He grunts, tapping his pen against his mouth.

Ruth sighs. Her shoulders feel heavy. She is tired. She listens to Dr. Steingold flipping again through papers and focuses on the wall hangings behind him. There are a number of diplomas and framed awards of merit; there is a painting of a pear against a blue background that might be a cloudless sky; there is a black-and-white photograph of the doctor as a very young man in front of a low, thatch-roofed hut, the dust from the ground swirling in the wind around his feet.

Africa.

Ruth sits up suddenly and reaches for her purse. She rifles through it for Isabelle's drawing, the one she promised Wilson she would show the shrink. Maybe, she thinks, maybe Wilson is right. "Doctor," she says.

Dr. Steingold looks up with an expression of surprise at the new, hopeful tone in Ruth's voice. Ruth holds the picture out for the doctor to see. He takes it from her and looks at it.

"Interesting," he says. He looks up. "Isabelle did this?"

"Yes," Ruth says. "Just last weekend. Do you think it means anything?"

"Art is always an important method of communication. And in this case it is even more important, since we don't have the benefit of spoken communication."

"And do you think she's trying to communicate something?"

"Whether consciously or not, certainly there is meaning in everything we make." He refolds the drawing and hands it out to Ruth.

"Wouldn't you like to keep it, then? Study it, or whatever?"

Dr. Steingold breathes out through his nose and retracts his hand. He tucks the drawing into Isabelle's file. "Mrs. Carter," he says, and he looks her in the eye. "We're going to get to the bottom of this. You wait."

Dr. Steingold has told her that he understands that she will not speak; instead, he has presented her with a series of puzzles, some consisting of as few as six pieces.

"My," he says, as Isabelle completes a fifteen-piece puzzle of a clown. "You're quick. You've got a good mind for puzzles." Isabelle watches as he jots something down in his notebook. He looks up at her with an earnest expression that makes Isabelle uncomfortable, somehow, because this man is trying, she understands, yet he is so very far off track. Being in the room with him is like watching a blindfolded person trying to pin the tail on the donkey and pinning it to the wall three feet away instead. "Isabelle," he finally says, tapping his pen to his lips. He crosses his legs. "I want you to look at the puzzle you've just completed. Look at it carefully."

Isabelle looks at the clown in the puzzle. He is sitting on a milk crate, and his shoes are red and long. His pants are blue-and-white striped, held high by yellow suspenders, and there is a wilted pink flower tucked into the brim of his hat. His chin rests in his gloved hand, and his mouth is painted into a frown. He looks tired.

Isabelle looks back at Dr. Steingold with a blank expression.

"Do you notice something unusual about this clown?"

Isabelle continues to stare at the doctor.

"Anything at all? You don't have to say it to me, of course, but maybe you could point to the part of the clown that seems strange."

Nothing. Dr. Steingold uncrosses his legs and crosses them the other way. He licks his lips.

"Or you could imitate the expression on his face. He's frowning, isn't he? But what should he be doing instead? Can you show me with your own face what a clown should do?"

Isabelle breathes in slowly through her nose as the pity she's been feeling for this doctor and his good intentions rapidly dissolves. Who does he think she is? She watches Dr. Steingold's tongue come snakelike from between his teeth and dab at his dry, cracked lips. His teeth are yellowing and lined; his top front teeth are ridged, sawlike, at the bottom. She can imagine the silver fillings that must line his back teeth, and the same cracks on the back of the tongue she used to notice in her old science teacher. She can tell that his mouth is dry as well as his lips; the little spit there clings like foam to the tip of his tongue as his mouth forms her name. *Isabelle,* she sees his mouth saying, but she has shut him out. She stares at his mouth as it moves, as the lips form words around the tongue, as the tongue darts in and out, licks, pauses, starts to move again. Mouths, she thinks, are strange things. If this doctor thinks something is wrong with the mouth of the clown in the puzzle, she wonders what he would think of a puzzle of his own mouth now. Maybe she'll make one and bring it in pieces for him to assemble next week. She bites the insides of her cheeks to keep from laughing, but to think of a puzzle like that and the doctor's expression once he'd seen it is too much, too funny, and Isabelle cannot help but laugh. She laughs silently; she shakes and reddens, and her eyes begin to tear, and the doctor's expression turns into one of utter stupefaction even as Isabelle does as he asked her to do and, like a proper clown, gives him a smile.

II

There is a constant parade of tiny ants that march up and down the back wall of the cabinet under the sink where the largest of the pots are kept. Some emerge from the crack where the back and top of the cabinet come together and disappear through the same space at the bottom; others make the journey in the opposite direction. Oftentimes, an upward traveling ant and a downward traveling ant will collide, each as if unaware of the other's presence until their tiny antennae have touched, or maybe, Isabelle thinks, their meetings are intentional. Maybe it's that they're greeting each other, imparting some kind of news— what kind of morsels have been dropped beneath the far chair at the kitchen table, what kind of mood the queen ant is in back at the farm, that the kitchen floor has just been washed and the cracks between the tiles are too flooded for crossing. She has been watching these ants for months now, and the more she watches them, so determined, so undistracted even by the huge face peering in at them from the world outside the cabinet, the more she senses that these creatures have a purpose, a goal, and the thought of that fills her with something close to jealousy, though she's not sure she'd ever say she'd like to be an ant.

"Isabelle." Isabelle hears her mother's voice behind her and slams the cabinet closed as she spins around and stands from where she's been squatting on the floor. Her mother stands in the kitchen doorway with a grocery bag under each arm, her head tilted slightly to the side in puzzlement. Isabelle hadn't heard her mother's footsteps, hadn't even sensed her presence in the room, and this makes her nervous. She wonders how long her mother has been standing there and whether her ants now will be discovered. "Are you finding what you need in there?"

Isabelle holds up the large silver pot she'd been looking for, the one she likes to use to cook her Wednesday-night specialty, which this year she thinks of as *spaghettini à la zucchini*. Wednesday night has been Isabelle's dinner night for nearly three years, ever since the time one winter when both her parents came down with the flu and she toasted up some frozen chicken nuggets for all of them to have with soup for dinner.

Her mother smiles, puts the grocery bags down on the table, and pulls her jacket off. Isabelle puts the pot down on the stove and turns to help with the groceries.

"I swear to God," her mother says, pulling a carton of milk and some bagels for tomorrow's breakfast from a bag. She puts the bagels on the counter behind her and the milk in the refrigerator. Isabelle hands her mother a jar of applesauce to put away while the fridge is open. "No matter how good a job I think we do shopping in the country, without fail I need to shop again midweek." She reaches into the bag. "I mean," she says, holding two zucchini out toward Isabelle, "how could we forget your zucchini? Where is my mind?" Isabelle takes the zucchini from her mother and puts them on the cutting board she's set beside the stove. "And your father's applesauce, though I didn't actually forget that—I bought three jars the weekend before that I thought would last him at least a little longer. But." She shrugs and hands Isabelle a fresh loaf of French bread to go with dinner. "And the cheese," she says, handing Isabelle the last of the ingredients required for her meal. "Which of course we can only get here. You go ahead and get started, though. I can do the rest of the groceries."

Isabelle fills the pot and sets it to boil. She's just begun to rummage through a drawer for the ivory-handled knife she likes to use for the zucchini when she hears above the clatter of the cookware the commotion in the hallway that means her father has come home. She hears Maggie skid to a stop at the end of the hallway, where she knows her father is crouched down with his arms wide open and ready to greet the dog, and then she hears Maggie's happy whine as her father rubs her vigorously and tells her through clenched teeth that *she's a good dog, yes she is, yes she is.*

Isabelle finds the knife she's looking for and turns around just as her father enters the kitchen, Maggie at his heels. He brings with him the smell of city cold; it wafts cold itself through the kitchen as her father removes his trench coat and throws it over a chair. "It is *cold*!" he says, pulling off his gloves.

"You're home early," her mother says, setting the paper grocery bags beside the garbage for recycling. She pulls out a chair and sits at the kitchen table.

Her father looks at the microwave clock. "A bit," he says. He pulls out a chair for himself and takes a seat. "But you know, I couldn't find those Africa slides this weekend, but I think I remember where they are now and I wanted to take a look before dinner."

"Ah," her mother says.

"Then maybe after dinner we can have a slide show."

"If you find them."

"Right. If I find them."

Isabelle slides to the floor with her back against the cabinets, and Maggie crosses from where she's been sniffing at the garbage can to drape herself across Isabelle's lap. Isabelle's legs will fall asleep this way, she knows, but she would never push Maggie away. Sometimes she wonders if Maggie has any understanding of her size: always she is trying to sit in the passenger seat of the car instead of stretching out in the back, always she wants to get into Isabelle's twin bed, to lie on the kitchen table, or to squeeze herself into the smallest of bathtubs on a hot day; she knocks people off balance with the force of her greeting, leans into them hard, sits down on their feet or lap like this and puts their limbs to sleep. Isabelle wonders what it would be like to be so very unaware of the vehicle that is the body, to exist as merely a self, an uncontained self. She looks at her toes on Maggie's other side. Already they are numb; without sensation, it is easy to imagine they have nothing to do with her.

"Belle. Belle!"

Isabelle blinks and looks up at the sound of her father's voice. From her seat on the kitchen floor, she can see both the top and bottom halves of her parents' bodies, split in two by the tabletop. Below the table, one of her mother's hands is in her lap, and her legs are stretched before her. Her feet are bare, and her heels are dry and cracked. Her father's shoes are covered by galoshes that are still wet and dripping a small puddle on the floor. His legs are crossed, the pant legs pulled high enough that Isabelle can see where the black socks give way to the white skin of his shins. Above the table, her father has his hands behind his head in a posture that suggests a good mood. Her mother's hand is cupped around a glass that Isabelle knows is filled with vodka, lime juice, and ice. Both her parents peer at her from above the table.

"Where are you?" her father asks, grinning. "My space cadet."

Isabelle smiles, but she's a little bit alarmed. When had her father fixed her mother a drink? Or had her mother fixed it for herself? When did the water she now hears bubbling over the top of the pot and sizzling in the flame beneath it begin to boil? She gently eases Maggie from her lap and stands to turn the flame down. Her feet feel like toeless stumps. She shuts her eyes and lets the steam from the water warm her face.

"I was asking you if you wanted to go down into the cellar to find those slides."

Isabelle feels her heart quicken. She loves going down into the cellar with her father. It is a terrifying place, dark and musty and huge with rows of storage stalls separated by chain-link fencing, the wire of it covered with dust and grime so thick that it looks like the hair on something living. Single bulbs hung from the ceiling are the only source of light.

"God." Her mother's voice sounds distant. "Better hope they haven't been ruined down there; remember how it flooded last spring."

"Oh, I think they'll probably be fine. I went down there after it flooded, and our stuff mostly seemed okay."

"Except for that rug of my mother's."

"Right, except for your mother's rug."

"Typical." The ice clinks in her mother's glass.

"So, what do you say, Belle?"

Isabelle opens her eyes and looks into the water bubbling before her and then at the zucchini on the cutting board beside the stove. She is behind schedule; already the water is ready for the pasta, but still she needs to wash and cut and sauté the zucchini. She needs to chop garlic for the bread. She needs to shred the cheese and wash lettuce for a salad, too. It is Wednesday night, and it is her responsibility to cook dinner. She lifts the zucchini from the cutting board and turns around, holding the vegetables out before her in explanation.

"Of course!" her father says. "It's Wednesday. Cook! Cook!"

Isabelle feels her face betray her disappointment.

"If you want to go down to the cellar, I can cook tonight," her mother offers.

Isabelle shakes her head. She would like to go down to the cellar, but she cannot. It is Wednesday night. She must cook. She *must* cook, like she *must* be silent, and she doesn't know why. What is she afraid of? She looks at the zucchini, and then at her fingers curled around them. Maybe in the end it is not her body that gets in her way; maybe it is her very self. She sighs.

"Hey," her father says. "We'll go down tomorrow. Tomorrow we'll go down and get the Christmas decorations out. It's December, it's winter, it's about time for that, no?"

"That's a good idea," her mother says.

Isabelle turns to rinse the zucchini in the sink and then begins to cut it into the thinnest slices she can manage. The slices that she cuts too thick she tosses into the sink.

"Speaking of Christmas," her father continues. "Maybe this weekend, Belle, we can go find ourselves a tree, huh? Cut one down?" They never get a tree this early, and they have never cut their own. Isabelle would be excited at the prospect, but she knows her father has hatched this plan only to soothe her disappointment.

"That might be jumping the gun," her mother says.

"Why?"

"Wilson, it's barely December. If we get a tree this weekend, the needles will have fallen off before it's even Christmas."

Isabelle bangs the knife down loud and hard against the cutting board. The noise startles her. She breathes deeply, clenches her teeth, and watches the yellow spots of oil quiver on the surface of the boiling water. Her parents are silent. She knows that if they weren't, if she hadn't interrupted them like this, their quarrel would have escalated, and all of it would have been because of her.

The memory of a Friday or a Saturday night, sometime in January, or maybe in February, before or after the squirrel, she can't remember, flashes into her mind. They were in the country. Her mother had been wearing a velvet evening gown, a maroon one with gold flecks across the chest, and her father had been wearing corduroys so old that the wales on the knees had worn away. She's not sure why she should remember these details so clearly, because she can't remember what she herself had been wearing. She's not even sure where in the room she'd been—she may have been curled in the old red armchair, but she might have been in the window seat or on the bench by the hearth—it's strange, she thinks now, because when she pictures the scene, she pictures it from overhead, as if she were strapped to the ceiling looking down. She can see her mother on the couch, supine, a book balanced on her chest. She can see her father standing up, a glass with ice and the dregs of scotch, maybe, in his hand, and he has asked her if she is bored. She doesn't know how she answers, except the wrong way, a heavy answer summoned from somewhere deep, with great effort, and for nothing good, in the end.

Bored? Her mother puts the book down. *There's no excuse for being bored.* Bored, *Wilson, is a boring word.*

And that, her father says, *is a tired cliché.*

How could anyone be bored here? There are books. There are games. I think we've offered to play every game in the house. There's the dog. There's homework. There's the yard.

Well, maybe bored *is the wrong word. But what is the right word? That's what I'd like to know.*

I don't know, her mother says. *Goddamned if I know. What is the word? Isabelle?*

She's not sure what she says. Something wrong.

Her parents' mouths continue to move, her mother's, then her father's, but she can't hear them anymore, and she is rising farther and farther above the scene, looking down at it from a great height. Her mother sits up and slams her book down on the table. Her father puts a hand on his hip. Her mother stands up, knocks a pillow to the ground. Maggie is a black oval, her mouth flashing red each time she barks. Her parents are heads and shoulders against the carpet. Her father strides toward the door, turns, and suddenly the sound of breaking glass explodes the silence.

The fire sizzles. Her parents look at each other, frozen, both of them standing now, then her mother is in her father's arms, sobbing. The dregs of her father's drink run in wet lines down the back of the fireplace, but only for a moment before the heat makes them disappear.

Isabelle blinks into the boiling water and opens the box of pasta.

"Well," her father finally says. "We'll wait and see about the tree. But the decorations we'll do tomorrow for sure."

She hears his chair squeak against the floor as he stands.

"Now I'm going to get changed and see if I can't find those slides."

He leaves the room. Isabelle listens to the swish of dregs as her mother swirls her glass in a circle on the table. Maggie sighs and shifts on the kitchen floor. Isabelle pulls a handful of pasta from the box, breaks it carefully above the boiling water, and drops it in.

The smell down in the cellar is moist and thick; Wilson can hear somewhere across the room the steady sound of water dripping. It echoes. The lightbulb hanging in the doorway of what Isabelle calls their cage of things is swinging still from when Wilson reached up to turn it on; the moving shadows make him dizzy. He looks up at the wall of boxes stacked ceiling high before him. Between everything in here and all the clutter in the garage and attic in the country, he wonders which amounts to more: the things they live with now, or these kept trappings of their former lives? He knows the box he's looking for will be somewhere near the bottom, among the first things stored away; part of him is loath to disassemble this stack of boxes, which to him seems some canyon wall whose geologic layers represent the stages of their lives.

At the top are things that are removed yearly, things like the Christmas decorations, their beach towels and umbrellas, a couple of plastic sleds for taking to the park in the snow. Next come mostly Isabelle's old things: outgrown books and clothing, toddler toys and baby toys, games that help you learn to read. Maggie's puppy cage is also in this layer, and the mat she liked to sleep on in the back of the car when she still understood she was a dog. Beneath these layers of parenthood and family are the layers of the early life he and Ruth shared together. Somewhere there's a box of cheap dishware from their first apartment and a roll of the posters that used to decorate their walls. There's a box of the magazines in which Wilson's articles appeared, and another box of things he kept in his desk during his journalistic years— things he knows he'll never need again but cannot bear to throw away: cracked rubber bands, twelve-cent stamps, an empty roll of tape, a jar of dried-out Wite-Out. It has been nearly eight years since he put this stuff away, although he continued for a few years after that to cover certain stories—the Bilderburg conference, for instance, which allowed him to travel to wherever all the major heads of state would gather for a week. He would bring back dolls for Isabelle from wherever he went: a Swiss doll in a dirndl, a Moroccan doll in gauzy scarves, a male Scottish doll in a kilt, which Isabelle found especially amusing. The last doll he brought home was an Egyptian doll riding on a camel, from the conference two years ago. Only two years, he thinks. So really, he hasn't stopped his writing entirely—he just skipped a year. He could go back to it, if he wanted to. He's getting proficient at "business," proficient enough that maybe in another few years he'll have saved enough to get Isabelle all the way through school, which he could never have done freelancing. Although at this rate he might as well go back to writing now; as of January, there'll be no school to pay for. The upside of all of this, he thinks, or tries to think, but truly the thought makes him sweat. If there's no school, he'll be paying for a trip to Africa, or anything in the world to get Isabelle speaking again.

And poor Ruth, Wilson thinks, gazing next at the boxes of the law books that aren't handy upstairs, papers from old classes, a rusted typewriter. Ruth has had to give up working entirely to tend to Isabelle's silence. She abandoned the law for however long it might take to get Isabelle back to being herself. A couple of weeks turned into a summer and then into an indefinite amount of time that in its open-endedness has forced her to officially resign her solo practice, to refer her clients elsewhere—though some took a while to really let her go. She used to laugh that she was more shrink than lawyer to these people, and Wilson laughed along, if nervously. He'd always sort of questioned the wisdom of letting these people into your home in the first place; imagining Isabelle and Ruth at home with the likes of some of them made him uneasy, even if Ruth insisted they were harmless.

At the bottom of this wall of boxes Wilson knows are the things from their separate lives: the odds and ends Ruth salvaged from her childhood home before it burned, the things Wilson saw fit to take with him from home and keep somewhere in the back of his life—his old guitar, a model airplane, his slides from Africa. Wilson crouches down to examine the labels on the bottommost boxes. His own shadow blocks the dim light, so he brings his face close to the cardboard to make out the letters. This close up, he can see the cardboard's corrugation; it is old and wearing thin. He touches the sides of several of the boxes. They are damp and flimsy, and he worries that Ruth might be right, that his slides may well be ruined, and other things besides. What he'll do is buy some plastic storage lockers for their things. He'll transfer the contents of these boxes into the lockers—when?—this summer, when on the hot weekday afternoons he comes home from work to an empty apartment, Ruth, Isabelle, and Maggie gone to the country. Yes, he thinks, the project will keep him occupied during those hot and lonely hours, and the cellar will be cool. He sniffs at one of the boxes; it is a deep and almost rotten smell. An earwig scurries across the cardboard before his nose. He grimaces, worried that the summer might not be soon enough, that it will be too late for their things by then. He makes a mental note to look into those lockers tomorrow; even if he doesn't start the transfer until summer, at least the presence of the lockers will be something of a start.

Wilson stands; his knee cracks as it straightens from his crouch. He's fairly sure that the slides are in the bottom left-hand box. It would be fastest to simply slide it quickly out and let the ones on top of it crash into its position, but he worries that the boxes might be too weak for such a fall. Instead, he thinks, he'll remove the boxes directly above the box he needs, and then he'll put them back. He will disrupt as little as he can. He opens the stepladder they keep in the cellar and carefully climbs until he's standing on the top step, where a semi-peeled sticker that used to read DO NOT STAND ON TOP STEP has been trimmed by Isabelle to read instead STAND ON TOP so that when they decorate the tree each Christmas he can no longer point to the ladder's rules when Isabelle climbs to that top step to reach the highest branches. He's amused by the ripple of guilt he feels to be standing on that forbidden step himself. If Isabelle were here she would surely comment; Wilson chuckles as he thinks that in response he could point to the abbreviated sign, just as she did last year. He'd say, *What, it's not my fault the ladder changed its rules.* And Isabelle would say something like—what? Wilson isn't sure, and then his smile fades as he realizes that his daughter would say nothing at all.

The kitchen is warm. Too warm. Ruth pulls her sweater off. In the winter this building is always overheated, and now, in the kitchen, with the water boiling on the stove, the heated oven waiting for the bread, and the zucchini sizzling in its pan, it feels almost worse than in summer.

She has been trying to read an article on Africa that Wilson has clipped out of a travel magazine, but she cannot concentrate. She is jealous of her husband and his ability to absorb himself so thoroughly in things like this Africa project when there are so many other things to think about, things like Monday's meeting with Mrs. Mason, or Isabelle's next appointment with this new shrink. Africa seems irrelevant. She pushes the article aside. Africa *is* irrelevant, but still her husband is down in the cellar searching for ancient slides that likely are beyond repair. She can picture him down there, rifling through old boxes and discovering all types of things he's forgotten but now suddenly feels he needs. He'll return with armfuls of things, armfuls of projects to fill his mind so full that there is no room left for Mrs. Mason, for psychiatrists and silence; these she'll have to bear alone.

Isabelle is standing stork-legged at the stove, flipping her zucchini so that both sides are evenly browned. One hand holds a spatula; the other is on her hip. Her feet, like Ruth's, are bare, and her pants are frayed at the bottom. She's had these pants for over two years now; Ruth wonders if she should worry at how little her daughter has grown of late. Isabelle's eyes make her look older than her eleven years, but from the back, like this, with her birdlike shoulder blades lifting through her shirt with every scoop of the spatula and her cowlick with this new haircut standing tall, she could easily be nine, maybe eight. Isabelle sets the spatula down and sidesteps to the counter to begin to grate the cheese. Beside her is the loaf of bread, cut through with deep incisions in each of which Isabelle has placed a pad of butter and a small spoonful of garlic.

Incisions. Ruth turns her eyes to the pile of homework Isabelle has left out on the kitchen table and pulls it toward her, a sickening reminder of what is at stake. It was difficult to imagine, before they'd had to pull her out of school, what it would be like to have Isabelle doing her schoolwork at home; it is even more difficult to imagine what it will be like *without* that schoolwork, which has, for Ruth, been the fine demarcation between temporary and permanent affliction, the hook on which to hang her hope, the reminder and promise of normalcy.

"Isabelle," she says. Isabelle pauses in her cheese grating and waits. She does not turn around. "Do you mind if I take a look at your homework?" Isabelle shakes her head, and Ruth opens the top folder, on which Isabelle has neatly written *English*. In this folder is the spelling list that Ruth remembers from Mrs. Mason's office on Monday—*decision, incision, license, precise*. There are several worksheets on the proper use of adjectives and adverbs, all of which Isabelle has completed in her tiny, perfect handwriting. There is a list of reading questions for *Tuck Everlasting,* the last of which asks the students to come up with an adjective that would describe how they might feel were they, like Tuck, to live forever. In the space that follows, Isabelle has written *lonely*. Ruth glances at her daughter, who is crouched before the open oven with the bread now wrapped in foil in her hand. Strands of her thin hair waver in the oven's heat. Ruth closes the English folder and sets it aside.

The next folder contains a graph charting the rise and fall of Coca-Cola stock. This had been a homework project from the year before, one that Isabelle had loved and chosen to pursue after the project had ended, with her own real money. Wilson has been helping her with this, a thought that instantly makes Ruth feel guilty.

In the folder marked *History,* there is on top a map of the United States on which, as directed, Isabelle has labeled the name and capital of each state. Beneath that, there is a sheet of paper asking the students to write by the following week a two-page paper explaining the causes for the entrance of the United States into World War II. Isabelle has made abundant notes, from which Ruth gathers that her daughter's understanding is that the primary cause for the involvement of the country in the war was to alleviate the negative effects of the Depression. FDR knew all along about the planned attack on Pearl Harbor, and he let it happen so that the country would *want* to go to war. Probably not the answer the teacher is looking for, Ruth thinks, but she is nonetheless amused by her daughter's response. On more than one occasion after reading over Isabelle's history homework, Wilson has shaken his head and called their daughter *pinko.*

Ruth is reaching to turn the paper over to read what Isabelle has written on the other side when she feels something hot and wet and sudden on her hand. Instinctively, she gasps and pushes back from the table, her chair legs screeching on the tile. She looks down at her hand; a thin wet line runs across it.

She looks at where her hand had been poised above Isabelle's notes. A single wet noodle lies limp on the page, causing the ink of the words it has landed on to bleed into a blue blur. She looks up at her daughter, who is standing frozen before the stove, a steaming fork in one hand, the other over her mouth, which Ruth can tell by the twinkle in Isabelle's eye is thin-lipped in an impish smile.

Ruth blinks at her daughter and then follows Isabelle's eyes with her own upward to the ceiling, where months' worth of Wednesday-night noodles cling to the plaster in a growing noodle web that until tonight Ruth has never noticed. She looks her daughter in the eye, and she smiles. "Well," she says, pulling her chair back to the table and tossing the fallen noodle into the sink. "I guess they need a few more minutes, then."

III

She is walking through tall blades of dried grass whose edges are sharp enough that they slice her legs with every step. The sun is so bright that it hurts to see; even when she shuts her eyes, the light is blinding and hot enough to burn her skin. She is desperate for clothing, water, shade, but the white of the sun swallows everything around her, and she cannot tell where she is going. All she can see are the blades of grass immediately around her and, when she looks down, her bare legs lashed and bloody.

Suddenly, the ground gives way beneath her, and her heart rises in her throat as she falls a long, cold distance through the dark. She is afraid to land; she lets her limbs go limp so that when she hits whatever ground there is she will crumple and not break. But then, as she falls through this black vacuum, she can feel her body begin to rotate so that she is no longer falling feet first but turning slow circles head over feet over head until she lands hard on her back, and for a moment she cannot breathe. Her eyes begin to adjust to the dark. The room that she has landed in is dark and cold and musty. It has no doors, no windows, and boulders for the walls and the low ceiling she's not sure how she's fallen through.

She hears in the corner of the room the hiss of a match struck into life. She turns her head to look in that direction; she follows the match with her eyes and watches as it shares its flame with a large torch that when lit casts a jumping orange glow. Isabelle blinks. Beneath the torch's flame, she can see a figure, a man, her father, seated backward on a chair, his head held down in some kind of vise. A black African wearing nothing but a loincloth even in this cold stands over him, digging into his skull with a sharp, thin knife. She tries to stand to save her father, but she cannot get her limbs to move. She tries to call out, but she cannot scream.

I am in a dream, she tells herself, *I am in a dream*. And with the same effort with which she tried to get her dream self to move her limbs, she tries to rouse her body out of sleep. *Wake up, Isabelle,* she tells herself, though now that she has entered into her own dream, she feels almost curious to see what will happen. She tries to hover in this midway state between dreaming and wakefulness, tries to live as both her dream self and an observer of that dream, but the dream's spell has been broken. She is aware now of the blankets around her, the sound of passing traffic on the street, the murmur of the television in the other room. Still, though, as after a scary ride or bad news, she is shaken. Her heart beats hard; she tries to breathe evenly and deeply to calm herself.

She opens her eyes. She is on her side, facing her desk, and there in her desk chair is the same African from her dream. He is sitting in his loincloth with his legs crossed, picking at his teeth with the same knife he used to dig into her father's skull. His teeth and the whites of his eyes glow startlingly bright; his skin is so black she can hardly make out his features, but when he sees that she is looking at him, he pulls the knife from his teeth and grins, his smile hovering white in his invisible face like a crescent moon, or the Cheshire Cat.

Isabelle pulls the covers up above her head and curls into a ball. She squeezes shut her eyes and tries to breathe. She tells herself that she is alone. She is alone. She is alone. After some minutes she dares to peer again from her covers; slowly, she pulls the blankets from over her head and opens her eyes. Her desk chair is empty. She sits up and looks around the room; she is alone. She takes a sip from the glass of water beside her bed, but she doesn't lie back down. She is not tired anymore.

She hears the sound of her father's recliner in the family room being raised upright. The noise from the TV stops, and after another minute she hears her father's footsteps coming down the hall, his slippers slapping against his heels. She wants to call out to him for comfort; she wants to run her fingers across the top of his skull to be sure that it is whole, even though she knows it was a dream. The footsteps grow louder as they near her room; they pause outside her door. *Come in,* she thinks, *come in.* She can see the shadows of her father's feet in the slice of light from the hallway shining underneath her door. If she called to him, the room would fill with a dim light as he opened the door, and her bed would sink down where he sat, and she would tell him about her dream until it seemed so strange and unreal that she'd come to wonder how she had ever let it scare her—if she could just call out to him, but her jaw clenches around the words, no longer of her own will. Sometimes, the safety she's created by her silence is more terrifying than the world from which she wanted to withdraw. The world is senseless, but it is peopled. *Please,* she thinks, *come in,* but the shadows pass on and the sound of her father's footsteps fades down the hall.

In her own bed, Ruth hears Wilson's footsteps approaching. It is after one; she knows her husband has likely spent the past hours asleep on the couch, the television tuned to late-night news and a magazine upside down across his chest. Their bedroom door creaks slowly open.

"It's okay," Ruth says. "I'm awake." Wilson's silhouette is dark against the light of the hallway as he stands in the doorway, and then it's gone as he reaches behind him to flip the hall light switch on the wall outside their door.

"I fell asleep," Wilson says, passing through the darkness to the bathroom.

"I figured," Ruth says. She props the pillows up behind her and listens to Wilson brush his teeth. He is thorough; the sound of the bristles passing over teeth is like a strange melody determined by the changing shape of Wilson's mouth as he opens wider or holds his mouth in an oval or a grin to best get at each and every tooth. He spits, then rinses, then turns the water off and makes his way to bed.

"Shit!" Ruth hears him say. He stoops down and lifts something from the floor. "Stepped on a bone," he says, tossing the rawhide onto the couch beside their bed. Ruth pulls back the covers on his side of the bed, and he gets in.

"I'm glad the slides were okay," Ruth says.

"Lucky they were. I'm going to get some proper storage lockers for the things down there. You know, plastic trunks or something. The cardboard just isn't doing it anymore."

"Well, still. They were good to see." Good, she thinks, and strange, almost sad, in a way Ruth can't quite understand. After dinner, Wilson had taken the painting down from the wall behind the couch, and the three of them had sat in the darkness of the family room and watched Africa flick against the wall: empty plains, flat and windswept trees, elephant herds and piles of enormous bone, black-skinned Africans with toothy grins. The images were grainy, some a little water-stained, some cracked with age. "See the lion in that one," Wilson had said, pointing to one. On the wall, Wilson, his brother, and their father stood in front of a safari jeep. They wore khaki shorts and knee socks, and Wilson's father wore a wide-brimmed hat. All of them were smiling.

"I don't see it," Ruth had said.

"I'll show you," Wilson said. He stood in front of the projection on the wall, pointing to a small lion in the corner of the image. Field grass and the headlights of the safari jeep seemed painted on his back. When he turned around, he stepped into the path of his own image. His young face hovered over his old face, his young body over the old. Then he stepped away, like a ghost of himself, leaving that young self grinning and pinned against the wall.

Ruth finds Wilson's hand with her own beneath the covers and gives it a gentle squeeze.

"I showed it to him," she says.

"Showed what to who?"

Ruth's mouth twists in frustration. "The drawing,

to the shrink! What did you think I was talking about?"

Wilson shrugs in the darkness, but his heart begins to beat a little faster as he thinks about Isabelle's drawing, and the way she loved those foreign dolls, and how when they go to Africa she can choose her own—one from Kenya, one from Ethiopia, maybe one from Madagascar. "And?" he says. "Did the guy seem any good? What did he say? What did he think about the drawing? Did he think Africa was a good idea?"

"Did he think Africa was a good idea?"

Wilson pauses. "Yes," he says. "Going to Africa. Getting Isabelle out of here for a while, showing her something she hasn't seen before."

"Wilson." Ruth turns her head to look at her husband. His eyes glint in the dark. He blinks. "I don't think you're thinking."

Wilson blinks again. Ruth looks up toward the ceiling so that he can see her profile, backlit by the green glow of the stereo lights on the shelf beside her. He *is* thinking, he thinks. "I am."

"Wilson. This has nothing to do with Africa."

"Sure it does," Wilson says. "She did that drawing. There's something to that drawing."

"I know it," Ruth says. "Whether consciously or not, there is meaning in everything we make." She feels herself blush. "The shrink said that."

"And the drawing is of Africa," Wilson says.

"What I think is that *you* want to go to Africa."

"I've been to Africa."

"I'd rather have her at school than in Africa come January."

Wilson turns his head, opens his mouth to say what he shouldn't have to, when Ruth interrupts him. "I know," she says. "I'm sorry, I know you would, too."

They are quiet.

Finally, Ruth takes a breath. "Regardless," she says, "I wanted to thank you for suggesting that we show that drawing to the shrink. Whatever she's trying to communicate by it."

Wilson flattens his lips.

"He seems good," she continues.

"Well, good."

"And he thinks there's really something to what she draws. I was thinking of finding an art class or something, something, I don't know." She turns her head toward Wilson as if asking him a question, or for his approval. He nods. "Anyway," she says, "I wouldn't have thought of showing him that drawing, so thank you."

"Don't thank me," Wilson says.

Ruth shrugs.

"When's the next appointment?"

"Oh, next Thursday, and I wanted to ask you about that. I have an appointment at noon on Thursday, and Isabelle's appointment is at eleven, which means I can't get her home and then get downtown for my own appointment. I was thinking that I could leave her off at the shrink and you could pick her up and take her out for lunch somewhere, and then I could meet you guys wherever you decide to go and take her home."

"Thursday?"

"Next Thursday, and her appointment ends at noon."

Wilson pictures himself and his daughter, sitting silent in a noisy restaurant, Isabelle drawing away on her placemat, Wilson making meaningless comments about the flower arrangement on the table, or the funny hairdo on the lady at the next table, or how he just can't decide whether to get the burger or something a little more healthful, like the chicken sandwich, and what did Isabelle think he should have? "Thursday," he says, and then he remembers that he's got a lunch meeting with clients flying in from California. "Shit," he says. "I have a lunch meeting Thursday. Do you think there's a chance the doctor could reschedule?"

"How about *you* reschedule?"

"They're from out of town," Wilson says. "They're flying in."

"Wilson," Ruth says. "I don't ask that much of you. I spend every day with Isabelle. I don't work anymore so that I can take care of her. I'm asking you for an hour of your time, two at the most."

"I know," Wilson says. "I know. I'll cancel." The meeting is an important one, and he knows if he explained the details to Ruth that she would understand, but he has to cancel. He has to cancel and he has to take his daughter to lunch because he doesn't want to, and this realization floods him with guilt. "Of course I'll cancel," he says. "Of course."

FOUR

Thursday

I

Ruth has shut the door of the den behind her in an attempt to sequester herself with her busywork; she has to pay the household bills, and she has to order tickets for the theater for sometime during the week after Christmas, though she has left this so late she suspects that they might be unable to get seats this year. She has to balance her checkbook and organize her receipts, of which there are so many she cannot close her wallet anymore; she's stuffed receipts in pockets and left them floating in her pocketbook, and she knows she'll never find them all. Somehow, she finds it harder to stay organized now that she's not working than she did when she worked full-time. While she was working, she knew the issues she was working with: Zeke Mueller, the nightclub owner who was sued every time a fight broke out in one of his nightclubs; Anastasia Koeppel, the Latvian landlady in the Bronx who demanded unreasonably detailed contracts for her tenants to sign; Cecilia Mirran, whose long-term care insurance Ruth arranged at the very last minute before she was officially diagnosed with Alzheimer's—though it was Marcel, her son, whom she always dealt with most. She shakes her head. Marcel, who called over his mother's every last toothbrush and hairpin. He's a little crazy, maybe, as Wilson's always said, but he's got a good heart, she thinks. And he's lonely; no matter how many times she reminds him, still he calls as if she were his mother's lawyer, though probably she's the closest thing to a friend he has. Last Christmas—Marcel's first since his mother had moved out of the house they shared and into the home—Ruth had invited him to spend the day with them, because, as he'd said to her and she said to Wilson, he had no one else. And he's not the first of her clients to become attached. Zeke Mueller invites them to his Halloween party every year—though they never go. Before he died, Sandy Lubbock, for whom Ruth won six figures for his severed finger, sent Isabelle a small stuffed animal on the first of every month. Probably that closeness came from working at home—her clients saw her in clogs instead of heels, were dribbled and drooled on by Maggie, had to tiptoe around Isabelle's train track set up in the foyer. Ruth has never been one to do things conventionally.

She lets her eyes wander to the bookcase beside her desk and to the bottom shelf, where she keeps her legal reference books. It has been months now since she last had cause to use one of them, and it seems that in only months a substantial layer of dust has settled across them. Although really there isn't anything "only" about months, she thinks; there has been nothing "only" about the months of living the life that hers has become. Aside from reminders like phone calls from Marcel or flowers from Zeke, she tries not to think too often about her old life; she rarely has the time. Her "old" life, she thinks sadly—but it isn't her old life, she tells herself, it is her life, and what she is living now is simply an interruption, a hiatus, a parenthesis within the life she will return to.

She fans through the art-class brochures she picked up at the Met this morning, looking for something for Isabelle. If art is her daughter's only form of communication, then by God Ruth is going to make sure she communicates. Of particular interest is a mother–daughter art class that meets Monday afternoons; if there's room, Ruth thinks, they should start immediately, next week, even if they'll be catching only the tail end of the series. And then after the holidays, when the new session starts, they'll already know the ropes. She is no artist herself, but it pleases Ruth to think of something she can do *with* Isabelle, not *to* Isabelle—dragging her around from shrink to shrink. The idea makes Ruth feel a little less helpless.

She is about to lift the phone and call about this art class when it begins to ring, once, twice. She looks at the thing, annoyed, sighs, and answers.

The colon blinking between the hours and the minutes on the microwave clock begs to be counted, though

Isabelle knows full well that in a minute, it will blink sixty times.

The corner of the newspaper flutters in the warm air from the vent. After checking on her stock, which to her pleasure has gone up, she had left the paper open, letting the strings of numbers and abbreviations hypnotize her eyes for a spell.

The kitchen's fluorescent light flickers and hums in what Isabelle is sure must be some sort of pattern, but one she can't quite discern.

Her sweater is pilled with raised wool that yearns for plucking.

Her fingers are rough with winter, the skin around her nails dry and easy to pull away in strips with her teeth, and when she pulls too far or a strip runs too deep she can make patterns with her blood on the paper towel she has set out on the table.

And of course beside the paper towel is this week's homework, from which she is distracted by everything else. She has finally finished looking up dictionary definitions of words that she already knows, but a definition never seems to encompass the real meaning of a word. She looks at her list. Desolate is not "joyless, disconsolate, and sorrowful," she thinks. No, desolate is the desert through which they'd driven last spring, that barren, red, and dusted landscape that she would never think to label joyless. Desolate is desolate, just as joyless is joyless and sorrowful is sorrowful. Words do not suffice, it seems to Isabelle, to define other words.

She shoves her vocabulary aside and scans the rest of the pile of homework her mother has brought home for her. She will do math next, she thinks. Unlike words, numbers *can* define one another, she thinks; while desolate isn't exactly joyless, disconsolate, and sorrowful, for instance, the number six, on the other hand, is inarguably one and two and three, but it is also one and five, and two and four, and two and two and two, and three and three—so many definitions for a single number! If there were ever a dictionary of numbers, Isabelle muses—but there could never be, she thinks. It would be an infinite project.

She rubs her eyes and pulls her math worksheet toward her. She frowns when she sees it; more probability. Probability, it seems to her, is not math. One might be able to predict the probability of something occurring, but whether or not the thing actually occurs is entirely out of math's control. Probability, in the end, has nothing to do with actuality; it doesn't matter if the probability of an occurrence is unlikely, only one out of a thousand; that one still exists in a very real way. She does not want to know what "might" happen, she wants to know what "will" happen; she has no use for a mathematics whose answer is "maybe."

She shoves her worksheet aside; she does not have the patience for it now. She eyes the back door. Her mother has asked her to listen for a knock; the doorbell is broken and she is expecting something— what, Isabelle doesn't know, probably her dry cleaning, or maybe the chocolates she always orders for Christmastime. Her mouth waters at the thought of those chocolates; she isn't hungry, but some hot cocoa would be good, she thinks.

She gets up from her chair and wanders to the fridge, pausing when the phone rings as if to answer it—but she catches herself as she reaches for the receiver, looking at her outstretched hand as if it were something separate from herself. She hasn't answered the phone in such a long time, she thinks, long enough that she's surprised that the impulse to answer when it rings still exists somewhere inside of her. It is because she was distracted, she thinks; she was thinking too much of her cocoa to remember her silence. What would have happened, she wonders, if she had picked up before she realized what she was doing? Would sound have made its way from her throat just as her hand had made its way to the phone before she could stop it? She blinks at the phone and finally lets her hand drop back to her side. If she had spoken now, that would have been 289 days of silence.

She swallows and opens the refrigerator door, scanning the shelves as she tries to remind herself of what she'd been looking for: orange juice, hummus, cold cuts, carrots, salsa, grapes, pizza left over from Sunday, Chinese left over from who knows when, a jug of milk. She pulls the milk from the fridge and pours just a small amount with cocoa into a mug, her stomach yearning now, and she has just put the mug into the microwave when she hears a knock at the back door.

Isabelle leaves her cocoa still cold in the microwave to hurry to the den for her mother. She knocks on the door only after she has already opened it so as to get her mother's attention; her mother is on the phone, but she looks up at the sound of the knock and places her hand lightly over the mouthpiece.

"Back door?" she asks.

Isabelle nods.

"Jimmy," she says into the phone. "Listen, I've got to run. . . . No. . . . I will, Jimmy. . . . Listen, I've got the exterminator at the door and he's not going to wait around. . . . I don't *know* if we have a bug problem, Jimmy. . . . No. . . . Good-bye." She hangs up the phone. "My brother," she says, getting up from her desk. "I swear to God."

Isabelle stands still in the doorway as her mother approaches, her palms gone sweaty and her shoulders tight with worry. Her eyes are fixed on her mother's desk chair, the cushion there unburdened now and rising. The exterminator, she thinks, remembering all the times in the past when the building exterminator has knocked on their back door and she has not given a thought to whatever creatures he was there to exterminate. But her ants! *Exterminate,* she thinks; such a violent, calculating word. Her mother brushes past her; Isabelle hurries after her toward the kitchen. Normally at a time like this, when there is a delivery or the superintendent has come to fix the toilet, Isabelle retreats to the safety of her room until whoever has come is gone; her mother looks over her shoulder with surprise at the sound of Isabelle's footsteps on the kitchen floor, and she pauses before pulling the back door open.

"Should I wait?" her mother asks, thinking, Isabelle thinks, that Isabelle wants to gather her homework or pour a glass of orange juice to take away with her before the exterminator comes in.

Isabelle shakes her head as the exterminator pounds on the door for the third time, stationing herself before the sink and the cabinet beneath it in which she can imagine her ants even now making their tireless march up and down the back wall. "Exterminator!" he calls. Isabelle swallows, digging her nails into her palms as her mother pulls the back door open. The door is heavy and opens with a familiar whine; Maggie appears at the sound, her eyes glassy with sleep, one ear flipped inside out. Maggie cocks her head, taking measure of the man in the doorway, her tail poised as if to wag, but uncertain yet. Isabelle looks from the dog to the exterminator, the man behind the voice she has heard so often calling from behind the door as he makes his quarterly rounds of their building. He wears white work pants gone brown with dirt on the thighs and knees and cuffs, a thick brown belt around his waist laden with sprays, a flashlight, a measuring tape, and, along the back, Isabelle can see when he turns around to set his tool kit on the floor behind him, a series of screwdrivers. His ponytail interrupts the T-shirt logo on his back, which Isabelle can make out as a foot descending upon an ant, the ant's cartoonish eyes big with worry. The man turns back into the room, and Isabelle lets her eyes travel up to his face; it is tan despite the winter, and Isabelle can imagine the rough feel of the bristles on his chin and cheeks, longer than her father's even when he hadn't shaved for a whole week one summer, just to see.

"Carter?" he says, looking at the clipboard in his hand.

"Yes," her mother says.

"Specific pests, or evaluation?"

"We don't have bugs that I'm aware of." Isabelle leans hard against the cabinet. "But Mrs. Drayton on three says they have terrible roaches, so I thought I'd have you just take a look while you're in the building."

"Evaluation," he mutters, checking a box. "Partial or comprehensive?"

"What's the difference?"

"Partial is kitchen, bathrooms, windows, fireplaces. Comprehensive is all that plus AC/water heater closets, TV/cable wall lines, plumbing penetrations, voids at baseboards, built-in cabinets, appliance conduits, and all other cracks and crevices." He looks up from his clipboard.

"God," her mother says. "I don't know. Do you recommend one or the other?"

"It's up to you, ma'am."

He runs his finger underneath his nose, sniffing. Isabelle wonders if he can smell himself; she can smell him from here, a putrid mix of cigarette and lemon cleaning fluid that she knows will trail him through the house and linger for days. She shouldn't have been so quick to get her mother, Isabelle thinks. She should have peered through the peephole to see who it was first. Why had she not even entertained the possibility of the exterminator? Why hadn't it even crossed her mind? Stupid, she thinks. Stupid, stupid.

"Well then, comprehensive, since we're doing this."

The exterminator makes another mark on his clipboard and picks up his tool kit. He gestures toward the kitchen table. "May I?"

"Oh, of course, come in," her mother says as the man sets his clipboard on the table among Isabelle's textbooks and worksheets. "Is all that in your way? Isabelle." She looks at Isabelle and points her chin toward the table.

"It's fine," the exterminator says, setting his tool kit on the floor again and crouching to dig through it for whatever he first needs.

"Isabelle." Her mother says her name firmly this time; Isabelle does not lift her eyes from the exterminator. Maggie enters into view, comes up to sniff the man, and Isabelle watches with clenched teeth as he runs his dirty fingers through Maggie's fur. "Isabelle," her mother says again, but the exterminator is standing up now, his clipboard again in hand.

"Should I start in here?"

"Ah, sure," her mother says, an edge of exasperation in her voice.

Isabelle glances quickly at her mother, leaning now against the fridge, and then back at the exterminator, who has opened the cabinet beneath the microwave where Isabelle's cocoa sits still unwarmed. He pulls out the pots and mixing bowls from the cabinet's shelves, and over the clatter Isabelle can just hear her mother ask the man if he's found many pests in his rounds so far today.

"What's that?" he asks, pulling his head from out of the cabinet.

"How have you found the building today, bug-wise?"

"Eh," the exterminator shrugs. "It's the city, you're always going to find something, roaches, fleas—plus you've got a dog, so that ups your chances." He pulls the flashlight from his belt and ducks back into the cabinet. "Looks okay in here." His voice is muffled. "But what I'm going to do"—and here his hand reaches again toward his belt and pulls from it a spray bottle with a thin straw attached—"is I'm gonna put a little of this gel we use along the seams." Isabelle can hear the hiss of the bottle as he applies the gel. His shirt is starting to come untucked in the back, and Isabelle can see hairs curling over his pant waist, dark and wiry. She looks from the exterminator to her mother, who is standing with a hand on her hip and her head tilted to the side as if, Isabelle thinks, she were really interested in what is going on, as if she really cared. "Just," he says, pulling his head out of the cabinet again, "as a preventive measure."

Her mother nods. "Whatever you say," she says.

He puts the pots and bowls back into the cabinet and moves to the wall perpendicular to inspect the cabinets on either side of the stove. Isabelle swallows; if he keeps moving counterclockwise as he is, then her cabinet is next. She slides her back down the cabinet so that she is squatting against it, her heart racing and her breaths coming quick. If she had only known the exterminator was coming, she thinks, if only, if only. She might have tried to collect the ants, maybe, tried to lure them away with crumbs into the safety of a jar. She might have tried to construct a fake back wall for the cabinet so that the ants' wall was covered. But what can she do now? She could try to distract the exterminator, she thinks, that might work. She could show him a spot in the living room or bathroom and swear that she's seen roaches there. Or she could ask if he could work in another room just while she finishes up her homework—but her heart falls, because she cannot do these things—but she *can,* she thinks; she *can* speak up, but she *won't* speak up. What is she afraid of? Hadn't words only minutes ago been on the tip of her tongue when she'd reached out for the phone? She is a selfish girl, she thinks, selfish and awful and cruel, and now, because of her, the ants will be killed. She feels her jaw begin to tremble; she sets it tight, seething inside, swollen with helplessness.

The exterminator is just putting back the contents of the cabinet before hers; Isabelle presses her toes into the floor and her back as hard against the cabinet as she can. She wraps her arms around her knees, each hand grabbing the opposite wrist and locking tight.

"Isabelle, you need to get out of the way," she hears her mother say. Isabelle stares at the red tiles of the floor, blurring the lines between them with her eyes; she will not look up. "Isabelle," she hears again. "What has gotten into you today?"

"I can move on to the next cabinet," the exterminator offers. Isabelle can see his boots on the floor now before her, one pant leg caught up in a tongue.

"No, you can't." Her mother sounds angry now. "Isabelle," she says. "Move out of the way, please, right now."

Isabelle breathes deeply through her nose. She can feel her nostrils flare, and she tightens her grip around her wrists. Her jaw is beginning to ache.

"Isabelle." Her mother is hissing now, her voice sharp and quick. "I'm sorry," she says to the exterminator, and Isabelle can hear her footsteps coming across the tiles. She shuts her eyes, tight, withdrawing into herself. She feels her mother's grip firm on her arm, trying to make her stand up; she clings even more tightly to her knees. *"Isabelle."* Her mother's voice seems distant now, belonging to a world different from the one Isabelle has entered into. She can feel the tiles sliding beneath her and

153

her mother's hands firm beneath her arms, and then she feels the tiles give way to carpet and then wood, and it splinters her bottom, but she does not yield. She does not uncurl herself, and she does not open her eyes, she *will not* open her eyes to see the world seeing her reduced to this, this cruel, silent rock of a child dragged across a floor.

II

The phone rings four times before it's answered; Wilson can hear a dog barking and the shriek of a teapot beginning to whistle, the unmistakable sounds of his mother's house, before his mother finally speaks. "Hello?" she says. The familiarity of her voice always strikes him; every time they speak, it is as if he had forgotten what she sounds like, and to hear her is like remembering a good forgotten memory.

"Mother," he says. "It's Wilson."

"Wilson!" she says. "I was just making tea. How are you?"

"I'm fine," Wilson says. "How are you?"

"Oh, well, it's frightfully cold, and poor Teddy cut his paw on the ice and the salt on the driveway hurts him dreadfully—can you hear him?—and I've got some French cousins coming this afternoon, and some of them might stay the weekend, but I never know what anyone's doing."

"How is the horsewoman working out, what's her name?"

"Oh!" Wilson can hear the clink of a spoon against china. "Sharon! She didn't understand the horses. I don't know what a person like that is thinking!"

"You got rid of her?"

"She was dreadful."

"She was there for all of a week, Mother. She came highly recommended."

"Well, I don't know by whom. I certainly don't recommend her."

Wilson sighs. "So now no one's there to help?"

"Sue comes by. It's fine."

Wilson lifts his pen and makes a note to call his brother; his mother is too old, he thinks, to be walking an icy driveway twice a day with bucketsful of feed.

"How is Isabelle?"

Wilson sits forward in his chair to doodle, circle after circle. "The same," he says.

"Still not speaking, then."

"No."

"Hmm. And Ruth?"

"Ruth is fine, I think," Wilson says. "Considering. Maggie's not, though. The vet called this morning. The biopsy was bad. She may need more treatment."

"She ought to see Dr. Marks when you come up. No more of this city veterinarian nonsense."

When you come up. It has been tradition since Isabelle was born to go see Wilson's mother the weekend before Christmas; this year, the thought of it takes him by surprise. Since nothing is as it normally is, he hadn't even considered their usual visit, and it is perhaps the realization that he had forgotten it that surprises him more than anything else. Normally, it is a part of their Christmas ritual, like the pageant on Christmas Eve and the opening of stockings Christmas morning. This year, silent, Isabelle won't be much of a visitor. This year, he will have to consult with Ruth.

"Dr. Bremer is a good vet," Wilson says finally.

"Well." He hears his mother sip her tea. Radio voices murmur in the background. He can picture the radio, an ancient, dusty thing, perched amid the clutter of catalogs and unopened mail on the kitchen counter. He loosens his tie and undoes the top button of his shirt; his office is so hot that, were the temperature in here the temperature outside, all the buildings would have their air-conditioning on. He looks up at the pictures on the shelf behind his desk; there is one of Ruth and Isabelle sitting on a rock, one of Ruth from years ago, when they'd first married, one of himself and his brothers, one of Maggie and Isabelle sitting in a leaf pile under the apple tree. There are dried leaves caught in Isabelle's hair, and her face is flushed with fall. She is mid-laugh, tossing a handful of leaves above Maggie's head. Wilson looks at that photograph, and his heart drops.

"She must be very sad," his mother finally says.

"What?"

"Isabelle," she says.

Wilson blinks. *Sad,* he thinks. Such a heavy, thudding word, so simple, so final, so wise. "We're thinking of going to Africa," he says.

"Africa!"

"We thought it might help her. We'd go only if the school disowns her, which they're going to do if she's not speaking by the time the semester starts. It's bad, Mother. Things are not getting any better."

His mother is quiet for a moment. "I remember when your father took you to Africa," she says.

"Yes, I showed her the slides."

"Nicholas was about Isabelle's age then, wasn't he?"

"About," Wilson says.

"I imagine it's a very different place now."

"Yes." Wilson looks at the paper before him; it is filled entirely with circles. Over the intercom, a voice announces that Mrs. Carter is on line two, and Wilson is puzzled for a moment, since Mrs. Carter is on line one, until he realizes the voice means Ruth. "Tell her I'll call her right back," he says into the intercom. "Mother," he says. "I have a few tax forms I need you to sign. I was going to fax them to Branwell and have him bring them over, but I guess I'll just bring them when we come up."

"Good. Do call before that," she says.

"I will, and I'm going to call Branwell about another horsewoman—"

"Wilson—"

"And I don't want any arguments."

He hears his mother sigh.

"Good-bye, Mother," he says.

He hangs up with his finger, a pause between Mrs. Carter and Mrs. Carter, the younger of whom he has been putting off calling ever since he heard from the vet. With another round of treatment, the vet has said Maggie's chances are about twenty percent. One in five, Wilson thinks. If there were a one-in-five chance that he'd, let's say, be killed, he'd consider those odds pretty good, and he'd be afraid. So shouldn't he be as hopeful that Maggie will live as he would be frightened if he had a one-in-five chance of being killed? Still, he's not sure he wants to tell Ruth about Maggie— not until the dog's been back to the vet anyway. There is, after all, a twenty percent chance she'll be okay, so shouldn't he spare Ruth the worry? He can hear his wife even now, blaming herself for insisting that they pick up Maggie a day early, though that has nothing to do with it at all—typical Ruth, to blame herself for everything. And Isabelle—if she knew Maggie is this sick—it's nothing Wilson will even consider! There is something about admitting a thing that makes it real, and Wilson doesn't want this illness to be real; if the treatment works, then no one will ever have to know.

"Hi," he says, when finally he's dialed and Ruth has answered.

"Did you know about the ants?"

"What?"

"The ants. Did you know about the ants?"

"What ants? What are you talking about?"

"The exterminator came today. Isabelle apparently had a little ant colony underneath the sink."

"An ant colony?"

"She parked herself in front of the cabinet and refused to move. I had to drag her out of the kitchen. Jesus, Wilson. What is going *on*? Where did I go wrong?"

"Ruth."

"I'm just glad I have no other children to fuck up."

Wilson bites the insides of his cheeks, which are ridged from the habit. He is glad he's said nothing about the dog; Ruth doesn't need to hear about Maggie right now. He decides to wait also, until the evening maybe, to mention their visit to his mother. He's not exactly sure what Ruth means by an ant colony, but it's clear that the issue is larger than that.

"You have been nothing but a good mother," he says.

He hears Ruth sigh.

"I did find an art class," she says, finally.

"You see?"

"Mother–daughter, although at this point it'd probably be better if it were a father–daughter class. You're much more creative than I am."

"You're creative."

"No I'm not. I can hardly do a stick figure."

"Well, you're the most creative lawyer I've ever seen practice."

"Please," Ruth says. "Was, maybe."

Wilson leans over to crack the window. "And will be again. As soon as she's back in school. As soon as she speaks again. Soon."

· Ruth sighs. "After today, I don't know. I don't know anything about anyone. Before the ants, Jimmy had called again."

"Ah. Still the helicopters? Or has he moved on?"

"Be nice, Wilson. I do worry about him. He's already lost the job he had for all of what, two months? And the landlord is threatening eviction."

"Eviction?"

"I don't know. Unwarranted, of course, according to Jimmy. They don't like the way he's 'decorated.' Which probably involves black sheets and tape over the windows and all the rest, who knows. I don't know. He's lonely. Delusional and all the rest, yes, but fundamentally a good person."

"You could invite him for Christmas," Wilson suggests, though he knows better.

"I don't think so. Not this year. I did ask him to come for the weekend, sometime."

"And?" Wilson puts his feet onto his desk.

Ruth sighs again. She is full of sighs. "Noncommittal."

"You do as much as you can, Ruth."

"I guess. But it's never enough."

There is a click on the line that neither of them really notices; for all Ruth knows, it is the cluck of Wilson's tongue against the roof of his mouth; for all Wilson knows, it could be a sound made as Ruth shifts the receiver from ear to ear. In the other room, Isabelle eases the kitchen phone back into its cradle, where her finger has already cut the line.

FIVE

Saturday

I

Her mug is almost too hot to touch, but still, Isabelle wraps both hands around it, imagining the heat traveling up through her arms and warming her entire body. She has eaten most of the whipped cream from her cocoa with a spoon, and her mouth is watering for the cocoa itself, but she knows that it is still too hot, and that if she takes a sip too soon her tongue will burn and feel scaly for the rest of the day. Despite the warmth beneath her hands, Isabelle shivers; she is chilled from a heatless night in the country.

"Coffee's warming me right up," she hears her father say. She does not look up from her cocoa. The steam from it curls in a beautiful patternless way.

"Not me," her mother says. "That was one of the most unpleasant nights I've ever had."

"It was cold," her father agrees. "Fucking furnace. I don't know how many times we've had to get that thing fixed, and still, without fail it craps out on us at least once a winter."

"I told you last time," her mother says. "Instead of paying someone to fix it when it's just going to break again, get a new one."

Isabelle has heard this conversation before.

"You might be right," her father agrees.

"Of course I'm right. It's what I've been saying all along. And you better do it soon. It's cold now, but I heard next weekend is going to be positively arctic."

"Well, it's a good thing we'll be at my mother's then."

There is a brief moment of silence.

Ruth sips her coffee. "God, I can't believe it. Is it already that time?"

"A week from Monday," Wilson says. "Christmas Day."

"If I didn't know better I'd think Christmas came at least twice a year."

Isabelle tests a tiny sip of her cocoa; it is the perfect temperature now, cool enough to drink and hot enough to trace as it travels down her throat and to her stomach. It makes her hungry; she scans the bakery for their waitress, hoping that soon she will come to take their order. Usually, Isabelle gets chocolate-chip pancakes whenever they come here for breakfast, but today she is going to get a breakfast sandwich, the same one that her parents always order: fried egg, a sausage patty, and American cheese on toasted rye. She took a bite of her father's last time they were here and was surprised by how much she liked it. Her mouth waters in anticipation.

She watches as their waitress delivers food to the table behind theirs. The woman at the table has ordered a Belgian waffle with whipped cream and berries, and the man has ordered some kind of omelet with toast and potatoes. He doesn't look at the waitress as she sets the food before him; nor does he look down at his food. His eyes are vacant, empty, and only when she notices the pole on the floor beside him does Isabelle realize that he is blind. He fumbles for his silverware. The woman with him unscrews the cap of the ketchup and pours some onto his plate. He reaches around for the salt and pepper, but there is none on the table, and the woman leans over and takes the salt and pepper from the empty table beside theirs. "Salt," she says, handing the blind man the salt. "Pepper," she says next, handing the shaker over.

"Isabelle."

Isabelle turns around, startled by the sound of her name.

"Don't stare," her mother says, her voice low.

Isabelle blinks. She looks down at her cocoa.

"Ah, here she comes," her father says as the waitress breathlessly approaches their table, pen and pad in hand. The waitress is named Beverly, and every time they come in here, she comments on how big Isabelle is getting, which bothers Isabelle only because it isn't true.

"Such a busy morning!" she says. "Sorry to keep you waiting."

"Not a problem at all." Isabelle holds her breath, willing her mother not to add something snide about being starving, or about how they must be understaffed, when she knows that there are always only two waitresses. But her mother is quiet, and Isabelle slowly lets her breath out.

"Okay, well, I know what the little lady over there wants; I already told the cook to get out some extra chocolate chips just for you."

Isabelle looks with alarm toward her father, hoping that he remembers how much she liked his sandwich last time and will step in just to make sure that that's not what she wants instead. But her father is peering through his reading glasses at the menu as if he doesn't know what he's going to have. Isabelle feels her heart flutter with frustration. A knot of anger tightens inside her chest.

"Well," her father says. "The usual for me: egg, sausage, and cheese on rye."

"Same," her mother says.

Isabelle had been planning, at this point, to hold up three fingers at Beverly to signify that she should bring three of these sandwiches. She kicks her father under the table as so often she has seen her mother do when trying to silence him, or to prevent him from picking at Isabelle's own food. He looks under the table; his legs are outstretched and he pulls them back toward him. "Sorry, dear," he says absently. She pulls her chair in closer to the table, hard and fast so that it shrieks loud against the floor. Her mother glances her way over the rim of her coffee mug as she takes a sip, and Isabelle tries to catch her eye, to hold it with her own long enough to impart meaning, but her mother has turned to ask Beverly for a refill when she gets the chance, and a glass of water.

"Anything else?" Beverly asks.

Isabelle looks from her mother to her father. Her chest pounds in panic, and she feels suddenly hot.

"I think that ought to do it," her father says.

"All right," Beverly says. "I'll place your order and come back with more coffee."

Isabelle grits her teeth so tight that her jaw begins to hurt, but there is something pleasing about the pain. Her father lifts yesterday's paper from the table. He hands a section to her mother and the business section to Isabelle before disappearing behind his own section. Isabelle sits rigid in her seat, breathing quickly through her nose, the business section untouched on the table before her. She doesn't care today to check how her stocks are doing. She hears the blind man clear his throat behind her and push his chair back from the table. She hears the woman he is with telling him the time, and saying how they'll have to hurry back if they're going to catch the game on the radio, and she wonders if the woman, if she were alone, would watch the game on television instead. She hears the tapping of the blind man's pole against the floor, and she badly wants to turn and watch him as he makes his way to the door, but she will not give herself that pleasure. She does not deserve it.

She stares into the hot chocolate before her, the whipped cream that remains soft now, without definition, the steam just a thread of its former self, and she pushes it away. She does not deserve this, either.

II

Wilson stands at the kitchen sink, looking over the counter and into the living room, where Isabelle sits in front of the fire, throwing dried pinecones into the flames one at a time and watching them burn. He thinks of telling her to stop, because the pinecones aren't just pinecones he collected but pinecones he bought, specially treated for use as kindling. But he says nothing. Isabelle has seemed distant today; there seems to be something on her mind. She didn't show any interest in checking the Coca-Cola stock she's given him her money to invest in. After breakfast at the bakery, they'd gone, as they always do after breakfast at the bakery, to the drugstore next door to buy the paper. On most mornings, Isabelle finds something or other to buy: a set of markers, a new pad, a candy bar, a barrette. But today she wandered listlessly through the aisles, and when Wilson asked her what she was going to get, she shrugged and looked away. At home, he asked if she wanted to sit with him and draw for a while; she showed no interest. She has been sitting for over an hour at the hearth, just staring and watching pinecones burn. Ruth has gone to run errands; her absence seems to increase the silence in the house, and Wilson wishes she were here.

"Hey, Belle," he says, remembering the zip cord he'd set up the weekend before that they hadn't had the chance to use before the Christmas tree lighting. "I want to show you something outside."

Isabelle turns around and looks at him.

"What do you say?"

Isabelle shrugs and turns back to the fire.

"It's a zip cord. I set it up for you last weekend. Know what a zip cord is?"

Isabelle turns around again. She looks at Wilson curiously.

"It's a wire, and you stretch it between two trees, and there's a swing attached and you ride the swing back and forth across the wire. You zip along the wire, I guess."

Isabelle licks her lips.

"Want to check it out? Give it a try?"

Isabelle nods.

"Let's go suit up," he says.

They bundle up in scarves, mittens, hats, and boots, Isabelle's new ones miniature versions of her father's.

Outside, the snow is crusty and deep; a layer of ice coats the trees.

"It's cold," Wilson says.

Isabelle nods. She is walking carefully, trying not to break through the snow's hard surface. On some steps, Wilson notices, she succeeds; on other steps she breaks through the crust, so that the path her footsteps make is uneven, footprints only here and there.

"All right," Wilson says as they reach the zip cord. "Here it is." He tells Isabelle to wait at the tree while he goes to get the swing where it hangs halfway down the wire. But when he pulls at it, tries to slide it along the wire back to the tree where Isabelle awaits, he finds that it is frozen solid in place. "Uh-oh," Wilson calls. "Minor problem, but"— he gives the swing a couple of yanks until it comes unstuck—"problem solved." But the problem is not solved. The swing is indeed unstuck, but there is a layer of ice coating the wire just as it coats the trees. Wilson tries to break it off; he cannot through his mitten, and even barehanded, when he tries, it is difficult to chip away. It would take an hour, he thinks, to clear the wire entirely of ice. He lets the swing go and stands for a minute watching his breath rise and disappear against the white sky. He sees some kind of bird, a raven or a crow, high in the branches of a nearby tree. The bird is still and seems to meet his gaze.

Wilson sighs and turns around. Isabelle is sitting in the snow by the tree, sucking on an icicle. "Where'd you get the icicle?" he asks, trudging toward her.

Isabelle gestures with her mittened hand to the rock ledge behind her, where a colony of icicles hang sharp and long.

Wilson nods. He takes a breath. "The wire's frozen," he says. "So it looks like we're out of luck."

Isabelle nods and shrugs, but Wilson can see disappointment in the way her eyes fall, the way her mouth twitches just a bit. She stands and starts back toward the house, and Wilson as he watches her is unnerved by how desperate he feels, desperate and helpless. "Belle!" he calls. "Wait, Belle!"

Isabelle turns around.

"A tree!" Wilson blurts out, his tongue working more quickly than his mind. "A tree. Remember, we were maybe going to cut ourselves a Christmas tree today. Since we're all bundled up anyway, we might as well stay outside and go find a tree." Isabelle nods, and Wilson is sure that he sees her eyes light up, even thinks he sees the trace of a smile. Usually, they buy their trees from a stand on the street in the city; Wilson has never cut a tree before, but he figures it will be easy enough. "Wait here," he says. "I'm going to go get the ax from the garage. Be right back." His heart is pounding as he hurries back to the house, whether with excitement or from the effort of walking through the snow he can't be sure. Every few steps he looks over his shoulder to where Isabelle waits, as if while he's not looking she might disappear. But every time, she's there, a dark shape against the snow, small, sucking on her icicle.

The roads have gotten slippery, and Ruth drives slowly, for once, though she's glad for some time alone. On either side of the road, snow has been shoveled into banks so tall they hide even the stone walls built by farmers centuries ago. This time last year, they hadn't even had a frost yet. Ruth remembers this specifically because on her birthday, which falls just after the new year, Wilson had presented her with rosebuds cut from his own rose bushes, which had begun to bloom early in the season's eerie warmth. She'd chastised him for clipping them before they'd actually unfurled, but he'd said it was better if he got to them before the winter, and he was right; it was only days later that the temperatures dropped and all the swollen tips of branches were cloaked in a layer of ice, the emerging crocus heads submerged again in snow.

But before that, before that week when it turned cold, they had taken a birthday picnic to what they called the Marsh Marigolds, though her birthday actually fell midweek. But midweek, Wilson had a business trip to visit clients in Louisiana, and Isabelle had a class trip to Washington, D.C., and Ruth herself had a court date on the day of her birthday. Yes, and Zeke Mueller had brought flowers for her to court, though how he knew it was her birthday she never understood.

But the day they celebrated was a warm Sunday, almost a year ago, and they'd followed the trampled path through the woods behind their house to the creek where all the season's water funneled its way to wherever it went. They followed the creek, then, to where it widened and collected around mossy rocks in pools deep enough to swim in, though it was too cold for that that day. Normally a lush and shady spot in springtime—which is when they usually visited—and dotted with the upturned eager faces of the marigolds for which the spot was named, in early winter the place had been transformed, and abundant stippled sunlight fell through the thinning canopy of leaves long overdue to have fallen, their hue a gold identical to that of the springtime marigolds. The moss was greener and thicker than they had ever seen it for all the rain they'd had, and Isabelle cut a small piece of it to bring back and replant by the house.

Ruth remembers the scene in flashes: Maggie chest-deep in the frigid water, burying her nose beneath the surface and then flinging her head upward, sunlight glinting in the resulting splash; Isabelle crouched down at the water's edge, releasing the tired goldfish she'd won at the fair the day before; Wilson supine on a mossy rock, the newspaper over his face, and then later the two of them, father and daughter, layering the glassy surface of a pool with floating golden leaves. Ruth tries to imagine herself in the scene—what was she doing?—but she cannot conjure herself there. What comes over her instead of an image is a feeling of release: her shoulders sink and her heart seems to slow its perpetual racing, and it is good.

She blinks. That was a year ago. What in the next three months had happened? What had gone wrong? What had steered them so drastically off course that they are where they are now? Ruth frowns. That picnic was the last time they'd been to the Marsh Marigolds, she thinks, and she wonders what other things they have allowed silence to let them neglect. She has tried to have them go on with their lives as normally as possible, given the circumstances, but that has been mostly in regard to larger things, like Wilson's birthday dinner, for instance, or celebrating the Fourth of July. She has neglected the little things, she sees now, things like the Marsh Marigolds and homemade macaroni and cheese and trips to the ice cream store or the zoo, things that seem pointless if they are done without joy. In the face of Isabelle's silence, these things came to seem small and insignificant. Who last spring wanted to go to the Marsh Marigolds when as a family they were so crippled by this new silence? Who wanted to go to the zoo? Instead, they have withdrawn into their separate quarters, waiting for things to get back to normal, each of them staring outward from him- or herself and into the vast silence between them. Last spring, instead of a trip to the Marsh Marigolds, a typical Sunday would have involved Ruth out weeding, Wilson tucked away behind the Sunday *Times*, Isabelle upstairs in her room or else drawing in the corner of the room, each of them as guilty of silence, really, as the next.

Ruth steers the car around the sharp bend in the road just before their driveway, surprised to find herself already almost home. It seems to happen to her more and more these days that she isn't aware of getting from point A to point B—she has no recollection of stopping at the stop sign before turning onto their road, or of changing gears to make it up the hill—but she knows she must have done these things to get to where she is. She slows down in front of Mr. Sullivan's old house, where she sees in the yard a man and boy rolling snow into the approximation of a man. The man has bent down to hoist a very large midsection up off the ground, but when he settles it down on the snowman's base, it shatters into clumps of snow. The boy throws his hands into the air and then rests them on top of his head before letting himself fall backward into the snow. Ruth blurs her eyes; the two of them could be Isabelle and Wilson, those two whom she left sitting silently by the fire.

Despite the cold, Wilson is sweating underneath his layers by the time he's dragged the tree he and Isabelle have cut down through the woods all the way back to the house, which is no short distance. Isabelle was particular about their tree, circling each one Wilson suggested so as to view it from every angle, shaking her head no before trudging on deeper into the woods to find another, more suitable tree. But Wilson doesn't mind. Good exercise, he figures, not to mention that Isabelle hasn't seemed more herself in some time, which is an especially welcome contrast to her mood this morning, which just about set Wilson over the edge of desperation. Maybe they don't need to go as far away as Africa, he thinks; maybe they should just hunker down up here for the rest of the month. A few more days like this one, and he can see Isabelle talking again, or forgetting not to. That's what it was, he thinks; both of them had been so intent on their search for a tree that they'd forgotten to fixate on her silence.

"Phew!" he says, releasing his grip on the trunk and letting the tree bounce down onto the packed snow of the driveway. "New tradition, don't you think?" He pulls his hat off and looks at his daughter, who is surveying the tree with her hands on her hips. She nods without looking at him.

Wilson sniffs. Ruth is home, he notes, and just beneath the hood the car's engine still clicks and purrs. "I wonder what your mother will think."

Isabelle gives him a skeptical look. He grins.

They climb up the back steps and bang the snow from their boots on the threshold. Wilson opens the door. "After you," he says, and follows his daughter inside, singing a version of the tune they'd marched home to: *"Hi ho, hi ho, we've drug a tree home through the snow!"*—but he stops short when they turn the corner into the kitchen and find that Ruth is not alone.

On stools across the island from where Ruth is dumping cocoa into mugs sit a man and a boy, each a different-size version of the other, both of them as red and wet with cold as Wilson and Isabelle are themselves.

Ruth smiles. "Hello," she says.

Wilson looks from his wife to his daughter, whose face seems to have turned to stone, her eyes gone glassy and doll-like, as if the lids would click shut if someone were to lift Isabelle and set her supine. He sets his jaw and manages a smile. "Hi," he says. He straightens up and runs a hand through his hair, which he knows must be at all angles, mussed by static and sweat. He extends his hand toward the man, who has risen from his stool. "Wilson Carter," he says. "And this is Isabelle."

"Jerome Dunlap," the man says. He shakes Wilson's hand, and then Isabelle's, and then he goes and puts a hand on the back of the boy's neck. "And this is Thomas. We're just moving in across the street."

Wilson nods. "Welcome to the neighborhood."

"I saw them out making a snowman as I was coming home with the wreaths," Ruth says. "They reminded me of you two guys. Thomas is Isabelle's age."

Wilson glances at Isabelle. She is staring at the floor, and Wilson feels a flutter of irritation toward his wife for inviting these people over here. He wonders, if she hadn't, how the rest of the day would have gone, whether the three of them might have sat down cheerfully to mugs of cocoa, maybe gone to see a movie in town or made Christmas cookies.

"It's nice to meet you, Thomas," Wilson says. The boy hasn't left his stool, and Wilson decides against reaching for his hand all the way across the island. Instead, he gives a little salute, which Thomas returns. Like Isabelle, Thomas is quite small for his age, but unlike Isabelle, the boy looks fragile, his skin pale, almost translucent.

"He can't hear you," Mr. Dunlap says, "but he can read your lips. He lost his hearing to measles when he was very young."

At this, Isabelle looks up.

"He doesn't speak much, but he signs. That's why we moved here, actually. They have a great school for kids who are deaf or mute. Shady Briar."

"I've heard of it," Ruth says. She clears her throat. "Isabelle doesn't speak much, either." It is a risky statement, and Wilson shoots his wife a look.

"That's okay," Mr. Dunlap says.

Isabelle looks back down at the floor, angry heat blooming through her body. Her initial anger had been that her mother had invited these new neighbors over while Isabelle was elsewhere and had no say in the matter, especially since she'd be expected to befriend the one her age—she could hear the coming suggestions: *Why don't you take Thomas outside and show him the tree? Why don't you kids go make snow angels?* When and if she wanted a playmate, she would find her own! She'd seen this coming last weekend; she does not need her mother arranging her friendships. But on top of this outrage, and worse, for her mother to humiliate her like that! *Isabelle doesn't speak much, either.* The words echo through her head, magnifying her humiliation—for her mother to compare her to a deaf boy like that, as if she could be shamed into talking! Wrong, wrong, wrong; she is ashamed of herself enough already, more ashamed than anyone outside herself could ever make her feel.

Inside her mittens, her hands are tight little fists, her fingernails dug deep into her palms. She reminds herself to breathe, and it is all she can do to walk to the back door and out into the snowy cold again.

She shuts the inner door firmly but quietly behind her. The screen door hisses shut on its hydraulic spring. She is embarrassed to have had to leave, especially when she considers what they must be saying about her right now inside—how are her parents explaining her rudeness?—but she hadn't known what else to do. And now that she's standing out here, she still doesn't know what to do. She has been outdoors for hours, and she is cold, and tired of being cold.

On the driveway below her, their tree is on its side, and the sight of it fills her with a dismay that she can't explain, but it is powerful enough to bring her to tears. Just minutes ago, she and her father were bringing that tree home, and she had been in a good mood, and just like that everything has changed, and really, she has no one to blame but herself. She tries to resummon her anger toward her mother—it is easier than sadness—but she cannot. Because really, what is wrong with her mother inviting the Dunlaps over? Why shouldn't she, even if it seems to Isabelle a transparent move, designed to get Isabelle to engage? But maybe it wasn't that at all. Maybe her mother had really just been driving by, and maybe the Dunlaps *had* reminded her of her father and herself, the way they used to be, the way she's made it impossible to be anymore. And maybe just to be polite her mother had asked them in for cocoa. What right does Isabelle have to be angry about that? And worse, what right does she have not to speak when Thomas Dunlap really can't? What must Mr. Dunlap think of her, with her self-imposed affliction, when his own boy *cannot* escape his world of silence?

She hurries across the driveway to the car. She locks herself inside, small in the driver's seat, which she imagines still holds the heat from her mother's body. There is still a trace of warmth in the car, and the smell of pine needles from the wreaths mingles with her mother's smell, at once indescribable and utterly familiar, and this, like the sight of the tree outside, fills her with a ragged sadness. She lowers her head onto the steering wheel, accidentally sounding the horn, and abruptly, startled by the sound, she sits back.

If the keys were in the car, she thinks, quickly checking the floor and visor to make sure they're not, she might drive away. She doesn't know exactly where she would go, because she doesn't really know how to get anywhere from here, but she'd go, following the roads wherever they took her. She reclines her seat all the way and stares at the drooping red fabric of the ceiling, from which still hang two sticky-bottomed caterpillars hatched from the plastic egg of a grocery store vending machine and attached there by Isabelle and her friend Phoebe two summers ago, when the car was a place where they played regularly. They'd roll down the front windows all the way and sit on the door with their legs inside, their bodies out, face-to-face across the roof of the car, where they'd set out their lemonades and plates of Fluffernutter sandwiches. Other times, when it was raining, they'd just sit in the car and read. One time, they'd even had a sleepover in the car. They'd flattened out the backseat and slept there, though they could just as well have reclined the front seats, Isabelle thinks now, and she wonders why they hadn't thought of that. It might have been more comfortable.

She sits up and tugs on one of the caterpillars, testing to see how stuck it is. To her surprise, it peels easily away from the ceiling's upholstery, and as she looks at the furry thing in her hand, she is filled with regret. She liked the fact that those caterpillars had been stuck there for so long, like bookmarks in time marking the days of a good friendship, or like place-holders, as if sometime, next summer, maybe, she and Phoebe could jump back in where they left off. She had seen Phoebe only once this past summer, in passing at the Fourth of July parade when they'd first arrived in Massachusetts for the summer. Even now she can feel her mother's hand steering her through the crowd in Phoebe's direction, can see Phoebe in her red-and-white-striped shirt, her blue shorts, her stubbornly downward gaze. Isabelle had known immediately that Phoebe's shyness wasn't the usual, temporary shyness of a winter's separation, but a different shyness—the shyness of not knowing what to say or do—and she'd known that her silence had preceded her, that she had no chance. *We've heard you had a hard year, Isabelle,* Phoebe's mother had said, and Isabelle had wanted to melt. She was not Isabelle anymore, even here where she hadn't been in a year; she was *the silent one.*

Isabelle blinks. She looks at the caterpillar in her hand—whether it is hers or Phoebe's she can't remember—and tries to reattach it to the ceiling. It stays for a moment, and then slowly, headfirst, it peels itself away and drops down onto the seat beside her.

SIX

Sunday

I

They'd spent the rest of yesterday silent, the last real words uttered being good-byes and nice-to-meet-yous as the Dunlaps, large and small, made their way outside into winter's early night, shortly after which Isabelle had reappeared from wherever she'd gone off to. They'd asked no questions.

Dinner was reheated split pea; Ruth hadn't felt like cooking. Evidently Isabelle does not feel like cooking either this morning; when Ruth appears downstairs, Wilson is fixing Sunday breakfast alone.

He cracks an egg into the waiting dish.

"Morning," he says, shortly.

"Good morning." Ruth pours herself a cup of coffee. It is not lost on her that Wilson neglected to bring up a thermos as he usually does. She leans her hip against the counter, watching as he cracks another egg, then another. "Where's Isabelle?"

"Outside." Wilson gestures with his chin. In the far corner of the yard, Isabelle is on her knees in the snow, all around her what looks to be the beginnings of a snow fort.

"She didn't want to do the eggs?"

"Evidently not."

Ruth grits her teeth. "Wilson," she says. "You have no reason to be angry at me."

Wilson lifts an eyebrow.

"You don't! And if you do, I want to hear what it is. I want you to explain it to me."

Wilson begins to whisk the eggs.

"Stop it. Put the fork down."

Wilson obeys.

"Now tell me what I've done."

Wilson swallows. Ruth can see it in the lurch of his throat.

"I invited the Dunlaps to come in for hot chocolate. That's it. And why the hell shouldn't I? They're our neighbors, they're new to the neighborhood, it's what you *do*."

"Not when your daughter won't speak! Not when she can hardly even stand the company of her own parents! How did you think she'd react, coming home to a roomful of strangers!"

"A roomful? A roomful?! Wilson, it was a man and his son, not a roomful!"

"His deaf son!"

"I didn't know he was deaf, and what the hell difference does it make, anyway! This is our problem, this is our fucking problem—we don't *do* things because our daughter won't speak. We don't go to the Marsh Marigolds, we don't go to the zoo, I don't work, we don't have new neighbors for fucking cocoa! Maybe if we *did* things, things would be different. We are *enabling* her, and we have got to stop!" Ruth takes a large sip of her coffee; it scalds. "Goddammit!"

She puts the mug down and walks over to the window. She can feel outside's cold even through the glass. Across the yard, Isabelle has added a second layer of snow bricks to her fort. Maggie is a black shape in the snow nearby, intent on rawhide, or a stick, Ruth can't tell for sure.

Behind her, Wilson stares into the eggs. "We had been *doing*. We went out and cut a tree down. We were in good moods. But you're right, too. You're right. Our *doing* just clashed with yours."

"Jesus. Wilson, what are we going to do? We cannot continue to live this way." She turns around.

Wilson shakes his head. "No," he says.

"So what do we do?"

Wilson sighs. He shakes his head again, all of a sudden filled with a terrible sense of hopelessness, which is the thing that he and Ruth now have in common.

She has just added the fifth layer of snow bricks to her fort when she is aware of someone else's presence nearby. She is inside the fort, and she's not sure what it is that makes her certain she is not alone; there are no sounds to suggest it, no shadows, and Maggie hasn't looked up from her rawhide, her ears perked as they'd be if she sensed someone coming. For some

183

reason, though, Isabelle suddenly senses she is not alone, and expecting that it is her father or mother come out to see if she wants breakfast or to give her a hand with the snow fort's roof, she lies down where she is inside the fort instead of crawling out through the space she's left as a door, knowing this will send the message that she wants to be left alone.

She studies the view from the snow where she lies: the crooked bricks loom in an oval around her, part of them blue in their own shadow, and part of them, on the other side of a sharp diagonal line between sun and shade, so bright they make the backs of her eyes ache when she looks at them directly. The snow bricks circle her five layers up, bright and shadowed, framing the sky, which seems a false shade of blue, almost three-dimensional, so that even lying on the ground, she feels as if she is in it. The tallest branches of the nearby trees tremble in a breeze she can't feel on the ground, tottering in and out of sight. She can count two clouds, both of them directionless wisps, thin and high. A small plane buzzes overhead, a silver flash.

Once, when they were on the beach, they had seen a plane like this one, high and silver and loud out over the water, and as they watched it, suddenly the engine stopped and in the sudden silence the plane tumbled wing over tail over wing toward the water, but then before anyone could even fill the space after a gasp, the engine choked to life and the plane caught itself, soared upward. She is remembering this moment, the horror and thrill of it, when suddenly, from behind, a shadow falls across her face. She tilts her head back and sees an unfamiliar pair of eyes peering over the top of her snow fort; abruptly, she gets onto her knees and turns around, and suddenly she is face-to-face over the top layer of bricks with Thomas Dunlap.

At first startled, she is quickly embarrassed and surprised at once; surprised to be intruded upon by someone so unexpected, and embarrassed first to think of her behavior yesterday, and then by her reaction to seeing Thomas Dunlap here right now—or, better, her lack of reaction. The two of them stare at each other over her wall of snow, Isabelle's mind racing. She has never encountered a deaf person so intimately. She's seen people signing before, and been aware that they were deaf, but she has never been face-to-face, one-on-one, with anyone who can't hear. Unsure of what to do, what to say, for a moment she desperately wishes that Thomas Dunlap were not deaf.

Finally, after what is probably a shorter time than it seems, Thomas waves. Isabelle waves back. To her relief, it is as easy as that.

II

Wilson looks at his old pickup parked at the edge of the driveway where just weeks ago it had still been warm enough to work on. Now the thing sits up to its wheels in snow so deep that in the back of the pickup it stands taller than the sides that hold it in. He should have cleaned out the garage after all, Wilson thinks, if only enough to make room for the truck, which left outside certainly won't make it through the winter—not this winter, anyway. In only a week there has been more snow than in the past two winters combined. He could clean the garage out still, he thinks; but then he'd have to dig the pickup out of the snow, and he suspects that the engine wouldn't turn over, that the battery would be dead. He tightens his lips in resignation; the truck is old, he thinks, and it's had a good life; he will let nature take its course.

He hears Isabelle's footsteps coming down the stairs behind him; she is running, and Wilson knows the steps are icy.

"Careful, Belle!" Wilson calls, turning around anxiously. But already Isabelle is safely at the bottom of the stairs, her breath white and fast in the air around her. Her parka is not done up, and the laces of her boots are not tied, but Wilson hesitates before saying anything more. It is unlike Isabelle to have her laces undone and her coat unzipped; there is something wonderfully childlike about such neglect, something lighthearted that Wilson cannot bring himself to check, and so he says nothing.

They cross the driveway to the station wagon; Wilson gets in the driver's side and watches through the glass as Isabelle struggles with the frozen door handle on the front passenger side. He leans across the seat and opens it for her from the inside, and then he watches as she gets in; she sits down before swinging her feet in, and she is small enough that she has to lean back out of the car to pull the door closed. She buckles herself in and then turns to Wilson as if to say that she is ready to go.

He drives slowly; the road is icy. But he is glad to drive slowly; it is beautiful, and the mall is no place to rush to. The trees that line the road are tall and thin; their limbs are heavy with snow and their branches glossy with a layer of ice. Off in the woods, Wilson sees a couple of deer grazing the snow, their heads to the ground, and he slows the car to a crawl. "Look, Belle, deer," he whispers, as if the deer could hear him. He holds his arm near Isabelle's face and points, so that she can follow his arm with her eyes to where the deer stand, alert now, frozen and staring. "See them?" he asks, and Isabelle nods.

After a minute, Wilson sees in the rearview mirror a car coming down the road behind them, and so he speeds up; at the sound of the revving engine, the deer startle and bound away through the trees, the white undersides of their tails glowing against their tawny hides. Isabelle lets her eyes linger in their direction, turning around in her seat so that she can see as the car moves farther down the road; finally, when the car has rounded a bend, she turns around and switches the heat on full blast, leaning forward in her seat to hold her hands over the vents, something Wilson has taught her to do.

Ruth jabs a macaroni with a fork and lifts it from the boiling water. She watches the steam rise above it as she holds it in the air, letting it cool for a minute before putting it into her mouth to test; the pasta is done. She carries the pot to the sink and empties its contents into the strainer waiting there, closing her eyes and holding her face above the steam. She cuts a chunk of butter from the stick and puts it into the pot, adds the pasta, the milk, the egg, the cheese, the salt. The little things, she tells herself. The little things. She dumps it all into a casserole dish and puts it into the oven to bake; it should be ready for lunch when Isabelle and Wilson return from the mall.

She looks out into the yard, where Maggie is lying in the snow not far from Isabelle's snow fort. Isabelle has shoveled paths through the snow across the yard: from the porch to her snow fort to the apple tree, around the far side of the house. Despite her best efforts, and despite all of their adherence to the rules of path-walking, there are still rogue footprints here and there. Some, of course, are from Maggie. Some lead up to the zip cord Wilson set up last weekend. Others lead off into the woods, distinguished from the prints returning by the marks left by the tree they'd dragged home through the snow. Ruth suspects that Isabelle will turn those prints into a path easily enough; the tree has done half the work for her. Then there are rogue footprints that Ruth can't account for, on the far side of Isabelle's snow fort. She frowns. These disappear behind a stand of trees. Whose prints are they? Ruth wonders. Isabelle's? But Isabelle of all people wouldn't wander without a path, especially around her fort!

Ruth pulls on her boots and coat and goes outside. She pauses by Maggie, tosses her a snowball, which the dog catches in her mouth. She follows Isabelle's path the rest of the way to the snow fort, which is more than waist high. Ruth is impressed. She touches the bricked wall; it is surprisingly solid. She takes a breath and looks at the footprints disappearing behind the stand of trees. They must be Isabelle's; they are small enough. But what was she doing? Ruth follows the footprints behind the trees, and to her surprise they do not stop there. She follows them where they lead, beyond the trees and along the edge of the road for a while until they vanish into pavement. Ruth steps into the road, puzzled. Where had Isabelle been going?

Just then a snowball crashes at Ruth's feet. She looks up. Thomas Dunlap looks out from behind the trunk of a tree at the edge of Mr. Sullivan's old yard, a big grin on his face.

"Hello!" Ruth calls, but Thomas has turned around, a skinny bundled figure running through the snow. Ruth watches him as he goes, leaving a trail of footprints the same as the ones she's been following.

The mall smells like wet wool and bad breath. It is stuffy and packed with Christmas shoppers; Isabelle allows her father to take her by the hand and lead her through the crowd. The faces of other shoppers seem to flash by Isabelle as they pass; she has time to look at each one for only a second, and it is interesting, Isabelle thinks, how when you just glance once at a stranger, the expression he or she is wearing in that moment is the expression you remember, as if with that glance you have taken a mental photograph. She looks down at her boots and watches the laces drag, trying to remember the faces she has glimpsed: a woman with her hand beneath her chin to catch the cookie crumbs falling from her mouth as she chews; a man with his nostrils flared and his mouth open as he takes a breath in for a sneeze; another man in the middle of a sip of hot coffee, his eyes watery behind the coffee's steam. She wonders if somewhere in her mind are mental photographs of everyone she has passed this afternoon, and she wonders why it is that these three are the ones she remembers first. If she thought hard about it, she is sure she could summon the images of other faces—like the boy with the cut beneath his eye, and the woman in the wheelchair digging through her purse. Yes, all the faces are in there somewhere, Isabelle is sure. They must be.

She looks up from her boots and glances over at a rough-skinned man with a blue silk scarf tied around his head. His face reminds Isabelle of the smell of stale smoke, and though she means to look immediately away, to preserve this face as a still photograph rather than an animated memory, she lets her eyes linger for a moment on the man. His eyes are trained intently on something to his left, and his brow is creased; Isabelle follows his gaze. But she cannot make out what or whom among the many shoppers and the signs for Christmas sales and the holiday decorations he is looking at, and then suddenly she has walked right into her father, who has paused before the window of a store.

"Let's take a look in here, Belle," he says. Isabelle looks once more at the man with the scarf; he is still staring, and for a moment Isabelle wonders if maybe he is blind, but then he has no stick, she thinks, and no dog, and his gaze is too intense to be the vacant gaze of a blind man. She almost wishes that he were blind; it frustrates her that he can be so captivated by something she cannot discern.

"Coming?" her father says, and Isabelle turns to follow him into the store. "I was looking through the catalog for this place," he says, his voice lower now in the store's relative quiet. "But I can never tell what something's really like unless I see it myself. And that way you save yourself the hassle of having to send the thing back if it's not what you had in mind."

Isabelle nods, looking around the store, which is spacious and dark and cool. It is what she could only describe as a store of gadgets, selling things utterly unnecessary along with elaborate models of everyday items, like the toaster oven her father is musing over now. "Electronic touch-pad control," he mutters, reading the description. "Nonstick interior, four rack positions, six-slice capacity. Six slices!" He turns to Isabelle with what seems genuine enthusiasm. "Two pieces for each of us at the same time, that means!" He turns back to the toaster oven. "Interior oven light, auto shut-off—that's good—and electronic toast control. Cool wall exterior." He bends down to look at the oven more closely. "Cool wall exterior," he repeats. "What do you suppose that means?" He opens the oven to peer inside. "The outside doesn't get hot, I imagine," he says. "That makes sense enough." He closes the oven and straightens up. "What do you think, Belle? Think Mom would want a new toaster for Christmas?"

Isabelle looks at him uncertainly. She doesn't want to hurt his feelings by shaking her head no, because her father seems truly impressed by the oven, but then again, she thinks, if she doesn't hurt his feelings, her mother will hurt them when she opens the gift. She has seen it happen too many times, with the banana hanger last year, and the bagel slicer, and the mini stereo the year before.

"Well?" her father asks again, running his fingers over the oven.

Isabelle hesitates, and then she shrugs.

"Keep looking?"

Isabelle nods, but just then a salesman walks by and her father grabs his attention. "Excuse me," he says. "Can you tell me about this toaster oven?"

The salesman starts to repeat the things that her father has already read; Isabelle wanders away from the two of them to the other side of the store. She sits for a minute on an electric massage chair, trying to enjoy the feel of it, but its vibrations make her feel more numb than relaxed. In a back corner of the room, she sees a specially lit shelf of geodes and mineral slabs, the crystals of them glinting at her through the store's darkness. She approaches the shelf to look more closely at these mineral slices, standing solid and calm. Agate, she reads, looking at the polished slabs of brown, orange, and red swirling into one another, the colors more deep and rich, she thinks, than colors normally are, as if they might have a taste or a smell. She blurs her eyes at the agate, and it seems to glow; it reminds her of what she imagines when she thinks of the center of the earth.

Beside the agate slabs sit opened geodes, the crystals clinging thick to their interiors. She wonders who was the first to open a geode, and whether it was done accidentally. She imagines someone long ago collecting rocks to build a wall, or to contain a fire, and dropping one that cracked open, revealing beneath the rock's rough surface the colony of crystals inside. Who would ever think that the exterior of a rock could hide something as beautiful as geodes do? She takes a step closer to the shelf, not noticing the alabaster slab on the floor until her toe hits it. It is large and heavy, a translucent orange, and she is captivated by the way it seems to absorb the light shining through. It looks warm, and she squats to touch it, but then she wishes she hadn't; it is cold.

She stands to return her attention to the shelf of rocks, noticing for the first time the counter beside the shelf, beneath whose glass are jewels made from these gems—jade bracelets, amethyst earrings—but what Isabelle finds most beautiful is a silver necklace, the pendant like a silver-black raindrop. She looks at this more closely; the rock of the pendant is called an Apache Tear, and she wishes she had thought of this herself; it is much more of a tear than a raindrop.

"Belle." She hears her father behind her. "Finding anything?"

Isabelle nods.

"I'm having luck in this store, too. I think I'll bag the toaster after all, but I found this," he lifts a box in one hand, "and I know it's wintertime, but they have this terrific hammock that comes with its own stand, and the way I see it, the old hammock's seen better days, and I doubt if the apple tree will be able to hold it much longer anyway. And you know your mother and her hammock."

Isabelle nods. Her mother does love to lie on the hammock when it's nice out; her father has chosen a gift that might not be so bad after all. She looks at the box in her father's hand, and he holds it out for her to see.

"It's a pedometer," he says. "It counts the number of steps you take."

Isabelle looks at the thing skeptically. She pictures Christmas morning, her mother opening the pedometer with disgust, her father sheepish, Isabelle herself filled with shame that she allowed him to purchase this gift knowing how it would be received.

"What do you think?" her father asks. Isabelle sucks in a breath through her teeth and shakes her head. "No? You don't think Mom would want one of these?" Isabelle wrinkles her nose and shakes her head again. "Oh," her father says, looking a little dismayed. "Well," he says, "there's also this shovel-type device, specifically for planting bulbs, and the good thing about it is that you don't have to bend over. Better for the back."

But Isabelle is only half listening. She has let her gaze wander back to the Apache Tear necklace.

"What did you find, Belle?" Her father takes a step closer to her and peers through the glass of the counter at the jewelry beneath. Isabelle points at the Apache Tear. "For Mom?" he asks.

She nods.

He bends closer to the necklace.

"It is pretty," he says. "You think Mom would like it?"

Isabelle nods again; she knows that her mother would like it. She knows that her mother will.

III

Isabelle has never liked Sunday afternoons. There is something about them that fills her with dread. She used to think it was because she knew she had to go to school the next day and start a whole new week, but she's concluded that the problem with Sunday has to do with Sunday and nothing else. There is something dark and lonely about those hours of the afternoon after they've returned to the city but haven't yet gathered for dinner, an awkward patch of time between day and evening that Isabelle is never sure quite how to fill. Today, sitting in the bath, she is even more eager than usual for the evening to begin; tonight, they will decorate the tree that she and her father chopped down. She sinks low into the water thinking about it, letting the water rise above her lips.

It is the perfect tree, symmetrical and full, and she likes it even more for having picked it out herself and having helped to cut it down and drag it out from the woods. Her father seems as proud of the tree as she is, and she smiles as she pictures him walking through the snow before her with an ax slung over his shoulder like a real woodsman. Much better than last year, when the three of them had stood shivering on a curb in the city and examined each tree a vendor had cut free of its netting. They must have looked at twelve or fifteen trees at least, and, at first, her parents had remarked on each one brightly—*this looks like a good one, don't you think?*—and she had shrugged her indifference from where she leaned against the building—*I don't care,* she'd said, because she *didn't.* So the vendor had unwrapped another tree, and then another and still another until finally, all possibility of fun bled from the evening, her parents had settled on a tree. They had walked home silently, one parent at either end of the tree, Isabelle trailing behind, and her father had dropped his end and chipped the bottom of the trunk, and her mother had said the tree would be crooked now, and then the top of the tree had snapped as they'd stood it in the elevator, and then the lights had gone on crooked. No, she thinks now, in the bath. Far better this year speechless.

But then she thinks of the hours before they went to cut the tree, when she sat sullenly and refused her father's company. She grits her teeth in shame. It wasn't her father's fault that she didn't get the breakfast that she wanted, yet she punished him for it anyway. Sometimes when she thinks about herself she can't believe she is the person that she is, a person she often doesn't like. What she's not sure of is whether she's more angry at herself for getting angry at her father, or for having been unable to order that breakfast sandwich. She pictures all their food on the table, and how she couldn't bring herself to eat more than a bite of the extra-chocolatey chocolate-chip pancakes that she knows would have been delicious.

She thinks of the blind man at the table behind theirs, and how something as simple as breakfast, something simple enough for her to refuse without thinking twice, had been for the blind man a challenge. She's thought about being blind in a new space, or walking down the street, but never before of being blind at breakfast. She's never considered the ketchups and salts and peppers of blindness, the brushing of teeth or the taking of baths. She closes her eyes and imagines that the blackness is permanent.

Suddenly, she is much more aware of the bathwater around her; it seems thick and somehow menacing. She notices for the first time the sound of the water dripping into the sink; the gurgling sound of water leaking down the drain groans louder than it seemed to before. She imagines she can even hear the rush of blood through her body.

If blindness makes sound that much louder, that much more detailed and precise, she wonders, then does deafness enhance sight? She shivers in anticipation of her thoughts and reaches for the hot water tap with her toes. She has been letting her mind roam carefully, knowing well where, eventually, she'd let it go but saving the best for last, as she would her favorite part of a meal, picking away at the turkey and stuffing with her eye all the while on the mashed potatoes in the middle of her plate.

Thomas Dunlap. She looks at the water flowing from the tap and tries to see it as he might, all the attention otherwise saved for sound fixed on what she sees. She carefully notes the rising steam, and how it is a fog, and different from the strandlike steam she notices lifting from a hot drink. She watches how when the water first emerges from the tap, it is an inch-wide solid band of water, clear as glass, and how as it falls it splits apart into so many messy drops. Watched carefully like this, the water seems to move in slow motion, to tumble slowly, if something can be said to slowly tumble. The water is hot around her toes; she lifts a foot to turn the tap off and settles back deeply in the water, ready now to replay the scene in her mind one more time tonight: his eyes peering at her over the edge of the fort, her scrambling up, and before he'd waved at her, that awful, panicked moment when she hadn't known what to do.

To think of that moment now is puzzling and wonderful. What hadn't occurred to her in that moment seems so obvious to her now: What difference would it make if Thomas Dunlap could hear? She wouldn't have said anything anyway! Confronted with his silence, she had forgotten her own.

He had clearly been working on his own brick of snow while Isabelle had been lying inside the fort, because next he bent down and lifted one perfectly formed snow brick from the ground outside the fort and offered it forward. Isabelle pointed to where it should be laid, and they worked silently on the fort together until, as quickly as he'd appeared, Thomas Dunlap was gone.

Now, in the bath, Isabelle sighs. She takes a breath and pulls her head beneath the water's surface.

Somewhere in one of the kitchen drawers, somewhere on one of the cluttered counters where magazines and old newspapers are stacked, somewhere in the kitchen, Ruth knows, there is a Chinese take-out menu. She has unpacked the crates of groceries they brought back from the country and put all the food away, even the steak she'd planned on cooking tonight to have with the leftover macaroni. She is tired and doesn't feel like cooking. She shuffles through a drawer of pencils, rubber bands, take-out menus to other restaurants. She looks underneath a stack of magazines, under the box of Christmas chocolates sent by one of Wilson's clients; she checks to see if maybe it has slipped beneath the microwave. She knows she saw it in here just last week. She pauses before the pile of newspapers; if the menu is not underneath these, she thinks, she will have run through all the possibilities of where it could be, and she'll have to order from memory. She begins to make a mental list of the dishes they like: spring rolls, spicy beef, moo-shu pork, vegetable lo mein. And there are the scallion pancakes that Isabelle especially likes, but she knows there are other dishes she's forgetting. She lifts the stack of papers. No menu. "Shit," she mutters, letting the papers drop.

She rests her elbow on the counter and her forehead in her hand. She should organize the kitchen, she thinks, scanning all the clutter before her. No wonder she can't find anything in here. As she surveys it all, her eye falls on something that part of her immediately wishes it hadn't. Near the small kitchen stereo and between two of the several cookbooks stacked there, she sees something bound in spiral, and when she pulls it out, she finds that it is indeed what she thought and hoped and feared it might be—one of Isabelle's sketchbooks. She looks down at the yellow cover on which Isabelle's name is printed neatly in the upper right-hand corner. Her daughter goes through sketchbooks sometimes as quickly as one a month, and she dates each one beneath her name. This one, Ruth notes, is from eight months ago, just after Isabelle stopped speaking.

Her heart quickens. She lifts the sketchbook, glancing nervously around her, and hurries to the bathroom down the hall, the narrow one at the back of the house where they keep their cleaning supplies in the bathtub, the one that no one ever uses. No one, she thinks, will find her here. She locks the door behind her and lowers the lid of the toilet to sit on. Her breath trembles as she looks at the sketchbook in her lap, running her fingers over it. She hesitates for just a minute before flipping the cover open. Going through Isabelle's sketchbook, she thinks, is equivalent to reading someone's diary, and she wants to be better than that. She doesn't want to be the kind of mother who snoops and spies. At the same time, she thinks, this is different. This sketchbook is from a crucial time, from the time Isabelle first began to cultivate her silence, and it could contain clues. And Dr. Steingold, hadn't he said that there was meaning in Isabelle's art? That she was trying to communicate something by it? Furthermore, Ruth reasons, what was the sketchbook doing in the kitchen, wedged between two cookbooks, anyway? Her daughter is neat, organized; she would never lose track of a sketchbook, Ruth is sure. Maybe, Ruth thinks, maybe Isabelle planted the notebook in the kitchen for her mother to find. Maybe she put it there as some sort of cry for help. Maybe, Ruth thinks, she put it there months ago and has just been waiting for Ruth to find it. The thought that this sketchbook might have been sitting here under Ruth's nose all along is maddening, and she takes a deep breath to calm herself before opening the thing up, almost afraid of what she'll find inside.

On the first page is the picture of a branch, done from above, it seems, and up close. The bark is textured and peeling in spots, and from the crooked way the branch bends Ruth can tell that this branch is a limb of the apple tree, the one where Isabelle so often sits. Isabelle has drawn springtime shoots sprouting from the limb, and the fragile curl of leaves beginning to open. If the apple tree doesn't make it through the winter, Ruth thinks, Isabelle will have captured its final spring right here.

Drawn on the next page is the corner of Isabelle's desk in the city. There is a glass of water on the desk, and a ruler, and a small basket of worry dolls, and a hand—Isabelle's own, Ruth can tell by the scar on the knuckle—sketching a drawing of Maggie. The drawing of Maggie within the drawing, it seems to Ruth, is as remarkable as the drawing itself, and she almost wishes that it stood alone—but, she thinks, looking again, there is something interesting about a drawing within a drawing.

On the next page is a view of the street below their house, done from Isabelle's bathroom window, Ruth can tell by the pattern of the curtains and the thin rails of the child guard that Isabelle has included in the picture. In the drawing it is a sunny day, and the shadows of the people on the street stretch long from beneath them, the people themselves, viewed from this angle, only heads and legs outstretched in a step.

Ruth hears Wilson's footsteps coming down the hall, and she freezes. She hears the hall closet door open and her husband rummaging through a plastic bag. She considers calling to him, but she is afraid that if she did he might disapprove of this invasion of their daughter's privacy. She returns to the sketchbook only after his steps have faded down the hall. She had expected drawings of fire and chaos, maybe, of crashing planes and car wrecks; instead, her daughter seems to draw simply what she sees. Or hears, Ruth thinks, thinking of the picture of the lion from dinner on Wilson's birthday. She flips through the sketchbook again and notices this time the picture of a field of oil derricks like grazing beasts with their heads to the ground. Ruth pauses over this drawing, trying to figure where it might have come from. This sketchbook is from April—and last April, she suddenly remembers, Wilson had taken a business trip to Texas to meet with clients who were in the oil business, and, she remembers quite clearly now, it was a Wednesday night when he got home, and he and Ruth sat in the kitchen while Isabelle prepared her spaghettini, and Wilson described driving down straight and endless roads through fields of these things bobbing their heads up and down, up and down, the sound of their groaning loud when he pulled over to check the map.

So Isabelle draws what she sees and what she hears, Ruth thinks. There must be something to that, something. If she herself were to draw the view of their street, she would have drawn the view alone, not the window in which the view is contained. And the apple tree—she would have drawn the tree in its entirety, and from the ground. And then the drawing of Isabelle's desk—or is it of Maggie? Or is it of Isabelle herself doing what she does best? Ruth shuts the sketchbook, anxious already for Thursday, when she can give this sketchbook to the shrink. Thursday seems forever away, though; maybe tomorrow, she thinks, she'll drop the sketchbook off at Dr. Steingold's office so he has time to study it before Isabelle's appointment. She wonders how long it will take before he can get her speaking again, because, she thinks, this doctor *will* get Isabelle speaking again, she is sure of it, feels it in her bones. She shivers with a surge of excitement.

She leaves the bathroom and stashes the notebook between the mattress and the box spring of her and Wilson's bed, and then she stands for a minute, trying to remember what it was she'd been in the middle of doing before this. Dinner! She was going to order dinner. She doesn't have the patience anymore to look for the menu; her mind is racing with images of Isabelle's drawings, and her eyes feel dry and wide with hope. She'll just call the place and order from memory, she thinks, and she'll ask Isabelle and Wilson if there's anything special they'd like to order tonight; she feels like celebrating. She hurries down the hall to Isabelle's room, so distracted by her excitement that she bursts into Isabelle's room without first knocking. "Isabelle!" she cries, and then she stops. Her daughter had been facing the bookshelf when Ruth entered, but whirled around at the sound of the opening door; Ruth now finds herself face-to-face with a blindfolded child trying too late to rip the blindfold—really a winter scarf—from her eyes, caught underneath the earmuffs on her head. "Isabelle," Ruth repeats, quiet this time, puzzled.

Isabelle has pulled the blindfold over her head and drops it to the floor. Her face is red, the earmuffs now around her neck. She glares at her mother.

"I'm sorry," Ruth says. "I should have knocked." She feels herself wither under Isabelle's gaze. She should have knocked, she thinks. Of course she should have remembered to knock; Isabelle has always insisted on it. Ruth stands lamely, unsure of what to do. For a minute, she can't remember why she even came in, and then when she does remember, it doesn't seem to matter anymore. Isabelle isn't going to want anything special; she probably won't want anything at all, just as she didn't want breakfast this morning. She looks at the blindfold on the floor, the fuzzy white earmuffs. Maybe her daughter is planning on going blind and deaf as well as mute, Ruth thinks bitterly. She looks at Isabelle, her wet hair kinky and wild, her eyes like ice. Ruth feels her own eyes begin to burn, and she lets them drop. "I'm sorry," she repeats quietly, and, quietly, she leaves the room.

Wilson is putting a string of lights on the Christmas tree for the second time tonight; the first string had taken him a good forty minutes, and then when he'd plugged it in he'd discovered that one faulty bulb had put out the lights on the entire string. He tested this second string before putting it on the tree. He is careful to space the lights as evenly as he can, but he has to work quickly so that there will be time to eat and to decorate the tree before Isabelle goes to bed. He started the first string of lights at the top of the tree, but this one he started at the bottom, just to try a new technique, and the whole process seems to be moving more easily this way, for whatever reason. He is pleased by his discovery—already he is more than halfway finished, high enough up along the tree to have to use the stepladder he brought up from the cellar along with all the decorations. Slowly, carefully, he leans out to drape the string of lights over the farthest branch he can reach without moving the ladder.

"They're totally uneven."

Wilson startles; he drops the coil of lights and grabs for the top of the ladder, which is at his knees. "Jesus!" he says. "You startled me." He turns around, his heart thumping. Ruth stands in the doorway, one hand on her hip. He comes down off the ladder and stands back to look at his work. The lights look fine to him. "What do you mean they're uneven? Where are they uneven?" he demands.

"Look at them, Wilson, they're all over to the left."

"What do you mean they're all over to the left?"

"I mean they're all over to the left. Come here. Come where I'm standing." Wilson obeys. "See?"

From this angle, there does seem to be a greater concentration of lights to the left; Ruth is right. "Yeah," he says. He sighs. "Okay, I'll do it over. Round three. I'm getting hungry, though. You order yet?"

"No, I didn't order, Wilson," Ruth snaps. "I can't find the fucking menu anywhere in that kitchen."

Wilson opens his mouth to fire back, but stops. There is something in Ruth's eyes that gives him pause; they are deep and troubled. And after the breakfast the two had eaten together, alone, she had seemed in an okay mood. She had complimented him on their tree, hadn't said a word about drying needles or fire hazards. He looks at his wife. She bites her lip and takes a long, trembling breath. He looks down the hall toward Isabelle's closed door. He doesn't ask what happened. "I'll do it," he says, because he's not sure what else to say. There is too much else to say. "I'll order."

They eat dinner in silence broken only by the clacking of chopsticks and the clink of glasses set back on the table after a sip. A few times, Wilson tries to start a conversation, but he goes unanswered.

"Good lo mein tonight," he says once.

"I heard we might get a big storm next weekend," he says later. "So much snow so early in the winter!" But his voice sounds loud to him, too loud.

When it seems as if everyone has eaten all they will, Wilson stands to clear the table. The white paper boxes of Chinese are all more than half full, still. He closes them one at a time and puts them in the refrigerator. Isabelle clears the plates and puts them in the dishwasher unrinsed. Wilson is always reminding his wife and daughter to rinse the dishes before putting them into the machine, but tonight he says nothing. Ruth sits at the table, swirling the last drops of wine in her glass.

"Should we do the tree?" Wilson suggests.

Ruth looks up. "Why don't you guys do it," she says. "I'm just exhausted tonight."

"No, if you're too tired, we'll wait. We'll do it tomorrow night."

Ruth shakes her head and takes her last sip of wine. "It's okay," she says. "Really. It's better if the two of you just do it."

Wilson gives his wife a questioning look, and she nods as if to reassure him. "I'm just going to head to bed." Wilson and Isabelle listen to her footsteps fade down the hall. They look at each other.

Isabelle stands small in her pajamas. She is pale, and Wilson thinks she must be hungry; she had no breakfast and barely touched her dinner, so all she's had today is some macaroni. She's wearing a pair of slippers that Wilson gave her last Christmas, huge, pink things shaped like pigs. He tries to imagine the sound of her voice, but to remember sound is not the same as hearing it, just as the memory of pain can never be as painful as the pain itself. Soon, he thinks, someday, this silence will be only a memory. He smiles sadly at his daughter.

Isabelle smiles back, though there is nothing, really, to smile about. Her mother has gone to bed at eight thirty instead of decorating the Christmas tree, and the lines around her father's eyes seem deeper than they ever have before, and she knows she is the cause of it all.

"I'm going to check on Mom, Belle," her father says after a minute. "Why don't you fix yourself a little dessert, and then we'll do the tree." He pauses, then turns and leaves the room. Isabelle stands another minute where she's been standing by the dishwasher, then she shuts the door of the machine and wanders down the hall toward the living room. Maggie is lying in front of the Christmas tree; even she looks small beside it. Isabelle turns off all the lamps in the room and plugs the Christmas tree lights in. She lies down on the floor with Maggie, her head on Maggie's stomach, which rises and falls with every breath. She starts to count the breaths: one, two, three, and when finally she's counted a hundred breaths, she nuzzles Maggie's soft stomach with her face and stands. Her father has laid out all the Christmas decorations on a nearby card table. There are many of them: shiny bulbs, silk balls, candy canes, glass sailboats, stockings, a teddy bear dressed as an angel, and a snowflake Isabelle made years before out of popsicle sticks. It looks nothing like a snowflake, Isabelle thinks now, looking at it in the dim light.

And then there are the ornaments she made for her parents, a red wooden *R* painted with wreaths and presents and elves, and a wooden *W*, painted in red-and-white stripes like a candy cane. She looks at these, and then she looks down the darkened hall toward her parents' room. Their door is half open, casting a small triangle of light into the hallway. She looks back down at her parents' ornaments, lifts them from the table, and carries them down the hall to their room.

SEVEN

Monday

I

Wilson looks at his watch as he turns onto their street; he is early. Ruth and Isabelle won't have left yet for this art class Ruth has signed them up for, followed by a visit to the popover café. So he will have to watch and wait until he sees them go. Part of him feels as if he should immediately go upstairs and tell them of Maggie's prognosis instead of sneaking her off to the vet like this, but a larger part clings to the hope that Maggie will be okay. The thought that she might not be would make him feel desperate even if it weren't for Isabelle; Isabelle's silence only doubles his desperation, even to the extent that it has crossed his mind, albeit fleetingly, that he could, if need be, replace Maggie with another dog—as if Isabelle wouldn't be able to tell the difference. He scoffs at himself; their daughter is nothing if not observant. He thinks of the sketchbook Ruth found last night and the images inside, far removed from the rainbows and unicorns of Isabelle's younger days. He sets his jaw; to think of the sketchbook and where it is now—on the secretary's desk at the new shrink's office—fills him with a terrible sense of guilt.

Last night, after he and Isabelle had somberly decorated the tree—neither had even pointed to the ladder's sticker—he returned to his bedroom not to find Ruth asleep, as he'd expected, or even lying glistening-eyed in the dark, but wide awake and hunched over what proved to be Isabelle's sketchbook. She said she'd found it in the kitchen. "I want the shrink to see it," she said. "Can you drop it off on your way to the office?"

"Don't you think she's missing it? Shouldn't you put it back? Or give it to her?"

"Wilson, it's from April! It's from exactly when she stopped speaking!"

And although it made him uneasy, he has dropped the thing off, as Ruth asked. He's not sure about this art business, though. It seems to him that Ruth is putting too much stock in *art*—this class they're going off to, the analysis of Isabelle's sketchbooks. It seems to him a sort of abstract way of dealing with her silence, or of understanding it, when it makes more sense to him to *do* something about it, or *go* somewhere. Like Africa. Wilson looks at his watch again. After Maggie's appointment, he's got a phone meeting scheduled with the travel agent. An exploratory meeting, he considers it, though if Isabelle is not at school come January, Africa makes perfect sense to him. As Ruth herself has said, they cannot go on this way.

Wilson sits down on the stoop of the town house behind him, where he has a view of their building across the street. There are wreaths hanging from the wrought-iron rungs of the door, and garlands have been wound around the poles of the canopy. Wilson can't remember if the decorations were there this morning, or if they appeared in the few hours he has been at work. For all he knows, they have been up for a week, and it unnerves him to be unsure; he likes to think of himself as an observant person.

A taxi pulls up in front of the building, and a doorman—a new one, and strikingly young-looking— emerges from inside to open the cab door. A woman gets out curbside and heads directly for the door; the doorman hurries to open it for her and to take her bags. Then a man gets out on the street side of the cab, and he closes the edge of his long scarf in the door as he slams it shut. Wilson sits upright, wondering if the man notices that his scarf is caught; he seems not to as he begins to walk away from the cab, the scarf slipping from his shoulders and finally dangling from the door to the ground. Wilson stands, ready to alert the man that he has left his scarf behind, and he is about to step into the street and call out when he sees the lobby doors open again and Ruth and Isabelle come out. He bites his lip, glancing from his wife and daughter to the cab, which is pulling away, dragging the scarf behind it.

He looks again at Ruth and Isabelle, and then he crouches behind a parked car so that he can see without being seen. Ruth has paused outside the lobby doors; she is introducing herself to this new doorman, who has taken off his hat in a show of old-fashioned manners. His hair lifts in the wind; Wilson half expects him to bow. Isabelle waits for her mother by one of the canopy poles, swinging herself around it in a way that surprises Wilson; if it were last year, he thinks, he would probably chastise her out of concern for the garlands; now, he would never interrupt this show of playfulness.

He shifts his weight from the ball of one foot to the other; his feet are sore from crouching, and his knees are beginning to hurt, and suddenly he feels keenly self-conscious, crouched down like this behind a car in the cold and spying on his wife and daughter. He looks around him for other people; the street is empty, and he is relieved. Still, he is glad when Ruth turns from the doorman and beckons Isabelle; Wilson finally stands as the two of them make their way down the street. Ruth walks ahead of Isabelle, who slows to walk on the low fence around each tree they pass and then hastens to catch up with her mother. Wilson wonders if Ruth is aware of her, and he wonders whether if Isabelle were following him rather than Ruth he would be aware that Isabelle wasn't simply trailing behind. Maybe he wouldn't, he thinks. Maybe Ruth isn't. Maybe that is the way Isabelle wants it.

The idea of an art class is not appealing. Isabelle does not need or want anyone telling her how to draw. She does not want to sit at a table and draw with other people, especially people she doesn't know, and even more especially if they are the kind of people who would voluntarily sign up for a mother–daughter art class. Her mother has told her that all drawing materials will be supplied, but she has brought her own sketchbook and her own pencils anyway; these she clutches as she walks with her mother on the park side of Fifth Avenue, staring at the hexagonal pavers passing beneath her feet. She has not looked up since they turned off their street and onto Fifth Avenue; she does not know where this art class is, or how far they're going to have to walk, but she has decided that she will not lift her eyes until they have gotten there and are seated at their table. Letting the ground roll by beneath her eyes is like watching trees flash by on the side of the highway; it seems that the ground and the trees are the things that are moving, and not she herself. She thinks of what it would be like if that's really how things were, if people only had the illusion of progress and really it was the world moving around them, like a giant treadmill. For all she knows, it could really be that way.

"Okay," her mother says. "Here we are."

The hexagonal pavers have turned into red bricks, and soon Isabelle sees steps beneath her feet, and her heart quickens almost against her will with excitement, not for the art class, but because she knows that they are at the Metropolitan Museum of Art. Before she can stop herself, she looks up, and she is not even angry at herself for lifting her eyes, because there before her are the huge columns of the Met, the banners for exhibits flapping large and heavy in the wind. She looks up the many stairs and past the people sitting there even in the cold with their pretzels and hot dogs and soda, toward the glass doors behind which she knows is a whole other world, like a good dream, but one you can return to.

The vast lobby of the museum is crowded and warm. It smells old, and Isabelle breathes in deeply, listening to the muffled echo of voices and the sound of heels on the marble floor. Her mother gets in line at the coat check; Isabelle hands her coat to her and points toward the Egyptian wing just off the lobby, at the end of which is the Temple of Dendur, her favorite part of the museum.

"You going off?" her mother asks.

Isabelle nods, and her mother looks at the clock on the wall above the door. "The class doesn't begin for another twenty minutes, but don't go where I can't find you. Just to the temple."

Isabelle nods and hurries away.

The getting there is as good as the temple itself. She passes through rooms filled with all kinds of ancient Egyptian artifacts: gold cups and chalices, ornate masks, the elaborate jewelry of pharaohs, slabs of wall taken from the insides of pyramids and marked with hieroglyphs. Isabelle peers closely at these markings. The Egyptian alphabet, she thinks, is far more beautiful than their own; one marking is a lion, another an owl, another a hawk, another a snake. There is something appealing about writing in pictures, about pictures standing for sound, about the way words and images and sound fuse as seamlessly as they do in hieroglyphics. She'd like to learn to write this way herself; before they leave, she thinks, she'll stop at the museum bookstore to see if there are any books on hieroglyphics.

The room before the temple is a relatively narrow one, more of a hallway than anything else. It is lined with huge stone coffins, the lids of some propped open. Inside one of the coffins is a model mummy, and even though she knows that the mummy is not real, it makes her uncomfortable. It is not really the mummy itself that bothers her, but the idea of being mummified, of being wrapped and wrapped and wrapped and trapped forever inside that thick, dark layer like some unforgiving skin, strong enough to hold your shape even after you are nothing more than dust inside. She looks at the dust motes coasting the air in the stark white light coming in through the window along the side of the room. This is the kind of dust she'd rather be. She lingers for a moment more before the mummy, and as she passes on she cannot help but run her hand along the cool stone of the coffin, as if in touching a spot that ancient hands have also touched she is touching the past, reaching into it instead of merely observing it from a distance.

She stands in the doorway of the final room and gazes at it all: the high, high ceiling, the wall of glass, the pool in the middle of the room. And then, behind the pool, guarded by sphinxes, the small set of stairs leading up to the ancient temple reconstructed with its massive bricks. She imagines the narrow hallways and small, ceilingless rooms of the temple, the sandstone bricks marked with the graffiti of nineteenth-century wanderers who didn't know what they had found, the graffiti itself another layer of history now. She likes how small and safe it makes her feel to be surrounded by these bricks, to be inside a room within a building within a room within a building, so many layers between her and the world.

She feels a hand on her shoulder, and she jumps.

"It's time," she hears her mother say. "We should find the classroom." Isabelle breathes out loudly as reality comes flooding back. She had forgotten about the art class entirely. She steps out from beneath her mother's hand and turns around. Her mother raises a paper bag from the museum gift shop. "I stopped for Christmas cards," she says. Isabelle feels her mouth flatten in irritation that her mother has been to the gift shop already without her. "Well," her mother says. "Ready?" Her mother turns and begins to walk away. *No,* she thinks, but she follows.

He is lucky; Wilson has to hail only two cabs before one stops that will take Maggie on board. He thanks the driver as he climbs into the warmth of the cab. Maggie strains at the end of her leash; she is particular about cars. "Come on, Maggie," Wilson says, pulling at the leash. "Come on, girl." Maggie sits back on her haunches, pulling away, her collar bunching the fur and extra skin around her face.

Wilson digs into the pocket of his coat for a doggie bag of spicy beef left over from dinner last night. Generally, the lure is steak, but under the circumstances, spicy beef is the best he can do. He pulls a piece of beef from the bag and holds it up. Maggie's resistance weakens as she eyes the meat dangling from Wilson's hand. He tells the driver the vet's address, and then "Come on," he says, and slowly, suspiciously, Maggie climbs in. Wilson reaches over and closes the door behind her and then offers her the meat. She takes it hungrily from his hand, and as she begins to chew he sees her lips go up in disgust and she lets the beef fall to the floor of the taxi. "Don't like the spice, huh?" Wilson says, stroking her. He can feel the cold from outside in her fur. "Thought you might not. Sorry."

"Dog sick?" the cab driver asks over his shoulder.

"Maybe," Wilson says.

"Nice dog. What kind dog?"

"She's a Newfoundland," Wilson answers.

"Big dog."

"Yes," Wilson says.

The voice from the front of the car has piqued Maggie's interest, and she positions herself in the middle of the seat so that she can put her head through the opening in the partition between the front and back of the cab.

"Maggie," Wilson scolds, pulling her back.

"No, s'okay," the cabbie says. "Nice dog. Nice dog have some jerky?"

"It was spicy beef. She didn't like it much."

"No, no. My jerky." The cab driver holds up a bag of beef jerky.

"Oh, sure," Wilson says. "Aren't you a lucky dog?" he says, running his fingers through the fur on Maggie's back as she devours the tough, dried meat. Even after she has eaten it, she hovers over the cabbie's shoulder and watches the road like a person, and Wilson is reminded of Isabelle, Christmastime maybe three years ago, hovering over a cabbie's shoulder in the same way on their way back from *The Nutcracker*. From the backseat, Ruth and Wilson hadn't been able to hear the words the two of them exchanged, but Isabelle stuck her hand through the partition to shake the driver's hand when they had arrived home. The next day, before they'd even noticed it was missing, one of their doormen handed Isabelle the rabbit hat she'd been wearing the night before. A cab driver had dropped it off.

She has covered her paper with four layers of red paint—red on red on red on red—and the paper has grown soggy and begun to tear. She eyes her sketchbook and pencils sitting on a chair in a corner of the room; the teacher has taken them from her and told her that while she is in this classroom, she will use this classroom's materials. She doesn't like this classroom's materials. She doesn't like paint, and she doesn't like crayon, and she doesn't like clay. Charcoal is fine, but to get to the charcoal table she must first pass through the other three, and it is not worth the effort.

Though she tries, the paper will not hold a fifth layer of paint, and so Isabelle sets her paintbrush down beside the nearly empty petri dish of red and folds her hands together in her lap. She stares down and blurs her eyes at the red until the rest of the table—the other dishes of colored paint, the jar of water, the paper towels, the half-done flowers and sunsets made by the other girls—disappears, and all she can see is a hot, pulsing red that seems to hum so loudly that she hears nothing else until the teacher grips her shoulder and says, "Young lady." The woman peers at Isabelle's name tag. "Isabelle," she says. "Have you finished?"

Isabelle blinks. The teacher's glasses swing on their chain before Isabelle's eyes as she bends down to examine Isabelle's work. Her smell is strong, a combination of perfume and coffee. Isabelle feels the teacher's breast brush against her shoulder; she recoils.

"It's very red." The teacher straightens up. "Have you finished?"

Isabelle swallows. She tries to nod, but her head is stiff; it is as if it is held in an invisible vise. She focuses on the red paper before her, trying again to lose herself in it, but the teacher's voice seems to follow her into the red, echoing "Have you? Isabelle, have you finished?" over and over again, and her heart begins to race in panic. She steers her eyes up toward a wall of glass on the other side of which her mother sits at a table with other mothers. Her mother's head is bent low over her own drawing, and she holds a black crayon awkwardly in her hand. She seems very, very far away, as if Isabelle were looking at her from the wrong end of a telescope. She wills her mother to look at her, look at her, look at her, but she does not, and so Isabelle clenches her hands more firmly in her lap and closes her eyes, as if she still believed that shutting out the world like this would make her disappear.

They should have turned around and walked out the minute they arrived, Ruth thinks; she should have known that this was a mistake the minute she saw the table with name tags in the greeting room; there is something about name tags that Ruth despises. All the girls wear the uniform pleated skirts of private schools, with thick tights and cardigans; Isabelle sticks out like a sore thumb in her blue jeans with ratty cuffs and Shetland sweater. Ruth should have thought to dress her differently, she thinks, should have remembered that all the other girls would be coming with their mothers straight from school.

This mother–daughter art class is not a mother–daughter art class at all; the teacher has herded the mothers into one classroom and the daughters into an adjoining one separated by a glass partition. Each room has four tables; there are paints at one table, crayons at another, clay at another, and charcoal at the last. The teacher has explained that the object is to create a piece of art at each of the four stations. When you have finished your work at one station, she's explained, you must raise your hand and have your work evaluated before moving on to the next station. At the beginning of class Ruth started to raise her hand, to say how nice it would be if the mothers and daughters could work together, but a menacing look from her daughter through the glass stopped her.

Ruth's crayon panda bear has met with the teacher's approval, though she knows that the drawing is terrible, and she has moved on to the clay table. She pulls a chunk of it from the pile in the middle of the table and starts to roll it into little useless balls. A panda bear and little balls, she thinks, and she begins to wonder what they're really doing here at all. What would Dr. Steingold think she meant by panda bears and little balls? Because by them, she means nothing at all. She feels a small pang of guilt at the thought of Isabelle's sketchbook now in Dr. Steingold's hands, delivered there by Wilson this morning. But then she tells herself that simply because *she* means nothing by her art—if you can even call it that—she is not Isabelle, and Isabelle does mean something by her art. Ruth speaks; Isabelle draws. She looks through the glass partition at her daughter, who is still at the table where she began. She has set her paintbrush down. The other girls move between their stations around her; most are at their third or fourth table, since they've been told they're allowed to make as many rounds in the two hours as they like. Isabelle sits quietly, her hands in her lap and her eyes down. *Raise your hand,* Ruth thinks. *You won't have to speak, just raise your hand!*

"Oh, what lovely work you're doing!" Ruth hears the teacher over her shoulder. "Are those going to be beads?"M

Ruth turns. "What?" she says, glancing again at Isabelle. Two girls are talking at her; they seem to have forgotten their art. Isabelle has not moved a muscle.

"Beads," the teacher says.

"They weren't going to be, but I guess they could be."

"Very creative," the teacher says.

"Listen," Ruth says. She points at her daughter through the glass. "That's my daughter."

"Yes," the teacher says. "She's the only one who hasn't moved stations yet."

"Would you mind telling her that she can move on? She's very shy, and I just don't think she's going to raise her hand to ask you."

"She's going to have to raise her hand. That's the policy. We're trying to teach discipline as well as art. Discipline is an important component of art. Something all artists must have."

"I understand that, but my daughter is eleven years old, and she's very shy."

"Well, she's going to have to overcome that. We're going to help her overcome that."

Ruth reminds herself to breathe; she will not make a scene in front of these other women, who are absently scratching their paper with charcoal or fingering bits of clay as they discuss how hideous the new building at the bottom of the park is. She gathers her little clay balls together in her fist and squeezes them into a single mass, which she sets firmly back on the original pile of clay. She wipes her hands on her smock and then pulls the thing over her head and drops it onto her chair.

"*We've* been trying." She snorts. "*You* have no idea." She pushes through the door in the partition into the other room and takes her daughter by the hand.

II

Ruth's dresser has become a collection of relics, things not so much kept as simply never thrown away, valued not in and of themselves, but because of their age, their attachment to the past. Or this is how it seems to Wilson, anyway. Tucked into the mirror frame is an old invitation to a cocktail party he can't remember attending given by people they haven't seen in years—people who might well have slipped forever through the cracks in his memory if he hadn't been reminded of them by this invitation, which Ruth has kept—why? Likely first as a reminder to attend, Wilson thinks, or maybe because of the bird painted so delicately in the corner of the card, and then kept out of habit—or not kept, but allowed to remain.

In the vase across from the live bouquet of somethings Wilson brought home for her one day last week is a single dried rose that he vaguely remembers having bought for her from a rose peddler come into a bar where they were drinking. But he has bought her more than one rose this way, and so which night was this rose from? When and where? How long has it been sitting here, so brittle that when Wilson lifts its vase to better visualize Ruth's dresser without it a petal falls to the floor? Without it, the dresser looks almost bare despite everything else on it—the lamp with Ruth's clip-on earrings dangling from its shade; the beaded necklaces hanging from the corner of the mirror; the old wooden jewelry box propped open and filled not with jewels but with old thread and rusted buttons, safety pins and dry-cleaning tags unfastened from a blouse or skirt and set down here again and again out of habit; the photograph of Isabelle on Halloween one year, a little Aladdin in yellow silk trousers that balloon around her legs.

Wilson sets the vase down where it belongs and lifts the photograph. The frame is an old one, engraved with Ruth's initials and a date from more than thirty years ago. And the photograph—what year was that from? Wilson wonders. Isabelle is very young in it, he thinks, only two or three—three, he decides; when she was two, he remembers quite clearly because it was her first real Halloween, she was a bumblebee, and he had half carried her from door to door in their building, crowding with witches and ghosts and Supermen into

226

the cramped space of the elevator. In the photograph, Isabelle is mid-step, and mid-speech, it looks like from her open mouth and almost indignant eyes—but is it indignation? Indignation, concern, worry, purpose, it could be any of these things. But her look is a serious one, he thinks; the camera has caught her in the middle of something that at that moment was, for her, important, wherever it was that that step was taking her, whatever it was that she was saying.

And what is he doing, lingering here before Ruth's dresser when the rest of the afternoon lies before him? He looks up from the photograph and glances around him, trying to relocate himself in the day. He needs to get going, he thinks, looking at his watch; Ruth and Isabelle will surely be home soon, and he's got that phone meeting with the travel agent. The vet had taken longer than he'd expected; Dr. Bremer had decided to give Maggie another round of treatment, which Wilson tries to see as a good thing. It *is* a good thing, he thinks, because now there is that much more medicine working to contain and kill Maggie's cancer—but he's fooling himself, he knows. A single round of treatment ought to have been enough, and it was not. He didn't dare ask the vet about Maggie's prospects this time; he didn't want to have to hang his hope on any number more meager than the 20 percent to which he clings.

He sighs and looks once more at the photograph before setting it down, and then takes the single step from the dresser to the window beside it. Their street is empty below him; garbage bags are piled on the curb awaiting pickup, and pigeons strut the gutter, pecking at scraps. A taxi careens into view, coming off Madison down their street; it could be Ruth and Isabelle, he thinks at first, but the taxi goes on by their canopy and disappears around the corner, where he knows it will merge with the flow of traffic on Fifth.

No one seems to be smiling today. From where she sits in the fogged window of the coffee shop, Isabelle has counted thirty-four people pass by, and only one had the trace of a smile on his face. No one is smiling in the line outside the popover café across the street. She looks across the table at her mother. She is not smiling, either. And neither is the woman behind the counter, or the man reading the paper at the table behind theirs. Isabelle spreads a smile across her face, the forced kind, the kind you put on not because you're happy but because someone has asked you to smile for a photograph, or because you've just opened a gift in front of the giver. She holds that smile until her muscles start to quiver and her cheeks to ache and twitch. It's strange, she thinks, that a smile should hurt.

She looks again at her mother. She is swirling the dregs of her hot cocoa with a spoon, where Isabelle knows rich chocolate has settled; Isabelle watches her take that last, best sip, and then she takes a sip of her own cocoa, which is still more than half full.

Her mother seems to feel her gaze, and she looks up. She takes a breath as if to say something, and

Isabelle can, quite clearly, hear the words catch in her throat; she tilts her head expectantly. Her mother takes another breath, and then, "Isabelle," she says.

Isabelle waits, holding her mother's eyes with her own. They sit like this for a moment, and then her mother shakes her head. "I'm not even sure what I was going to say," she says. "But I'm going to run to the bathroom," she says. "Okay?"

Isabelle nods and turns back to the window. She reaches her fingers out to trace designs through the fog there, and this suggestion of drawing makes her suddenly remember her sketchbook and pencils on the chair in the corner of the classroom. She sits upright and whirls around to look for her mother, but she has already vanished into the bathroom at the back of the place. She reaches hastily down for her mother's pocketbook to pull out the six dollars she knows they owe for their hot chocolate; she cannot sit here for another moment knowing her materials are where they are. She snatches the pocketbook up, and as she does, the shopping bag from the museum gift shop, which has been resting against it, falls sideways, and then, louder than the drone of background voices and the throaty idling of the bus outside, the beautiful, fragile sound of pencils rolling across tile fills Isabelle's ears—the sound of *her* pencils, she knows, and she drops to her knees to collect them from where they have rolled out of the shopping bag and onto the floor. She clutches her pencils in her fist and, still on her knees, she rights the shopping bag, which contains, she sees, not only the Christmas cards but also her sketchbook. This she pulls from the bag, just to be sure it's really there, just to hold it, and she is overwhelmed by a feeling that surprises her, not a feeling of relief or of gratitude, but one of an almost painful guilt. She pictures her mother through the glass of the classroom partition, bent awkwardly over her drawing, and then she pictures her mother storming, like an angry angel, it seemed to Isabelle then, through the partition door and sweeping Isabelle out of there. That she had remembered to pick up the sketchbook and pencils on their way makes Isabelle's heart drop, and she feels her throat tighten around the familiar lump that has formed there.

"Isabelle," she hears her mother say above her. "Are you okay down there?" Isabelle returns her materials to the shopping bag and sits down again in her chair, nodding. "I thought you might be hungry since we didn't get our popovers." She sets down a huge chocolate-chip cookie before her daughter. "Otherwise we can just take it home."

Isabelle looks sadly from her mother to the cookie. Even though she isn't hungry, she wants to say thank you. She wants to say I'm sorry. She wants to reach across the table and squeeze her mother's hand or, even more, to bury her head in her mother's shoulder, a familiar yet now distant comfort.

Instead, she reaches for the cookie and breaks it carefully in half. Then she pours half of what she has left of her cocoa into her mother's mug.

"Thank you," her mother says, but Isabelle shakes her head and puts her fingers to her lips.

III

"Hold the elevator!" Isabelle hates to share the elevator with other people; there is something about being trapped in such a small space with someone for even the short length of time it takes to ride five stories that makes her nervous. She had seen their downstairs neighbor paying for a cab outside their building as she followed her mother inside, and she had quickened her step so that they could take the elevator up alone, before their neighbor entered the building. But they hadn't been quick enough; now her mother fumbles for the button to hold the door open for the man. Isabelle hears his footsteps click faster across the lobby floor as he jogs nearer and then bursts into the elevator, panting slightly and smelling faintly of old taxi.

"Thank you," he says, setting his briefcase down between his legs to shove his gloves into the pocket of his coat. "Four, please," he says, but Ruth has already pressed the button for his floor.

He looks down at Isabelle as the elevator door slides shut. Isabelle looks back at him. He is older than her father; his hair is graying and his skin loose, but there is something young about his eyes, she thinks.

"You're not the little girl who lives upstairs from me, are you?"

Isabelle nods. "This is Isabelle," her mother says.

"Isabelle!" he says. "But you're not the pianist, are you?"

Isabelle glances at her mother and then looks quickly to the floor. As far as her mother knows, she has not touched the piano in months.

"Isabelle used to take lessons," her mother explains. "But not for a few months now."

"Well, I'd say she doesn't need them," the man says. "She plays just fine on her own."

Isabelle hears her mother clear her throat, but she doesn't look up. She watches her mother shift her weight from one wet foot to the other, and then she sees the man's hand reach down to lift his briefcase from between his legs as the elevator stops at his floor.

"Young lady," he says as the door opens. "My wife and I enjoy your music very much."

Isabelle gives a quick smile, then returns her eyes immediately to the floor before her mother can catch them with her own.

"Have a good Christmas," her mother says.

"The same to you," the man says as the door closes again, leaving Ruth and Isabelle to ride the last flight up on their own.

The painting in the foyer is of a marsh, but when Wilson looks closely, it doesn't look like a marsh at all. What looks like textured sunlit marsh grass from across the foyer is instead simply swatches of paint:

green, gold, orange. And what looks from afar like the reflection of the sky in the water reveals itself, up close, to be a large patch of light gray. It's no wonder he can't paint, he thinks, though Ruth has tried again and again to get him to take a class. He would never think that the reflection of the sky was as easy as gray, or that the marsh could be painted in three colors.

He hears the elevator nearing their floor; he has changed into a fresh shirt and put a sweater on beneath his coat, and he's left Maggie by the tree, her water dish refreshed. He glances at his watch; there are less than a couple hours left of the workday, and he wonders if it's even worth his while to go back to the office. Though he has no place else to go, he thinks, and he can't stay here without giving himself away. He sighs and lifts his collar as he hears the elevator reach their floor. The door opens, and Wilson sees Isabelle and Ruth inside.

He hardly has time to think before Ruth exclaims, "Wil! What are you doing home?"

"Ruth!" Wilson says. "Belle. Hi."

Ruth and Isabelle step out of the elevator, and Wilson, though he has summoned it, lets it go without getting in. He bends to give Isabelle a kiss on the forehead, then gives his wife a kiss on the cheek.

"Hi," Ruth says. "So?"

"So?" Wilson says, searching a mind that feels suddenly empty for some sort of excuse.

"So what are you doing home?"

"Nothing. I forgot some important papers. You're back early. How was the art class?"

"It wasn't," Ruth says. "Or it won't be anymore." She looks down at Isabelle beside her. Isabelle sniffs and tucks her hair behind her ears; her fingers are red and swollen with cold. "Maybe, Isabelle, you should be wearing gloves," she says. "It's probably not good for those fingers to be so cold."

Isabelle shrugs and leaves Ruth and Wilson standing in the foyer.

"So what papers?" Ruth asks.

"For the Levitt deal. Remember I told you about the Levitt deal, right?"

"No," Ruth says.

Maggie has wandered into the foyer and leaned herself against Ruth. Ruth reaches down to stroke her. "And why is Maggie wet?" she asks.

"I took her out," Wilson says.

"I see."

They stand in silence. Ruth looks at Wilson. He knows she does not believe him; he is not good at telling lies. He doesn't, he realizes, even have a briefcase in his hand.

"Maggie is sick," he says finally. "I took her to the vet."

"Sick?"

Wilson nods. As he had feared, the utterance has made the illness real, too real.

"How sick?"

"The cancer spread," he says. "It's all through her lymph nodes."

"And you weren't going to tell me? You weren't going to tell Isabelle?"

"I didn't want to worry you."

"What do you mean you didn't want to worry us?"

"She has a chance. She needed another round of treatment."

Ruth has stooped down now to put her face in Maggie's fur as so often she sees her daughter do. She thinks of how small Isabelle's hand had seemed when she grabbed it to leave the art class today, and how before they'd left Ruth had found Maggie and her daughter asleep beside the Christmas tree. She pictures Isabelle's face across the table from her at the coffee shop, the way she had given Ruth half her cocoa, the way she'd put her fingers to her lips in a way that seemed to Ruth the gesture of a kiss more than a command of silence, the sad smile that is so rare these days, that will never be again, she is sure, if Maggie dies right now. This cannot happen; Maggie cannot die. Ruth lifts her face toward Wilson, worry eclipsing her anger at his secrecy. "You're right," she says, and she stands. "No worrying." She clears her throat and says, loudly, "Do you have those papers?"

"What?"

"The papers you came home for. Do you have them?"

Wilson nods uncertainly.

"Good, well. Pork for dinner tonight, so don't be late. And bring some ice cream, will you? Coffee."

"Okay," Wilson says. Ruth leans over to peck him on the cheek, and then she goes inside. Wilson stands for a minute more in the foyer, his hands heavy at his sides. He does not want to go back to work; he is tired, and he does not want to go back out into the cold. But he has to, he knows. He has to finish this day as he would any other, so he lifts his hand and rings again for the elevator.

EIGHT

Thursday

I

Once, years ago while driving through Missouri, Wilson had come upon a town just minutes after a tornado had ripped through. The corrugated tin of trailer roofs lay strewn over the ground; storefront windows were shattered. A shower stall lay tipped on its side by the only gas station, and a woman's long-haired wig hung from the branches of a tree. Downed power lines draped the wreckage like webs. But what was most remarkable, what made Wilson pull off the road and just stare, was how things were still falling from the sky: a plywood door, the cushion from a sofa, a plastic lawn chair. He got out of the car to look up and watch these things grow from dark specks against the sky into things familiar, falling onto the land like some bizarre rain. The air was eerily still in the wake of the force that had stirred it, thick with a smell deep and electric, sweet and rotten at once—the smell of ozone, he had told himself, though it struck him more as the smell of death.

Wilson hasn't thought of this story in years, and he's not sure why he's thought of it now, but he's glad to have unearthed the memory before it was lost for good, buried somewhere deep in the southern hemisphere of his mind beneath so many other memories. At the same time as he is glad to have remembered, the fact that he had forgotten makes him uneasy, worried about the other memories he might be missing. He'd like to be able to pour all the memories out of his mind and spread them on his desk, just to remind himself of everything he has in there.

"Mr. Carter," a voice suddenly bursts through the intercom on his desk. "Your wife on line one."

Wilson looks at his watch; it is ten fifteen, and he was meant to let Ruth know by ten where he plans to take Isabelle to lunch today so that she can meet them there after her appointment. Maybe, he thinks, the reason he thought of the tornado was to distract himself from what he is supposed to be thinking about—the papers on his desk and where to take Isabelle to lunch.

"Tell her I'll call her right back," Wilson says through the intercom. "Tell her I'm on another call." The truth is that Wilson hasn't yet decided where to take Isabelle to lunch, but he knows this will make Ruth furious; she can't understand his indecision and had wanted an answer before he'd even left for work. He's narrowed it down to three options: the pizza place around the corner to which they've always gone when Isabelle has come with him to the office for a day, a new diner he's read about, and the Mexican place where they make the guacamole at your table.

Ruth is right; it's silly to make such an issue about where to have lunch, but really he knows the where of it is only part of the issue. The where of it has nothing to do with what kind of food he'd rather eat; the where of it matters only insofar as *where* silence would be the easiest, *where* there would be enough around them for Wilson to comment on in order to break the silence now and then—but he cannot tell this to Ruth. He doesn't even like to admit it to himself. What kind of father is he, he thinks, to dread lunch with his daughter? To think of this dread fills him with shame, but he cannot help it.

The Mexican place would be good because of the guacamole preparation—it would be something to remark on, certainly, along with the decorations—the piñatas hanging from the ceiling, the handwoven rugs and hats on the walls. And the musicians who come to the table and serenade—that would take things out of Wilson's hands for ten minutes, anyway. He hasn't been to the diner, but he knows it's done in fifties style, so he assumes there's probably a jukebox and photographs of people like James Dean hanging on the walls, maybe a motorcycle in the corner—all good distractions.

The pizza place is least appealing. It's the standard pizza place—a counter with a couple of swivel stools, plastic booths, tiled floor. It's where they always go, which is why it made it to Wilson's list of finalists; he's afraid it either would seem strange to Isabelle if they broke tradition and went elsewhere, or, worse, would be obvious to her what he was up to. But then he thinks of Marco, the owner, and how he always leans up against the counter to talk to them as they eat, how he always gives Isabelle candy from the stash he keeps in the back. Wilson can picture Marco's face at the change in Isabelle, his puzzlement that this sweet little girl he's known since she was a baby is now silent and unsmiling. And what would Wilson do? Would he pretend nothing was out of the ordinary? Would he lie and say that Isabelle had lost her voice in this cold? Or would he tell Marco the truth when Isabelle went to the bathroom, or over to a table to get oregano or pepper, that his daughter simply will not speak? No, Wilson thinks, the pizza place is out of the question.

He sighs, tired though it's early. The Mexican place or the diner; it makes no real difference. He lifts the phone to call Ruth. He'll ask which place is easier for her, which is closest to her doctor's office—if she's even going to the doctor. For all Wilson knows, Ruth could be going to the dentist or the chiropractor. He frowns. He should know what kind of appointment his wife has; they used to know these things about each other—what book the other was reading, what their plans were for the day, whether the other was feeling tired, or nervous, or excited about something. He knows none of this now, and this, too, like his dread at the idea of lunch, fills him with guilt.

He dials their home number and listens to it ring three times before Ruth answers.

"Hello?" she says. She sounds weary, and suddenly Wilson wishes that he weren't calling for any particular reason, that he'd just decided to call and say hello. He wishes that he'd decided about lunch earlier, before he'd gone to work, so that with this call he'd have no agenda but to check in.

"Ruth," he says quietly. "Ruth."

The vet has instructed Wilson to be sure that Maggie gets three hundred milligrams per day of omega-3 fatty acids, as well as prednisone, to maintain her appetite, and so, as she has each day since Monday, Ruth wanders into the living room with a pill-filled cream cheese ball in one hand and the daily stack of Christmas cards in the other. Normally underneath the tree, this morning Maggie is lying before the fireplace on the picnic blanket still spread on the floor from dinner last night. Picnics before the fire are something Isabelle has always loved; last night's was the first of the season, and, Ruth thinks, the first in silence—but at least they'd gone ahead and picnicked anyway. The room still smells a bit of smoke, though the ashes in the hearth are long cold.

Maggie's tail thumps the ground as Ruth squats beside her; Maggie lifts her head in greeting. "How's my girl?" Ruth says, running her hands down the length of Maggie's back. She offers the cream cheese, and Maggie gobbles it up, hardly bothering to chew. "You don't seem so bad," Ruth says, sitting back on her heels. "You're going to be okay." She takes

Maggie's ears between her fingers and lowers her face close to the dog's. "You have to be," she whispers.

She wipes her fingers on a Kleenex in her pocket, gathers the Christmas cards from where she set them on the floor, and stands, taking a step closer toward the fireplace to put the cards out on the mantle. She studies the faces of other people's children as she stands the cards up one at a time. They sit smiling on a sunny rock in summer; they stand side by side on their skis, grinning from beneath their goggles; they sit in matching nightgowns side by side before the fire. She thinks of their own Christmas cards this year, the ones she bought at the Met of a lonely lighthouse standing in the snow—the kind of cards single people send out, or people without children, or people like Jimmy, whose card is next in the pile. His card has a drawing of a quiet house, candles in the windows, a wreath on the door, Santa headfirst down the chimney, visible as a red rear end and a pair of big black boots. Jimmy, she thinks. She wishes she had more time for him.

She sighs as she sets down the last card that the mantle can hold, and then she crosses the room to put the remaining cards out on the piano. The lid is open, and without first thinking, she begins to lower it so as to provide a flat surface for the cards—but then she stops. Last week, she remembers, the piano lid was closed; she knows this with certainty because she had set a vase of short-lived poppies on it. That it is now open means that Isabelle must have been playing; neither she nor Wilson knows how. So the downstairs neighbor really has been hearing Isabelle play, Ruth thinks with a little envy; though he had aroused her suspicion, she thought it possible that he might have been mistaken, that what he was hearing was music from the stereo, or that he was remembering the music that Isabelle used to play, when she still did. Or when she still played when Ruth was home.

She runs her fingers over the keys, imagining Isabelle's fingers there. She glances toward the Christmas tree then, and the needles that have fallen to the carpet beneath it. Though part of her resists the urge, she crosses the room and gathers up a small handful of the needles. These she spreads out across the keys—just a few, but enough so that Ruth will be able to tell by their absence when her daughter next plays. Though why she wants to catch Isabelle like this she's not sure; what does it matter whether or not Isabelle plays if Ruth isn't going to hear it anyway? But, somehow, it does matter. She steps back to survey her work, pleased. She lifts the last cards from where she has left them on the piano bench and sets them instead on the windowsill, leaving the lid of the piano open as Isabelle has left it.

In the other room, the phone is ringing, and so Ruth sets the final card down and hurries to answer it before the machine picks up and Isabelle's voice announces that no one is home—a recording that seems both inappropriate to keep yet a terrible admission to erase, and one that she tries at any lengths to avoid hearing.

"Ruth," she hears Wilson say. "Ruth."

The somber tone of his voice frightens Ruth. She swallows. "What is it?" she says.

There is a pause. "Lunch," Wilson says finally. "What would be better for you—if we went to the Mexican place on the West Side or this new diner in Midtown?"

Relief and annoyance flow through Ruth's body at once. Why is it so difficult for Wilson to settle on a restaurant? A restaurant is a restaurant is a restaurant. "What do you mean, better for me? I'm not the one eating."

"No, I mean which is closer to your appointment? Which is more convenient for you?"

"Oh," Ruth says. "It really doesn't matter."

"Well, which do you think Isabelle would prefer?"

"Wilson, it really doesn't make that much difference. I don't know, go to the diner."

"It's on Fifty-eighth," he says. "Fifty-eighth and Third."

"Okay," Ruth says. "I shouldn't be much later than one thirty. As soon as my appointment is through."

"All right," Wilson says. And then he asks, almost tentatively, it seems to Ruth, what her appointment is for.

She hesistates, caught off guard, because her appointment isn't a doctor's appointment, or a dentist's appointment, or anything warranting Wilson's canceling of his meeting to take Isabelle to lunch; she is going to the spa. But the appointment had been hard to get; she'd had to make it two weeks in advance, and, she thinks, she needs it. But still. "Eye doctor," she says. "My contacts have been killing me, so I'm going to see if I can try another kind. Maybe the soft ones."

"Oh," Wilson says. "I didn't know they were bothering you."

"Well, they have been, Wilson," she says, defensively, angry at herself for having lied; why shouldn't she take a fucking hour for herself? She can't remember the last time she did.

"I'm sure they have," Wilson says quietly.

II

The shrink's office is off the lobby of a residential building uptown. Wilson sits on a stiff Victorian chair in the waiting room, which is paneled in dark wood; it is cavernous and dim. The dish of potpourri on the table beside him smells like something distant and familiar, but what about it is familiar he's not sure. He can't tell if the feeling it gives him is one of comfort or fear, and that the two can be indistinguishable like this is disconcerting. He shifts in his seat, his hands curled around the clawlike ends of the wooden arms, and glances at the clock on the wall. There are ten more minutes until Isabelle's appointment is over.

The sound of the doorbell breaks into the room's formal silence, and the secretary, tucked away behind her counter, buzzes the ringers in— a boy maybe seven or eight years old and his mother, both without hats or scarves. Their ears are red. The mother wipes snot from her son's face with her glove. She hangs his coat and then her own on the rack by the door, and she nods to the secretary as she passes her counter. The secretary smiles; they seem to know each other well enough, Wilson thinks, and he wonders how long this mother and her son have been coming here.

They sit together on the couch perpendicular to Wilson's chair. The boy pulls a comic book from his mother's purse; the mother herself digs through the pocketbook for her lipstick, which seems to Wilson colorless. She looks older than Ruth, her hair graying and skin beginning to loosen at the cheeks—but maybe it's that she's tired. Because there is something young about her eyes, and the hand she uses to apply her lipstick is smooth, almost fragile-looking. He wonders what is wrong with her son—if he won't speak, like Isabelle, or if maybe he won't eat or sleep. The woman glances in Wilson's direction and gives a small smile; Wilson lowers his gaze. He does not want to be this woman's ally. He does not want to compare symptoms and swap shrink stories, the shop talk of parents of troubled children. He almost resents this woman's smile; he resents that she must pity him just as he has been pitying her. He wonders if when Isabelle emerges from Dr. Steingold's office this woman will herself wonder what is wrong with Isabelle, just as he himself has been wondering about the woman's son.

The woman clears her throat, but before she can speak, if she was going to speak at all, Wilson takes a magazine from the coffee table to hide behind. It is a *National Geographic,* which is a magazine he enjoys; there was a time in his life, when he was younger, when he wanted to be a *National Geographic* reporter and travel to many of the exotic places featured in the magazine. Today, though, he can hardly focus; he flips blindly through the pages, and only when he comes across a photograph of a yawning grizzled lion does he realize that the main article in this edition is on Africa. His heart begins to race—Africa, again. It cannot be anything but a sign, he thinks, that he should stumble across a long article on Africa sitting here in the waiting room as, on the other side of the thick wood door, some man, a stranger, is trying to get his daughter to speak. The doctor won't succeed, he thinks; not one of them has. But Africa, he thinks—he is more certain than ever that somehow, the answer lies in Africa.

Her thumbs are raw from where she has been scratching at them with the forefingers of each hand, digging her nails in hard and dragging them across the skin over and over again. Her feet are hooked solidly around the legs of her chair and have fallen asleep, and her jaw is sore from clenching, but she will not release—not her feet, not her jaw, and she will not stop the scratching. She cannot; in this posture she feels anchored and as much in control as she can be; if she were to shift positions, she's not sure what would happen.

In the chair across from her, Dr. Steingold holds one of her sketchbooks in his lap; she stares at it covetously as the doctor turns the pages slowly, examining each drawing individually and making comments that Isabelle can hardly hear over the roaring in her ears. Her mind has been racing ever since the doctor produced the sketchbook from his desk drawer, this precious, private, utterly familiar thing emerging from a place so entirely unexpected and wrong. No one looks at her sketchbooks. No one has ever looked at her sketchbooks, and to watch this doctor doing just that makes Isabelle hot, nauseous, dizzy, as if she had awakened to find that he had been watching her while she slept. In this setting, her drawings seem foreign to her. Each time he turns the page, Isabelle wants to cringe as yet another of her drawings becomes something other than what it had been, somehow violated by this doctor's eyes. But she holds her face still; only her fingers move, up and down and rough against her skin in the only way she can think to contain her desperation.

She is not sure whether she is more angry at her mother for giving the sketchbook to the shrink, or at herself for having allowed it to be discovered. Her mother would never have found her hiding place— behind the cabinet in her bathroom—and if she had, Isabelle would have known, because she has set a bobby pin just on the crack between the cabinet and the wall, so that if the cabinet were moved forward, the bobby pin would fall, and it hasn't, which means that Isabelle herself must have left the sketchbook out in the open, but where? How? When? How could she have been so careless as to leave such a private thing out in public? Had she left it in the car? Or maybe beside her bed one night after she'd drawn herself to sleep? Or in the kitchen, where it might have gotten mixed up with her homework, or the newspapers stacked there? She wishes she could remember; she wishes that she knew so that she could relive the scenario, pinpoint the exact moment of forgetfulness, and punish herself for it. She does not like to forget.

And then her mother. She imagines her mother stumbling across the sketchbook and hurrying to some private place to pore greedily through it. Isabelle can understand why her mother would have looked at the drawings herself, but to give them to the shrink? To a stranger? To land Isabelle in a situation like the one she's in right now, her privacy excavated before her eyes? Her heart surges with new fury to consider this betrayal.

Finally, the shrink closes the sketchbook. He holds it out for her to take; she does not move. "Don't you want it?" the shrink asks, and she will not give him even a silent response, a nod or a shake of the head. She sits stiff in her chair, working her fingers back and forth across her thumbs. "Well," he says. "I'll set it on my desk, and if you want it back, you can take it on your way out." He looks at his watch. "So I'll see you next Thursday, Isabelle," he says.

Isabelle unhooks her feet from around the leg of her chair and quickly stands, and when she takes a step forward, it is as if the ground is giving way beneath her; she cannot feel the floor beneath her sleeping feet, and she stumbles. "Easy there," the shrink says, reaching to catch her; she recoils. Her feet feel like stumps, lifeless and numb, and were she at home Isabelle would sit down again to rub them back to life. But she cannot do that here; she will not, and so, carefully, with each off-balance step shooting needling pain up both legs, she makes her way to the door.

III

"You're not breathing."

The masseuse is right, Ruth realizes, releasing a breath she's been holding in, for how long she cannot remember. She feels the hands working her lower back press down on her more firmly, as if to squeeze every last bit of breath out of her.

"Now breathe in." Ruth does, a long, deep breath. "And out." But it is hard to let the breath go; it is as if the breath has not yet done its work, the lungs not yet absorbed the oxygen they need, and so Ruth holds it in. "Out, out, breathe out. You need to relax. You cannot relax if you do not breathe." Ruth blows the air out and takes another breath in. "Now out," the masseuse says, and Ruth complies, breathing this way four or five breaths, until she feels like she is beginning to hyperventilate. The masseuse takes her hands from

Ruth's back, and Ruth opens her eyes. The circular face rest of the massage table pulls the skin tight at the corners of her eyes, blurring her vision so that in the room's dim light she can hardly make out the nubbly texture of the carpet. A white set of feet appears below her face, and she can hear the masseuse lubing her hands up with yet more oil. The smell of it makes Ruth's lungs cold, and she shivers beneath the oily hands as they travel up and down the length of her back in strong, sweeping strokes. "It's cold, but this is where the hot rocks come in." Ruth feels a thin sheet spread across her back, and then the pressure of oven-heated stones being laid one at a time on either side of her spine. "Now I'm going to leave you for ten minutes. Let the stones absorb your tension. Release it. Breathe."

Ruth hears the door click quietly closed as the masseuse leaves, and she closes her eyes again. The stones along her back are not heavy, she knows, but they feel heavy. Their heat is soothing, and though she knows she is supposed to let them absorb her tension, she concentrates more on absorbing their warmth, on letting herself be held flat by their weight. She imagines that they are boulders, the same hot boulders that jut through the dry grass along the road in Mexico, too hot in the August sun to lay a hand on and large enough to crush a truck. She imagines that she is pinned down by them, that she could not move if she wanted to, and the feeling is one of relief. There is nowhere she can go, she thinks. There is nothing she can do except lie here and remember things she normally doesn't have time for, like those boulders in Mexico that she and Wilson had marveled over when they were there for their fifth anniversary, or the empanadas they had had one of those nights, the sauce so spicy that Wilson had broken into an hours-long sweat, or how they had brought a sombrero home to New York for Isabelle, which Ruth is sure must still be in the dress-up trunk in Isabelle's closet. She should go through Isabelle's closet, she thinks, and take all the old clothing out; Isabelle hasn't grown out of the clothes she bought when she was nine, but it's high time for a new wardrobe. Maybe this afternoon, Ruth thinks. Maybe this afternoon they'll go shopping, after she's met Wilson and Isabelle at the diner. They can stop at a few stores on their way home, and then, she thinks, her heart beginning to quicken, and then, as soon as they get home, she'll call Dr. Steingold to find out how their appointment went, whether he made any progress. She takes a breath, deep and quivering with anticipation, so sudden that with the heave of her body two of the stones slide from her back, and the noise of them hitting the floor through the thin carpet reminds her of what she is meant to be doing—she is meant to be letting these stones absorb her tension, she is meant to be breathing, in and out, evenly—but she cannot. The rocks feel all of a sudden too heavy, their weight oppressive rather than freeing, and though she wants now to get up, she will not. This is time she paid for, her time, and she will suffer through it.

To Wilson's relief, there is, as he had hoped, a jukebox for every booth in the diner. But the relief does not last long; Isabelle does not even glance at the stack of quarters he puts before her to choose the songs she wants. "Too many good songs to choose from," Wilson says as cheerfully as he can, flipping through the selection as if he were really reading the titles. "Want to choose a couple?" Isabelle blinks at him. "Well, I'll choose a couple. Some good songs in here." He deposits six or seven quarters into the machine at once before he realizes that there was already money in the thing, two dollars' worth, which at a quarter a song leaves him with fifteen songs to choose—fifteen songs he doesn't even care to hear unless it is Isabelle who chooses them and not himself.

He smiles at Isabelle and leans close to the machine, but before he has time to begin to select his songs, a waitress appears. She leans over their table to wipe it down with a wet cloth; she smells like grease and ketchup, as Wilson knows he will, too, after they have left this place. Her forearms are remarkably large, Wilson notices, ridged and firm, the skin stretched tight around muscle. He can see muscles and tendons twitch as she rubs her rag across their table, and then as she sets the placemats down, and then the silverware, and then a dish of crayons. Crayons. Wilson's chest warms with relief. Crayons are better than the jukebox waiting with his fifteen songs, better than the statue of Marilyn Monroe across the room, better than the letter jackets with their ivory leather arms hanging on the walls, or the old finned convertible in the corner. Isabelle likes to draw, and Wilson can draw too, and have something with his daughter that more closely resembles a conversation than if he sat there and talked to the air or sang along to music. He lets his eyes follow the arm up from the crayons and to the waitress's face. She is young. "Thank you," he says.

She looks at them through glassless cat-eyed glasses. She wears a fifties-style uniform, an apron around her waist and a hat pinned to her head. Her name tag reads Mona.

"Can I bring you all something to drink? Soda? Coffee? Water?"

Wilson orders a lemonade for himself and a milkshake for Isabelle. Coffee; he has never known her to order any other flavor.

The waitress leaves them menus and goes to get their drinks. Isabelle lifts her menu so that Wilson cannot see her behind it. She seems subdued today, more so than usual, and he wonders what is wrong. *What is wrong,* he thinks, and he smiles sadly, wishing that what is wrong were something as simple as being tired, or not feeling well, or having cold toes, or simply having gotten up on the wrong side of the bed—anything that has a name.

After a minute, Isabelle sets her menu down.

Wilson looks at her. "Did you decide?" he asks.

Isabelle shrugs. Wilson hasn't yet looked at his menu; he scans it quickly to see what Isabelle might like, since clearly she is not going to help him.

"Grilled cheese?"

Isabelle shrugs.

"Or chicken fingers. Would you rather chicken fingers?"

Isabelle shrugs again, and Wilson feels a small quiver of annoyance.

"Well, I'm going to have a BLT. Do you want to join me?" He bites his cheek to control the desperation he can hear on the edge of his voice.

Isabelle gives him a small smile and nods.

He tries to smile back. "Extra T and crunchy B?"

Isabelle nods and lets her eyes drop. Wilson can see that she is eyeing the crayons between them, and he lifts a blue crayon from the dish of them on the table. Then he lifts the dish and extends it toward her. "Want one?"

Isabelle makes a move toward the crayons with her hand, but then she hesitates and puts her hands down in her lap.

"Did you want the blue one?" Wilson offers, desperate at the thought that in trying to initiate this activity, he has ruined it by taking the blue crayon. Blue is Isabelle's favorite color; how could he have been so careless?

Isabelle shakes her head, and Wilson sets the blue crayon back into the dish. The light from the jukebox is flashing; he watches the neon pink flash in Isabelle's eyes as he looks at her. She looks down, and Wilson swallows. He has never known Isabelle to turn down a chance to draw.

"What is it, Belle?" The words are out before he has a chance to consider them.

Isabelle looks up at him again, quickly, and for just a moment, he thinks he sees her eyes begin to fill with tears. But then, just as quickly, they are dry, and he is almost disappointed. He wants her to cry. He wants her to be able to cry to him.

The waitress returns with their drinks then, bursting loud and sudden into their silence and knocking over the briefcase that Wilson has set beside their booth. "Oh!" she says. "I'm sorry!"

"No," Wilson says. "I shouldn't have left it there." He leans down to move it underneath the table by his feet.

"Lemonade," the waitress says, setting the drinks down, "and a coffee milkshake. Extra thick. And what can I get you all to eat?"

Wilson clears his throat and orders for them, two BLT's, extra T, crunchy B, and the waitress leaves. Wilson sips his lemonade and watches Isabelle suck her milkshake through a straw, her cheeks fishlike with the effort.

"Good?" he asks. She nods.

Wilson moves to cross his legs and knocks his briefcase again. He bends to move it farther under the table, and as he does, he remembers the *National Geographic* he'd swiped from Dr. Steingold's waiting room.

"Belle!" he exclaims, banging his head on the table as he straightens up. He pulls the magazine out from under the table and puts it in front of his daughter. "I meant to show this to you," he says. "I thought you might be interested."

Isabelle pulls the magazine closer. She looks at the cover; it is a photograph of a herd of elephants at evening, and their shadows seem to stretch all the way to the horizon. She looks at her father, and then she opens the magazine to the article on Africa and begins to read. Wilson sits back in his seat. He watches his daughter read, her face bent close to the page, her hands holding the magazine open, her hair hanging down over her eyes. Every now and then she sips her milkshake, and, Wilson thinks, he'd even dare to say that if not happy, she looks content. Wilson smiles. He lifts the blue crayon from the dish again and begins, alone, to draw.

The women's locker room is mostly empty when Ruth returns for her clothes after showering. There is one other woman in there, a woman in her late sixties, maybe. She is naked, bent over to towel off her legs, and as Ruth, wrapped in a bathrobe, stands at the sink drying her hair, she cannot help but watch in the mirror this woman behind her.

The woman places the towel on the bench beside her and then reaches into her large bag for her clothes. Carefully, she lifts a foot to step into her underwear; Ruth watches her legs tremble as she balances on one foot and then the next, her spine protruding sharply as she bends. Then, carefully, the woman straightens up, working her underwear up slowly around her. It is large underwear, large enough to come up all the way over and contain the woman's belly. She is a thin woman, but her skin has sagged badly, so that it is more a belly of skin than of fat, but a belly nonetheless. Her breasts are long and small, the skin of them wrinkled. Ruth has seen naked older women before, but suddenly the idea of wrinkled breasts strikes her as strange; her own face has wrinkles, and her arms around the elbows, but she has never considered that one day her breasts might wrinkle, too. The woman pulls a turtleneck over her head. She wears no bra, and her breasts sit low on her torso and then vanish beneath her sweater.

Suddenly Ruth smells the rich, sickening smell of burning hair and realizes she has been drying the same lock of hair over and over again as she's been watching this woman dress; the hair above her right ear is wiry now, stiff and burned. She looks at herself in the mirror, standing there in a bathrobe with a dryer to her head, pale with winter and suddenly older-looking than she had thought—but then she realizes that she hasn't really looked at herself in months, maybe even years—not closely, anyway. She turns the dryer off and leans in toward the mirror. There is darkness beneath her eyes, and the lines around her mouth seem deep, her lips scarred with pursing. But the light is bad in here, she tells herself, and it is, after all, winter. Still, her birthday is soon; she will be forty-one. Birthdays have never bothered her, but this year, the idea of a birthday dismays Ruth. It's not that she's afraid of getting old; age is just a number. No, instead it's that she feels she's losing time. She is no longer working. She can't remember the last book she read, or the last time she went to lunch with friends. And today, she thinks, she couldn't even enjoy a goddamn massage. She grits her teeth, filled with both frustration and resentment and, at the same time, guilt about feeling these feelings. She is a mother, she tells herself. This is exactly what she bargained for. She sets the dryer down, though her hair isn't really dry except in one spot, and turns to dress. It is five past one; Wilson and Isabelle will be expecting her.

Her BLT is good, the bacon perfectly crunchy and the tomato generous, but after only a few bites, Isabelle is full, and this disappoints her. Usually when she has a milkshake with her lunch, she is sure to drink only half before her meal comes, and then if she's not full after she's eaten, she drinks the other half if it hasn't melted too much. But today she'd unwittingly finished her milkshake before her sandwich arrived, so distracted was she by the magazine that she hadn't realized how nearly empty her glass was until the straw began to guzzle against the bottom. She looks longingly at her sandwich now, wishing that she had more appetite, both because the sandwich is so good and because she wants to finish it for her father. He has been commenting on how good their matching sandwiches are the whole time he's been eating, and though Isabelle has nodded in agreement, she can see her father eyeing her nibbled sandwich with concern. She picks it up and takes another bite and chews until the food has all but dissolved in her mouth and she barely has to swallow at all.

She glances at the magazine beside her and opens it just a crack to look again at the page she has marked with a napkin. The photographs of Africa themselves are interesting to look at, the color so vibrant and the images so clear as to make the scenes seem almost three-dimensional, but what has really caught her attention, in the end, is the section of the magazine devoted to the ancient African systems of writings. These African symbols are even more beautiful than hieroglyphs, Isabelle thinks; they are symmetrical and precise and simple. There is one symbol that represents a crocodile, but instead of standing for a sound, as in hieroglyphics, the symbol stands for adaptability. There's another that represents a ram's horns; it stands for humility and strength. The ladder of death stands for mortality, and the yellow-flowered plant for jealousy and envy. The wooden comb stands for beauty and hygiene, and, perhaps Isabelle's favorite, the symbol that represents the weight of the earth stands for the earth's divinity. She likes that these symbols stand for ideas instead of letters that make up words—they are enough to communicate only what is essential; there isn't an excess of words to clutter things up. It is a simple system, beautiful and quiet, better even than hieroglyphics.

"You can keep that, if you want, Belle," she hears her father say. She lets the magazine close and smiles at him, and seeing him once again glance toward her sandwich, she lifts it and forces down another bite. She looks at the jukebox, which her father has put money into but neglected to play. She looks at the dish of crayons, and her own blank placemat beneath her plate.

"Can I clear those for you?" Isabelle looks up; she hadn't noticed the waitress approach.

"I think we're finished," her father says. "Do you want to take your other half home, Belle?"

Isabelle nods and watches as the waitress lifts their plates. And then she sees that although she has left the crayons untouched, her father has not; she blinks at the upside-down blue image of herself on her father's placemat, reading, stained in places with ketchup, a wet ring from his lemonade on the corner.

From across the street, Ruth sees Wilson and Isabelle standing on the corner just outside the diner. Isabelle is without a hat, and the wind is whipping her hair in every direction. Wilson is standing behind her, rubbing his hands up and down her arms to warm her; she is chattering with cold. The street is busy; bundled people eclipse her family from Ruth's view as they pass down the street, and a Salvation Army Santa rings his tinny bell.

The light changes, and Ruth hurries across the street. "Aren't you freezing?" she asks. "Why aren't you waiting inside?" Isabelle's nose is red and runny; she'll probably get a cold, Ruth thinks, and she looks at Wilson incredulously.

"We are cold, but unfortunately there's no room to stand inside."

Ruth looks through the glass of the diner door and sees that there is indeed a crowd of people squeezed into the doorway waiting for tables. "Well," she says. "How was lunch?"

"It was good," Wilson says, and he hands her a plastic bag. "Leftovers," he says.

"I thought it was good," Ruth says.

"It was good. But we got full."

Ruth can hear the annoyance in Wilson's voice, and she knows that she is picking, but she cannot help it. "Well, I'm glad you had a nice lunch," she says.

"What's on the agenda this afternoon?" Wilson asks.

Ruth holds up a grocery bag filled with baking ingredients she picked up on the way to the diner. "I thought maybe we'd make cookies," she says; she is simply too tired to go clothes shopping this afternoon. She looks at Isabelle for a reaction; Isabelle stares vacantly down the street. "How does that sound, Isabelle?" she asks. But Isabelle is frozen where she is; she doesn't blink; she doesn't move; she does not look in Ruth's direction.

"Well, that sounds good to me," Wilson says. "I'd come bake, too, if I could."

They are quiet for a minute. The Santa's bell rings in a constant rhythm, loud even against the noise of traffic.

"How was your appointment?" Wilson asks.

"It was fine."

"Good."

"Ready, Isabelle?" Ruth asks. Still, Isabelle won't acknowledge her. Ruth looks at Wilson, asking with her eyes if there is something wrong, and suddenly she feels sad, sad that her daughter will not even look at her, sad because she is short these days with the only person in the world with whom she can have a conversation with her eyes.

"I'll get you a cab," Wilson says, stepping into the street to hail a passing taxi.

Isabelle gets in first; Ruth hesitates before getting in herself, taking Wilson by the arm.

"What?" he asks.

She hesitates; she doesn't know. "Nothing," she says, finally. "We'll see you later." She gives him a kiss on the cheek, which tastes metallic with cold, and then shuts herself into the warmth of the cab beside her daughter. She tells the driver their address, lets out a breath, and sits back. She looks over at her daughter. Isabelle has pulled up her sweatshirt hood and drawn it tight around her face so that only her eyes are showing. She seems to sense her mother's look, and she turns sharply toward the window, clearly furious at something. Ruth sighs and looks out her own window. She shuts her eyes to the world passing by outside the cab and does not open them again until she feels the taxi lurch to a stop and hears the meter tick its final reading. Isabelle is already opening the cab door, and before Ruth can say anything, Isabelle has vanished into their building. She digs through her purse for money and pays the cabbie before sliding across the backseat to the open door to get out on the curb side. She shuts the door behind her gently, and instead of going directly inside, she stands in the cold, looking up at their building swaying against the sky. She imagines her daughter upstairs, still red-faced but warm now, maybe lying down with Maggie, maybe sitting at the window, maybe going to her bedroom for her sketchbook. Her daughter, Ruth thinks, one of the hundreds of people in the building behind those small and many windows; her daughter, to Ruth the only person in the building. It is cold, too cold even to shiver, but Ruth doesn't mind it; she'll stand where she is until she is numb enough to go inside.

IV

Wilson has been describing to her what he's learned about Africa, about what kind of trip they'd take if they went, and instead of resisting—she is too tired to resist—Ruth finds herself listening intently, imagining herself far, far away from the city, their apartment, the living room where they're sitting now, the tree looming in the corner behind them, Peter, Paul, and

Mary singing "Go Tell It on the Mountain" from the speakers, Isabelle off wherever she is, furious at Ruth for reasons that became more than clear this afternoon, when Dr. Steingold finally returned her call.

"How was the appointment?" she had asked. "And the sketchbook—what do you think?"

"Today's appointment was difficult," he said.

"Well, these things take time," Ruth said, unwilling to give up hope. "Isabelle takes her time warming up to people. But you've seen her drawings now, so you've got some insight."

"I think you might be placing a little too much emphasis on her drawings, Mrs. Carter. It's going to take a lot more to understand what is troubling Isabelle than a sketchbook."

Ruth was silent for a moment. "I thought you said her art would be meaningful," she said. "You said there is meaning in everything we make."

"And there is. But what we make doesn't hold all the answers. Isabelle's sketchbook doesn't hold all the answers. For therapy to work, Isabelle has to understand what is causing her to use silence. My job is to help her understand."

Ruth did not respond. She wasn't sure how to respond. She felt misled, deceived, incredulous, but at the same time what the doctor was saying seemed suddenly obvious, but something to which she'd willed herself oblivious.

"Isabelle is a willful child," Dr. Steingold said into the silence.

"Are you telling me that my daughter is a willful child?" Ruth said, the desperation behind her silence suddenly breaking through. "Is that your diagnosis? My daughter is willful," she scoffed. "Do you think anyone knows that better than I do?"

"I know your situation is difficult, Mrs. Carter."

"You have no idea."

"And I know that all you want is for your child to be happy, to be well, and I want to try to help you."

"I let you have my daughter's sketchbook," Ruth said. "That is like giving you her diary. It's something I would never do. But I let you have it anyway, under the impression that it would help. You led me to believe that it would help."

"And maybe it will, Mrs. Carter. I'm not saying that it won't. I still have it, and if you'd like, I can take another look through it, perhaps see what a colleague thinks."

"You still have it," Ruth repeated.

"Yes."

"What does that mean?"

"I've still got it here in the office. Isabelle opted not to take it with her."

Ruth shut her eyes. "You showed her the sketchbook."

"Yes."

Ruth swallowed, the reason for Isabelle's fury suddenly clear. "I thought that the sketchbook was going to be just between you and me." Her voice was low and fast, just under control. "I let you have that sketchbook to study her drawings, not to discuss them with her. I thought I'd made that quite clear over the phone."

"I must have misunderstood," the doctor said. "I was not under that impression at all."

"I see."

"I'm sorry."

"So am I." Ruth breathed in deeply through her nose, trying to steady her voice. "If you'd please leave the sketchbook with your secretary, I'll be by later to pick it up."

"I'll do that. Again, I apologize."

"Well."

"We'll see you next week, then?" the doctor said after a pause.

"No," Ruth said. "I don't think you will."

"I'm sorry about that, Mrs. Carter. I would like to help Isabelle."

Ruth snorted; she'd heard this too many times. "Well," she said.

"I'll leave the sketchbook with the secretary. But I would urge you to reconsider."

Ruth hung up.

She laid her forehead down on her desk, pressing her skull as hard as she could against the wood until her head ached, the pain traveling dully from front to back, wrapping itself around her. It was not Dr. Steingold who misled her, she realized; it was hope that misled her, and she had allowed it—but it wouldn't happen again, she thought bitterly. It couldn't, because she had no more hope. The sound of Isabelle's voice seemed suddenly a thing impossible to achieve, and she could only feel that she was the one to blame. Somewhere, she knew, everywhere, she went wrong.

Now, by the fire, Ruth shifts, tucks her legs beneath her, listening to Wilson talk about Africa. He wants to start out in South Africa and make their way north. First, he has said, he wants to spend time in Botswana, which to Ruth's surprise he has described as lush, green, and swampy; when she thinks of Africa, she thinks of what he is describing now—vast grasslands with the occasional acacia tree.

"See, in Tanzania," he is saying, "you have the Serengeti National Park—*serengeti* means 'endless plain' in the language they speak there, I can't remember what it's called. So you have the grasslands, but there's also a huge crater, what's it called, Ngorongoro, and also Mount Kilimanjaro. So there's a lot to see in Tanzania."

Ruth nods, taking a sip of her drink. "Yes," she says. "And then what would be next?"

"From Tanzania, I'd say we keep going north through Rwanda. It's very hilly, I read. They call it Land of a Thousand Hills, which I kind of like. Like I like *serengeti*."

"And what's in Rwanda?"

"Well, really it's just on the way to Kenya, but the hills are supposed to be beautiful. And there are gorillas."

"Huh."

"I mean, we can just pass through, we wouldn't have to stay."

"No," Ruth says. "I was just—go on."

Wilson takes a breath. "Kenya," he says. "Kenya's your real Africa, you know. Lots of lions, leopards, gazelles, zebras, buffalo, all those guys. I was thinking we'd get a guide and go on safari. Casey says it's really the way to go. The trouble is, you've got to book well ahead."

"Casey?"

"The travel agent I've been working with. She's looking to see if there'd be anything left for January, if it came to that, which it seems to be doing."

All of a sudden, Ruth plunges back to reality, to where they're sitting right now, their daughter silent in the other room. "Wait a second, Wilson. All of a sudden you're talking about this trip in awfully concrete terms. January? January is soon! January is in a couple of weeks! Maybe June, maybe next year—Africa sounds like a wonderful trip—but I thought we'd settled it that going to Africa in January is totally unrealistic."

"I thought you said that going on this way is totally unrealistic."

"And it is. But Africa is not the cure, I'm fairly sure. I don't know *why* you've gotten such a bee in your bonnet about Africa." She can see the hurt in Wilson's eyes, and for a moment, she feels guilty; she is taking out the day's frustrations on him.

"It's not a *bee in my bonnet,* Ruth," he says defensively. "It's something to *do.* You're the one all hyped over *doing.*"

"Oh, come on. *Doing* does not mean flying off to another continent. It would be an interesting trip. It is not a cure."

"Is art a cure? Going to that art class sounded like an absolute disaster. And you really think that she's spelled out some hidden message in her sketchbooks? That some shrink is going to be able to decipher? I think you've got a *bee in your bonnet* about art, is what I think."

After this afternoon's conversation with Dr. Steingold, Wilson's criticism stings doubly. "I never said art was a cure. Anyway, wasn't it that *drawing,* the one of the lion, that put this Africa idea into your head in the first place?"

"No, it was you, trying to make conversation at dinner that night. If you recall, that's why she did that drawing in the first place."

They are quiet for a moment. They stare at each other. "Jesus," Ruth finally says. "You're right. Wilson, we are fooling ourselves. That drawing of Africa—you've run with the Africa bit, I've run with the art bit—and where the hell are we going? We are getting nowhere!" She sighs loudly, stares into the flames. After a moment, she speaks again. "You know I fired the shrink?"

"What?" Wilson says. "Why?"

"I shouldn't have. But I did. I was angry. He showed her the sketchbook. He wasn't supposed to show her the sketchbook, and he fucking showed her the sketchbook, and now she is absolutely furious. I mean, she is never going to trust me again. Fuck!"

"Ruth."

Ruth brings her fist to her forehead and begins to cry.

"Ruth."

"I don't know what to do anymore. I never knew what to do."

"This isn't going to last forever," Wilson says, leaning over to take his wife's hand. "It can't last forever."

This is the posture they are in when Isabelle appears like a shadow in the doorway—Ruth with the knuckles of one hand against her forehead, the other hand in Wilson's, Wilson himself half out of his chair, almost on his knees, his free hand outstretched, as if beseeching his wife to stop, please stop crying.

It is past her bedtime, but no one has been in to say good night. She had tucked herself into bed and turned off the lights, but she could not fall asleep. It was the anticipation of her father cracking her door, whispering good night, that kept her awake at first, and then it was the fear that he wouldn't at all, and that she would lie awake all night waiting. She crept down the hall in search of her parents, increasingly aware of a sound she didn't immediately recognize, one that both lured her on and warned her off. It sounded at first like the strange, choking call of some animal, but Isabelle knew as she neared the living room—really had known all along—that it was the sound of her mother crying, and her chest went cold with fear.

As she stands in the doorway, any anger she felt earlier toward her mother evaporates; all she wants now is for her mother to stop crying. *Please stop!* she wants to beg. *Please, please stop!* and she knows that if she said this, then her mother would stop. It is all within her power, she thinks, but at the same time it *is not* within her power, not anymore.

Quietly, unseen, she backs away from the doorway and hurries down the hall to her bedroom. She takes her sketchbook from her desk drawer and goes to sit on the radiator underneath the window, where earlier she'd left the *National Geographic* her father had given her. She looks at the sketchbook in her lap, which was waiting on her bed for her after dinner. She hadn't doubted even for a second that it was what it was, and her certainty then surprises her now, because it was the last thing she expected to see there. She pictures the places it has been: in the shrink's dark desk drawer, on the corner of his desk for her to take or leave, in her mother's hands, and then safely in a plastic bag swinging home through the cold to lie waiting on her pillow. She pictures her mother quietly setting it there, maybe even pausing to sit on the edge of Isabelle's bed, and she is overcome all over again with a gratitude that feels very much like sadness.

She sets the sketchbook aside, opens the *National Geographic,* and rests it in her lap. The heat blowing from the radiator flutters its pages, but she doesn't move. She turns to the page of African symbols once again, and she studies them carefully for a while before closing the magazine and lowering it to the floor. She tears from her sketchbook a single white sheet of paper and lifts the charcoal she has set on the windowsill. Carefully, she begins to draw the design she has memorized from the list of them, a line that chases itself endlessly around a square, looping back over itself at each corner and then rushing again forward. Mpatapo, it is called, the knot of reconciliation.

II

NINE

Friday

I

She sets her charcoal down and looks at what she's drawn so far, which isn't much for the hours she's been working. In the open space framed by the symbol she drew last night, she has begun to sketch the image of her parents as they were last night by the fire: the two of them joined hand to hand; the long, slender length of her mother's neck, her fist against her forehead; the fire-cast shadows; the looming Christmas tree; her father's outstretched hand, the white space of his palm, which she cannot bring herself to fill in. Everything else she has done from memory, but she is afraid to do the palm from memory. Because it wouldn't be from memory; she does not know the lines of her father's palm. It would be from imagination, and this to her seems not only inaccurate but dangerous. What if she were to somehow curse her father by giving him a short life line or an unlucky love line? She does not want to take the chance.

She sighs and rubs her eyes, remembering too late the charcoal on her fingertips, and she is just about to stand to wash her face when she hears the elevator door clank shut and Maggie begin to bark. Isabelle looks at the microwave clock, puzzled; her mother isn't meant to be home for another hour at least; probably it is the dry-cleaning, she thinks, or someone has sent flowers, or a Christmas package has arrived. Curious, she makes her way down the hall to the door.

A large man is bent over in the doorway, trying to push Maggie away from him, even slapping her snout a few times, Isabelle notes with indignation, and she is relieved when Maggie leaves the man and runs toward her, still barking. She holds Maggie by the collar and kneels beside her, stroking her beneath her chin, and when she looks back at the man in the doorway, he has straightened up so that she can see his face; it is her uncle.

"Hi-ya, Isabelle," he says. She looks at him warily. She does not know him well, but she knows that there are times when he has made her mother cry. "Your mom home?"

Isabelle blinks at him, his wide, round face. The snow from his boots is melting on the floor. Maggie has finally stopped barking, but she is tense still, alert.

"You sick?"

Isabelle shakes her head again.

"Snow day?"

Isabelle stares at him.

"Lucky. Enjoy them while you can." Isabelle lowers her gaze back to her uncle's boots; there is an actual *puddle* around them now. "Mind if I come in?"

Isabelle stands and lets Maggie's collar go; the dog approaches her uncle tentatively, her tail stiff. Her uncle steps inside, unzipping his coat.

"I had a meeting in town," he says. "Foundation wanted to discuss some things with me. Important people. Important stuff." He tosses his coat onto the hall bench. "Your mom going to be home soon?"

Isabelle nods.

"Haven't seen her since the summer. Thought I'd drop in while I was here. She mentioned me coming to see you all anyway. Think she wants to see me." He looks at his watch. "'Bout what time'll she get here? Because there are other people I could see."

Isabelle stares at him.

"What's that, cat got yer tongue?"

Isabelle looks at the floor.

"Well," he says, and his boots step out of their dirty puddle. "Coffee. Kitchen's this way, right?" he says. She watches with horror as his boots stain their way down the hallway, and then she hurries after him toward the kitchen as if her presence could protect things from him there.

He pauses in the kitchen doorway; Isabelle skirts around him and rushes to her drawing on the table, which quickly she begins to roll.

"Don't!" Her uncle's voice is loud, and she freezes. "It's going to smudge that way." Isabelle lets the drawing fall flat against the table. Her uncle is right; the Christmas tree is blurred now—and of course it is! she thinks; she feels her ears begin to burn. What had she been thinking rolling up a charcoal drawing? What kind of artist must she seem, to have to be told by a soldier of all people that charcoal will smudge?

"That yours?" her uncle asks. He is standing behind her, looking over her shoulder at the drawing.

Isabelle nods and starts to pull the drawing quickly from the table; it is unfinished and unfit to be seen. But her uncle puts his hand on her shoulder. "Wait," he says. "You did that?"

His hand is heavy and hard, more like stone than flesh.

"You did that," he says again.

Isabelle nods, steps out from beneath his grip.

"You know I do some drawing myself," he says. "You didn't know that, did you?"

Isabelle shakes her head. That her uncle is an artist surprises her; she has always imagined him with a gun.

"I bet your mom didn't tell you that, did she?"

Isabelle shakes her head again.

"No, she wouldn't have." He takes a step back from the drawing and tilts his head. "Huh," he says. He squints his eyes and tilts his head the other way. Isabelle looks from her uncle to the drawing, squints her eyes at it, and tilts her own head to see it as her uncle does; the drawing only looks the same, but blurry.

"You heard of mystics?"

Isabelle gives her uncle a questioning look.

"You know what a mystic is?"

Isabelle shakes her head.

"No, you wouldn't," he says.

She waits for him to tell her about mystics, but instead he puts his hands on his hips.

"Where's that coffee?"

Isabelle points to the cabinet where the coffee is kept.

"Where'd that cat get off to, anyway?"

Isabelle glances around her—as if they really had a cat. Maggie has settled in the kitchen doorway, eyes wide, brows twitching. Isabelle kneels to stroke her.

Her uncle turns from the cabinet with the coffee tin in his hand. "Think he'll bring yer tongue back soon?" he says. *That* cat; Isabelle smiles, surprising herself. Her uncle spoons coffee grounds into the machine. "What kind of contraption is this?" he mutters. He shakes his head. "In the war we had to make our coffee instant. Sometimes with puddle water." He pours water into the coffeemaker, and then he pulls out a chair and sits down at the kitchen table. "Know I was in the war?"

Isabelle nods, getting up from beside Maggie on the floor. She moves her drawing to the counter and sits down across the table from her uncle.

"Yeah, I bet your mom told you that. Korea. Ugly time," he says. Isabelle can hear the coffee start to drip behind her; the smell of it makes her mouth water. "Your mom tell you not to speak to me, too?"

Isabelle looks at him quickly and shakes her head, alarmed at this misunderstanding.

"Then what? Just shy?"

She shrugs.

Her uncle nods slowly. "Silent spells," he says. "Julian of Norwich had one. After she was sick. She's a mystic, too, like us."

Isabelle blinks. *Mystic,* she thinks. Mystical, mystery—a mystic must be something good. She wants him to go on about mystics, but he gets up to take a mug from the cabinet. She watches him. The coffee hasn't finished brewing yet, but he pulls the pot out anyway and pours what's there into his mug; Isabelle cringes at the hiss of coffee dripping onto the hot plate while the pot is gone. It will burn, she knows, and stain.

"I lost my whole platoon in the war, know that?" Her uncle sits across from her again, stirring his coffee with his finger. "Found them later, though." His mouth grimaces around a sip. "When I was a kid," he says, "I was looking through family photos. Knew everyone in the pictures, but then I came to one where I didn't recognize anybody. Lot of guys around a big table. Young guys. Tons of food, silver platters, wine, flowers on the table—big table, like a banquet table— everyone all smiles. Went downstairs and found my dad to ask him who these people were, brought him back upstairs, picture was gone. Nowhere." He takes another sip, frowns around this one, too. "And it had been there. I saw it." He points at his eyes.

"Got back from the war and started seeing this minister, good guy, been in a war himself. Dead now.

But what he said was that when you die, you get welcomed into heaven with a big banquet, and what he described was *exactly like that picture.* Course, I hadn't thought about that photograph in years, but I pictured it, and I could remember every detail. The banquet like the minister described, and all the people eating and smiling, and all of a sudden I knew." He leans forward. "All of a sudden I recognized the faces." He sits back. "My men," he says.

Isabelle blinks. This is unlike any story she's heard before.

"I don't tell that story to just anyone."

Isabelle licks her lips.

"But you're different," her uncle says. "I can tell that. I can recognize that in you."

Isabelle breathes in deeply and sits forward, eager for her uncle to go on, to tell her more.

He points to his eyes again and smiles. She waits. Then, "Charcoal," he says. "You look like a raccoon."

Ruth sits back and looks out the taxi window. The sun is out today, and in the white winter light the city looks overexposed; she squints as they hurtle past storefront windows frosted with white paint, streetlamps wrapped in garlands, buses kneeling at their stops, a reclining Grinch stretched along the sides of many of them to advertise a movie or a Broadway play, Ruth doesn't read the fine print. She lurches against the door as the driver changes lanes to avoid an idling truck, and her stomach drops as the taxi bounces over a rise in the pavement. Madison is mostly empty, the lights so wonderfully in sync that they have been able to ride a single wave of green all the way uptown.

She pulls her list of errands from her pocket; she's ordered the groceries for Christmas lunch, and she's found a scarf for Wilson's mother for Christmas. She's found Isabelle a new art set, though she's promised herself to stay out of Isabelle's art from now on. It's one thing that makes her daughter happy, and she won't compromise that. And she's found the perfect gift for Wilson, a desk lamp, penholder, and radio in one, a gift she recognized as one that he might choose for her, as random and unnecessary as a bagel slicer: perfect.

She straightens up as the cab turns down their street, and she puts her errand list away; all she needs to do now is pack for the weekend, and then she can relax for an hour or two before they leave for New England, which is a chore in itself, but she will be a good sport about it, she thinks, for Wilson's sake. She hands the cab fare to the driver and goes inside, gratefully settling onto the elevator bench as she ascends, realizing suddenly that she is very tired. She is tired of being tired.

The elevator arrives at their floor. Ruth gathers her parcels together and stands. The door opens onto the bright light of the foyer; it smells like Christmas tree and coffee. She hangs her coat on the coat stand and steps out of her shoes; her bare feet are white with cold, she notes, toeing at the residue of salt on the floor just inside. She can't remember how many times she has asked Wilson to *please* take his shoes off *before* he comes through the door. "Belle!" she calls out. "I'm home!" She doesn't expect an answer, but sometimes when she calls out Isabelle will appear from the kitchen or her bedroom or the study, wherever it is she's been spending her time. Ruth listens for a moment for the sound of footsteps; she hears none. "Isabelle!" she calls again, heading toward the kitchen. She pauses in the hallway to examine large, wet shoe prints. "Wilson?" she calls, hoping that the shoe prints are his, wishing that what she felt was more annoyance than concern. "Isabelle?" she calls, hurrying now, then she stops short in the kitchen doorway. "Jimmy!"

Her brother and her daughter are seated at the kitchen table, each with a mug of coffee. "Coffee!" she says, and she snatches Isabelle's mug away. "Do you ever want to grow?" she asks, splashing the coffee into the sink. She whirls around, her heart pounding. Isabelle is looking up at her with wide, bewildered eyes, a look of interrupted happiness on her face; instantly, Ruth feels awful. Her brother isn't Isabelle's fault.

"It was decaf."

Ruth turns to face her brother at the sound of his voice. "Jimmy," she says. She clears her throat. "What are you doing here?" She tries to ask this nicely, with an inquisitive rather than accusatory tone.

"Isabelle and I were just having a nice chat."

"I see. And what brings you to the city?"

"Business. Also, you asked me to come. You said any old weekend, so since I was here anyway . . ."

"Of course," Ruth says. She wants to point out that it's really not any old weekend, that they are meant to go visit Wilson's mother, that Sunday is Christmas Eve. She holds her tongue.

"Coffee?" Jimmy asks.

Ruth smiles tightly. "No, thanks," she says. "So, what were you guys talking about?" She looks nervously toward Isabelle; her daughter glares at her.

"Well, I was doing most of the chatting, actually," Jimmy says, and he winks at Isabelle. "Jungle stories, mostly."

"Ah," Ruth says. "And what did Isabelle have to say?" She looks again at her daughter, who is looking at Jimmy.

"Lots," Jimmy says. "Lots and lots, but I don't know what it was." He leans toward Ruth. "Because she didn't say it." Their eyes meet; they stare.

The doorbell rings with startling suddenness; all of them jump, as if an electric jolt has pulsed through the room.

"The groceries," Ruth says. "Isabelle, would you get the door, please?"

Isabelle's eyes shift back and forth between her mother and her uncle, uncertain.

"Please?" Ruth asks.

Isabelle hurries to the door, leaving Jimmy and Ruth alone in the kitchen.

"How long have you been here?" Ruth asks her brother.

"Hour," he says. His eyebrows lift and sink, lift and sink, as if he is trying to clear his eyes of a nasty vision.

"And how long are you in town for?"

"Just the weekend. Monday's Christmas." He clears his throat loudly of phlegm.

"It is." Ruth takes Jimmy's mug from the table. "More coffee?" she asks.

He nods.

"If you've been here for an hour," Ruth says, pouring the last of the coffee into Jimmy's mug, "you've probably gathered that Isabelle isn't speaking these days."

"Course not." His tone of voice is almost scornful, as if silence were a phase every child went through, like puberty. Ruth looks at him questioningly. He clears his throat and leans toward her. "She's a mystic," he says.

"A—" But she stops short as Isabelle enters the room, bent over double beneath the weight of the grocery bags she's slung over her back.

The buildings across the park jut jaggedly into the horizon like a jawful of crooked teeth, it seems, the sky itself, then, the gaping hole of a throat open wide to the world, so wide it's nearly inside out. Like

Isabelle's lion, Wilson thinks. He sighs: Isabelle's lion. They'd grabbed that one by the coattails, all right; Ruth is right, he sees that now. But who can blame them? It was nice to have coattails to cling to at all; now it's just the three of them, free-falling.

All day the sky has been clear; with nightfall it seems that the air itself is clear—though air always is, he thinks—but it seems tonight that he can see farther, that things are in better focus. He imagines he can even see figures in the windows of those distant toothlike buildings, vacuuming or cooking or putting things away. One year, Isabelle charted the season's progress by keeping record of where on this horizon the sun set each day; with the approach of winter, he remembers, it moved farther and farther to the left until it seemed the sun was nearly setting in the south. He wonders where the sun is setting now, behind which two buildings over there, and he realizes that yesterday was the solstice, and so the sun has begun its journey back to the right and days will slowly start to swell with light until they all are nearly drunk with it, everyone outside late and marveling that a day could go on for so long. Though winter has only just begun, Wilson finds comfort in the thought of the sun, at least, starting to make its way toward the spring.

He turns from the reservoir fence, where he has been standing, and makes his way out of the park. He has walked home tonight, through the park. He knows Ruth would likely scold him, and he'd probably scold her, too, if she walked in the park at night, but there is something so different between the actual park at night and the idea of it. The idea of it is dangerous and foreboding, the park peopled by the imagination with muggers and killers and drunks. But to actually *be* here, Wilson thinks, looking around him—it is gentle, quiet, calm. The snow beneath each decorated lamp glows; squirrels perch furtively on the backs of benches, nibbling their finds; a branch breaks; bursts of traffic pulse the drive, released by mid-park stoplights.

Leaving the park is like reemerging into the world. Wilson puts his hands in his pockets and keeps his head down as he walks the few blocks up Fifth toward home. He's already called to get the car from the garage, and he got his things for the weekend together this morning, so as long as Isabelle and Ruth are ready to go, they should make it to his mother's well before midnight. He turns the corner onto their street and looks up from the ground as he hurries the few yards left to their building. The light atop the canopy shines like a beacon; he can anticipate the warmth inside, and the musty smell of marble, and the soft, dim light—he needs to bring holiday bonuses down to the doormen, he's thinking as he passes through the door, tonight, on the way out—and then, right there in the doorway, he stops short.

In one of the green armchairs, just by the lobby's Christmas tree, Isabelle is sitting, a book on her lap. Her feet don't reach the floor, and her hair clings with static to the velvet upholstery, and the sight of her there—small and smiling and so utterly herself—makes Wilson hurt with love. It has been months since she last waited for him to come home.

"Belle!" he says. "What are you doing down here?"

Isabelle looks up from her book, momentarily surprised to see her father in the doorway, though it used to be when she sat in the lobby that her heart would race in anticipation of her father's arrival each time the door opened. He gathers her up and spins her as he always used to do, and she feels herself blush, because this makes her feel less like a mystic than a little girl. She glances at Brian, the new doorman, who is rising from his seat. Her father sets her down.

"Belle!" Brian says. "So that's your name!"

"Isabelle, actually," her father says. "Wilson Carter," he says, extending his hand.

"Brian," Brian says. "Nice to meet you. Isabelle has been keeping me company."

"How thoughtful!"

Isabelle blushes to have both sets of eyes on her, each of these men under the impression that she is down here for him when in truth she has come down in the hopes of making her mother worry. *Go answer the door, please. Go water the tree, please*—transparent requests; there seemed no reason at all why she should be banished from the kitchen and Jimmy's company, but since she had been, she'd wanted to leave the apartment entirely. She has brought a dictionary with her, and memorized the definition of mystic: *one who claims contact with an order of reality transcending the world of the senses and the ordinary forms of discursive intellectual knowing.* She's not entirely sure what this means, but it is a good thing, she can tell that much.

"I hope you'll come visit me again," Brian says.

"Shall we go up?" her father asks, extending his hand toward her.

II

From his seat at the dining room table, Wilson can see through the room's glass doors his duffel in the foyer, packed and ready to go to New England. And if things had gone as he'd envisioned, it would be well on its way there now, and he and Ruth and Isabelle would be in the car eating the sandwiches they'd have picked up from the deli for the drive, and they'd be listening to Garrison Keillor on the radio.

Ruth sits at the other end of the table, six leaves away; they never use the dining room, and the table is still extended from last Christmas. She has set the table with the real silver and put new candles in the candlesticks and cooked the filet mignon that she had sent Wilson out to get the moment he'd come home, before he'd even taken off his coat. Knives click against the china as they eat.

"Good meat." Jimmy sits along the length of the table across from Isabelle, each of them with room for two or three on either side. He chews loudly, his hands in fists around his silverware.

"It is good, Ruth," Wilson says—almost calls it down the table. "The potatoes are good, too."

Ruth looks from Wilson to her brother and smiles.

"Should get these knives sharpened, though," Jimmy says, brandishing his fork against his knife. He brings the knife closer to his face. "This Mother's silver?" he says.

Ruth glances at Wilson and then down at her plate. "It is," she says.

"Huh. Wondered where that got to."

"Jimmy!" Wilson says loudly, shifting in his seat, racking his brain for a topic, any topic. "Have your travels ever brought you to Africa?" he says.

Jimmy's knee bumps the table as he crosses or uncrosses his leg. The plates rattle and the wine in their glasses sways. "Seventy-five," Jimmy says. "Kenya."

"I was there in seventy-five," Wilson says. "Isn't that funny."

"Visiting, I suppose." Jimmy's eyes narrow.

"Yes," Wilson says. "My father took me and two of my brothers."

"Jimmy was there on his way around the world," Ruth says. "Isabelle, have I ever told you about your uncle's trip?"

Isabelle looks from her mother to her uncle with a look of interest that makes Wilson almost jealous.

"It was not a trip, Ruth. Don't trivialize."

Ruth's cheeks tighten. She blinks quickly. "I'm sorry," she says. "What was it then, Jimmy?"

"I was on my way to New Guinea."

"Fine, then."

"But Africa!" Wilson interjects. "How long were you there?"

"Long enough." Jimmy looks at Isabelle. "Met a mystic there," he says. Isabelle sits forward, and Wilson glances at Ruth. "First black mystic I ever met," he says. He straightens up. "Isabelle here is a mystic." He looks from Wilson to Ruth.

"Is that so?" Wilson says.

"Jimmy," Ruth says. "Would you pass the potatoes, please?"

Jimmy looks at the potatoes beside him, then up at Ruth, and then he slides the dish across the table a little too hard. "Your mom doesn't think we should talk about it," he says to Isabelle.

"You can talk about anything you'd like," Ruth says, spooning potatoes onto her plate. "I simply asked for the potatoes."

Jimmy winks at Isabelle.

"Well." Wilson clears his throat. "I hear it's going to warm up next week. Maybe start acting a little more like New York instead of Alaska."

"That would be nice," Ruth says. "Otherwise I think I'll have to retire early to a warmer climate!"

"It rained in Istanbul today." Jimmy shovels a bite of peas into his mouth and chews loudly. They watch him. He swallows and then stabs a bite of meat. He turns to his sister. "How is the law, anyway, Ruth? Still working with that lesbian?"

Ruth blinks at him. The phone rings. "Excuse me," she says, setting her napkin onto her seat.

"How are the girls, Jimmy?" Wilson asks. He can hear Ruth's voice low in the kitchen as she answers the phone.

Jimmy nods. "Martha gets her license next week," he says through a mouthful of food.

"Is that right."

Jimmy points at Isabelle with his knife. "Your dad teach you to drive yet?"

Isabelle shakes her head.

"This spring," Wilson says hastily. "We were going to start this spring."

"Start what?" Ruth asks, returning from the kitchen. She gazes at the food on her plate as she pulls her chair in behind her.

"Driving lessons," Wilson says.

Ruth looks up. "I thought we'd decided twelve was a good age," she says. Isabelle glares at her mother.

"Had Marth driving when she was nine," Jimmy says.

"Hadn't we, Wil?"

Wilson looks from his daughter to his wife. "I guess I'd forgotten," he falters. The phone rings again.

"Goddamn fucking phone!" Ruth says, pushing her chair back so hard that it nearly tips over as she stands. It balances for what seems to Wilson long, long seconds on its back legs before finally coming to rest on all four. He lets out his breath. Ruth has disappeared into the kitchen. The door flaps back and forth behind her.

"Stick," Jimmy says, arranging his silverware on the side of his plate. He has finished eating. "Got to learn on stick."

Wilson blinks at Jimmy. "I'll keep that in mind, Jimmy," he says.

But Jimmy is looking at Isabelle. "I'll take you driving if your folks won't," he goes on.

"We'll take her when we think it's the right time, Jimmy," Wilson says. He turns to his daughter. "Isabelle, do you want to start to clear?"

Isabelle's mouth goes tight with displeasure. She gives her father a steely look.

"Right now," Wilson says. Isabelle's nostrils flare once, and then she stands. She has lifted her plate and is about to clear Wilson's when Ruth emerges from the kitchen.

"Are we clearing already?"

"We were starting to," Wilson says. "You hadn't finished?"

"Does it look like I've finished?"

"I'm sorry," Wilson says. "I didn't realize. Isabelle, why don't you set your plate back down for another minute—"

"No," Ruth says. "No, just go ahead and clear."

"You keep in mind what I said." Jimmy says this in a low voice to Isabelle as she goes to take his plate.

"Jimmy," Wilson says, just as the phone rings again.

"Jesus fucking Christ!" Ruth cries.

"Just let it ring."

They all look at Jimmy. "Let it ring," he says again. Ruth sits down. Isabelle stands above her uncle, a plate in either hand. The phone rings.

"I'll help you clear, Belle," Wilson says, standing himself now. He gathers the dish of peas from the table. The phone rings again, and then the answering machine clicks on, and even in the dining room, they can hear the sound of Isabelle's voice coming from the kitchen, telling whoever is calling that *no one is home.*

III

She has erased so thoroughly that the paper is beginning to wear away, but she wants to be sure to undo this curse she's set. She cannot get the image out of her head: her uncle's hands on her father's shoulders, bulbs dropping from the tree as her father falls against it, Maggie barking up at them, her mother pointing over Isabelle's shoulder through the doorway and shouting at her *Go back to bed!* She hadn't dared disobey.

She wonders what happened next. She wonders if her father had fallen all the way to ground. She wonders if her mother had had to help her father up, or if she had knelt down to calm Maggie. She wonders if anyone had cleaned up the mess of Christmas bulbs that must have shattered on the floor.

The paper finally tears beneath her eraser. She pauses and looks at her drawing, and the rip in her father's palm. Now she'll never be able to draw the lines of his palm as they really are, not on this drawing, anyway, but better no lines at all than any trace of the lines she drew after her father had sent her early to bed. She had been angry, but she hadn't meant to curse him. She wouldn't have known how. Still, by filling in the lines of his palms she had taken a knowing gamble, and it wasn't long after that she'd heard the shouting in the other room and seen her father—her *father*—falling down. She had never seen her father fall before. What if she had caused worse things to happen? What if the lines she had drawn cursed him to something really terrible? Sickness or death? The idea fills her with anxiety and shame. She should have known better, she thinks. She is a mystic and should be careful with her powers. This incident proves to her that she has powers—powers she's not sure she wants.

She sets her eraser down. It has been quiet in the house since she was sent to her room for the second time, but now she hears a knock on her bedroom door. She turns her drawing upside down on the table and goes to answer her door; her father is standing on the other side. She looks down.

"I saw the light under your door," he says. Isabelle crosses the room to climb into bed.

"It's late," her father says from the doorway.

Isabelle nods. She imagines her father falling into the Christmas tree, knocking away ornaments and snapping branches, and then she pictures her father pulling the same tree through the woods, an ax over his shoulder; the contrast makes her want to melt into herself. She keeps her eyes down and picks at her toes.

"Not tired?"

She shakes her head. Her father crosses the room and sits on the edge of her bed.

"Hey," he says. He tilts her chin up. "It was a crazy night," he says.

She nods.

"I'm sorry you had to see all that."

She looks at him.

"We all sat down and had a talk," he continues, "and your uncle understands he can't behave the way he did."

She looks down. If only her father knew that it was her fault her uncle had behaved that way, her fault her uncle had pushed him into the tree—but she is glad he doesn't. She would never want her father to think that she had wanted to hurt him. Because she hadn't, not really.

"He didn't hurt me, you know." She looks up again; it is as if her father has read her mind. "And he didn't hurt Mom, either. Or Maggie." She feels her eyes beginning to tear up. "We're all okay," he says. "You're okay, right?"

Isabelle nods, but she is beginning to see double through her tears.

"Hey," her father says. "It's okay," he says. "There's nothing to be scared of." He pulls her toward him.

He is glad that she lets him. She had been angry at him, he knows, for making her clear the dishes, and then for sending her to bed before it was her bedtime. Jimmy had seduced her, and she didn't want to go to bed, but Wilson wanted to spare her the chaos that the look in Jimmy's eyes promised, whatever form the chaos ended up taking. He hadn't been surprised when later Jimmy broke the porcelain dish their great-aunt had left to Ruth, and then launched into his sister for leaving heirlooms out like that to be broken, and for hoarding the heirlooms, like the silver and all the other goods he knows she's stashed away in some vault—Wilson is used to these tirades. But not to the violence; Jimmy has laid a hand on him only once before, and this was years ago when he'd first come back from New Guinea. And though he'd tried, Wilson had been unable to spare Isabelle the violence. He pictures her standing in the living room doorway as he felt the branches of the Christmas tree against his back. The memory makes him hot. He tightens his grip around his daughter as if to reassure her of his strength, and she doesn't pull away.

TEN

Saturday

New England is infinitely more dreary than New York this time of year. The sky seems lower. Everything looks thinner than it should—the trees, the posts of highway signs, the metal of the cars around them. The passengers in every car they pass are bundled up as if it were as cold inside their cars as it is outside.

Ruth pulls her own sleeves up and snaps the heat off. She sits back and returns her gaze to the scenery, but she can feel Wilson glancing at her, once, then again. She clears her throat as if of the irritation she cannot hide.

"What," he finally says.

Ruth turns to her husband. "What?" she asks.

"What's wrong."

Ruth raises her eyebrows. "Nothing," she says, but she cannot quite control the edge to her voice. "Why do you ask?" She blinks and looks out the windshield at the lines passing beneath their car. She sees Wilson shrug out of the corner of her eye.

"You could have stayed, you know."

She rolls her eyes toward him. "Wilson."

Wilson shrugs.

"What bothers me," Ruth says after a minute, "is that he just *shows up,* and then he makes it out as if I've specifically *asked* him."

"Well, you did, didn't you?"

Ruth shifts in her seat. "I *offered,*" she says. "I said *some weekend.* I didn't say *this weekend.* I would never suggest Christmas weekend. Tomorrow is Christmas Eve!"

Wilson sniffs.

"And of course I get made out as the villain in all this. Of course everything is my fault."

Wilson glances in the rearview mirror. "No one thinks you're a villain, Ruth."

"My brother is furious because we had plans, even though I'd *invited* him," she continues, and here she lowers her voice, "I'm sure Isabelle's furious because her uncle charmed her, and you're furious because we're a day behind in getting to your mother's."

"I'm furious?"

Ruth pictures her brother as she'd seen him early this morning through the glass doors of the den, his suitcase open at the foot of the fold-out couch, the blankets twisted around the hulk of his body, a bath towel draped over the back of an antique chair. She groans inwardly. "We shouldn't have left him there," she says.

"Like I said, Ruth, you could have stayed."

"I didn't want to stay, Wilson. I didn't want him to stay either, but what was I supposed to do?"

The highway bends; around the corner, brake lights glow. "Shit," Wilson mutters, slowing the car. "We're never going to get there."

"See, you *are* furious," Ruth says.

"Ruth," Wilson says.

"Well, I'm sorry."

Wilson says nothing.

Ruth shuts her eyes. She is tired, but she will be a good sport, she tells herself again, just as Wilson was last night, rushing to get dinner for her brother as if it had been the plan all along. "Wil," she says, opening her eyes. "I need to pee."

Wilson pulls into the next rest stop as smoothly as he can, but when he glances at Isabelle in the rearview mirror as they come to a stop he sees that the change in momentum has woken her anyway.

Ruth opens the door partway and then turns to Isabelle. "Do you need to go?" she asks.

Isabelle shakes her head. Her cheek is ridged from pressing against the upholstery.

"We've got a couple more hours," Wilson says. "Sure you're okay?"

Isabelle nods. Exhaust fumes and cold air waft into the car as Ruth gets out and hurries in only her shirtsleeves to the bathroom. Wilson cranks the heat and pulls at a hangnail with his teeth. The trip to his mother's as planned would have been short enough; to come all this way for only a night seems absurd, almost a waste. He feels rushed—there are things he wants to be sure to do. He wants to show

302

Isabelle his old things, the stuffed animals and toys still in the upstairs closet, and he wants to have a bonfire, maybe, and he wants to ice-skate on the river, and he wants to have tea and boiled eggs and English muffins with his mother when it's teatime. But by the time they get there, the weekend will already be half gone. He shouldn't have agreed to this change of plans, he thinks, but then again when he'd walked in the door last night and seen Ruth's face as she sat across from Jimmy at the kitchen table, the tired, plaintive look she'd given her husband, a look that seemed to say, if nothing else, *please*, and *help*, he had been filled with a sense of responsibility and without question stepped into the role he knew was expected of him.

The taste of blood fills his mouth. The blood from his hangnail has leaked around his nail. He glances again in the rearview mirror as he sucks at his finger, and then again, this time letting his eyes linger on the mirror, where Isabelle's own eyes have come to rest. Wilson blinks at her, and she looks back at him, and neither of them looks away until the click of the door handle unlatching sounds and Ruth, with another gust of cold, lowers herself into the car.

The drive takes almost twice as long as it should. They hit traffic from three different accidents, and taking these as warning, Wilson drives cautiously. Things have gone colorless with evening by the time they arrive, though it is not quite dark yet; beneath the cloud line on the far horizon the sky glows. Wilson turns the engine off and looks up at his mother's house, the house that he grew up in. It looms. The upper windows are dark, but the kitchen lights are on, and the lights of the Christmas tree are on in the large picture window. He can already smell muffins toasting, can already hear the kettle's shriek. It is almost teatime.

"Well," he says. "We're here." They have been quiet for the past hour, all of them lulled by oncoming headlights and the engine's warm murmur. In the back, Maggie lifts herself, and Isabelle yawns.

"I'm starving," Ruth says.

"We should be just in time for tea."

Wilson carries their bags from the car and sets them just inside the door. It is warm inside. A small dog with ratty hair appears from the other room; she and Maggie regard each other warily. "Mother!" Wilson calls. He stamps the snow from his feet. "Maybe in the kitchen," he says over his shoulder to Ruth and Isabelle. They follow.

The kitchen is the mess it usually is. The radio is on. There are piles of Christmas cards and catalogs on the table. Dried soup crusts a pot on the stove, and a fly buzzes around a greasy pan. A mug of coffee sits half drunk on the counter, and a gnawed slipper lies on a dog bed in the corner. A starling hops from one rung to another in its cage by the window. "Mother!" Wilson calls again. "Huh," he says. "I thought she'd be in here."

He wanders back into the foyer and calls up the stairs. No one answers. He returns to the kitchen. Ruth stands at the table, her hand on a newspaper but her eyes worriedly on Maggie, who has collapsed herself onto the dog bed in the corner. Her breaths seem short, labored. Ruth looks up as her husband enters, then lets her eyes fall again to Maggie, and then to Isabelle. Isabelle has squatted down before the bird, following its leaping with her eyes.

"That's a wild starling," Wilson says. Isabelle looks up at him. "Or it was wild. It fell out of its nest last spring, when it was a baby, and your grandmother found it."

Isabelle turns back to the bird and puts her finger through the bars of the cage to touch his tail.

"It can speak," Wilson goes on. "He can say his name. Gilbert." He crouches beside Isabelle. "Gilbert," he says. "Gilbert. Gilbert. Gilbert." The bird pauses and cocks his head. "Gilbert. Gilbert." Wilson takes a breath. "Oh well," he says. He stands.

"Where do you think your mother is?" Ruth says. She has lifted a Christmas card from Wilson's brother's family from the table. "We haven't gotten this one yet," she remarks.

"I don't know," Wilson says. "I thought she'd be here, but"—he looks at his watch—"she could still be with the horses."

"The horses, Wil? I thought you'd gotten someone to do that for her."

Wilson shakes his head. "I had."

"And?"

Wilson shrugs. "The woman 'didn't understand the horses,' according to my mother."

"Well, maybe you ought to go down there," Ruth says. "It's icy, you know, she could fall and break her hip again."

Wilson turns to Isabelle. "Do you want to go see the horses, Isabelle?" She looks up from Gilbert and nods. He turns to Ruth. "Shall we?" he says.

"You go," she says. "I'll stay here with the dog. Maybe I'll start tea. Your mother is going to want tea, isn't she?"

"I'd assume so," Wilson says. He takes a step toward the doorway and then turns around. "You sure?"

Ruth nods rigorously, as if to reassure him, Wilson thinks. He frowns.

"Really," she says brightly. "Go, go!"

"We'll be back," Wilson says.

Dusk has gotten deeper, and the driveway is icy; it makes him uneasy to think of his mother making this trek to the stables alone. Across a blue field of snow Wilson can see the barn lights glowing, and he can imagine his mother inside, her white hair bound, her fingers bare and raw and numb against the horses' noses as she strokes them, speaking to each one as she passes, he is sure, a dog or two at her feet, a cat in the rafters. He breathes in deeply and turns around to look for Isabelle behind him. He extends his hand. She gives him her fist; she has pulled her fingers up into her gloves. Behind them, the windows of the house are lighting up one by one, as Ruth wanders from room to room turning on the lights while she waits for the kettle to boil.

Isabelle has cut each half of her English muffin into fourths. On one piece she has spread raspberry jam, on another clear honey, and on another clouded honey, and on yet another marmalade. The raspberry has been the best, so far. She sits forward and puts the marmalade in its place and gives the lazy Susan a little spin to see what her other options are. The blackberry jam she hasn't yet used; this she takes and spreads on another bit of muffin.

"Did you want another egg, Isabelle?"

She glances up from her muffin. Her mother has a knife poised against a soft-boiled egg, ready to crack it open, but Isabelle shakes her head; she has muffin to eat.

"Eleanor?"

"Thank you, Ruth, dear, no. But Wilson will have it, won't you, Wil?"

"I suppose you could twist my arm," he says. "I'm not going to be able to eat dinner, though!"

"You sure, Isabelle? This is dinner, for you," Ruth says.

Isabelle nods again, chewing, and reaches for another spread from the lazy Susan.

"Marmite!" her grandmother exclaims. "A girl after my own heart!"

"Do you like Marmite, Belle?"

Isabelle pauses to inspect the brown stuff now on her knife. She has never had Marmite before, and it smells terrible, but all eyes are on her, so she spreads it on thick. She looks up and nods.

"God," her father says. "I hate the stuff."

Isabelle puts the muffin in her mouth and starts to chew. A taste like rubber fills her mouth.

"You like it?" her father asks.

She looks from her father to her grandmother and nods. She wants to be a girl after her grandmother's heart, though to swallow this bitter mouthful is a struggle. She reaches for her tea and takes a large sip; it burns her tongue.

"Marmite is good for you," her grandmother says to her father. "Lots of vitamin B."

"Protein, too, right?" Her mother breaks a piece of cookie from the plate of them; Isabelle reaches for the other half to try to clear her palate.

"Protein, too. I give it to the horses sometimes. They like it on apples," her grandmother says. "It's good for their eyes, too."

"Is that right?" her father asks.

"Well, I think so." Isabelle watches her grandmother's fingers curl into the sugar dish for a cube; the joints seem too swollen to bend. Her grandmother drops one sugar cube and then another and another into her tea. "Dr. Marks says Brodie's eyes are exceptionally good for a horse his age, and he's had Marmite all his life." She brings her cup to her mouth; the cup seems to tremble in her hand more than her hand seems to tremble. Her hand is too thick to tremble, it seems to Isabelle. Her grandmother's lips purse around the rim of her cup as she takes a sip. The lines gather deep around her mouth, and Isabelle can trace them upward to where they disappear into her cheek. She has never seen wrinkles quite like these before. They aren't the kind of loose wrinkles made by sagging skin; instead they seem chiseled, and beautiful. The wrinkles around her eyes are still wet with tears from the cold.

Her grandmother sets her cup back onto its saucer. "You know, Wilson, Dr. Marks might be coming tomorrow to rebandage Adrien's leg. I told you how he cut it?"

"No," her father says.

"Awful story." Her grandmother shakes her head. "But if he does come, then while he's here I thought maybe he should take a look at Maggie."

"Oh!" her father says, quickly. Isabelle catches his eye, but he looks away. "We have a wonderful vet at home! And Maggie was just there the other week, as a matter of fact."

"You were telling me," her grandmother says. "But since she's still unwell I thought you might like another vet to take a look at her. A real vet."

Since she's still unwell. Isabelle sits up straight.

"Dr. Bremer is a real vet," her father says. He looks at his hands on the table.

Since she's still unwell, Isabelle thinks, looking around her for the dog; she isn't in the room. But Maggie *isn't*

309

unwell. They had taken care of that, and she is fine now. That's what the vet had said, isn't it? She breathes quickly and looks hard at her father, but he does not look up. She looks at her mother; her mother blinks and looks down. Isabelle lets her eyes dart from one parent to the other; their silence is a confession. That scalding sip of tea feels as if it's spread all throughout her body; her limbs feel hot and numb at once.

Finally her father looks up. "Belle," he says.

It is all she can do to stand and steer herself from the room, though she has no destination in mind, no plan other than to remove herself from the kitchen, to take herself off display.

They watch her leave.

"Oh dear. She must be very upset about Maggie. I wouldn't have mentioned it. I didn't know."

"It's all right," Wilson says. "I suppose she had to find out sometime."

"You mean you hadn't told her?" Wilson looks down. "Wilson."

Ruth sighs loudly. "Oh, this is exactly what we need."

"I am sorry."

"No," Ruth says. "No, no, you did nothing wrong. You didn't know. Just, yet again, we've fucked up." She takes a breath. She is tired.

Wilson takes a breath. "Now what?"

Ruth shrugs. *I give up,* she wants to say. "I don't know."

*   *   *

I give up, she thinks later. What a wonderful, awful thing to allow herself to think. To imagine giving up was blissful, like falling into sleep, but awful, awful. She bites the insides of her cheeks as she scrubs the soup pot with an old sponge. The water steams, but the burning hardly bothers her. What kind of mother is she to have even *thought* of giving up? She turns off the faucet and looks at the kitchen clock: six fifteen. Isabelle left the kitchen an hour ago, and when several minutes later Wilson went after her, he could find her nowhere in the house.

She cups her eyes against the glass of the kitchen window and stares intently down the driveway, her eyes turning every tree, every shrub, into Wilson returning, Isabelle in tow. She holds her head against the glass until it fogs. The glass is cold, and Ruth knows that outside is colder, and Isabelle has been out there for an hour almost, maybe even without a hat or gloves, or even a coat—to think of it again is beyond distressing. She just needs time, Ruth tells herself yet again tonight. Some time alone, and then she'll come back, and she should *have* that time—but Ruth finds less and less comfort in that reasoning as the minutes pass. The possibilities that Isabelle has run away or tried to hurt herself, possibilities that initially seemed unlikely, have come to seem increasingly real, and there is nothing else in the kitchen to distract her—she has cleaned it inside out and emptied the fridge of rotten food— and goddammit! she thinks, she won't just sit here waiting any longer in case her daughter should return. If she hasn't returned by now, then Ruth is better off helping Wilson search.

Even through the thick front door, Ruth can feel the cold from outside in the foyer, and her fingers tremble as she buttons up her jacket. Isabelle's coat had been beside hers, and it isn't any longer, she notes with relief—at least she has her coat. But what if she's been in an accident? Fallen through ice? Anything? She fumbles with the laces of her boot. Stupid, stupid, she thinks. Of course they should have told her about Maggie. What had they been thinking? Now Isabelle is not only devastated about the dog, but furious at her parents on top of that, and really, who knows what she might do? They should call the police, she thinks. Of course! They should have called the police right away!

"Ruth, dear." She looks up. Wilson's mother is standing above her. She puts her hand on Ruth's shoulder. "Are you going out, too?"

"Yes!" Ruth says. She almost does not recognize her voice. "Shouldn't I? Don't you think? I should have right away. We both should have. Shit! Fuck!" She stands up.

"You said yourself she needs time."

"But an hour! In this cold!"

"There are many places to hide here. There's the barn, and the greenhouse, and the toolshed, and the pool house."

Ruth blinks.

"Wilson knows these spots from experience, I can tell you that."

She squeezes Ruth's shoulders. Ruth takes a breath. Her mother-in-law is right. Isabelle is probably fine. *Time,* she tells herself. Time, time. It is Isabelle.

"Here," Eleanor says. She opens the door of the closet behind them. "Here," she says, handing Ruth a flashlight. "You go help him."

"Isabelle!" Wilson turns around at the sound of Ruth's voice. The beam of a flashlight scans the driveway just around the house, and though he can't see her, he knows that Ruth is behind the light. "Isabelle!" The light bounces as Ruth makes her way through the snow. She is headed across the sweep of the lawn toward the river. "Isabelle!"

It had been Wilson's impulse, too, to call his daughter's name when he first came out to find her, though he knew better, and Ruth knows better, too. He'd thought Isabelle would be easy to find; he'd thought he could just follow her footprints, but the snow around the house is too tracked out for footprints to be distinguishable.

"Isabelle!" The beam from Ruth's flashlight pauses and sweeps the area around the river; Wilson has already been that way and knows that no prints lead out onto the ice. Ruth turns and heads toward where Wilson stands just outside the sugarhouse, where they used to bring sap to be boiled down and filtered into syrup. They'd always had their own syrup when Wilson was growing up, and every time he's taken Isabelle to visit his mother, for whatever reason she takes endless interest in the sugarhouse. He thought maybe she might be in there, but the sugarhouse behind him is empty except for the rusted boiling vat and, in the corner, old filtering wool that mice have made a nest of.

Ruth's flashlight shines for a second directly into Wilson's eyes, and he expects it to return to him again as Ruth realizes what she has seen, but it continues to bounce along, veering away from the sugarhouse and more in the direction of the toolshed. It is easy to be invisible out here. Wilson has been holding his own flashlight by his side; now he raises it and shines it at Ruth. Her beam halts and then jerks in Wilson's direction. He puts his flashlight down again and squints into the light.

"Wilson?" Ruth calls. The light begins to bounce toward him. He shields his eyes in the glare. "I didn't see you there," she says.

"I know," he says. He turns his flashlight off.

"You haven't found her."

Wilson shakes his head, though the comment requires no response.

"Fuck," she says. "I'm worried, Wilson."

The worry in her voice surprises Wilson, because he *isn't* worried.

"It's cold out here," Ruth says.

"I know."

"It's been an hour."

"I know."

"And no trace of her? Nothing?"

Wilson shakes his head.

"Do you think we should call the police?"

"The police?"

"Yes!"

He pictures a handful of police stalking the property with flashlights, the beams passing over Isabelle as easily as Ruth's had passed over Wilson. "What would we tell the police, Ruth?"

"That our eleven-year-old daughter who hasn't spoken for nine months has been missing for an hour in the dark out in the freezing cold!"

"Ruth."

"What!"

"Do you think that Isabelle ran away?"

Ruth falters. "No."

"And do you think she's gotten lost?"

"No, but—"

"She's out here because she wants to be. Just like you were saying earlier. If she wants to be found, she'll be found."

"Well, I'm glad you can be so nonchalant about it," Ruth says, spinning around. "As usual, I'll do the worrying for the both of us." She resumes her trek toward the toolshed. Wilson switches on his flashlight and heads toward the barn.

From where she sits on the roof, Isabelle sees her parents' flashlights, having come together for a moment, go their separate ways through the dark, and she feels a stitch of guilt to see them looking for her out in the cold. There was a time not very long ago when she might have reveled in watching their fruitless search, but from up here, tonight, her parents look very small and very human. She doesn't have the energy to be angry. And for all she's put them through, she doesn't have the right. She leans back into the pillow of snow behind her and looks up. The wind whisks her breath away, and now and then the moon gleams through holes in the clouds. She turns her head to watch snow blow through the patch of light shining through the dormer window through which she crawled, fine as sand or ash. She's left the window open just enough that she can slip her fingers underneath to raise it to come back in, but even through a crack that small the snow is blowing into her room. Or her father's old room, she corrects herself. It is strange to imagine her father as a boy, sleeping in the same bed she'll sleep in tonight beneath the faded fire engines stamped along the wall.

She puts her hand into that patch of light and brushes up a spray of snow. The tiny flakes glint. Just then, a shadow appears in the light. Isabelle freezes, hardly dares to breathe. The shadow gets larger, and Isabelle waits for the window to open and her grandmother's head to emerge, or else for the window to be closed, shutting her out. She shuts her eyes and wills the shadow away, away, away. She will not be found. She will not be found. She will not be found. She counts to one hundred, and then slowly, she opens her eyes. The snow quietly blows through the window's cross-hatched light. The shadow is gone.

Of course it is, she thinks; she is a mystic. Her uncle has told her so. Look what had happened with her father's palms, and look now how she has been able to will away this shadow.

She is a mystic, and with her powers, she will make Maggie well.

ELEVEN

Sunday

I

At six thirty Wilson finally allows himself to get up. He has been awake most of the night, or semi-awake, in that restless place between sleeping and wakefulness where thought and dream merge. He gets out of bed as quietly as he can and begins to dress in the light by the window. It is still too early to tell whether the gray outside portends the day to come or it's leftover from the night and waiting to be colored by the sun. He looks from his robe to his corduroys. At home on a Sunday morning he would put his robe on, but here he's more inclined to dress completely, the way you would in someone else's house. He frowns. *Someone else's house,* he thinks to himself. *Someone else. He* is someone else, someone other than who he was when, young, he *would* wander these halls in a robe and slippers. He reaches for his corduroys.

Ruth lies curled on her side. She looks younger asleep, Wilson thinks. Her skin is smoother, her expression softer. She breathes quietly, long, deep breaths. He considers waking her to let her know that he is getting up; she won't be happy to wake and find herself alone. But if he wakes her, he knows she'll never fall back to sleep, and she looks at peace, for once, even if it's an unconscious peace. He watches her body rise and fall. Quietly, he leaves the room.

It is cold in the hallway. The doors of the other bedrooms on this floor are closed, and, he imagines, the furniture is covered in sheets, as if this were a summer home put away for the winter. At the end of the hall is his mother's old room. He pushes the door open and stands on the threshold. Even though she can manage stairs again, his mother has been living downstairs for a year now, since she broke her hip, but her old bedroom looks as if she lives there still; it is exactly as she left it. Old mail is stacked by the bed. A few shirts lie wrinkled on the chaise longue, and an old pair of sneakers sits beneath the dresser. There are photographs on the dresser, of Wilson's father, of his brothers and their families, one of Ruth and Wilson on their wedding day. It is as if his mother plans to move back up here one day, even though the space she has created downstairs is similarly cluttered, similarly her own.

He shuts the door behind him and goes to the staircase. He looks down the stairs; the light from the kitchen just illuminates the foyer. His mother's dog lies on his bed in the corner. Wilson coughs once, and the dog opens an eye. He is uninterested. Wilson then looks up the stairs to the third floor, where the hall light has been glowing for Isabelle all night. This floor was the children's floor; it is where Wilson and his brothers slept, where they played in the large nursery playroom. In a closet off the nursery are all his old things, his model airplanes and stuffed animals and building blocks and an old-fashioned bingo machine. Some of this stuff, he thinks, might interest Isabelle.

His footsteps are muffled by the staircase carpet. It has been treaded thin in the middle and faded over the years into a color Wilson can't name. It used to be green—or it may have been more of a golden color, he can't quite remember now. In the hallway, he passes his oldest brother's room on the right, another older brother's on the left, then his youngest brother's, and then Samuel's, who died the same year as their father, which was the year Isabelle was born. His own room is the last before the nursery. There are stickers on the door still: a Red Sox sticker, a Nixon-Lodge sticker, a sticker with his own name, handwritten. Inside, the walls are still pasted with the fire engine wallpaper he chose at age six, the bed the same he slept in, the little red dresser in the corner the one he kept his clothes in. Aside from being emptied of many of their things, all the Carter boys' rooms are the same as they have been for more than forty years, but hollow, dusty, barren, and cold, like some abandoned village. If he were Isabelle, he would never have chosen to sleep up here alone, but the fact that she is here, just on the other side of his door, is comforting. Her presence up here makes it seem more like a place than a memory.

He continues to the nursery, though a large part of him wants to wake Isabelle and bring her with him to rummage through old things, just so he feels more certain that his rummaging is for her sake and not his own, so that what he finds are toys rather than relics, things not to reminisce over but to be put to use. But it *is* for her sake, he tells himself; he needn't wake her so early to make it so. He thinks of the bingo machine, the old globe of a cage and the wooden numbered balls inside that roll out one by one with the turn of a handle. He imagines the three of them in front of the fire in the country, Isabelle cranking the handle and calling out numbers. Then he remembers his railroad set, the pieces of track he'd lay out across the nursery floor, around the life-size rocking horse in the corner, underneath the table where his sisters would sit with their puzzles. They could do this in the country, too, he thinks, excited now, pleased. These things will have new life; they've not been in retirement, but merely hibernation.

In the nursery, the wall of shelves still holds their childhood books, and the Oriental carpet lies thin as always and curled as always at the edges. A cuckoo clock hangs from a wall, across from the rocking horse. It reads 4:28. The hands aren't moving, and Wilson wonders what hour it was when the cuckoo emerged from his home for the last time. The couch along the other wall is draped with a sheet, has been for years, but on the coffee table before it, usually bare, is some kind of magazine—an L.L.Bean Christmas catalog, Wilson sees when he picks it up, and from this year. He sets it back on the coffee table and gazes at the couch, imagining his mother sitting there, marking down pages: a bathrobe for Wilson, a pair of gloves for his sister. When Wilson and his mother speak on the phone, he pictures her downstairs in the library, the fire going, the TV on, the dog at her feet, clutter on the floor beside her armchair, or else he imagines her in the kitchen having tea. He wonders how many times when he has pictured her down there she has actually been up here, in this museum of the family's past.

He crosses to the picture window. Outside, the trees on the horizon are darkening as the sky begins to glow behind them. He blows on his hands, imagining the cold outside. Still, it looks like it will be a nice day after all, clear, if cold. The traffic won't be too bad, that means, so they can stay at the very least until after lunch before they have to leave. A short visit, Wilson thinks, but worthwhile. Last night, when after another half hour of searching he and Ruth had returned to the house—both of them at the same time, which coincidence set Wilson's heart racing, because he thought that their approaching the house at the same time, their giving up the search at the same moment, could only be a bad sign—and gone inside and hurried to the kitchen, perhaps to use the phone (they hadn't exchanged words, just looks), they had found Isabelle there, at the table with her grandmother. Eleanor and Isabelle had looked up at Ruth and Wilson as if surprised to see them there, as if it had been Ruth and Wilson and not Isabelle herself who had gone missing into the night and then just as suddenly returned. Aside from Ruth's and Wilson's empty seats and the comparative cleanliness of the kitchen, the scene seemed to pick up exactly where it had left off nearly two hours before: there was a pot of tea on the table beneath a cozy, a plate of English muffins and another one of oatmeal cookies, and eggs on the boil.

They didn't ask what happened. They didn't ask where Isabelle had gone, or when she had returned, or how the two of them, Isabelle and her grandmother, happened to be sitting once again where they had been before as if they'd never been interrupted, as if the news about Maggie's sickness had never been let loose. Maggie herself lay on the dog bed in the corner, chewing on a piece of rawhide too intently to acknowledge Ruth and Wilson with more than a glance. Ruth caught Wilson's eye. Wilson blinked and gave her a semi-smile, and she followed his lead and pulled out a chair at the table, too cold and dazed with worry and relief to do more than take the tea she was offered and watch the steam curl upward from it, every now and then glancing through that curling steam at Isabelle, as if the steam would offer protection from what she expected to be Isabelle's looks of fury.

But Isabelle hadn't seemed angry at all. In fact, she looked calm, assured—the same way she looks this morning, Ruth thinks now, looking at her again across the kitchen table. Isabelle is fixing her third cup of tea, slowly dripping honey into the liquid with a spoon. Remnant Cheerios float fat and soggy with milk in the bowl beside her. Wilson's mother is at the stove, cooking bacon she's found stashed in the freezer. The sound of sizzling gets louder with each strip she adds to the skillet.

"Well, the bacon may be old," she calls, "but it still smells good!" She turns from the stove and settles at the table. "You like bacon, don't you?" she asks Isabelle.

Isabelle looks up from her tea and nods.

"Good. Sensible girl. Your cousin Monica has taken up this vegetarian nonsense." She shakes her head. "I keep telling Ellen not to let her, you know, one *must* have meat in one's diet." She sips her tea. The sun coming in through the kitchen window is almost blinding in her white hair. Ruth can feel the sun on her own back, can see her shadow falling with the shadows of the window sash and the shadow of the jams and jellies across the table. She picks at a mound of candle wax dried on the checkered tablecloth. She shifts in her seat. She feels left out of something, but what, she doesn't know.

"Ruth, dear." Ruth looks up. Her mother-in-law is buttering a muffin. The knife clatters against the butter dish as she puts it down. "I've got some things in the cellar you might want," she says. "An old table for outdoors, really lovely, iron, you know, but . . ."—she shrugs—"it's just sitting there, and Wilson mentioned your garden, and it might be just the thing."

"That sounds great," Ruth says. "I'd love to take a look."

"And an old toboggan. I've no use for it, and Darryl and Ellen's kids have several, I'm sure, and—Isabelle, do you have a toboggan?"

Isabelle shakes her head.

"Oh, well then, you *must* take it. *Such* a waste for it to just sit down there rotting. Oh!" she exclaims. "The bacon!"

The bacon does smell as if it's starting to burn; Ruth puts her hand on her mother-in-law's shoulder before the woman labors herself to the stove. "Let me," she says.

She turns the flame down and starts to flip each piece of bacon. The meat shrivels into itself, dancing on the grease and popping. Behind her, Wilson's mother is asking Isabelle if she'd like to visit the horses again this morning when the vet comes to look at Adrien's leg. There's a mare who's expecting, too, she is saying, and if Isabelle comes back to visit in the spring she can name the foal. If she's speaking by then, Ruth thinks bitterly, still standing over the bacon though she has already flipped every piece. What is her problem? she thinks. Why the cynicism? Why should part of her *want* Isabelle to be distraught, except for her suspicion that the only reason she *isn't* distraught is that her grandmother was somehow able to soothe her while Ruth and Wilson were out searching in the dark and cold?

But she is being silly, she tells herself. Isabelle is taking the news about Maggie well, and no matter what the reason, that is all she can ask. She clears her throat and turns around. "That's a real honor, Belle," she says, brightly, "to name a foal."

Isabelle smiles.

"I once let your father name a foal. And do you know what he chose?" There is a pause. Wilson's mother sits forward.

"My goodness!" The three women turn. Wilson is in the doorway, a large box under his arm. "Early birds! I thought you'd all still just be getting up."

Ruth purses her lips. "*You're* the early bird," she says.

"I didn't want to wake you." Wilson crosses to the table and sets the box down. "I've been in the closet upstairs." He sits down. "Found some things."

"Just a second, Wilson," Ruth says. "Your mother was in the middle of saying something."

"I beg your pardon," Wilson says. "Excuse me, Mother, go ahead."

"Well, I was just telling Ruth and Isabelle about how you named Mussolini."

"Mussolini?" Ruth's laugh is genuine. "You named a horse Mussolini?"

"I was six," Wilson says.

"Horribly inappropriate, but there we had it. Mussolini!"

"Do you know who Mussolini is, Belle?" Wilson glances at Isabelle as he pours himself a cup of tea.

"Of course she does, Wil. I've nearly bought the bookstore out of books on World War Two."

"That's right," Wilson says. "Of course. I guess I was still thinking of the Roman Empire kick." He looks at his mother. "Isabelle likes to read up on things pretty thoroughly," he explains.

Ruth looks at her husband. "Kick?"

"Yes, dear, I remember when it was that poet, that Emily Dickinson, and I found that old biography at Chamber's. Wonderful place, Chamber's. Goodness, I did send it, didn't I?"

Isabelle nods.

"Yes," Ruth says, glancing at her mother-in-law. "It came just in time for her birthday, actually." She looks again at Wilson. *Kick?* The Roman Empire was more than a month ago! Where has Wilson been?

They are quiet. Wilson's spoon clinks against the china as he sets it down. "Well," he says. "In any case."

Ruth turns back to the bacon. "Your mother is going to let Isabelle name a foal in the spring," she says, lifting the bacon one piece at a time from the skillet and setting each on a plate she's made ready with a paper towel.

"Is that so?" Wilson says.

Ruth watches bacon grease spread across the paper towel. She imagines Isabelle nodding her head, that mysterious smile still on her face. She wonders if Wilson finds it strange.

"Lucky girl!" he says.

Ruth turns from the stove. "Bacon," she says. She sets the plate down.

"Here she is," her grandmother says. "Agnes." The horse lifts her head and gazes at them. She blinks slowly, her eyelid lowering itself heavily over a big black globe of an eye. Isabelle has never seen eyelashes so long. "Hello, girl." The horse shifts her weight. Her nostrils quiver as she sighs. "Still tired, huh? Come here. This is Isabelle."

Her grandmother clicks her tongue at the horse and extends a hand. "That's right," she says. The horse sighs again and takes the few slow steps to the stall door. Her belly sways. "That's a girl." Isabelle watches her grandmother run her hand, clumsy and firm, down the horse's face. "Now where are those sugar cubes?"

Isabelle reaches into her jacket pocket for the handful of sugar cubes she's brought from the table. She holds them out for her grandmother to take. "No," she says. "You give them to her." Isabelle looks at the horse uncertainly. She has never been brave enough to feed the horses herself. "Go ahead."

Isabelle takes a cube between her fingers and holds it out for the horse.

"No." She feels her grandmother's hand on her shoulder. "Like this." Her grandmother takes Isabelle's hand in her own and presses it flat. She puts the sugar cube in her palm. "Keep your fingers together," she says. "They're very gentle, but they have bigger teeth than they know what to do with." Isabelle timidly extends her palm toward the horse. "That's it," her grandmother says. She feels the horse's hot breath in her hand, and the tickle of her huge lips as they scoop the sugar cube up.

"She'll foal in April. She's the only one this year."

The horse has stretched her neck over the stall door and nudges Isabelle's chest.

"She likes you." Isabelle reaches up and strokes the horse's face just in the way she has seen her grandmother do. Her face is solid and warm. "Go ahead and give her another sugar cube, if you want."

Isabelle flattens out her hand and places another sugar cube carefully on her palm. Agnes's lips are searching for it before Isabelle has even reached out all the way, her big yellow teeth flashing. "Get a good look at her so you can think of names that might suit her babe. They always look quite a lot like the mare, I think. They always seem to have the mother's eyes." Her grandmother cups the horse's cheeks, round and solid and strong. The hair looks softer there, and even softer on the neck, where it looks long enough to run fingers through. "Of course, we won't know whether it's a filly or a colt until it's born, so you'll have to come up with both boy and girl names."

Isabelle blinks at the horse. The horse blinks at her. She can see herself reflected in that eye, swallowed up again and again behind the heavy lashes. She traces the white streak that runs from the horse's forehead to her nose. She will have to be careful in choosing a name, she thinks. It is no small thing to be responsible for telling someone who he or she is.

"Knock knock," a man's voice calls. Isabelle and her grandmother turn around. A man stands just inside the door. He's wearing a long black coat with a bright red flannel scarf. White hairs curl from beneath his black wool hat, and behind a crooked pair of glasses his eyes glisten deep in their sockets.

"Dr. Marks!"

"Eleanor, my dear," he says. He pulls his hat from his head and gives a little bow. His curls waver. He returns the hat to his head, but with one free hand— the other holds a doctor's bag—all he can do is set it there. Isabelle watches it slide slowly to the side of his head and then to the floor.

"Ah, well, there goes the hat," he says.

"It's too cold to be polite, Dr. Marks," her grandmother says. The man has set his bag down and squatted to retrieve his hat. "You know you're losing heat by the second now. Up and out the top, like a chimney."

"And you," he says, standing, tugging the hat back over his ears, "in nothing but a handkerchief!"

"I've got lots of hair up here to keep me warm," she says. She pats the blue silk kerchief, stained and frayed along the edges. Underneath, her white hair is coiled and pinned. Isabelle wonders what it looks like down.

Isabelle looks from her grandmother to the man and the bag on the floor beside him. It is a triangular black leather bag, the kind old-fashioned doctors used. She wonders how old this doctor is. One of the bag's handles has broken and been mended with thick silver tape. "And who's this?" the man is saying. Isabelle looks up.

"This is Isabelle. Wilson's daughter."

"Isabelle!" he says. He crosses toward her. "It's very nice to meet you," he says. He grips her hand firmly with both of his. His eyes are a cold blue and seem to be peering past wrinkles and lashes and curls and the lenses of his glasses from somewhere very far away. They glow, it seems to Isabelle, and when she focuses on the glass before them instead of on the eyes themselves, she can see the reflection of Agnes behind her, and she imagines that in this reflection she can see in the horse's eyes her own self reflected there, staring at the reflection of a reflection.

"Isabelle is quite shy," her grandmother explains.

"Ah," Dr. Marks says. "Wilson's daughter, you said?"

"Yes."

Dr. Marks turns back toward Isabelle. "Your father was very shy, too, you know."

"It's something she'll have to work on, isn't it, Isabelle?"

Isabelle looks at her grandmother and then at the ground. The stable floor is cracked and strewn with scattered hay.

"Well, in good time," Dr. Marks says. He sniffs. Isabelle watches his boots cross back to his bag. They disappear beneath folds of coat as the man stoops down to open the bag. He pulls out a bandage roll and scissors. "And how does Mr. Adrien seem today?" he asks.

"We haven't been in to him this morning yet, but he seems to be doing remarkably well considering he cut his ankle, when was it, only a week ago?"

"Any limping? Visible signs of pain? Staining through the bandage?"

Isabelle watches her grandmother and this doctor walk slowly toward a stall. She follows at a distance. Her grandmother is shaking her head to each listed symptom.

"Appetite changes? Sometimes comes with infection."

"No." Her grandmother shakes her head. "I tell you I've never seen a horse heal so quickly. I don't know how you did it."

"Magic touch," Dr. Marks says. He has opened the stall door and crouched down. He runs his hand down the back side of Adrien's lower leg, and the horse curls his foot to be held. This horse is much bigger than Agnes. He is black and towering, his eyes quick. Isabelle watches nervously as he lets out a whinnying breath.

"Hey. Hey." Dr. Marks stands up and brings his face close against the horse. He whispers things that Isabelle can't hear. The horse's blinking slows. His stomach swells with deepening breaths, and he hangs his head. "That's a boy," the doctor murmurs. "Yes, you know. You know."

He pulls a stool from the corner of the room and sits at the horse's front feet. The horse allows him to hold the hoof this time long enough to cut away the bandage from around his ankle. "Yes," the doctor says. "Good boy." He looks up. "That was a nice-looking cut, too," he says.

"It's remarkable, didn't I say?"

Dr. Marks pulls a tube of ointment from his pocket and begins to massage it into the horse's leg.

"He cut it on a rusted fence wire," her grandmother says to Isabelle in a low voice.

Dr. Marks mutters to the horse as he rewraps the leg. The horse keeps his head low, as if he is listening. When the vet has tied the bandage off, he stands up and takes the horse's head in both his hands, bringing his own face close to the horse until they are touching, head to head.

Ruth stands by the bedroom window, her arms clutched across her chest. Behind her, Wilson is crouched on the floor, fiddling with the pieces of a phonograph player. The sky has clouded over after only a few hours of sunshine; it is barely noon, but dusk already seems well on the horizon.

"Are you going to have him look at Maggie?" Ruth squints in the direction of the barn, where her daughter and her mother-in-law have been since just after breakfast. Something clatters to the floor behind her.

"Shit," Wilson mutters.

She turns around. Wilson's elbows are perched on his knees. He holds a slender wire in each hand before his face, stares at one, then the other.

"Wilson," Ruth says.

"Yuh," he grunts.

"Are you going to have him look at Maggie?"

Wilson fastens the wire in his left hand to the back of the phonograph base. "Who?"

Ruth sighs and turns back to the window.

"Dr. Marks?" he asks.

"Yes, Wilson. The vet. Do you think we ought to let him take a look at the dog?"

"You've been talking to my mother," Wilson says. She hears a click as Wilson sets another piece of the phonograph machine into place. "Dr. Bremer has seen Maggie twice now," he says. "I think he's probably done for her everything there is to do."

"She doesn't seem well."

"She's not well."

"I'm just never going to forgive myself if we don't do everything we can," Ruth says, turning around again.

"Forgive yourself?" Wilson says. He looks up from his fiddling. "I think we've done everything we can and more. Believe me, if there was anything I thought Dr. Marks could do, I'd be the first to let him."

"Well, maybe there is. . . ."

"Ruth, the man's been in retirement for over a decade. But if you want to, then by all means."

Ruth follows his gaze toward Maggie. She lies

curled on the rug at the foot of the bed, her eyes half closed and glassy.

"She doesn't look well," Ruth says.

"No." Wilson frowns.

"I should never, never have insisted on getting her early. Shit. Shit." She turns around again.

"Getting her early?"

"From the vet, Wilson. Picking her up a day early." A cat slinks through the opened crack of the barn door and makes his way darkly along the side of the building, pausing there and then darting across the field, a tiny black bolt against the snow.

"Ruth."

She says nothing.

Wilson fiddles in the silence.

"The strange thing is, she seems fine about it," Ruth says.

"About what? Who?" His voice is distant, coming from a world of bingo machines and record players.

"About the dog, Wilson. When we got back last night, and then this morning. I'd think she'd be, I don't know. I expected worse after she disappeared to wherever she did. But she just seems to be taking it so well."

"Isabelle? Is that necessarily a bad thing?"

Ruth hesitates. "No," she falters. "I don't know." The trees outside bend as one in a gust of wind. Ruth hadn't noticed any wind until now. She shivers. "It's cold up here."

"Mmm."

"I think a front might be coming through."

"Mmm."

She turns around, holding her lips tight around a mouthful of frustration that swells and evaporates almost at once at the sight of her husband on the floor. His cowlick is raised and his eyes are triangled in concentration as he works on the silly old machine before him, the box of other finds away to the side. He sat proudly at the kitchen table this morning, pulling from the box an old bingo machine and a railroad set and a stuffed animal leaking cotton at its seams, and then, after his mother took Isabelle out to the barn, he led Ruth upstairs to show her the best of his finds, an old phonograph player, which with a little work, he has said, will be good as new, and wouldn't it be just the sort of thing that Isabelle would love for Christmas?

Wilson feels her gaze and looks up; against the bright background of white snow, white sky out the window behind her, she is mostly silhouette, her face and body dark. "What?" he says.

She sighs. "Nothing," she says. "I just wish you'd focus."

"I'm trying to," he says, unfastening the tone arm from its hinge.

"Not on the phonograph machine."

He doesn't answer; he wants to make sure he's got all the pieces he needs to this machine before they leave his mother's this afternoon; it would be typical, he thinks, if they got back to the city and he realized only then that he'd left some important part behind. And the cousins are coming, when? He glances at his watch—in just an hour, and then, if there really is a front coming through, they should get on the road, and so it's now or never. He swallows. The cousins. He hasn't yet told Ruth that they are coming; he didn't know himself until his mother mentioned it as they'd stood side by side at the sink, elbow deep in breakfast suds. *Laurie's family,* his mother had said, meaning her late brother's wife; Wilson isn't sure if he's even met these cousins before.

He lifts the tone arm of the player. The needle seems to be relatively well intact, and the table spins, and so as long as the transducer works—and he thinks he's got it all hooked up right—the machine should be good to go. He connects the wires from the amplifier to the speaker and looks up.

"Ruth," he says.

She looks at him.

"My mother mentioned that a few cousins might be stopping by for lunch."

Ruth shuts her eyes. "How considerate of you to let me know," she says.

"I just learned myself."

"What does that mean, 'a few'?"

"Laurie's family," he says. "Benton's wife."

"And that means . . ."

Wilson puts the tone arm back in place, struggling to screw it in with his fingertips.

"*Wilson.*"

337

He looks up. "Sorry," he says. "I don't know what that means."

"Knowing your family, that could mean a small village," she says.

"Well, I don't know what to tell you, Ruth," Wilson says. "It wasn't my idea, it wasn't my plan, but we're here, and they're coming, and as soon as lunch is over, we can get out of here and we never have to come visit my mother again. *Fuck*. This goddamn piece of shit!" But just as he says it, he gets the screw to catch the thread, and the tone arm is affixed. He feels himself turn red. "I'm sorry," he says. "It's not my ideal plan either, but you know my mother."

"Yes, I know your mother, Wilson, and I adore your mother, you know that, so don't pull that on me."

Wilson raises an eyebrow.

"It's just—cousins?"

Wilson sighs. He pulls a record from its jacket and blows it free of dust. "I don't think you're exactly in the position to give me shit about my family," he says. His voice is low. "Let's remember exactly why we were a day late in getting here." He swallows and looks up.

Ruth has turned back to the window. Her head is down, and a strand of hair arches up from her head on its way back to where her elastic has gathered all her hair together.

"And we can go as soon as we've finished lunch. We can use the weather as an excuse."

"No, Wil, I'm sorry. You shouldn't have to apologize." She lets out a loud breath. "It's just Jimmy, and then here, and now cousins, and the dog, and do you know school starts two weeks from tomorrow?"

Wilson sniffs and puts the record onto the turntable. "I know," he says, though he hadn't been aware of the precise date, and liked it that way. Now there's a countdown: fourteen days. What the hell in fourteen days is going to change things he can't imagine.

Ruth puts her hands on her hips and turns around. "I just don't know. I don't know. I don't know. I don't know what we're going to do." She squeezes her eyes shut and then opens them wide. "About anything." She brushes her hands against her thighs, as if she has put away the topic. She sniffs. "I just saw your mother and Isabelle on their way back from the barn," she says. She looks at the phonograph player, the record finally ready on the table. "Finished with that?"

Wilson nods. "Think so," he says, and gently, he places the needle in the record's groove. The speaker crackles as the record spins, and both Ruth and Wilson stare at the machine. The record wobbles and spins, wobbles and spins, and they watch and they wait for the music to come, the air thick with anticipation, but finally it is clear that even after all Wilson's work something isn't right—maybe the wires are wrong, or the needle is too worn after all, or the amplifier isn't picking up its signals, or the transducer isn't converting—and the needle traces the groove deeper into the record, far beyond where the music should have begun, but no, something is not right; it could be anything, really, Wilson has no idea. It seems a long moment of just staring, a moment, he thinks, like that after a child has fallen and cannot decide the best way to react, whether to let loose a wail or to brush off and keep on. Finally he blinks and looks up at his wife. Ruth has a hand over her mouth, covering what Wilson fears is an expression of pity, but then when his eyes meet hers, though hers are filled with tears, she lowers her hand and starts to laugh.

Wilson blinks at her again, and slowly starts to laugh himself, and Ruth starts laughing louder, and he laughs louder, too. He lowers his head into his hands and laughs, big, heaving laughs, and they laugh, and they laugh, and the record player silently spins.

TWELVE

I

The highway has narrowed to a single lane for the snowbanks spilling onto the road, and Wilson can't stop himself from flinching as snowflakes flash into the headlight beams and swoop up against the windshield, even though he knows there is a pane of glass between them. The windshield wipers flap in slow motion, it seems, calling his attention away from the road; he snaps them off.

Ruth chuckles lightly; he glances toward her.

"I'm sorry," she says. "I don't know why I find it so amusing still."

"The phonograph player?"

"No!" she says, her tone more subdued. "No, that wasn't really funny."

Snow is gathering fast at the bottom of the windshield; Wilson will have to turn the wipers on again soon. "Then what?"

She laughs again. "They were French!"

Wilson nods. "That they were."

"Don't you think that's funny, a little?"

"I guess."

"No, you don't. You don't see the humor in it at all." Ruth shakes her head and runs a finger beneath her eyes. "It's just . . ." She shakes her head again and sniffs. "I don't know, there was nothing we could do. Nothing we could say. *Bonjour, oui, Je m'appelle Ruth, c'est Isabelle,* and that's about fucking it. How liberating!"

Wilson flips the wipers back on. They groan as they heave the load of snow that has settled in only minutes up and off the glass; for a minute, Wilson worries that they might break under the weight. The golden arches of a McDonald's glow up ahead, the post that holds them invisible in the dark; they seem to float. He glances in the rearview mirror, as if he might again catch a glimpse of his mother standing in her driveway, the blue kerchief flapping around hair so white it was hard to tell where hair ended and snow began, the French cousins beside her with their arms raised and their hands fluttering good-byes. *"Au revoir,"* he says.

"What?"

"Au revoir," he says, more loudly. "That's another one."

"Oh," Ruth says. She uncrosses her legs and sets her feet on the dashboard. *"Bouche de Noel."*

Wilson slows to squint at a highway sign; he clears his throat. *"Bon appétit."*

Ruth looks at him, her head tilted in amusement. *"Merci beaucoup."*

Wilson pauses. "Caviar."

Ruth laughs, a full, throaty laugh. "Caviar!"

"Why not?"

"Translate caviar."

"Little mini fish eggs." He grins to himself. "Salty. Delicious. Expensive."

"I don't know, Wil. Caviar might be pushing it."

Bonne nuit, Isabelle thinks in the back. Her father has put the seat down so that she and Maggie can stretch themselves out their full lengths. *Bonne nuit,* she remembers, was stitched across one of her earliest nightgowns. She gazes past her toes toward her parents' heads, dark shapes against the speckled windshield. Their voices have woken her, but she hasn't stirred; she doesn't want to distract them from what they do when they think that she's asleep. She lets her eyes roll upward through the back windshield; the wiper clunks from side to side, smudging an arch of dirt that glows a hazy orange under each infrequent roadside light. Beside her, Maggie stretches and lets out a series of tired grunts; Isabelle rolls onto her side and takes Maggie's head in her hands. The dog opens an eye, shuts it. The fur of her ears spills from between each of Isabelle's fingers.

Isabelle shuts her eyes and makes quiet whispering sounds, shaping soundless air around her tongue. She brings Maggie's forehead to her own and holds it there, just as Dr. Marks had done with Adrien. *Magic touch,* he'd said, and he'd winked at her, and in that moment she knew that he was a mystic, and that he knew she was one, too. She had watched him carefully, learned just what she'd need to do to make Maggie well, just as Dr. Marks had made Adrien well.

She shivers with relief at the magical, lucky timing of it all—her uncle's visit to the city, and then their visit to her grandmother's—and how in only a weekend she had learned about both a terrible problem—Maggie's illness—and a miraculous solution—her own mystical powers. Normally, she might question those powers, but she has *evidence:* her silence like Julian of Norwich's silence, the lines in her father's hands, the shadow outside the window, Dr. Marks's knowing wink. She holds her eyes shut tight, concentrating, concentrating, feeling the point of Maggie's skull against her head, her nose against the white strip that runs up Maggie's big black face, giving Maggie strength, making her well.

"Wilson, you are driving like my mother."

Wilson glances at the speedometer; he is driving well under the speed limit. "Not your mother," he says. "Maybe someone's. Not yours."

"You know what I mean."

The closer to the city they have gotten, the more Wilson has slowed their speed. Now he puts his foot more firmly on the gas. "Sorry," he says. He clutches the wheel and takes a breath, willing himself out with it. But he shuts his mouth, breathes out loudly through his nose.

Ruth looks over at him. Her feet are on the dashboard, toes to the glass. "What?" she says.

He gently clears his throat and glances in the rearview mirror. He can see neither Isabelle nor Maggie where they lie stretched out in the back. "I think your brother might still be there," he says. His voice is low. He scratches the side of his head, though it doesn't itch.

Ruth faces forward again. He sees her blink rapidly out the windshield from the corner of his eye. "You think what?" she says.

"I called to check the messages, and someone answered."

Ruth shakes her head. "Wait a second, Wilson, what are you talking about? What do you mean you called to check the messages? I'm not following you. What do you mean someone answered?"

"The answering machine I bought this fall. You can check the messages, and I called before we left to check them and someone answered. Your brother answered. I think."

Ruth pulls her lips over her teeth as she ponders this. "And what did he have to say?" she says finally.

"I hung up."

Ruth grips her temples with a hand: thumb and pinky. "Are you saying you think my brother is still at the apartment?"

"I think so." Wilson takes a breath. "But it could have been the wrong number. I could have misdialed."

"Well, did you try back? After you hung up, did you call back?"

"Yes."

"And?"

"The machine picked up."

"And why didn't you say anything until now?"

Wilson doesn't answer; he doesn't know why. The ridges in the highway thunk beneath them, one-two, one-two, one-two.

"Wilson?"

He stares at the bumper sticker on the car in front of them. *Morning Has Broken,* it says.

"Wilson," Ruth repeats, loudly.

He glances again in the rearview mirror, checking for Isabelle. "It could have been the wrong number," he says quietly. "And what difference would it have made?"

Now Ruth is silent.

"Would we have stayed at my mother's? It's Christmas Eve. Of course we're coming home." He changes lanes to pass the car with the bumper sticker, driving quickly now.

"It's the principle," Ruth says. "That's all."

She shivers in the chill as her father rolls down the window to pay the toll above the West Side Highway. She can hear the voice of the tollbooth operator, but she cannot make out the words.

"Thank you," she hears her father say. "Merry Christmas."

The window whines as it goes up, and Isabelle's ears pop in the muted vacuum of the car; the sounds of outside had sounded so crisp in the cold, and clear.

She sits upright for the rest of the drive to look out at the dark ice floes on the Hudson, the occasional hooded figure hunched along the river rails, the George Washington Bridge aglow, the swooping lights of its cables. There is traffic on the bridge tonight. It goes both ways.

Her father sets the blinker long before their exit; the flicker of the arrow on the dashboard lights his face so that she can see the lines running back from his eyes; he might be squinting, but she can't tell for sure. She's not sure why he would squint in the dark.

She clucks her tongue along with the tock of the blinker, keeps clucking even after they have made their turn.

"Isabelle," her mother says.

She stops.

The traffic is slow-moving as they cross the city. She rests her elbows on her knees and lowers her chin into her hands, letting herself lurch back and forth as the traffic stops and starts. They slowly pass a Christmas tree stand set up in a lot where she has seen flea markets before, and once a school fair; the trees are still stacked against one another three deep at least, the lanterns strung above them swaying gently. There are only a few hours left until Christmas Day, and she wonders what will happen to all the leftover trees. It makes her sad to think of a tree, grown its whole life to be decorated and loved, instead left to dry out and die on a curb, or to be tossed with trash onto one of those garbage islands where seagulls scream and dead bodies are found. She can picture it: a mound of dented car parts, garbage bags, cardboard, Styrofoam, bent bicycle frames, old tires, body parts, and Christmas trees. She frowns. The trees deserve better than that.

She hears her mother suck a breath in loudly through her teeth as the car stops abruptly. A car has pulled out fast in front of them; its window goes down and a fist comes out, but the cars behind them have begun to honk, and the car squeals away, the last to make it through the light.

"I swear to God," her father mutters, peering up at the stoplight.

A church on the corner is letting out; men standing in each door of the church hold baskets of candy canes, which they hand out to the members of the congregation as they leave, a flow of people in their best winter coats all hurrying home to hang their stockings or light a fire, the girls Isabelle's age in the black patent-leather shoes and white tights that she knows she would be wearing were she now coming home from church. She is glad to be in her blue jeans instead.

The light changes, and everything gets dark as they cross the park. She lies down again beside Maggie. She strokes the dog absently, staring up through the window at the topmost branches of trees reaching against the orange sky, and she is just getting dizzy when the car comes to a stop. She can tell from the arched streetlamp in her view that they have come to the other edge of the park. The blinker is on again, signaling their right-hand turn, and she clucks twice, then stops; she does not want to irritate her mother. If Jimmy really is at home, as she has overheard he might be, Isabelle wants her mother to be in the best mood she can be in. She puts her feet up against the ceiling and watches her dangling laces sway as the car resumes its motion, bringing them closer to home. Her socks are striped, red and green for Christmas. It's *Christmas,* after all, she thinks. Even if he hasn't been invited, Jimmy has no one else to spend the holiday with, and it seems unkind not to let him stay.

She rolls herself upright as her father stops the car in front of their building. In the front seat, her parents are looking at each other, neither one of them reaching for door handles or unbuckling seat belts. She looks from one of them to the other, waiting. Her father takes a breath, as if to speak, but her mother breaks in. *"Ne dis rien,"* she snaps.

"Ruth—"

"Eh!"

Her father shakes his head, unfastens himself, and gets out of the car. Her mother follows suit. Isabelle waits in the back for someone to lift the tailgate; she can see out the window her parents discussing, planning. Her mother's mood is *not* good, she can tell. Finally, the tailgate whines upward and she scrambles from the car. "Hey, my friend!" She looks up; it is the new doorman, Brian, who has released her. She smiles at him gratefully.

"Isabelle." She turns at the sound of her father's voice. "Why don't you go with your mother and take the dog across the street?" Isabelle puts a hand on her hip. She isn't stupid, she thinks. She's going to be banished across the street while her father goes upstairs and gets rid of Jimmy. She frowns and shakes her head.

"Isabelle," her father says. "I need you to cooperate."

Brian leans down to her. "I think you might be spoiling a Christmas surprise," he says in a low voice. "Better go with your mom."

She swallows; she does not want to embarrass herself in front of Brian; she does not want to be scolded.

Her mother is helping Maggie from the car. Her father gestures toward them with his chin, and grudgingly, as her mother leads Maggie toward the crosswalk, Isabelle follows. The light is just beginning to blink, warning them that soon it will change, but she knows there is time enough to make it across if they hurry. She steps off the curb; her mother puts a hand on her shoulder.

"Let's wait," she says, looking down at Maggie. Maggie settles on the corner, chin between her paws.

Isabelle turns around. Her father is in discussion with Brian. She can see his mouth moving, his hands gesturing. Brian nods, nods again, his eyes getting smaller and smaller as her father continues to talk at him. She glances up at her mother. Her mother has also turned around, but instead of watching Brian nod at gestures and commands, her eyes are raised to the building's windows. Isabelle follows her gaze, counting five flights up to their floor—where the windows are lit! So Jimmy must be there, she thinks, and just as she is thinking this, a shape appears in the living room window, and "Isabelle!" she hears her mother say, sudden and panicked.

"I want you to go! Go! Hurry, go with your father!"

Isabelle looks back toward the car and the awning where her father and Brian had been standing; they have gone inside. She feels her mother's hand on her back, urging her back toward the building, and suddenly she is afraid. She doesn't know what she is afraid of, exactly; she is afraid because her mother is afraid, and her mother is never afraid. She looks at her mother; her mother's eyes are wide and worried. "Go! Go! Go, hurry, go!"

Isabelle feels hot, feels cold, doesn't know what she feels as she races back to the building, stumbling over her laces twice. She is aware of the oddest sensations: her pulse in her ear, the ragged edge of toenail catching on her sock, a quivering just beneath her right eye. She does not wait for the lobby doors to open for her; she thrusts the weight of her entire body against them, but her fingers cannot work the latch, and she peers through the bars and glass in panic as Brian crosses the lobby to open the doors for her, almost falls through them when he does.

"Isabelle!" he calls after her as she runs through the lobby. *Stop,* she is thinking, willing it as she's never willed anything before—the shadow away, or

Maggie's health—summoning up all and any powers she might have, even if it means she'll use them up forever. *Stop!* She rushes to the end of the front room, where she'll turn a corner and at the end of the hallway either will or will not see her father standing there still waiting for the elevator, where she'll know whether or not she is too late. Her sneakers squeal against the marble as she takes the turn, and she can just see her father's heel following the rest of him into the elevator, and she knows she will not make it there in time, the doors will close and the elevator will rise without her, and her father will be alone upstairs with Jimmy, and if anything happens it will be her fault, it will be because she did not make it there in time. She can hear the elevator hum as it gears up to shut its old doors and take her father away, and she staggers again over her laces, cannot quite catch herself, falls, and "Dad!" she cries.

And she is gone. Not gone: but above it all, looking down. She sees herself on the lobby floor, a growing puddle of bright red blood on the tiles. She sees herself bring a hand to her nose; she watches the blood drip down her fingers, roll down her wrist and into her sleeve. She sees the books from her backpack scattered around her, and suddenly she is in her father's old bedroom again, putting her books into her backpack when her mother comes to tell her that the cousins have arrived, slinging her backpack on before it is zipped and following her downstairs, and her backpack is unzipped in the hall as they eat Yorkshire pudding and roast beef, and it is unzipped in the car as they drive home, and it is unzipped as she runs through the lobby and crashes to the tiles, but it is only now, as the blood from her nose seeps into the cuff of her sweater and the books lie all around her, that she realizes that it has been unzipped all this time.

She sees her father's foot caught cartoonlike in the elevator door, holding it open, and she can hear the confused shifting of the elevator's gears; she sees her father's hands prying open the door, and then she sees him kneeling before her, his head from above a funny lump on the platter of his shoulders, and he is pulling away the hand she's put to her nose, asking her, *Does it hurt? Does it hurt?*

Next she sees her mother hurrying through the lobby, not checking to see that the door has closed behind her before dropping Maggie's leash, and then dropping her pocketbook, and then shrugging her coat from her shoulders, shedding these things as she nears Isabelle as if in shedding them she will get there faster, leaving them all in her wake, finally kneeling also before her daughter and saying, *Jesus Christ, do we need a doctor?*

And then Brian is there, and he is holding her mother's pocketbook, her mother's coat, and he has gathered up Isabelle's books, and Maggie is yipping at the end of her leash at the commotion, circling them, and then all of them are in the back elevator, because Wilson has jammed the door of the front elevator, and the back elevator smells of mildew, and they can see the bricks of the shaft passing as they rise in the cagelike enclosure, can feel the *thunkthunk, thunkthunk* of the ancient wheel turning high in the shaft above them, hoisting them up, up, and up. Isabelle puts a hand to her nose, and that slightest touch zaps back through her head like jagged lightning, blooming and branching in a sudden, shocking way that forces Isabelle to shut her eyes. Blood thunders through her brain.

When she opens her eyes they are all crowded at the back door by the garbage and recycling bins, Brian rattling through his giant ring of keys, but before he has found the key that will open their back door, the door opens in what seems a flash, seems to simply disappear, and hulking there in the doorway, a silhouette against the kitchen's stark fluorescent light, is Jimmy, a large cutting knife in his hand.

"Fuck!" Isabelle cries, her heart pounding in fear, her head pounding in a matching pain. "Fuck!" and with that, it is as if she is released from whatever distant place she has gone, she is slingshotted into the now: Christmas Eve, their kitchen in the city, everything suddenly in precise and startling detail.

The smell of garlic is thick enough to taste. Water runs in the kitchen sink, giving rise to a cloud of steam that fogs the window above. A marbled rack of lamb sits on the table in a pooling sauce of wine and rosemary, the rib bones skinny fingers, clawing the air. On the stovetop, oven-ready, is a tray of new potatoes, the white flesh beneath the pink of their skins exposed where they have been cut in two. A spillage of flour dusts the countertop near the fridge, where an egg carton holds empty shells. Relief and disbelief at once surge through Isabelle's limbs, which feel heavy and hot. Her head pounds, and she can taste the blood from her nose when she licks her lips. She blinks up at her uncle. "You're cooking dinner?" she says.

II

Later, Isabelle lies in bed with her eyes closed, an ice pack across her nose, waiting for the pain in her head to subside. A tray with dinner and a glass of milk sits untouched on her bedside table. In the kitchen, her parents sit with Uncle Jimmy; she can hear the click of the cutlery and the distant hum of their voices. Periodically, one of them comes in to check on her, holding open her eyes to peer in at her pupils, which are still not big and black enough to mean concussion. She doesn't think they'll get that big; the pain has diminished enough that she imagines that if she could see it, it would be quite beautiful, her brain like one of those clear globes slivered through with pink electricity. She is sure that this image would not have occurred to her earlier, when it was all she could do to sit down at the kitchen table before her legs buckled beneath her, the noisy coursing of blood like little subway cars thundering through her head.

Though not as noisy as the sound of her own voice crying out *Fuck!* and before that *Dad!* She opens her eyes. Two hundred and ninety-nine days of silence broken just like that, and nothing had *happened*. When she thinks about it now, she's not sure what she'd been expecting, what exactly she'd been afraid of; in this case, all that had happened was exactly what she wanted to happen: her father heard her, and he turned around. She frowns; what she could not achieve through force of will, she achieved through speech. She hadn't *meant* to speak, but out the words had come, and now that she has spoken, she has no excuse not to speak again. She knows now that she can. And her parents know it, too. What's puzzling to her is that while *Dad* and *fuck* had been accidental exclamations, it was she, Isabelle, and not panic that had caused her next utterance: *You're cooking dinner?* Those words had come so easily, as if *Dad* and *fuck* had punctured the balloon of her silence, had broken some kind of spell.

Her silent spell, she thinks, though she wonders if that's what it was at all, if she was even a mystic to begin with. She may have drawn those lines in her father's palm and then Uncle Jimmy might have pushed him, and she may have willed that shadow away at her grandmother's house, and she may have sensed that connection with Dr. Marks, but then when she really needed to make something happen, as a mystic, she had failed. She had not been able to will her father to turn around. She shuts her eyes again. Maggie, she thinks. But what about Maggie? What if, in speaking, she has jeopardized whatever powers she might have had? It was, after all, her silence that made Uncle Jimmy think she was a mystic to begin with. The thought makes her desperate.

"Knock knock." She hears Uncle Jimmy outside her door. A triangle of light from the hallway falls onto her carpet as he pushes the door open and turns on her bedside light. "How you doing?" he says. "Let's see." Uncle Jimmy, claiming expertise gained during the war, has proudly taken the role of doctor, and to Isabelle's surprise, he is very gentle, very kind.

Obediently, she turns her head toward him, lets him pry open her eyelids to check the pupils. "Still good," he says. "Not too big. Let's see the nose." He lifts the ice pack. "Rudolph," he says. He winks, and there is a glimmer in his eye that makes Isabelle grab his hand before he can turn away.

"Uncle Jimmy," she says, because she has to know. "What can a mystic do?"

He looks down at her. "A mystic," he says, "can only be." He winks again. "Want me to reheat this dinner?" he says.

Isabelle shakes her head.

Jimmy returns to the kitchen, where Wilson and Ruth sit at the table, each of them looking as shell-shocked as they feel.

"She'll be okay," Jimmy says. "Pupils aren't dilated. And she's alert. Nose isn't broken, either."

"Thank you, Jimmy," Ruth says. She swallows. "I'm glad you're here. I'm glad you were here to help."

"Wouldn't have been if it weren't for the snow," he says. He pulls out his chair. "I don't expect the

airports will be running smoothly tomorrow either."
He looks at his watch. "I'm going to take the first
train I can. Want to get back for the girls."

"Of course you do," Ruth says.

Across the table, Wilson fiddles with a meatless
lamb bone.

"Wilson," she says.

He looks up.

"Let's go to the country tomorrow. If the roads are
clear enough."

"Really?"

"Let's get out of here. Let's just go. There'll be so
much snow."

"What about presents?"

"We can do presents when we get back. We'll bring
a few, but we can have another Christmas when we
get back. What do you think?"

Wilson nods. He turns to Jimmy. "We can drive
you partway, then," he says. "Put you on a train in
New Haven or somewhere."

"Yes," Ruth says. "And then you won't have to
deal with getting to Grand Central and all that."

Jimmy nods. "That's good," he says. "That'll work
out fine."

III

He has cracked the window, as Ruth has asked;
though it is still warm in the room, as he stands at
his dresser he can already feel the cold air around his

feet. He imagines it pouring in through the half-inch opening, pooling on the floor, rising all night like a cold tide under which, come morning, they will be fully submerged, the two of them huddled against each other underneath the blankets.

He scratches at his ankle with a bare toe. His toenail is sharp; he winces. He stares at Isabelle's lion on his dresser, retrieved by Ruth from the shrink along with the sketchbook. Isabelle's voice echoes through his head, calling him, *Dad!* At the time, he had wondered if it was a creation of his mind. There were things he knew he heard: Brian's voice calling Isabelle's name, her footsteps on the lobby floor, the squeal of her sneakers and the rattle of the chain that dangles from her backpack coming closer toward the elevator doors, the dull sound of her crashing, knees and elbows and nose against marble—and all of this punctuated by her calling out for him, he had thought, but wasn't sure— wasn't sure until they stood there at the back door and she'd cried out exactly what her mother would have: *Fuck!* And in that moment, whatever segment of life they'd been living for the past nine months had ended. He blinks. What he's unsure of is what new segment they've begun. They don't need Africa, he thinks. They don't need shrinks. He thinks.

"Wil."

Wilson looks over his shoulder. Ruth has turned out her bedside light, her head a dark shape against the pillow.

"You coming to bed?"

Wilson turns back to his dresser. "Yes," he says. He folds the lion into fourths and tucks it into the drawer that holds his medicines, their passports.

Ruth throws back the covers on Wilson's side of the bed. "Come," she says.

Wilson pauses at his dresser, his hand on the light switch. The bottom of his nightshirt wavers in the draft from the window, and she can see where his leg hairs end at his sock line. She pictures him crouched with Isabelle on the lobby floor, the helpless look on his face as he held their daughter, who could hardly catch her breath through her tears, and it makes her want to run and hold them both again.

Wilson turns off the dresser light. He is a dark figure making his way to bed. "Now what?" he says.

She feels the mattress sink under his weight. "What do you mean?" she says, although she knows what he means. He means, what will they do next? He means, what will happen tomorrow? He means, yes, their daughter said *Dad,* and *fuck,* and *you're cooking dinner?*—but will she speak again? "I know what you mean," she says.

There was a time when she imagined that any word coming from Isabelle's mouth would be a burst of light, a sunrise, the beginning of a new day on which they'd embark full force, leaving the silent night behind them; she feels instead as if they are beginning a march through a minefield, where any misstep might be the end of them.

"I think," she says finally, "we just have to take each day as it comes."

Wilson nods.

"We don't know what will happen," she says.

"What about school?"

"First, tomorrow," she says. "Tomorrow first."

THIRTEEN

Christmas Day

I

They stand, the three of them, shin deep in snow, their eyes slits against sun that seems to come at them from all directions, the morning an explosion of light. A bird cries out somewhere in the woods behind them. A branch cracks. A gust of wind blows a shimmering cloud of snow from the needles of an evergreen.

"Well," Wilson says.

The apple tree lies horizontal before them, snapped at the trunk. Jagged splinters rise from the stump.

"Firewood," he says, shrugging.

Ruth turns to him. "Don't joke."

Isabelle lifts the shovel from where she's stood it upright in the snow. She looks at the path she's shoveled to get them here, a perfect line from house to tree through an unbroken field of snow. She turns and sets off shoveling toward the swing set.

Ruth follows the path back to the house.

Wilson stands where he is. A bird lands on a branch of the fallen tree and stops to preen beneath its wing. Wilson thinks at first it is a robin, but it is only December, Christmas Day. The hook for the hammock juts up from the tree's trunk, the silver glinting in the sunlight. The bird looks up at Wilson, puffs itself, and flies away.

The microwave is broken; the split pea will take an hour at least to thaw completely. She knocks it from its Tupperware; it thuds against the bottom of the soup pot. She turns the burner on and jabs at the soup with a wooden spoon, but she hardly makes a dent. Carrot coins that have frozen where they settled at the bottom of the plastic stare up at her now like wide orange eyes; she covers them with a silver lid.

The glass slider opens, clicks shut. Ruth can hear Wilson stamping the snow from his boots in the doorway. He comes up behind her; his lips are cold on the back of her neck.

"Lunch already?"

"It has to thaw."

She hears his footsteps passing through the kitchen.

"Where are you going?"

The footsteps pause. "Garage."

"Wait, Wilson!"

"I know," he calls. "I know. The goddamn door."

Ruth looks at the milk in the saucepan beside the soup pot; it is steaming and ready for cocoa. The back door opens. The back door shuts. Ruth shakes her head and smiles.

She stirs the milk and cocoa and turns around to gaze out the window. A path leads from the house to the apple tree, from the apple tree to the swing set, and from the swing set to somewhere Ruth cannot see from here—to Isabelle, neatly heaving snow aside with a shovel bigger than she is.

Somewhere in the garage there is a chainsaw. He'd know where, exactly, if only he'd clean things up a little, get rid of the clutter. But how often has he thought this?

His eyes scan the back wall, where a rusty saw hangs. He stands on a box to reach it; the cardboard is weak, and his foot falls through and into the box. Inside, mice have made a nest among Isabelle's old schoolbooks, but no one is home. He pushes the box aside and reaches on his toes for the saw. He holds it up in the light streaming in through the high, boxy windows; the teeth are dull.

The power drill is where he left it weeks ago, on the floor beside a flashlight and spare hooks for the zip cord, which by now, if the wire's even free of ice, will be too low to the snow-raised ground for riding. In the spring, he thinks. When the snow melts.

His eyes wander from the drill to his father's old toolbox to the trash can full of rags to the workbench he'd built from a kit but never used. Piled on this are loose screwdrivers, a level, a staple gun, a coiled hose and sprinkler, an emergency roadside kit, paddles for a canoe, which now is upside down and wholly buried under snow down by the swamp; winter came on so suddenly he'd forgotten to bring it in. He lowers his eyes, and he's almost forgotten what he's doing in here at all when he sees beneath the workbench, between a folded tarp and an ancient pair of ski boots, the chainsaw he's been looking for.

The legs of the old piano bench are rickety. The piano is an upright, cherry wood. Half-moon ruts from fingernails scar the wood above the keys. A mug of cocoa steams on the lid. She is hot from shoveling, but her extremities are numb: her feet, her nose, her fingers. It is as if they are gone, as if her arms and legs both end in stumps. She has often heard that a chicken runs around even after its head has been cut off, that amputees can feel pain or itching in a missing limb, and she wants to know if, similarly, her fingers can play without her, or if she can play without her fingers, whichever it is.

Her mother is in the other room, but she doesn't care. It is too much energy to care, to restrain herself from playing for no good reason she can remember. She wonders if there ever was a good reason, for any of it. Hearing her play will only make her mother happy. She can make her mother happy, wants to. And Maggie used to like to hear her play, would come and settle beside the bench, and if this is all she can do for her dog now, she will. Her father has explained to her that Maggie has a one-in-five chance, and though Isabelle has no use for probability, she takes comfort in these numbers, and the fact that they have nothing to do with her.

She looks at the keys, imagining where her fingers will go, and how the piece will sound, and then she holds her fingers just above them. They are red and swollen, her fingers, little sausages. She tells them to bend, and though she can't feel them, or what she is sure must be creaking in her knuckles, they do. She looks at the cocoa atop the piano. The marshmallows will have melted already, and the bottom of the mug will have left a ring of fog on the wood.

In the kitchen, Ruth pauses above Maggie's dish, which is still full with this morning's breakfast. Ruth frowns. She wanders into the family room, where Maggie lies by the picture window beside the heating vent. Ruth peers at her closely, watches the gentle rise and fall of her ribs, too easily visible.

"Maggie." She says it quietly. Maggie breathes.

Ruth kneels beside the dog; Maggie opens a glazed eye. The fur beneath her ears is matted.

"Here." Ruth takes a single piece of kibble from the measuring cup. Maggie sniffs it without lifting her head. Her nose is dry. "Please, eat." The dog takes the kibble from Ruth's hand, mouths it, and lets it fall to the floor. "No, eat," Ruth says. She takes a new piece of kibble. The dog lifts her head, and again she takes the kibble from Ruth's hand. This piece, she grinds and swallows. "Good dog," Ruth says. "Good dog." She takes another piece of kibble from the many in the cup and holds it out. Maggie eats. "Good, good dog." Maggie lets out a labored breath.

Ruth pauses before holding out the next piece of kibble she takes from the cup. She can hear the sound of music coming from the other room, tentative and gentle, and it is a moment before she is sure that it is Isabelle playing, and not the radio or stereo. Is it? She strains her ears. It has been a long time since she has heard this piano played, but yes, the sound is unmistakable, the notes old and tinny and distinct.

"Maggie," she says. "Here. Will you, please?"

Maggie will, and does. The sound of the piano gets louder.

"Good girl," Ruth says. "Good girl." Her hair wavers in the hot air blowing up from the vent, and her knees are sore from crouching, and so she lowers herself completely to the floor. She will feed this meal to Maggie piece by piece, if that's the only way to do it, as she quietly listens to her daughter play.

She rests her head against the cold glass of the window and looks into her own eyes dimly reflected there. She blinks at herself, and then looks beyond the glass into the yard. Wilson is out there in his shirtsleeves. His coat flaps from a branch of the fallen apple tree he's not yet cut and added to the modest pile near the tree's stump. She watches as he guides the blade through a branch, and she is glad not to be able to hear above the sound of the piano the chainsaw's buzzing whine. The limb falls; Wilson straightens up and runs an arm across his brow, then throws the limb aside, onto the pile with the rest of the wood.

II

"I don't think we've ever spent Christmas Day in the country before." Wilson looks into his soup bowl as he speaks. He scrapes with his spoon at the green streaks of split pea still left.

"No."

"It's nice to be here, though."

"It really is. Better than being cooped up in the city. Easier just to *be*," Ruth says. Through the window, she can see Isabelle outside, at work on a path from what was the apple tree to the woodpile at the edge of the woods. The day has lost its brilliance as it's passed, but the sky is still blue. "I should probably get her nose looked at, though. Don't you think?"

Wilson shrugs. "Your brother seemed to think it wasn't broken."

"True," Ruth says. "But still." She sighs. "You know, I'd almost feel better if he'd greeted us with a gun."

She feels Wilson's gaze.

"I would," she says. "Then at least I'd feel somewhat justified, sending her after you like that. I'm not sure exactly what I was so afraid of." She shakes her head. "But dinner? He greets us with dinner?"

"But how would you know that, Ruth?" Wilson says. "I mean, after last week."

They watch their daughter shoveling.

"What matters," Wilson says, "is that she spoke. That is what matters."

"Yes," Ruth says. "She spoke for you. And who knows if she will again." She swallows. "I'm going to have more soup. Do you want more soup?"

Wilson shakes his head. Ruth puts her spoon beside her bowl and her napkin onto the table, but she doesn't get up.

"She didn't speak for me, Ruth. She spoke."

They are quiet for a minute. Wilson blinks into his bowl. "Maybe I will have more soup," he says. He gestures toward Ruth's bowl, but she shakes her head. He brings his own bowl into the kitchen. "It's bubbling," he calls. "Should I turn it down?" He waits for a response, but hears none. He fills his soup bowl, scooping up as many of the carrots as he can.

"I turned it down," he says when he returns to the table. He puts his napkin onto his lap. "It was bubbling." Wilson seeks Ruth's eye. "And she sounded like you," he says. "She did. Her mother's daughter."

Ruth smiles, holds his eye for a minute, and then looks away. Wilson follows her gaze toward Isabelle, halfway along to the woodpile. He offered to help her shovel this path, but she turned him down.

"She played the piano this morning," Ruth says.

"Isabelle?"

Ruth answers with a look.

"What did she play?"

Ruth settles her chin into her hand. "Beethoven."

Wilson blows at a spoonful of soup.

369

"The *Moonlight Sonata*. The one they always played at the Plaza when my mother would take her there for tea. Remember how she loved it?"

"Yes," Wilson says, and he does remember, vaguely.

"I'm not sure how she managed to learn it. Or when." Ruth reaches over and spoons up a bite of Wilson's soup. He pushes the bowl toward her, so that it is between them. A carrot coin surfaces in the soup.

"She's almost made it to the woodpile," Ruth remarks.

Wilson turns to the window. There are three paths that end at the apple tree now, one from the house, one from the swing set, one from the woodpile. The stump of the apple tree he has carefully smoothed out. "It was one hundred and three or four or five," he says. "Somewhere around there. I lost count." The stump looked better jagged, he thinks now, but it had been somehow important that he be able to count the rings.

He turns back from the window. Ruth is looking at him. She doesn't say anything. "Stay here," he says. "I'll be right back."

She watches as he opens the sliding door and steps outside, no hat or coat. He follows the path that leads to Isabelle, whatever words he says made visible as white puffs in the air. Isabelle sets the shovel down and follows her father back down the woodpile path and onto the path that leads around the house to the driveway, out of Ruth's sight.

Ruth lifts the spoon out of the soup bowl, puts it back. She gazes at Maggie. In a minute, she hears the back door open and Wilson and Isabelle stomping the snow off their boots. "I'm closing the door!" Wilson calls. She hears his footsteps going upstairs, Isabelle behind him.

Upstairs, on his dresser, neatly wrapped, is the black box from last weekend, the necklace that Isabelle chose for her mother inside. Wilson forgot to bring it back to the city last weekend, and he is grateful to have something to give Ruth today, to make her smile. He picks it up and turns around. Isabelle's eyes glisten with cold. "Ready?" he says.

She nods. He offers the box to her, but she shakes her head; she wants her father to bestow the gift. She follows him eagerly downstairs, to where her mother is sitting at the table, not eating the soup in front of her. Isabelle wants her to eat that soup, wants her to smile.

"Merry Christmas," Wilson says.

Isabelle watches as her mother carefully unwraps the small box, neatly folding the square of wrapping paper and setting it aside in the way that Isabelle would. It is more satisfying, in Isabelle's opinion, to open gifts this way, to relish every step, though to watch her mother work so deliberately is frustrating when she so badly wants her mother to get to the thing inside.

At last, her mother opens the box. The Apache Tear sits black and brilliant against the velvet lining.

As her mother lifts the necklace from its box the slender silver chain seems to cascade from her hand like something liquid. "I don't think you've ever given me jewelry before," she says, bringing the tear closer to her face. "I mean, except for my engagement ring—but, Wil!" she says, looking up at him. "This is beautiful!" Isabelle's breath quivers with satisfaction and delight at the expressions on both her parents' faces, her mother's one of wonder, her father's one of pride, both of them happy.

"It's called a— What is it, Belle?"

"An Apache Tear," she says, because she can.

Both her parents look at her, quiet for a moment. "That's right," her father says. "An Apache Tear."

Isabelle has shoveled the path to the woodpile wide enough that there is room for her and Wilson to pass each other on their ways to and from the apple tree. Between the two of them, they are making quick work of the stack of limbs.

He carries a piece of wood under each arm and tosses them one at a time onto the pile. They make a dull thunk as they land. He passes his sleeve beneath his nose. Come spring, he'll have a lot of firewood to split for the next winter, to chop and stack neatly on the rack. He'll get a new ax for the job. Either that, or they could just set fire to it all. He likes the idea; it seems somehow a more fitting fate for the apple tree.

A small log hits the pile. He looks down. Isabelle is beside him, her breath puffing white and quick.

"It'd make some bonfire, huh?" he says. They gaze into the pile, at the thick, firm pieces of lower limbs and then the jagged branches that stick up every which way. "Remember that bonfire we had? When the decade changed?" He doesn't look at her for a response. There had been no snow that year, and he'd constructed a small rock wall around the woodpile to keep the fire contained. No snow, but it had been cold, and they sang "Lord of the Dance" as they danced around the fire to keep warm. "A spark burned a hole in your mitten," he says. He sighs. "Well," he says.

He pauses, then he turns and trudges back toward the stump. There are only a few more loads to haul, then they'll be done. "Dance, dance, wherever you may be," he sings as he goes.

Isabelle watches her father go. "I am the Lord of the Dancing Dee," she sings quietly, finishing the tune her father has begun in the way she always used to, with the words all wrong. She looks beyond her father, beyond the stump of the apple tree, and across the street to where smoke is threading its way from Mr. Sullivan's old chimney. The Dunlaps' chimney, she corrects herself. She will have to start thinking of it as the Dunlaps'. She wonders what their Christmas is like, what the two of them are doing over there. Tomorrow, she thinks. Maybe tomorrow she will go over herself and say hello.

Acknowledgments

I am indebted to many people for their help along the way in the writing of *December*.

Thanks go, of course, to Amanda Urban and Jordan Pavlin for believing in the book and in me, and thanks also to Leslie Levine.

Enormous thanks goes to the thoughtful early readers whose feedback was invaluable: Mary Jo and Stephen Foley, Hartford Gongaware, Geoffrey Wolff, and, last but certainly not least, Richard Trenner.

I am endlessly grateful to Michelle Latiolais, without whose constant encouragement, support, wisdom, and friendship this book would not have been written.

And, of course, thanks and love always to my parents and my sisters, Adin and Mona.

ELIZABETH H. WINTHROP

Fireworks

Hollis Clayton is in trouble. Still haunted by the death of his young son two years earlier, stalled in his writing career and overfond of the bottle, he finds himself abandoned by his wife for the summer – or, if he doesn't shape up, for good.

Here, in the daily rhythms of Hollis's disintegrating life, lies a viscerally comic portrait of suburban despair. With this deeply affecting tale of grief and renewal, a young writer makes a striking debut.

'A lovely, touching novel: intelligent,
wry, at once lush and spare'
Andrew Solomon

'Winthrop sketches her hapless hero with
uncommon charm . . . As his summer slips by, both he
and the reader learn to appreciate anew the "non-stories"
that make up life.'
Observer

'Winthrop proves to be a bitingly intelligent writer who infuses
otherwise unremarkable moments with bittersweet pathos'
New York Times Book Review

'Combining a light comic touch with a compellingly
honest portrayal of her flawed, yet loveable, protagonist,
Winthrop has produced a work of psychological acuity and
gentle absolution.'
Mslexia

S

SCEPTRE

Melt into a book with Galaxy

Curled up on the sofa,
Sunday morning in pyjamas,
just before bed,
in the bath or
on the way to work?

Wherever, whenever,
you can escape
with a good book!

So go on...
indulge yourself with
a good read and the
smooth taste of
Galaxy chocolate

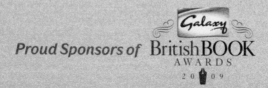